新式
**英文流行/
慣用語**

Trendy!
Express it!
Must-know
words!

Nice!

英文流行語	解釋
ASMR 自發性知覺經絡反應	Autonomous Sensory Meridian Response 的縮寫。用來指一種受到特定聽覺、視覺或感官刺激，進而觸發愉悅感的身心反應。其中，聽覺的效果通常大於視覺。
be chasing clout 刻意地撈粉	講網紅迎合大眾，以獲得更多網路聲量或粉絲追蹤數的行為。如果要用來表示某個人，可以使用名詞片語 a clout chaser。
cancel 取消追蹤；掉粉	cancel 原意為「取消」，現在常用來表示某名人或網紅說了或做了不適當的事，導致大眾取消追蹤、不再關注。用法：The singer is canceled.（那名歌手掉粉了。）
COVID-19 新型冠狀病毒肺炎	2019 新冠肺炎的正式名稱。CO 代表 corona（冠狀）／VI 代表 virus（病毒）／D 代表 disease（疾病）／19 代表 2019（發現病毒的年份）
glow up 改頭換面	glow（發光）+ grow up（長大）的組合單字，形容隨著年齡而變得更美、更帥，整個人閃閃發光，有女／男大十八變的意思。
infodemic 假消息	隨著新冠肺炎流行而出現的單字。info 指 information（資訊）；demic 則指 epidemic（流行病），用來表示「與疫情相關的假消息」氾濫現象。
I feel you. 我懂；我能理解你	I feel you. 或 I'm feeling someone. 並不是指「我感覺到你」，而是指「我懂」、「我了解你」的意思。美國人與朋友聊天談心時，常用 I feel you. 來表示理解朋友想表達的感受。
salty 惱羞成怒	遊戲常見用語。salty 通常用來形容某人被羞辱或是發生丟臉的事情後，生氣或是很激動的樣子。形容一個人 so much salt，表示那個人很容易哭哭。
sharent 狂曬小孩的父母	share（分享）+ parent（父母）的組合字。指那些在社群網站上發布大量孩子照片與近況的父母。網路上的 #sharenting 標籤表示這篇是曬小孩的文章。
showrooming 體驗後網路購買	去實體店體驗後，在網路上用更低的價格購買商品。
slay 做得超棒	slay 的原意為「殺害」，年輕人用這個單字表示某人或某事物「棒極了」，比如 You slayed it.（你做得很棒）；sth. slay me 表示某物讓我大為驚豔。
staycation 在家中（或附近）度假	由 stay（停留）+ vacation（假期）組合而成，表示放假期間不出國，也不出遠門，只待在家裡，或在住家附近逛一逛。用法：have a staycation。
a total snowflake 非常玻璃心	snowflake 原指雪花。用來形容人時，表示那個人就像雪花一樣，一碰就碎，因而用來戲稱別人的「玻璃心」。total 加強玻璃心的程度，可視語意省略。

傳訊好用極短字

CD9 ▶ Code 9 爸媽出沒警報
1. 爸媽在旁邊，不方便講話。
2. 你也別講話，免得被看見。

ELI 5 ▶ Explain Like I'm 5
請用最簡單的話解釋（把我當五歲小孩）。

IMHO ▶ In My Humble Opinion
個人淺見

NSFW ▶ Not Safe For Work
上班不適合看或聽（包含敏感圖片等）

tl; dr ▶ too long; didn't read
訊息太長了，懶得看。

網路鄉民必備

GG ▶ Good Game
源自線上遊戲的對戰，輸家表示風度用，後用來指人或事物「結束」了。

OP ▶ 文章重複了；太強了！
over post（重複文章）或 over power（太強）的簡寫。

PUA 男 ▶ 註❶ Pick-up Artist
直譯搭訕藝術家，後指「渣男」。

RIP ▶ Rest In Peace
希望過世者得到安息。

WFH ▶ 註❷ Work From Home
因新冠肺炎而崛起的工作型態「在家工作」。

多合一縮略語

chillax ▶ 冷靜一點
chill out 冷靜 + relax 放鬆

stan ▶ 瘋狂粉絲；腦粉
stalker 跟蹤狂 + fan 粉絲

smize ▶ 用眼神笑
smile with your eyes

hangry ▶ 餓到生氣
hungry 飢餓 + angry 生氣

netizen ▶ 網友；鄉民
internet 網路 + citizen 公民

音譯流行語

斗內
donate 贊助；捐獻

黑特
hater 討厭特定事物的人

魯蛇
loser 輸家；失敗者

7pupu
台語「氣噗噗」的諧音

OSSO
中文「喔是喔」的音譯

網路標籤 #hashtag

#instagood
Instagram + good 好照片

#latergram
照片不是今天拍的，而是幾天前照的。

#nofilter
炫耀照片完全沒有加濾鏡

#ootd
Outfit Of The Day 今日穿搭

#tbt 註❸
沒有時間拍新照片，只好拿舊照充數。

註❶ PUA（Pick-up Artist）原指那些學習社交技巧，且懂得自我包裝的人，後用來形容很會吸引異性的渣男。

註❷ 另一個相似詞彙為 work at home，通常表示自由工作者，工作地點在家裡。

註❸ Throwback Thursday，直譯為「懷舊星期四」，也就是週四那天 PO 以前的照片。因為歡樂週五夜的前一天，通常最忙碌，沒有時間拍新照片，只好拿舊照來湊數。

GREAT!!

超強

Just Like Natives!
Let's Talk in English Slangs.

關鍵慣用語
口說提升術

張翔 著

時代在走，英語也要跟著進化！

聯想 × 答題 × 詞彙起源，

開口一字就讓老外驚豔！

使用說明

User's Guide
一開口就破功？這些英文慣用語，不懂千萬別裝懂！
Oops! That English Idiom Means This.

① 釐清讓人困惑的慣用語

Part 1整理出華人最容易搞錯意思的慣用語，清楚點出不能按照字面猜意思的英文。

② 情境分類，便利性MAX

將老外使用頻率最高的慣用語，依照情境分門別類，例如：個性與特質、行為舉止、場所與物品…等等，同性質的英文整理在同一個主題，學習效率飆升。

目錄 CONTENTS

Part 1

這些英文，原來是這個意思！
～1+1≠2，千萬別用字面的意思猜英文。

| Topic 1 | 個性與特質 Personality UNIT 001～UNIT 039 | 014 |

英文慣用語當中，常常會用物品或行為去比喻人的個性與特質，乍看之下與特徵無關，但其實這些用法包含了外國文化的幽默感，例如butter face、Spanish athlete、on one's high horse…等等，本主題將幫助你理解老外在說什麼。

目錄 CONTENTS

Part 2

這些講法，原來應該這樣說！
～中式英文狂NG？英文其實要這樣說。

| Topic 1 | 個性與特質 Personality UNIT 177～UNIT 201 | 192 |

描述個性、特質的詼諧中文很多，像是「頭腦簡單，四肢發達」、「舌燦蓮花」等，這些其實都有英文的說法可用，只是我們在教室裡都學不到而已，其他用法還有on the ball、an eager beaver…等等，想知道這些英文表達的是哪些中文俚語嗎？翻開本主題就能學會囉！

③ 介紹中文俚語的英文說法

Part 2精選有英文對應的中式詼諧用語，最適合想甩開正經八百的教室英文、學會生動表達的華人學習者。

只要花**20%**的力氣搞懂慣用語，就能講出**100%**的道地英文！
巧妙運用慣用語，讓英文語感飆升、實力脫胎換骨！

Part ❶

這些英文，原來是這個意思！
～1+1≠2，千萬別用字面的意思猜英文。

一遇到不懂的英文，許多人都容易望文生義，
依著每個單字的意思，推測複合字的含意，
但是，有些英文慣用語不能用這種方式破解。
butter face是在講人皮膚水嫩？
nosebleed section是流鼻血的地方？
get one's goat是搶走誰的山羊？
如果不想因為NG的理解方式鬧笑話，
就請務必閱讀本章內容，搞清楚這些用詞。

學習POINT！
學會看起來容易，意思卻不簡單的英文慣用語，
深入老外的想法，快速培養英語腦思維！

❹ 一目了然的 學習POINT

在進入每一章的內容之前，將點出學習POINT，幫助讀者建立明確的目標，也才能更有效率地吸收接下來的內容。如果你總是埋首於厚重的英文工具書，讀了又讀，卻不見期待中的實力激增的話，就請務必體驗一次擁有明確目標的學習方法。

❺ 明確的 單元分類

在每一個主題後方點出該主題所囊括的單元，在日後複習的時候，就能更快速地找出自己想學習的類型，無須從頭開始查找。

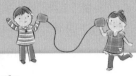

6　利用聯想與推測強化效率

利用每單元的標題思考該單元的慣用語，以循序漸進的方式引導讀者，增進效率。

PART ❶ 這些英文，原來是這個意思！

UNIT
047
a pack rat
把老鼠裝進箱子？

🎧 047

暖身猜猜看 Warming Up

Ruby: Your sister seems to be in a panic over moving next month.
Ian: Definitely. She's **a pack rat**. I bet she has tons of stuff to pack.
露比：你妹妹看起來很擔心下個月搬家的事。
伊恩：肯定的，她是個囤積狂，肯定有一堆東西要打包。

原來是這個意思！

a pack rat 習慣囤積東西的人
　　pack rat是北美洲的狐尾大林鼠，這種動物習慣將找到的東西拖回去，以便築巢時使用，或者將食物拖回巢穴儲存；用來比喻人的話，則是比喻「為了紀念意義或不時之需等理由，囤積沒有用途與舊東西的人」。

7　活潑生動MP3，口說力倍增

跟著外師讀誦，學會慣用語的口氣，邊聽邊開口，訓練出最道地的發音與語調。

8　暖身猜猜看，吸收加速度

Part 1 設計雙人對話
Part 2 則利用選擇題，讓讀者推測其意。與標題不同的是，此處將提供情境，有了上下文，讀者自然能更貼近慣用語的意思。

PART ❷ 這些講法，原來該這樣說！

UNIT
177
一個「喜怒形於色」的人，
就是很會給人color瞧？

🎧 177

暖身猜猜看 Warming Up

情境：你和朋友在討論某男同事喜怒形於色，這時應該怎麼說？
(　　) Bill is one of those guys who wears his heart on his _____.
　　　 (A) shoulder　　　 (B) head　　　 (C) sleeve
正確解答：(C) 比爾是個會把感受表現在臉上的人。

原來應該這樣說！

wear one's heart on one's sleeve 喜怒形於色
　　從字面上來看，這個慣用語是指將心穿在袖子上，也就是將心思顯露在外的意思。早期的西方社會有個習俗，會將女性的緞帶別在愛人的袖子上，所以有這樣的說法，wear可以用have和pin取代。

⑨ 解答慣用語的真實義

不管是容易讓人猜錯意思的英文、還是不知從何開口的中式詼諧語，都可以在解析中找到正確用法。

⑩ 深入老外思維的解析

解析將提供慣用語的起源、意象、以及其他補充，理解字面背後的意思，才能真正像老外一樣活用這些慣用語。

原來是這個意思！

a pack rat 習慣囤積東西的人

　　pack rat是北美洲的狐尾大林鼠，這種動物習慣將找到的東西拖回去，以便築巢時使用，或者將食物拖回巢穴儲存；用來比做人的話，則是比喻「為了紀念意義或不時之需等理由，囤積沒有用途與舊東西的人」。

Ian: I suggest you get rid of some useless stuff.

Eve: I can't. Every item has a special value to me.

Ian: Even this tattered notebook?

Eve: It's my first notebook; the sketches are the marks of my youth.

Ian: You are such **a** hopeless **pack rat**.

伊恩：我建議你丟掉一些沒有用的東西。

伊芙：不行啦，每件東西對我都有特殊意義。

伊恩：這本破爛的筆記本也有意義？

伊芙：那是我的第一本筆記本，裡面的塗鴉是我青春的紀錄。

伊恩：你真是個無藥可救的囤積狂。

字彙 / 片語充電區 *Words and Phrases*

hoard 動 貯藏 / perpetuate 動 留存 / disorderly 形 雜亂的 / arrange 動 整理
stock up (為某種目的)儲備 / tidy up 整理；清理 / sit on the fence 猶豫不決

⑪ 更進一步的對話練習

提供超擬真生活對話，建議搭配MP3的內容，學會語調，就能拋開僵硬的口語表達，像母語人士一樣開口說。

⑫ 完整補充進階字彙和片語

除了以樂趣為主軸，帶領讀者理解英文慣用語之外，也重視學習的質與量，該補充的一個都不會少。

善用英文慣用語，
開口就讓老外驚艷！

　　在我自身學習英語的過程中，一直很重視基礎的紮實度，像是單字、片語、文法，不斷強化自己的英文實力，教學的時候，也嘗試不同的方式來讓學生融入英語，但是，有一項領域，是我一直在思考的，就是道地的英文俚語、慣用語。

　　之所以會思索這部份的英文，是因為有許多學生，明明一直很努力加強字彙量，各種英文檢定考的分數也都相當優秀，但是一出國唸書，往往都會和我聊到同一件事：因為難以理解的英文慣用語而鬧笑話。像我就有一個學生，國內幾項被人重視的檢定考，他都取得優異的成績，在他順利出國後，就和我聊到，曾經因為室友的一句hit the books而以為對方非常生氣，後來才知道那是「用功唸書」的意思，他的室友其實是想邀請他一起去圖書館。

　　其實，這是許多英文學習者的苦惱，因為文化差異，無論自己多麼勤奮地背單字與片語，一聽到母語人士使用慣用語的時候就碰壁，但偏偏這些用語又是實用度相當高的英文，和老外交談個沒幾句就會出現，因為學生們這個普遍的煩惱，我才有了規劃本書的想法。而就在我規劃這本書內容的期間，某次學生的提問又給了我一個方向，他遇到的困擾是，和美國人聊天，想要形容人「頭腦簡單，四肢發達」，但無論如何都想不出英文該怎麼講，結果繞了一大圈，講了很長串的英文，但他的美國朋友最後還是霧煞煞，不太確定他想要表達的是什麼意思，他問我：「老師，其他人都說中文俚語沒辦法用英文表達是真的嗎？」就是他的一句提問，讓我突然想到，其實有很多中文的詼諧用語是可以用英文表達的，只是很多用法無法直接翻譯過去，

在以升學為主的英語課上，又很少會教給學生這些用語，所以才會有很多人以為中文的講法沒有辦法轉成英文，結果許多人都像我那位學生一樣，講了一長串的英文，卻無法確定外國朋友是否能理解自己想要表達的想法。

如果，能用比較活潑的方式讓學生理解老外常用、但字面上很容易猜錯意思的英文慣用語；能教給學生那些中文詼諧語的英文對應，這樣不僅能幫助他們理解外國文化，減少溝通時的尷尬情形，也能因為融入了中文生動用語，在教學時更能激發學生的學習動力。

在想法漸漸成熟了之後，我開始著手於這本書的編寫，一方面解釋那些「從字面上容易猜錯意思的英文慣用語」，二方面介紹一些「能用英語表達的中式詼諧說法」，除此之外，為了幫助讀者理解，我堅持介紹這些慣用語的起源、意象解釋和其他補充，因為慣用語有趣歸有趣，如果沒有一個透徹的了解，依然很容易忘記為何要使用那些單字，下一次遇到時可能還是會誤解、用錯英文。

也藉著這樣的一本書，我想將學習語言的樂趣帶給讀者，並藉著慣用語的解析，幫助讀者去理解母語人士的思維，有了文化的思維，自然能擺脫中式英語，也能在開口的幾句英文中，讓外國人肯定學習者的程度，畢竟，我們使用英文的情況，多半是在與人溝通，所以我很希望能藉由這些慣用語，改變那些認為只要單字背得多，就等於英文好的學習者，也期望幫助那些曾經因為難以理解的慣用語而鬧笑話的人，下一次，就用這些英文，扭轉母語人士對你的印象吧！

張翔

Part 1

這些英文，原來是這個意思！
～1+1≠2，千萬別用字面的意思猜英文。

Topic 1　個性與特質 Personality
UNIT 001～UNIT 039　　014

英文慣用語當中，常常會用物品或行為去比喻人的個性與特質，乍看之下與特徵無關，但其實這些用法包含了外國文化的幽默感，例如**butter face**、**Spanish athlete**、**on one's high horse**⋯等等，本主題將幫助你理解老外在說什麼。

Topic 2　行為舉止 Behavior
UNIT 040～UNIT 079　　053

在描述一個人行為上的特徵時，也有許多聽起來有趣的慣用語可以形容，例如**backstabber**、**a pack rat**、**henpeck**、**put on airs**⋯等等，什麼樣的行為舉止會與這些詞彙扯上關係，想知道的話就別錯過本主題喔！

Topic 3　抒發情緒與評論 Emotion
UNIT 080～UNIT 095　　093

母語人士在抒發情緒的時候，和我們所知的**happy**、**angry**相比，更常用慣用語來表達不滿、無奈、或其他想法，對他們來說，慣用語更能傳達自身的心情，非常實用，例如**see red**、**eat crow**、**Over my dead body!**⋯等等。

Part 2

這些講法，原來應該這樣說！
～中式英文狂NG？英文其實要這樣說。

描述個性、特質的詼諧中文很多，像是「頭腦簡單，四肢發達」、「舌燦蓮花」等，這些其實都有英文的說法可用，只是我們在教室裡都學不到而已，其他用法還有on the ball、an eager beaver…等等，想知道這些英文表達的是哪些中文俚語嗎？翻開本主題就能學會囉！

說到人的行為舉止，英語學習者往往會用do、make等萬用動詞去拼湊，放棄像「破釜沉舟」之類的活潑描述。其實，中式俚語的英文對應並不少，像是rise from the ashes、egg on、eat dirt…等等，學會之後，就能與那些特色不強烈的萬用動詞說掰掰。

抒發情緒的中文會想到類似「手舞足蹈」、「熱鍋上的螞蟻」、「面不改色」等用詞，如果這些都能用英文表達，是不是活潑多了呢？其他甚至有in stitches、over the moon、in a stew…等等，其實可以轉成英文的情緒用詞遠比想像中的多呢！

評論或讚賞的用詞在中文裡，其實不只有好、壞這麼簡單，例如「用膝蓋想也知道的事情」，不直接說好壞，就能完美地表達自己的想法，本主題將介紹在英文當中有對應的用法，像是**at cross-purposes**、**straight from the shoulder**…等等，快學會這些說法，替你的評論加分吧！

在描述場所或物品時，中文裡約定俗成的說法有「中看不中用的東西」、「搖錢樹」等等，每次想要讓自己的描述更有趣，卻總是苦無英文可說的話，就來看這個主題的內容吧！你將學會像**a rip-off**、**a page-turner**…等讓人微笑的生活化用語。

提到身體狀態，我們常常會用「神采奕奕」、「鐵胃」、「皮包骨」等用詞去形容，將這些用法轉成英文時，單字會與我們想像中的不同，像是**spare tire**、**feed the fishes**…等等，其實這些看似簡單的英文單字，組合起來都會成為中文的幽默俚語，強烈建議學起來，下次與老外聊天的時候就能讓人驚艷囉！

和英文較為不同的是，除了明確的時間以外，中文會用其他詞彙描述時機，例如「時機成熟」、「有的是時間」等等，可以用英文表達的趣味用語還有**cut things fine**、**in a good time**、**donkey's years**…等等，學會之後，就能用英文傳達中式幽默。

Part ①

這些英文，原來是這個意思！

～1+1≠2，千萬別用字面的意思猜英文。

一遇到不懂的英文，許多人都容易望文生義，
依著每個單字的意思，推測複合字的含意，
但是，有些英文慣用語不能用這種方式破解。
butter face是在講人皮膚水嫩？
nosebleed section是流鼻血的地方？
get one's goat是搶走誰的山羊？
如果不想因為NG的理解方式鬧笑話，
就請務必閱讀本章內容，搞清楚這些用詞。

學習POINT！

學會看起來容易，意思卻不簡單的英文慣用語，
深入老外的想法，快速培養英語腦思維！

UNIT 001　towhead
拖著頭？是什麼懲罰嗎？

🎧 001

暖身猜猜看 *Warming Up*

Parker: Do you know Anna, the new pharmacist?

Debby: You mean the **towhead**? I think she's really cute.

帕克：你知道新來的藥劑師安娜嗎？

黛比：你是說有淡金髮色的那個安娜嗎？我覺得她很可愛。

原來是這個意思！

towhead 擁有一頭淡黃髮色的人

　　這個慣用語起源於美國獨立前的十三州殖民時期，tow在現代英文中，為拖繩、拖輪之意，但在那個時候，tow有「亞麻或大麻」的意思，為縫製衣物的原料，亞麻本身就是淡金色，因此被用來形容「有淡金髮色的人」。

Neil: Genie said that you two went to the same high school.

Lisa: That's right. She used to dye her hair maroon.

Neil: She is very talkative and friendly.

Lisa: I do recall that she was in the cheerleading squad.

Neil: Wow. She is truly a bright **towhead**.

尼爾：吉妮跟我提到你們是高中同學。

麗莎：是啊，她以前都把頭髮染成褐紫色。

尼爾：她真是健談又友善。

麗莎：我記得她以前是啦啦隊的一員。

尼爾：哇，她還真是個開朗的淡金髮女性呢。

字彙／片語充電區 *Words and Phrases*

brunette 名 深褐髮色的女子 ／ rinse 名 染髮劑 ／ countenance 名 面容；臉色

in vogue 時尚的 ／ have one's eye on 目光放在 ／ hit between the eyes 讓人驚喜

UNIT 002 southpaw
南邊的腳爪與動物有關？

🎧 002

暖身猜猜看 *Warming Up*

Danny: I never thought I could pitch a whole game.

Linda: I know! You are incredibly powerful for a **southpaw**.

丹尼：我從沒想過自己可以投完一整場比賽。

琳達：就是啊！你實在是個超強的左投手。

原來是這個意思！

southpaw 左撇子棒球投手

　　在棒球賽中，打擊手都是面對東方，以避免西曬，而投手在打擊手對面，自然是面對西方；左撇子的投手站在投手丘時，投球的那隻左手此時位於南方，所以被稱為southpaw，paw（爪子；腳爪）在這個慣用語中指的是手。

對話練習 *Let's Talk!*

Linda: Did you watch the baseball game yesterday?

Mike: I missed it. I had to take on an additional shift.

Linda: What a shame! Danny is the best **southpaw** I have ever seen.

Mike: I know. It's too bad that I missed it.

Linda: Guess what? I've got the game recorded.

琳達：你有看昨天的棒球賽嗎？

麥克：沒有，我錯過那場比賽了，因為我得加班。

琳達：太可惜了！丹尼是我見過最厲害的左投手。

麥克：我知道，真遺憾我錯過了比賽。

琳達：跟你說，我有錄下整場比賽喔。

字彙／片語充電區 *Words and Phrases*

left-handed 形 左撇子的 / **habitual** 形 慣常的；習慣的 / **adroit** 形 靈巧的；熟練的 **the dominant hand** 慣用手 / **a pinch hitter** 代打 / **blow the whistle on** 揭發

UNIT 003 butter face 誇獎人細皮嫩肉？

🎧 003

 暖身猜猜看 *Warming Up*

Laura: Didn't you ask the girl with long hair out?

Adam: Well, I didn't because she is actually a **butter face**.

蘿拉：你不是去約那個長髮女孩了嗎？

亞當：當我發現她只有身材可以看的時候，就放棄了。

 原來是這個意思！

butter face 身材好，長相卻不佳的女性

　　這句慣用語是取其諧音，butter聽起來是快速念過的but her，意即「除了她的」；所以這個慣用語的意思是「一切條件都很好，除了她的臉以外」；即指一個身材很好，但是臉不好看的女生。

 **對話練習** *Let's Talk!*

Robert: I don't think I will date Jenny again.

Hannah: Didn't your date go well?

Robert: No. We didn't click. Besides, she is a **butter face**.

Hannah: Aha! You were turned off by her appearance.

Robert: Not just that. She gossiped too much. She's not my type.

羅伯特：我想我不會再和珍妮約會了。

漢　娜：這次的約會不好嗎？

羅伯特：不太好，我們不合拍，而且她只有身材可以看。

漢　娜：啊哈！你是因為外貌才對她失去興趣的。

羅伯特：不只是這樣，她太愛講八卦，不是我喜歡的類型。

字彙／片語充電區 *Words and Phrases*

belle 名 美女 / hideous 形 醜陋的；可怕的 / figure 名 身材 / buttery 形 像奶油的 wear off the fat 減肥 / make up 化妝；補足 / not give a damn 沒興趣；不在乎

UNIT 004
big shot
是指很大的槍響聲？

🎧 004

 暖身猜猜看 Warming Up

Alice: Recently, I've been feeling dizzy all the time.
Fred: You can go see Dr. Hammer. He's a **big shot** in neurology.

艾莉絲：最近我一直感覺頭暈。
弗瑞德：你可以找漢默醫師看診，他是神經科的權威。

 原來是這個意思！

big shot 有權有勢的大人物；有份量的人

　　big shot是非正式的說法，起源於十九世紀初期，當時是指大砲之類的大口徑武器，這個慣用語在1920年代開始流行，被借用來指大人物，或是有份量、不可輕忽的人，也可以寫成big gun。

 對 話 練 習 *Let's Talk!*

Gary: What did that woman say to you?
Helen: She said she likes my hair. Is anything wrong?
Gary: She is a **big shot** in the industry!
Helen: Really? No wonder I felt she had special charisma.
Gary: Ha, maybe she can help your career someday.

蓋瑞：那位女士剛剛跟你說了什麼？
海倫：她說她喜歡我的髮型，有什麼不對嗎？
蓋瑞：她可是我們這一行的大人物呢！
海倫：真的？難怪我感覺她有一種特殊的魅力。
蓋瑞：哈，她或許能給你的事業帶來幫助。

字彙／片語充電區 *Words and Phrases*

tycoon 名 (企業界的)大亨 / **authority** 名 權威人士 / **influential** 形 有權勢的
top brass 重要人物；要員 / **play hard ball** 有影響力 / **small fry** 小人物

UNIT 005　blue blood
藍色血液與科幻小說有關？

🎧 005

 暖身猜猜看 *Warming Up*

Betty: My new manager is very genial but distant.
Sara: I heard that she's a **blue blood** from London.

貝蒂：我的新經理很親切，不過有點距離感。
莎拉：聽說她來自倫敦的貴族家庭。

 原來是這個意思！

blue blood 名門貴族

　　blue blood（藍色血液）直譯自西班牙文的sangre azul，十九世紀時，有一些西班牙望族，宣稱自己的血統純正，沒有摩爾人、猶太人或其他種族的血統，而這些望族白皙的皮膚，讓藍色的血管清晰可見，因此用此慣用語形容。

 **對話練習　*Let's Talk!***

Andy: What are you watching? A soap opera?
Emma: It's a love story of a **blue blood**. It's quite popular.
Andy: Does it involve time traveling?
Emma: Yes! I am obsessed with it. The story is really unconventional.
Andy: Too bad I have been too busy to keep track of it.

安迪：你在看什麼？肥皂劇嗎？
艾瑪：是關於一個名門貴族的故事，現在正熱門的。
安迪：是不是有穿越時空的那部電視劇？
艾瑪：沒錯！我正著迷呢，故事情節不落俗套。
安迪：真可惜我忙得沒時間追劇。

字彙/片語充電區 *Words and Phrases*

status 名 地位；身分 / **magnificent** 形 高尚的 / **gracious** 形 雅緻的；優美的
the royal court 宮廷 / **salt of the earth** 高尚的人 / **smart aleck** 自認高人一等的人

UNIT 006
senior citizen
過了法定年齡的成年人？

🎧 006

暖身猜猜看 Warming Up

Helen: We're throwing a retirement party for you this Sunday.

Joey: Thanks. I can't believe I am a **senior citizen** now.

海倫：這個星期日我們會為你舉辦退休派對。

喬伊：謝謝，真不敢相信我加入銀髮族了。

原來是這個意思！

senior citizen 老年人；銀髮族

　　senior citizen所界定的長者，不只是年齡和生理狀態上的年長，而是在社會統計和行政體制中，以多數人為對比所界定出的範疇；一般而言，是指六十到六十五歲之後，已經從職場退休，享有退休金和社會福利的人群。

對話練習 Let's Talk!

Peter: My pension will help pay the cost of my round-the-world cruise.

Tracy: What a life! I still have three more years to go.

Peter: Well, I sometimes wonder if I'll miss the nine-to-five life.

Tracy: I am sure you will enjoy all the free time you have now.

Peter: You're right. I should enjoy being a **senior citizen**.

彼德：我的退休金族以支付我搭郵輪環遊世界的費用。

崔西：這生活也太棒了！我還得再工作三年才能退休。

彼德：不知道我會不會想念朝九晚五的生活。

崔西：我相信你會很享受自己的空間時間的。

彼德：也對，我應該好好體驗銀髮族的生活。

字彙／片語充電區 Words and Phrases

seniority 名 年資 / **retirement** 名 退休 / **pension** 名 退休金 / **routine** 名 日常作息
a golden-ager 長者 / **the golden handshake** 豐厚退休金 / **all the time** 無時無刻

UNIT 007 stuffed shirt
塞滿東西的衣服？

🎧 007

 暖身猜猜看 Warming Up

Mark: I can't believe you invited Bob. He is such a **stuffed shirt**!

Sally: He's our supervisor. I can't invite the entire office but him.

馬克：你竟然邀請了鮑伯，他很裝模作樣耶！

莎莉：他是我們的主管，總不能邀請了全公司就不請他吧。

 原來是這個意思！

stuffed shirt 自命不凡的人；裝模作樣的人

　　stuff是填充的意思，而stuffed shirt是指襯衫裡面只用紙張塞滿內部，而非靠活生生的人撐起來，但是，這句英文可不是指襯衫的狀態，而在形容一個「過度包裝、自視甚高的人」，如同用紙撐起的襯衫，沒有實在的內涵。

 *Let's Talk!*

Billy: Your party was awesome. The marinated steaks were fabulous!

Cathy: Thank you. But I guess Wilson didn't enjoy it.

Billy: Actually, I was surprised to see him there.

Cathy: My fault. I really didn't know he's such a **stuffed shirt**.

Billy: I agree. After all, who'd wear a white suit to a barbecue?

比利：你的派對真棒，那些醃牛排真好吃！

凱西：謝謝你，但我想威爾森不怎麼喜歡吧。

比利：老實說，在派對上看到他的時候，我很驚訝。

凱西：是我的錯，我完全不知道他是這麼裝模作樣的人。

比利：我同意，畢竟，誰會穿白西裝來烤肉啊？

字彙/片語充電區 Words and Phrases

stuffiness 名 自負 / **pompous** 形 愛炫耀的；浮誇的 / **fusspot** 名 小題大做的人
big cheese 自認重要的人 / **stick-in-the-mud** 頑固保守者 / **out of place** 格格不入

UNIT 008
brown-noser
咖啡色鼻子在描述膚色？

🎧 008

暖身猜猜看 *Warming Up*

Mary: Adam has risen to the position of manager within six months!
Joey: I am not surprised after seeing what a **brown-noser** he is.

瑪莉：亞當只花了六個月的時間就當上經理了！
喬伊：在我看過他是多麼厲害的馬屁精之後，就不訝異了。

原來是這個意思！

brown-noser 馬屁精

　　這個慣用語的動詞為brown-nose，源於軍中的美式俚語，指的是每天鞠躬哈腰地跟在別人後面親人家的屁股，以至於鼻頭沾到糞便，成了咖啡色鼻頭；注意這是屬於較粗俗的用語，使用時請多加留意。

Let's Talk!

Amy: Have you heard the news of a major personnel movement?

Tom: Yeah, I know the entire management team will be replaced.

Amy: Do you know why?

Tom: Our boss has had enough of those **brown-nosers**.

Amy: Now they know ass-kissing is not their only responsibility.

艾咪：你有聽到關於大幅人事調動的消息嗎？

湯姆：有啊，我知道整個管理團隊都要被撤換掉。

艾咪：你知道原因嗎？

湯姆：我們的老闆受夠那些馬屁精了。

艾咪：現在他們終於知道拍馬屁不是他們唯一的任務了。

字彙/片語充電區 *Words and Phrases*

flatter 動 奉承 / **subservient** 形 卑躬屈膝的 / **gush** 動 裝模作樣 / **praise** 名 讚揚
curry favor with sb. 拍某人馬屁 / **fawn over** 奉承 / **be hard-nosed** 理智的

UNIT 009　yes man 和Yes, sir.意思差不多？

🎧 009

暖身猜猜看 Warming Up

Henry: Should I get Mike to help you with the project?

Ruby: Never mind. He won't contribute much. He's a real **yes man**.

亨利：要不要我找麥克來幫忙你做這個企劃？

露比：不用了，他不會有什麼貢獻的，他是個應聲蟲。

原來是這個意思！

yes man 應聲蟲

　　yes man最典型的用法，是指完全聽從上司的員工，後來也擴及其他對象（例如朋友），對於所有的要求，都回答yes，總是附和別人，就是我們中文所說的「應聲蟲」；要注意的是，即使是女生，也一樣稱她為yes man。

對話練習 Let's Talk!

Roy: What do you think about Thomas and Lynn?

Linda: I don't know. I personally don't like Thomas.

Roy: Why not? He is pretty nice.

Linda: Well, I think he is a bit of a **yes man**.

Roy: I see. I never gave much thought to that before I set them up together.

羅伊：你覺得湯瑪斯跟琳登對嗎？

琳達：我不知道，我個人並不喜歡湯瑪斯。

羅伊：為什麼？他人滿不錯的啊。

琳達：嗯，我覺得他有點濫好人的性格。

羅伊：原來如此，我撮合他們的時候倒沒仔細考慮過這點。

字彙／片語充電區 Words and Phrases

temperament 名 性格；氣質 / **obedient** 形 順從的；服從的 / **respond** 動 回應 **approve of** 贊成 / **turn down** 拒絕(請求、忠告) / **argue the toss** 反對某項決定

UNIT 010

confidence man
信心滿滿，走路有風的人？

🎧 010

 暖身猜猜看 *Warming Up*

Lucy: I can't believe that Mike stole our client!

Danny: Well, our advisor has turned out to be a bit of a **confidence man**.

露西：麥克竟然接手我們的客戶，真令人不敢相信！

丹尼：我們的顧問原來是個騙子。

 原來是這個意思！

confidence man 騙子

　　confidence是信心、信賴的意思，那麼，「信賴的人」為什麼會被用來形容「騙子」呢？其實，這個慣用語當中的confidence指的是雙方的互信基礎，如果有人利用對方的信賴，背叛了彼此的互信基礎，當然就是「騙子」了。

 **對話練習** *Let's Talk!*

Lucy: We need to do something since Mike swindled us.

Danny: Nobody knew he was a **confidence man**.

Lucy: I can't believe we fell for his double-dealing tricks.

Danny: What about our targets for this month?

Lucy: Don't worry. We'll find a new client in no time.

露西：被麥克擺了一道，我們得想想辦法。

丹尼：沒人知道他是個騙子。

露西：不敢相信我們竟然中了他雙面人的計。

丹尼：那我們這個月的目標該怎麼辦？

露西：別擔心，我們很快就會找到新客戶的。

字彙／片語充電區 *Words and Phrases*

trickster 名 騙子 / **fraud** 名 騙局 / **distrust** 動 不信任 / **watchdog** 名 監視者

count on 依賴；指望 / **see through** 看穿 / **stake sth. on** 以某物作為賭注

UNIT 011　Spanish athlete 西班牙籍的運動員？

🎧 011

 暖身猜猜看 *Warming Up*

Maggie: Jack just told me about his new, big house.

Peter: Don't buy it. He is a **Spanish athlete**.

梅姬：　傑克剛才告訴我，他新買了一間大房子。

彼德：　不要相信他的話，他是吹牛大王。

 原來是這個意思！

Spanish athlete 吹牛的人

　　十六世紀時，西班牙的「無敵艦隊」獨霸一方，當英國開始積極擴張領土及商貿活動時，西班牙便出兵英國，當英國以奇襲大敗當時號稱最強的艦隊後，他們便以Spanish athlete來譏諷西班牙的自誇，之後引申指「吹牛的人」。

 **對話練習** *Let's Talk!*

Jack: Thanks for joining my housewarming party.

Maggie: Your friends are all interesting.

Jack: I just hope you weren't offended by their jokes.

Maggie: Not at all. But I need to apologize for doubting you.

Jack: Never mind. I know some people think I'm a **Spanish Athlete**.

傑克：謝謝你來參加我的喬遷派對。

梅姬：你的朋友們都好有趣。

傑克：希望你沒有被他們的玩笑嚇到。

梅姬：完全不會，但我必須為了懷疑你道歉。

傑克：沒關係，我知道有些人認為我愛吹牛。

字彙／片語充電區 *Words and Phrases*

bluff 動 虛張聲勢 / disclose 動 揭露 / counterfeit 動 仿造 / admonish 動 提醒
boast of 自吹自擂 / blow one's own trumpet 自我推銷 / cover up 掩蓋；掩飾

UNIT 012
a man of straw
農田中常見的稻草人？

🎧 012

暖身猜猜看 *Warming Up*

Lily: Why don't you invite Dan to join our team?

Kent: I think he is **a man of straw**. We can't count on him.

莉莉：你怎麼不邀請丹加入我們的團隊呢？

肯特：我覺得他靠不住，我們不能依賴他。

原來是這個意思！

a man of straw 靠不住的人

　　這個慣用語的一個可能起源，是指過去遊蕩在英國法庭附近的人，會為錢作偽證（鞋子裡會塞稻草），後藉以形容「靠不住的人」；這個慣用語與straw man同義，也可以理解為像稻草人一樣只是個空殼子，不足以被依靠。

對話練習 *Let's Talk!*

Keith: Can you help me with all these invitations?

Emma: Sure. But wasn't this John's job last year?

Keith: He is **a man of straw**. He missed the mailing date.

Emma: I see. I will make sure everything is on schedule.

Keith: Thank you. I hope the charity ball will be a success.

基斯：你可以幫忙處理這些邀請函嗎？

艾瑪：可以啊，但這去年不是約翰負責的嗎？

基斯：他是個不可靠的傢伙，上回還錯過了寄送時間。

艾瑪：原來如此，我會確保事情都按預定的時間進行。

基斯：謝謝你，希望這次的慈善晚會能成功。

字彙／片語充電區 *Words and Phrases*

untrustworthy 形 靠不住的 / reliable 形 可信賴的 / consign 動 交付給；委託給
a straw in the wind 事態的徵兆 / be dependent on 依賴 / entrust with 委託

UNIT 013
yellow-belly
黃色肚子是在講亞洲人？

🎧 013

 暖身猜猜看 Warming Up

Hunter: Gary left the office early today. What's wrong?

Carol: What a **yellow-belly**! He stole my idea for his project and is trying to avoid meeting me.

杭特：蓋瑞今天提早下班了，怎麼了嗎？

卡蘿：那個膽小鬼！他在企劃中盜用了我的創意，現在還試圖想避開我。

 原來是這個意思！

yellow-belly 膽小鬼

　　這個慣用語最早源自英國，專指林肯郡（Lincolnshire）的居民，並無負面意涵；直到十九世紀，yellow-belly才首次帶有「膽小」的負面意思，當時美國用此說法稱呼將成為交戰國的墨西哥人，但此是否與膚色有關，並無定論。

 **對話練習** *Let's Talk!*

Laura: Do you really believe that Gary stole Carol's concept?

Hunter: I don't know. But he shouldn't avoid her like a **yellow-belly**.

Laura: True. Stealing her idea could cost him his job and hurt his future.

Hunter: I heard that they will investigate it.

Laura: Alright. I'll see if I can talk to Gary later.

蘿拉：你真的認為蓋瑞盜用了卡蘿的創意嗎？

杭特：我不知道，但他不該像個懦夫般躲著她。

蘿拉：也是，剽竊卡蘿的創意可能會害他失去工作跟前途。

杭特：我聽說他們會調查這件事。

蘿拉：好吧，我看看晚點能不能與蓋瑞談談。

字彙／片語充電區 *Words and Phrases*

coward 名 懦夫 / pretext 名 藉口 / courageous 形 勇敢的 / dauntless 形 無畏的
step forward 自告奮勇；向前一步 / in Dutch 處境困難 / in a tight spot 走投無路

UNIT 014 dirtbag
裝灰塵的袋子？

🎧 014

暖身猜猜看 *Warming Up*

Mary: Did you see that scoundrel on the news last night?

Sam: Yeah. That **dirtbag** was finally arrested.

瑪莉：你昨天晚上有看到新聞裡的那個惡棍嗎？

山姆：有啊，那個下流胚子終於被逮捕了。

原來是這個意思！

dirtbag 卑鄙的人

　　dirtbag 從字面上來看，是裝滿泥沙的袋子或麻布袋，這也是這個詞彙一開始所指稱的意思，直到二十世紀，這個詞才初次被用來評論人，帶有「不整潔的、髒的、粗野的」等負面意思，之後逐漸引申指下流、齷齪的壞胚子。

對話練習 *Let's Talk!*

Mary: The news said that a gang committed the robberies.

Sam: So you are saying there are more of those **dirtbags**?

Mary: I am afraid so.

Sam: I believe the policemen will bring that scum's accomplices to justice.

Mary: Well, I will ask my friends to be careful until that happens.

瑪莉：新聞說那些搶劫的罪行涉及幫派組織。

山姆：你是說還有更多那種可鄙的歹徒？

瑪莉：恐怕是這樣。

山姆：我相信警察會將那個無恥惡徒的同謀繩之以法的。

瑪莉：在他們被逮捕之前，我得警告身邊的朋友小心點。

字彙／片語充電區 *Words and Phrases*

notorious 形 惡名昭彰的 / **vile** 形 卑鄙的 / **accomplice** 名 同謀 / **hideout** 藏匿處

put away 關起來；送進監獄 / **on the lam** 在逃 / **hold the bag** 承擔所有指控與責任

UNIT 015 black sheep
黑色的羊有什麼特別？

🎧 015

 暖身猜猜看 *Warming Up*

Earl: I have three brothers who all are well-disciplined.

Cindy: Aha! So you are the **black sheep**!

厄爾：我有三個哥哥，都非常嚴謹自律。

辛蒂：啊哈！那你就是那匹害群之馬囉！

 原來是這個意思！

black sheep 害群之馬

　　在工業發達前的年代，白羊的毛可以染成其他顏色，被視為有價值，黑羊的毛無法染色，因此被認為沒有經濟價值，後來就被用來表示「害群之馬」，不過，這個詞彙後來漸漸跳脫負面意思，用以形容「特立獨行的人」。

 對話練習 *Let's Talk!*

Allen: I have always been the **black sheep** in my family.

Mandy: What do you mean by that?

Allen: Ha-ha. I bother everyone with my surprises.

Mandy: I bet you are the youngest of your family.

Allen: You're right! I am the baby of the family.

亞倫：我向來都是家裡的害群之馬。

曼蒂：什麼意思？

亞倫：哈哈，我老是讓大家被我的驚喜搞得人仰馬翻的。

曼蒂：你肯定是家裡的老么。

亞倫：你說對啦！我在我們家的排行最小。

字彙／片語充電區 *Words and Phrases*

obey 動 服從 / sheepish 形 羞怯的 / disturb 動 擾亂 / offbeat 形 非主流的；特異的
abide by 遵守 / get sb. off my back 讓…不要來煩 / a party-pooper 掃興的人事物

UNIT 016 tosspot
被拋的平底鍋？

🎧 016

 暖身猜猜看 *Warming Up*

Karen: I didn't know Tom had such a low tolerance for alcohol.

Jerry: Yeah. He turned into a **tosspot** after just two beers!

凱倫：我不知道湯姆的酒量這麼差。

傑瑞：就是，才兩杯啤酒下肚，他就變醉漢了！

 原來是這個意思！

tosspot 醉漢

　　這個用語最早出現於十六世紀，莎士比亞的劇本"Twelfth Night"《第十二夜》中。toss是丟擲的意思，pot則指陶壺，早年的酒都是存放在陶壺裡面；tosspot是形容人已經醉到開始亂扔空的酒壺，用其醉態來比喻醉漢。

 對話練習 *Let's Talk!*

Karen: How are you feeling today?

Tom: Not good. My head is killing me.

Karen: I can't believe you got drunk on only two beers.

Tom: Those were two huge mugs! Did I do anything silly?

Karen: Well, I have a video of a certain **tosspot** in my cell-phone. Anyone interested?

凱倫：你今天覺得怎麼樣？

湯姆：不怎麼好，我的頭痛死了。

凱倫：我真不敢相信你竟然被兩杯啤酒打敗。

湯姆：那是兩大杯耶！我沒做什麼蠢事吧？

凱倫：這個嘛…我的手機裡有醉漢的影片喔，有沒有人感興趣啊？

字彙/片語充電區 *Words and Phrases*

drunkard 名 酒鬼 / **hangover** 名 宿醉 / **drowsy** 形 困倦的 / **alcoholic** 形 含酒精的
propose a toast to sb. 敬酒 / **feel rotten** 覺得不舒服 / **break down** 情緒失控

UNIT 017 a queer fish
奇怪的魚究竟有多古怪？

🎧 017

 暖身猜猜看 *Warming Up*

Connie: Did you see that guy? He is acting very strangely.

Randy: What **a queer fish**!

科妮：你看到那個男的嗎？他的舉動好奇怪。

藍迪：真是個怪人！

 原來是這個意思！

a queer fish 怪人；瘋子

　　fish在口語用法中可指人，ex. odd fish怪人、poor fish小可憐；queer這個字則需要小心使用，因為他不只有特異、古怪之意，更有暗指同性戀傾向的意味，因此，a queer fish除了怪人之外，也會被解讀為具同性戀傾向。

 對話練習 *Let's Talk!*

Matt: The fashion design competition was beyond my expectations!

Rita: I was hoping the designer from France would win.

Matt: I guess the judges wanted something more astonishing.

Rita: But the winner is really **a queer fish**. His works are so odd.

Matt: I suppose people have different tastes in fashion.

麥特：那個時裝設計比賽真是跌破我的眼鏡。

芮塔：我本來還希望那個法國設計師贏。

麥特：評審可能想要更令人為之驚豔的效果。

芮塔：但冠軍是個怪胎耶，他的作品都很怪異。

麥特：我想每個人對時尚的定義都不同吧。

字彙／片語充電區 *Words and Phrases*

lunatic 名 瘋子 / **weird** 形 奇特的 / **behavior** 名 行為 / **astonishing** 形 驚人的
scare away 把…嚇跑 / **fish out of water** 不熟悉環境而尷尬的人 / **fish out** 探出

UNIT 018 bird of passage
飛過迴廊的小鳥？

🎧 018

 暖身猜猜看 *Warming Up*

Vicky: I wonder how long Tom plans on being a **bird of passage**.

Carter: It's not a bad thing for him to see the world before settling down.

薇琪：不知道湯姆還打算漂泊多久。

卡特：在他定下來之前，多看看這個世界，不是件壞事。

 原來是這個意思！

bird of passage 居無定所的人

　　bird of passage有兩個意思，原始義為「侯鳥」，與migratory bird同義；第二個意思為「居無定所、經常搬遷的人」，此為衍生意義，因為這些人就像侯鳥一樣，只在一處待一陣子，就又遷移了。

 對話練習 *Let's Talk!*

Vicky: Don't you think being a pilot would be better than being a sailor?

Tom: Can't you have a little more faith in me?

Vicky: But you can't be a **bird of passage** forever.

Tom: Don't worry. I will come up with a long-term plan.

Vicky: I hope you'll figure it out before your next sea trip.

薇琪：你不覺得當飛行員比船員好嗎？

湯姆：你就不能對我有點信心嗎？

薇琪：但你不能永遠當個居無定所的人。

湯姆：別擔心，我會做長遠的打算。

薇琪：希望你能在下一班船之前打算好。

字彙／片語充電區 *Words and Phrases*

migrate 動 遷移 / movement 名 移居 / residence 名 住所 / passageway 名 通道
knock about 漂泊 / a long and difficult trek 長途跋涉 / a passage of arms 交戰

UNIT 019
bag lady
拎著大包小包的購物女性？

🎧 019

 暖身猜猜看 Warming Up

Kyle: Why are you carrying so many bags? Do you need a lift?

Mary: Thank God! These groceries made me feel like a **bag lady**.

凱爾：你幹嘛拎著一大堆袋子？要載你一程嗎？

瑪莉：謝天謝地！這些雜貨害我活像個街友。

 原來是這個意思！

bag lady 女性的街友

　　美國在1970年代時出現bag lady的說法，是shopping bag lady的簡化寫法，指的是城市中無家可歸的女性，將自己所有的家當都裝在購物袋裡，在城市裡流浪，尋找夜晚的棲身之所，並於垃圾桶找尋可用之物。

 **對話練習** *Let's Talk!*

Phil: What have you been up to these days?

Tina: I've been volunteering at a homeless shelter.

Phil: Really? You must see a lot of **bag ladies** there.

Tina: No, the shelter is full of men mostly.

Phil: I see. Well, what you are doing is certainly a good deed.

菲爾：你最近都在忙些什麼啊？

蒂娜：我在遊民收容中心當義工。

菲爾：真的嗎？你在那裡一定看到很多女街友吧。

蒂娜：沒有耶，那間收容中心裡大多數都是男性。

菲爾：了解，但你在做的事情絕對是件有意義的好事。

字彙／片語充電區 *Words and Phrases*

vagrant 名 漂泊者 / **dawdle** 動 遊蕩 / **freezing** 形 極冷的 / **welfare** 名 福利；幸福
fool around 遊手好閒 / **doggy bag** 剩菜袋 / **go from rags to riches** 由貧致富

UNIT 020 backseat driver
坐在後座的駕駛？

🎧 020

暖身猜猜看 *Warming Up*

Sara: I can't stand Dan. He keeps proposing lame ideas!

Ian: I didn't know he was such a **backseat driver**.

莎拉：我實在受不了丹，他一直提出爛主意！

伊恩：我不知道他原來是個愛亂指揮的人。

原來是這個意思！

backseat driver 胡亂給建議的人

　　這個慣用語起源於二十世紀初的美國，於汽車駕駛慢慢開始普及之時；backseat是汽車後座，這個慣用語指的是「坐在後座的人，明明看不到路況，卻還是想指揮駕駛」，藉以比喻「愛亂指揮、亂給建議的人」。

Let's Talk!

Nora: Did you know Carl applied for extra funding for your project?

Sam: No, I didn't. He is such a **backseat driver**!

Nora: I suppose you weren't informed about it.

Sam: What am I supposed to do now?

Nora: Calm down. Mr. Lee sent me over to figure this out.

諾拉：你知道卡爾為了你們的企劃，申請了額外的補助經費嗎？

山姆：我不知道，他真是個不清楚狀況還愛亂搞的傢伙！

諾拉：我猜大概沒有人告知你這件事。

山姆：那我現在應該怎麼辦？

諾拉：冷靜點，李經理讓我來了解情況。

字彙／片語充電區 *Words and Phrases*

conduct 動 引導 / indicate 動 指示 / annoying 形 惱人的 / chauffeur 名 汽車司機
give orders to 指揮 / clear up the mess 收拾殘局 / over one's head 越過上級

UNIT 021　a busy-body 忙得昏天暗地的人？

🎧 021

 暖身猜猜看 *Warming Up*

Ann: How did Tom find out about our trip last weekend?

Joe: Eddy must have said something about it. He's **a busy-body**.

安：湯姆怎麼會知道我們上週末去旅行？

喬：一定是艾迪說出去的，他很多管閒事。

 原來是這個意思！

a busy-body 多管閒事的人

　　a busy-body也可以寫成a busybody，在1520年代將busy（忙碌的）和body（意指person）兩字相結合，所產生的慣用語，用來形容「愛插手他人事物或私事的人」，即中文的「愛管閒事的人」。

 對話練習 *Let's Talk!*

Megan: Marcus is prying into our project.

　Joey: Well, you know what **a busy-body** he is.

Megan: We can't afford to lose this proposal.

　Joey: That's true. We worked on it for several days and nights.

Megan: I hope Marcus doesn't keep bugging us.

梅根：馬卡斯在打聽我們的提案。

喬伊：你也知道他有多愛管閒事，

梅根：這個案子絕不能出差錯。

喬伊：這倒是，這可是我們日以繼夜趕出來的案子。

梅根：我只希望馬卡斯別來找我們的麻煩就好了。

字彙／片語充電區 *Words and Phrases*

pry 動 打聽 / **snoop** 動 窺探 / **meddler** 名 愛管閒事的人 / **gossip** 動 閒聊；傳播流言 **make discreet inquiries** 打探 / **burn sb. up** 使惱怒 / **brush sb. off** 不理睬某人

UNIT 022

class act
某一階級的舉動？

🎧 022

暖身猜猜看 *Warming Up*

Allen: George is really a **class act**.

Judy: Indeed. He has excellent taste and style.

亞倫：喬治真的是個很出色的人。

茱蒂：的確，他很有品味，又具備個人風格。

原來是這個意思！

class act 出類拔萃的人

　　class act可用來指在某個領域表現十分出色，足以成為他人目標或模範的人，也可用來指某個氣質與風度出眾或品味不凡的人。此外，這個慣用語也可以用來指事或物，例如一個很有社會責任的成功企業也可以稱為a class act。

 對話練習 *Let's Talk!*

Paul: What a concert! No one sings like Robbie Williams.

Cathy: That's so true. He is a great musician, a **class act**.

Paul: Yeah. I love all of his songs!

Cathy: Did you know his latest album is a real hit?

Paul: That's great! I guess I should buy it.

保羅：好棒的演唱會！羅比・威廉斯的唱功真是獨一無二。

凱西：真的，他是名優秀的音樂人，非常出色。

保羅：對啊，他所有的歌我都喜歡！

凱西：你知道他的新專輯很熱銷嗎？

保羅：真棒！我想我該去買一張來聽聽。

字彙/片語充電區 *Words and Phrases*

exceptional 形 優秀的 / phenomenal 形 傑出的 / inept 形 無能的 / trait 名 特點
have the goods 很有才能 / have on the ball 有聰明才智 / fair to middling 過得去

UNIT 023

a good sport
一項很好的運動？

🎧 023

 暖身猜猜看 *Warming Up*

Roy: Tim lost the arm wrestling contest. Boy, was he ever pissed off.

Jenny: That's weird. He is usually **a good sport**.

羅伊：提姆比腕力輸了，怪了，他有為此生氣過嗎？

珍妮：真奇怪，他平常都很有風度的。

 原來是這個意思！

a good sport 有風度的人；精神可嘉

　　除了我們熟知的「運動」外，sport也有「玩笑、被戲弄的對象」之意，英式口語英文中，也指朋友或老兄這樣的稱呼，採用這些用法的a good sport，指的是「一個有風度的人」，即使在遊戲或運動中輸了，或被開玩笑也不介意。

 **對話練習** *Let's Talk!*

Jenny: Tim, is everything all right?

Tim: I shouldn't have taken my frustrations out on Roy.

Jenny: I guess something is bothering you.

Tim: Well, I got eliminated after the job interview.

Jenny: So that's why **the good sport** has turned sulky.

珍妮：提姆，你還好嗎？

提姆：我不該把我的沮喪發洩在羅伊身上。

珍妮：我猜是有什麼事讓你感到困擾吧。

提姆：嗯，我在面試後被刷下來了。

珍妮：原來是這個讓一個好好先生繃著臉啊。

字彙／片語充電區 *Words and Phrases*

demeanor 名 風度 / frustration 名 挫折 / displeased 形 不悅的 / outdo 動 超越
take out on sb. 拿某人出氣 / see red 火冒三丈 / laugh up one's sleeve 竊笑

UNIT 024 dreamboat 一艘夢寐以求的船？

🎧 024

 暖身猜猜看 Warming Up

Mary: Pete is such a gentleman. He is handsome and caring.

Carl: He sounds like your **dreamboat**.

瑪莉：彼特是個十足的紳士，他又帥又體貼。

卡爾：他聽起來像是你的理想情人哦。

 原來是這個意思！

dreamboat 理想的對象或物品

　　在美國的文化中，有艘自己的船可以去冒險或出遊，代表著一種夢想成真。dreamboat的字面意義是「夢寐以求的船」，由此義延伸，就能用來比喻理想的對象（通常指男性，也可以用來形容心目中理想的汽車等交通工具）。

 *Let's Talk!*

Sandy: My new neighbor, Chad, is so cute!

Will: So, you have found your **dreamboat**.

Sandy: You must see for yourself. I've never met anyone like him before.

Will: So what now? You can't just be a secret admirer, right?

Sandy: This is exactly why I am here. I need your help!

仙蒂：我的新鄰居查德真的超有魅力的！

威爾：看來你找到你的夢中情人了。

仙蒂：你親眼見過他就知道了，我以前從沒遇過像他這樣的人。

威爾：那你現在在打算怎麼做？總不能就當個小粉絲吧？

仙蒂：這就是我為什麼會來這裡，我需要你的幫忙！

字彙/片語充電區 *Words and Phrases*

eyeful 名 引人注目物(尤指美女) / charming 形 魅力十足的 / affection 名 鍾愛

a head-turner 萬人迷 / set one's cap for 追求 / be smitten with 對…一見鍾情

UNIT 025 bird dog
既是鳥又是狗？

🎧 025

 暖身猜猜看 *Warming Up*

Bob: I think Troy is a **bird dog**!

Lisa: Are you sure about that? What makes you suspect him?

鮑伯：我覺得特洛伊是監控我們的人！

麗莎：你確定嗎？是什麼讓你懷疑他的？

 原來是這個意思！

bird dog 監管人；挖人才者

　　bird dog原指專門獵鳥的獵犬，因其作用在捷足先登地叼回被射中的獵物，所以被用來比喻搶他人對象的人（負面意思）；另外，這個英文也可以當動詞用（bird-dog），意指「偷偷地監管他人、嚴密監視」。

 **對話練習** *Let's Talk!*

Teddy: I think my supervisor is **bird-dogging** me.

Elaine: What makes you think so?

Teddy: I've caught her sneaking up on me several times.

Elaine: Could it just be you being too suspicious?

Teddy: I hope so. I don't think I've done anything wrong.

泰迪：我覺得我的主管在偷偷監管我。

伊蓮：你怎麼會麼想？

泰迪：她有好幾次都被我發現在偷偷觀察我。

伊蓮：會不會是你太多疑了？

泰迪：希望如此，至少我不認為自己做錯了什麼。

字彙／片語充電區 *Words and Phrases*

suspicious 形 可疑的 / monitor 名 監視器 / strictly 副 嚴格地 / retrieve 動 補救
do one's bit 盡本分 / make allegation 指控 / be strictly for the birds 無價值的

UNIT 026 criminal lawyer
犯了罪的律師？

🎧 026

暖身猜猜看 *Warming Up*

Susan: I've decided to be a **criminal lawyer**.

Terry: Well, it's more serious compared to business law.

蘇珊：我打算成為刑事律師。

泰瑞：比起商事法，這更嚴肅。

原來是這個意思！

criminal lawyer 刑事律師

　　這個慣用語所要強調的是，lawyer前面的詞彙是說明律師的專業領域，並非用來形容這名律師；因此，criminal lawyer是刑事律師；正如同drug lawyer中的drug，是毒品、管制藥品的意思，不能看成嗑藥的律師。

對話練習 *Let's Talk!*

Maggie: I can't decide which law firm I should apply for.

Parker: I thought you were interested in commercial law.

Maggie: But I'm also interested in being a **criminal lawyer**.

Parker: Why? Have you been watching too many CSI episodes?

Maggie: Stop teasing me! I just think it is a meaningful profession.

梅姬：我無法決定要申請去哪間律師事務所。

帕克：我以為你對商事法很感興趣。

梅姬：但刑事律師其實也滿吸引我的。

帕克：為什麼？你看太多《CSI犯罪現場》了嗎？

梅姬：不要笑我！我只是覺得這工作很有意義。

字彙/片語充電區 *Words and Phrases*

attorney 名 律師 / lawsuit 名 訴訟 / practicing 形 執業的 / victim 名 被害人

file a lawsuit 提出訴訟 / a civil case 民事訴訟案件 / pore over 鑽研；專心閱讀

UNIT 027 blue-stocking 一雙藍色的褲襪？

🎧 027

 暖身猜猜看 *Warming Up*

Joey: Are you sure becoming a **blue-stocking** is what you want?

Ivy: I know it won't be easy, but I will put all my efforts into it.

喬伊：你確定你想要成為女學者嗎？

艾薇：我知道那不容易，但我會盡一切努力的。

 原來是這個意思！

blue-stocking 女學者；女才子

　　1750年代間，倫敦的Elizabeth Montagu女士比照巴黎人的做法，發起了女性的文學沙龍，她們定期聚會，暢談文學作品，不再只是玩紙牌或盛裝出席派對；stocking為褲襪，藍色的褲襪是用來比喻這些女性簡樸的裝束。

 對話練習 *Let's Talk!*

Mark: I've heard your grandmother was a well-known **blue-stocking**.

Vicky: Yeah. She did influence me a lot.

Mark: That must inspire you to study literature.

Vicky: I've always loved reading. Books have been my guide.

Mark: Good for you. I didn't know you're such a book lover.

馬克：我聽說你祖母是位知名的女學者。

薇琪：是啊，她對我的影響很大。

馬克：這肯定是你之所以想唸文學的原因吧。

薇琪：我一直很喜愛閱讀，書是我的嚮導。

馬克：那很好啊，我都不知道你這麼愛書。

字彙/片語充電區 *Words and Phrases*

scholar 名 學者 / compose 動 作詩 / celebrated 形 著名的 / recognize 動 表彰
think highly of 極重視 / put one's thumb up 認同 / point of view 觀點；看法

UNIT 028

cheerleader
專指啦啦隊的隊長？

🎧 028

 暖身猜猜看 *Warming Up*

Lucy: Betty told me that the head **cheerleader** is bossy.

Randy: Really? But I think she is actually considerate and gracious.

露西：貝蒂告訴我，那個啦啦隊的隊長很愛指使人。

藍迪：是嗎？但我覺得她其實很體貼有禮。

 原來是這個意思！

cheerleader 啦啦隊的一員

　　leader為「領袖；領導人」之意，光看這個慣用語的字面意思，會讓人誤以為是指啦啦隊的隊長；其實，這裡的leader所隱含的是「帶領觀眾的人」，整個慣用語為「帶領觀眾整齊劃一地歡呼、加油的人」，也就是啦啦隊員。

 對話練習 *Let's Talk!*

Rita: Watching baseball games in a stadium is the best!

Andy: I know! Nothing can compare to the ambiance.

Rita: Everybody waves and cheers with the **cheerleaders**.

Andy: It is the cheerleaders' and the audience's job to raise morale.

Rita: You're right. We are actually taking part in the game.

芮塔：在球場觀看棒球賽最讚了！

安迪：就是啊！這種氣氛沒有什麼能比得上。

芮塔：在場的每個人都跟著啦啦隊一起揮手和歡呼。

安迪：激發鬥志可是啦啦隊員跟觀眾的責任。

芮塔：說得對，我們也是參與賽事的一員呢。

字彙／片語充電區 *Words and Phrases*

stimulate 動 刺激；激勵 / **passion** 名 熱情 / **cheerful** 形 興高采烈的；使人愉快的 **cheer up** 使振作；使高興起來 / **cheerleading squad** 啦啦隊 / **accrue to** 帶給

UNIT 029

sea dog
海洋的狗就是指海狗？

🎧 029

 暖身猜猜看 *Warming Up*

Rose: Are you sure sailing is safe?

Kyle: I promise. We'll go with Sam. He is a **sea dog**.

蘿絲：你確定出海會很安全？

凱爾：保證安全，我們會跟山姆一起，他是名經驗老到的航海人。

 原來是這個意思！

sea dog 老練的水手

　　在英國伊莉莎白女王時代（十六至十七世紀），sea dog這個詞被用來指稱橫行於海上的海盜或冒險者，由dog一詞可以看出比喻的是不討喜之人；而後，引申這些人的特質，這個慣用語就被用來描述「經驗老道的水手」。

 **對話練習** *Let's Talk!*

Kelly: This novel is about an adventure of a **sea dog**.

Harry: Sounds like "Moby Dick". Have you ever read it?

Kelly: I have. Ernest Hemingway is one of my favorite writers.

Harry: Actually, the book was written by Herman Melville.

Kelly: Well, both Melville and Hemingway were great American writers.

凱莉：這本小說是關於一個老水手的冒險。

哈利：好像《白鯨記》的內容，你看過那本書嗎？

凱莉：看過啊，海明威是我最喜愛的作家之一。

哈利：事實上，這是赫爾曼‧梅爾維爾寫的小說。

凱莉：嗯，梅爾維爾與海明威都是很棒的美國作家。

字彙/片語充電區 *Words and Phrases*

experienced 形 老練的 / stun 名 驚嘆 / wreck 名 失事 / dogmatic 形 固執己見的
set sail 出航；啟航 / be awkward with 不熟練的；笨拙的 / take a chance 冒險

UNIT 030
greenhorn
與園藝有關的綠色號角？

🎧 030

暖身猜猜看 *Warming Up*

Anna: Even though you're a **greenhorn**, you are doing pretty well.

Roy: Thank you. That's because Mark has helped me a lot.

安娜：雖然你只是個新手，但做得相當不錯。

羅伊：謝謝，那是因為馬克幫了我很多忙。

原來是這個意思！

greenhorn 新手；生手

此說法起源於十八世紀的珠寶手工業，當時流行用動物角做成具浮雕的胸針，加工時須用火烤，再鑄型，燒出漂亮的咖啡色；若溫度過高，則會烤出綠色的失敗品（多為學徒作品），因此greenhorn被引申為「無經驗的新手」。

對話練習 *Let's Talk!*

Irene: How have you adapted to our department?

Kyle: I think everyone is so nice to a **greenhorn** like me.

Irene: If you have any questions, don't hesitate to ask us.

Kyle: Hopefully, I haven't caused you too much trouble.

Irene: Don't be silly! Our doors are always open.

艾琳：你還適應我們的部門嗎？

凱爾：我覺得大家都對我這菜鳥很好。

艾琳：有任何問題的話，就問我們，不用猶豫。

凱爾：希望我沒有帶給大家太多麻煩。

艾琳：別說傻話了！隨時歡迎你來找我們。

字彙／片語充電區 *Words and Phrases*

apprentice 名 學徒 / veteran 名 老手 / consult 動 請教；與…商量 / adapt 動 適應
help out 幫助；解決困難 / take one's time 慢慢來 / feel ill at ease 感到不安

UNIT 031　man Friday
星期五的男性？

🎧 031

 暖身猜猜看 Warming Up

Scott: How was your family trip?
Lesley: Well, our **man Friday** saved us big time.

史考特：你們的家庭旅遊如何？
雷思麗：我們的男管家省下我們很多時間。

 原來是這個意思！

man Friday 男性的忠實僕人

　　這個慣用語的起源來自小說《魯賓遜漂流記》。Friday是小說中的一個角色，是忠實、奉獻的黑人男僕，男主角魯賓遜經常以my man Friday稱呼他，因此，man Friday後來就被用來形容忠誠的男管家或僕人。

 **對話練習** *Let's Talk!*

Matt: Our family is planning to go on vacation.
Nancy: You'd better stay in a resort that fixes you up with a butler.
Matt: I was thinking of one with a kid's club. I'll take my kids there.
Nancy: Trust me. A **man Friday** can save you a lot of time and effort.
Matt: Alright. I'll think about that.

麥特：我們家打算去度假。
南西：你最好找間提供管家服務的度假村。
麥特：我在考慮一家有兒童活動中心的，我會把小孩帶到那裡。
南西：相信我，一個管家可以讓你省下很多時間與工作。
麥特：好吧，我會考慮。

字彙／片語充電區 *Words and Phrases*

butler 名 男管家 / servant 名 僕人；僱工 / competent 形 能勝任的 / assist 動 協助
avail oneself of 利用 / devote oneself to 專心致力 / breathing space 喘息時間

UNIT 032

ghost writer
專寫鬼故事的作家？

🎧 032

暖身猜猜看 Warming Up

Ian: Being a **ghost writer** is almost like having an under-the-table job.

Amy: Don't look at it that way. Your time will come.

伊恩：當代筆作家其實不算是上得了檯面的工作。
艾咪：不要那樣想，你的機會一定會來的。

原來是這個意思！

ghost writer 代筆寫作的人

　　ghost writer是個相當晚才出現的慣用語（1890年才出現於美國），指像鬼魅一樣看不到的作者；意思就是「為他人撰稿書籍、文案、演講稿等，而不具自己名字的職業」；ghost本身當動詞則有「替人代筆、捉刀」之意。

對話練習 Let's Talk!

Judy: The politician's words were very effective.

Mark: Who knew that he could be so incisive?

Judy: He truly has a powerful team behind him.

Mark: What do you mean?

Judy: Don't you know? He has a crew of **ghost writers** and advisors.

茱蒂：那個政客的話可真有力。
馬克：誰能想得到他竟能如此犀利。
茱蒂：他背後的智囊團確實很了不起。
馬克：什麼意思？
茱蒂：你不知道嗎？他有一群代筆的人跟顧問啊。

字彙/片語充電區 Words and Phrases

composition 名 作品 / **authentic** 形 真正的 / **anonymous** 形 匿名的；不署名的
affix one's signature 具名 / **let out** 洩露 / **steal one's thunder** 剽竊某人的想法

UNIT 033 busboy 搭公車的男孩？

🎧 033

 暖身猜猜看 *Warming Up*

Martin: I just found a **busboy** opening at Big Joe's Café.

Wayne: I'm wondering if they have enough dirty dishes for another one.

馬丁：我在Big Joe's Café找到一個雜工的缺。

韋恩：不知道他們的髒盤子夠不夠多，可以再請一個。

 原來是這個意思！

busboy 餐館的打雜工

　　這個慣用語起源於十九世紀的法國（omnibus），指幫忙清理桌子的雜工，到二十世紀才簡化為busboy；這裡的bus用來比喻餐廳裡收髒碗盤的推車，像公車一樣載滿各式各樣的食器，來回忙碌的模樣。

 對話練習 *Let's Talk!*

Nancy: Congratulations on winning the best-manager award.

Roger: Thank you. It has taken me quite a long time to get here.

Nancy: I heard that it's quite a story.

Roger: True. I started as a **busboy**, doing all the heavy-duty jobs.

Nancy: That must have been tough. And it's very inspiring.

南西：恭喜你得到最佳經理獎。

羅傑：謝謝，這一路我可是走得很辛苦呢。

南西：聽說你的心路歷程不是三言兩語可以講完的。

羅傑：的確，我從一個做粗活的雜工開始做起。

南西：那一定很辛苦，同時也很激勵人心。

字彙／片語充電區 *Words and Phrases*

restaurant 名 餐館 / strive 動 努力 / haste 動 匆忙 / proprietor 名 業主
do odds and ends 打雜 / work part-time 打工 / clear up 清理；整理

UNIT 034

have two left feet
擁有兩隻左腳的人？

🎧 034

暖身猜猜看 *Warming Up*

Rose: Hey! This is our wedding song. Let's dance!

Larry: Give me a break. You know how I **have two left feet**.

蘿絲：嘿！這是我們的婚禮主題曲，我們來跳舞吧！

賴瑞：饒了我吧，你知道我的舞姿很笨拙的。

原來是這個意思！

have two left feet 舞姿笨拙

　　想像一下，如果一個人用兩隻左腳來跳舞，是不是會顯得很笨拙呢？所以，have two left feet就用來形容人「舞姿生硬、笨拙的模樣」；這樣的說法比 not good at dancing（你不會跳舞）好，因為後者帶有評論，語氣比較傷人。

對話練習 *Let's Talk!*

Lucy: I've signed us up for a ballroom dancing lesson!

Mark: No way! I'm not going to expose myself to ridicule.

Lucy: Don't worry. It's a small class for tenderfoots.

Mark: I **have two left feet** by nature. It's hopeless.

Lucy: Come on! Just do it as an exercise.

露西：我幫我們兩個報名了國標舞課喔！

馬克：不是吧！我才不要去丟人現眼。

露西：別緊張，那是小班制的初學者課程。

馬克：我天生就不會跳舞，沒救了。

露西：拜託！你就當是運動嘛。

字彙/片語充電區 *Words and Phrases*

motion 名 移動 / **shimmy** 名 狐步 / **socialize** 動 交際 / **etiquette** 名 禮儀；禮節

get vibes 焦慮；恐懼 / **back down** 放棄；打退堂鼓 / **itch for a try** 躍躍欲試

UNIT 035

crackerjack
和小點心有關？

🎧 035

 暖身猜猜看 *Warming Up*

Anna: Can you hook me up with a professional in investment?

Josh: Sure! My college roommate is a **crackerjack** banker.

安娜：你能不能介紹一個熟知投資的專業人士給我？

喬許：沒問題！我大學的室友就是出色的銀行家。

 原來是這個意思！

crackerjack 傑出的；上等的

　　Jack在英文中是男孩跟男人的代稱，而crack作為形容詞時，意思為一流的、最棒的；兩者放在一起時，jack可以與cracker中的[k]押韻；這個慣用語形容的是一個具備某種專長、擁有某項長才的人。

對話練習 *Let's Talk!*

Anna: Josh referred you as a **crackerjack** banker.

Matt: He is exaggerating. Well, how can I help you?

Anna: I'm looking for some suitable investment products.

Matt: Let's start from figuring out your acceptance of risk.

Anna: Wow. I didn't know I would need to fill in a questionnaire first.

安娜：喬許說你是最頂尖的銀行家。

麥特：他太誇張了，我可以為你做些什麼呢？

安娜：我在找合適的投資商品。

麥特：我們先從了解你的風險承擔程度開始吧。

安娜：哇，我不知道我還必須先填問卷呢。

字彙/片語充電區 *Words and Phrases*

remarkable 形 卓越的 / **splendid** 形 極好的 / **inferior** 形 較差的 / **evaluate** 動 評價
a hard act to follow 難以超越的人事物 / **all thumbs** 笨手笨腳 / **drop the ball** 出錯

UNIT 036

write one's own ticket
自己填票是在開支票嗎？

🎧 036

暖身猜猜看 Warming Up

Helen: Have you prepared for your job interview next week?

Tony: Don't worry. With my experience, I can **write my own ticket**!

海倫：下週的工作面試你準備好了嗎？

東尼：別擔心，有過去的經驗，我可說是勢在必得呢！

原來是這個意思！

write one's own ticket 佔有絕對優勢

　　ticket指「門票、入場券」，那麼，假如你可以自行填寫門票上的訊息，自行決定時間與票價等資訊，可就很厲害了；引申形容一個人可以照自己的意思開條件，不怕他人不接受，也就是「取得決定權及全部優勢」之意。

對話練習 Let's Talk!

Nina: I heard you're going to conduct the press conference!

Carl: Yeah, my boss has assigned me to market the product.

Nina: Congratulations! All your hard work has been worth it.

Carl: Thanks. I think I'll be able to **write my own ticket** after this project.

Nina: That's great to hear!

妮娜：聽說你要主持這次的記者會。

卡爾：是啊，老闆要我來負責這個產品的行銷。

妮娜：恭喜！你的努力得到回報了。

卡爾：謝謝，我想在這次的案子過後，我能取得更多的優勢與決定權。

妮娜：那真是好消息！

字彙/片語充電區 Words and Phrases

advantage 名 優勢；優點 / predominate 動 佔主導地位 / position 名 地位；身分

hinge on 取決於 / cut to the chase 切入正題；開門見山 / by the book 照規距來

UNIT 037 on one's high horse 在高大的馬背上？

🎧 037

 暖身猜猜看 Warming Up

Nina: What David said last night was very rude!

Ian: He gets **on his high horse** while talking about business.

妮娜：大衛昨晚說的話實在太無禮了！

伊恩：每次談到生意，他都一副目中無人的樣子。

 原來是這個意思！

on one's high horse 目中無人

　　十八世紀的時候，騎士、國王和要人都是騎乘高大的戰馬，而女士和普通人只能騎一般的承載用馬；因此，當說一個人是坐在他高大的戰馬上時，也暗指他的位階較高，這種姿態就被引申用來形容「頤指氣使或目中無人的態度」。

 **對話練習 Let's Talk!**

Betty: Don't you think you are provoking your colleagues?

David: Do I have to be responsible for others' grudges?

Betty: No one likes to be treated as inferior all the time.

David: I am not here to make friends.

Betty: Well, you can't win people's hearts up **on your high horse**.

貝蒂：你不覺得你是在激怒同事嗎？

大衛：我難不成還要為他人的妒忌心負責嗎？

貝蒂：沒有人喜歡老是被輕視。

大衛：我又不是來交朋友的。

貝蒂：一副高高在上的樣子是沒辦法贏得人心的。

字彙／片語充電區 Words and Phrases

obnoxious 形 令人討厭的 / improper 形 不合禮儀的 / aggressive 形 積極進取的
get under one's skin 令人感到不舒服 / off one's high horse 放下某人的身段

UNIT 038 think a great deal of oneself 形容某人想得太多了？

🎧 038

 暖身猜猜看 *Warming Up*

Lily: I keep getting the cold shoulder from the newcomer.
Jack: Yeah. She really **thinks a great deal of herself**.

莉莉：那個新人對我一直很冷漠。
傑克：對啊，她太自視甚高了。

 原來是這個意思！

think a great deal of oneself 自視甚高

a great deal of用來形容「大量、多數」，但是，這個慣用語並非指「某人想得很多」，而是用來描述某人一直在想自己，似乎把自己想得多麼至關重要，也就是「自視甚高」的意思。

 對話練習 *Let's Talk!*

Marvin: How's your new job?
Sandy: It's okay. I haven't had any challenging tasks yet, though.
Marvin: Well, just don't **think a great deal of yourself**.
Sandy: I know, Dad. You want me to be humble and friendly.
Marvin: Remember, building a career is not just about abilities.

馬文：你的新工作如何？
仙蒂：還可以，但目前完全沒遇到什麼有挑戰性的工作。
馬文：你可別太自視甚高了。
仙蒂：我知道，爸爸，你希望我做人謙虛和善一點。
馬文：要記得，經營一份工作，靠的可不全只有能力而已。

字彙 / 片語充電區 *Words and Phrases*

snob 名 傲慢的人 / arrogant 形 傲慢的 / despise 動 看不起 / braggart 名 吹牛的人
have one's nose in the air 高傲的；傲慢的 / make a big deal out of 小題大作

UNIT 039 too cool for school
學校的風雲人物？

🎧 039

 暖身猜猜看 *Warming Up*

Jenny: Did you see how arrogant Bill was at the meeting?

Earl: He totally thinks he is **too cool for school**.

珍妮：你看到比爾在開會時那副自大的樣子嗎？

厄爾：他完全是自以為了不起。

 原來是這個意思！

too cool for school 自以為了不起

　　美國1960年代時流行反社會主義，嬉皮份子反政府、對抗體制，認為反文化優於主流社會，too cool for school就是指這些人自認為主流體制配不上自己，也被沿用來形容「自以為是、自視甚高的人」。

 對話練習 *Let's Talk!*

Simon: I wish somebody could teach that stubborn man a lesson!

Fanny: You mean Spencer? What happened?

Simon: He opposed every idea we proposed at the meeting.

Fanny: But he doesn't know a thing about this case.

Simon: That's the point! He just thinks he's **too cool for school**.

賽門：我真希望有人給那個老頑固上一課！

芬妮：你在說史賓賽嗎？發生什麼事了？

賽門：他在會議上反對我們提出的所有想法。

芬妮：但他根本不了解這個案子。

賽門：這就是重點！他就是自以為了不起。

字彙/片語充電區 *Words and Phrases*

pompous 形 自負的 / radical 形 激進的 / resist 動 抵抗 / righteous 形 正直的
rebel against 對抗 / full of oneself 自以為是 / all hat and no cattle 浮誇而不實際

UNIT 040
go-to guy
走向某處的人？

🎧 040

暖身猜猜看 Warming Up

Sara: Can you please check my computer out for me?

Leo: Why don't you talk to Sam? He is my **go-to guy**.

莎拉：你可以幫我檢查一下我的電腦嗎？

里歐：你何不去找山姆幫忙？他是我的萬事通。

原來是這個意思！

go-to guy 能搞定事情的人

　　這個慣用語源自於體育比賽，指的是在關鍵時刻，能幫隊伍得分的球員（隊友會將球傳給他，倚靠他得分。）go to本身也有「求助於」的意思，所以後來就被拿來形容「在某方面可以求助的對象」。

對話練習 *Let's Talk!*

Allen: I can't believe Bert is quitting!

Nicole: Maybe he is sick of being the **go-to guy** at all hours.

Allen: Or, maybe he has found a better way out.

Nicole: Anyway, let's throw him a farewell party.

Allen: Good idea! We should send him our best wishes.

亞倫：我不敢相信伯特要辭職了！

妮可：也許他厭倦當大家的萬事通了。

亞倫：搞不好是找到更好的出路。

妮可：無論如何，我們來幫他辦個歡送會吧。

亞倫：好主意！應該向他致上我們的祝福。

字彙/片語充電區 *Words and Phrases*

capable 形 有能力的 / **oblige** 動 答應…的請求 / **troublesome** 形 麻煩的；討厭的
give a helping hand 幫助 / **straighten out** 解決；改正 / **be no slouch** 俐落能幹

UNIT 041　smart cookie
餅乾還分聰明還是笨的嗎？

🎧 041

 暖身猜猜看 Warming Up

Sandy: Who should I send to negotiate with that difficult client?

Tyler: How about Emma? She is quite a **smart cookie**.

仙蒂：我該派誰去跟那個難搞的客戶協商呢？

泰勒：艾瑪如何？她是個精明的人。

 原來是這個意思！

smart cookie 精明能幹的人

　　十八世紀時，cookie指餅乾，而後也被用來稱呼人，一個可能的起源是用來形容廚師，smart用來形容廚師的悟性，因為當時廚師只需要接受實際訓練，無須文憑；後來，smart cookie就用來形容「聰明、機靈的人」。

 **對話練習 Let's Talk!**

Emma: I think I can convince Mr. Lee to make a concession.

Henry: Just don't forget to stand on our margin and limit.

Emma: No problem. I will keep that in mind.

Henry: Be a **smart cookie**. Good luck.

Emma: Thank you. I won't blow the deal.

艾瑪：我相信我能說服李先生做出讓步。

亨利：別忘了要守住我們的利潤和底線。

艾瑪：沒問題，我會記住這點。

亨利：機靈點，祝你好運。

艾瑪：謝謝，我不會搞砸這個案子的。

字彙/片語充電區 Words and Phrases

intelligent 形 聰明的 / **clumsy** 形 笨拙的 / **reception** 名 感受 / **seemly** 形 適當的 **sound out** 試探；探聽 / **tinker with** 笨拙地修理 / **a tough cookie** 不易動搖的人

UNIT 042

backstabber
從背後攻擊人的行為？

🎧 042

暖身猜猜看 *Warming Up*

Bonnie: I can't believe Mark stole our idea for the project!

Wayne: How could we have known he's actually a **backstabber**?

邦妮：不敢相信馬克竟然偷了我們企劃的點子！

韋恩：我們怎麼知道他實際上是個背後插刀的小人？

原來是這個意思！

backstabber 從背後出賣別人的人

　　二十世紀初期的英國，政治人物跟勞工之間的關係時而緊張、相互牽制，在政治活動和社會活動的領域中，產生了backstabber這個詞彙，意指因為信任對方而放鬆警戒，以致於被對方從背後插刀，比喻「從背後出賣他人者」。

對話練習 *Let's Talk!*

May: My heart goes out to our CEO, Mr. Brown.

Dan: Same here. The board meeting was awfully inequitable.

May: Tom even proposed replacing Mr. Brown with someone else.

Dan: I know! He's such a **backstabber**.

May: Let's talk to the others. Maybe there's something we can do.

梅：我真為執行長布朗先生感到不值。

丹：我也是，董事會根本就不公平。

梅：湯姆還建議要以其他人取代布朗先生的位子。

丹：就是啊！他真是個從背後插刀的小人。

梅：我們去找其他人談談，也許我們可以做點什麼。

字彙／片語充電區 *Words and Phrases*

traitor 名 背叛者 / forsake 動 拋棄 / deceive 動 蒙蔽；欺騙 / fidelity 名 忠誠

sell sb. out 背叛 / stab sb. in the back 中傷 / be two-faced 表裡不一的

UNIT 043　downer
往下移動的人？

🎧 043

 暖身猜猜看 *Warming Up*

Larry: I'll pass on the party. I want to go home early today.

Sara: Come on. Don't be such a **downer**. It's Friday!

賴瑞：我不去派對了，我今天想早點回家。

莎拉：拜託，不要掃興嘛，今天是星期五耶！

 原來是這個意思！

downer 掃興的人

　　down有低落、沮喪、憂鬱之意，downer一開始是抗憂鬱藥物和鎮靜劑的代稱，在1970年代時，用於形容「心情沮喪或低落的人」，後來才慢慢衍生其義至「將低氣壓渲染給他人者」，即「掃興的人」。

 對話練習 *Let's Talk!*

Willie: Are you going to the basketball game this Sunday?

Erin: Of course. It's the championship.

Willie: Great! Shall we ask Emily to come?

Erin: I don't think so. She didn't like it much last year.

Willie: Oh, right. She was quite a **downer** at the auditorium.

威利：你要去看星期天的籃球賽嗎？

艾琳：當然，這可是冠軍賽耶。

威利：太好了！我們要不要約艾蜜莉一起去？

艾琳：我想不要了吧，去年她就不怎麼喜歡。

威利：對喔，她在觀眾席上還挺掃興的。

字彙／片語充電區 *Words and Phrases*

disappoint 動 使失望；使挫敗 / dispirit 動 使氣餒；使沮喪 / atmosphere 名 氣氛 / a wet blanket 掃興的人或物 / give sb. a flat denial 斷然拒絕 / brace up 打起精神

UNIT 044

freeloader
坐車不付錢的奧客？

🎧 044

 暖身猜猜看 *Warming Up*

Lily: Tim has been coming over several times a week. What's he up to?

Tony: Well, I think he's kind of a **freeloader**.

莉莉：提姆一個禮拜來我們這裡好幾次，他到底想做什麼？

東尼：這個嘛，我覺得他有點愛佔便宜。

 原來是這個意思！

freeloader 白吃白住的人

　　loader是裝貨機及載貨人的意思，免費把東西載走，意指想不花任何代價地享受福利，也可以用free rider取代。freeloader原本是指「濫用社會資源、不事生產的人」，後來才用來形容「在別人家白吃白住的人」。

 對話練習 *Let's Talk!*

Betty: Here you are again. What do you want?

George: There's a good game on Channel 5. Let's get some pizza.

Betty: You are such a **freeloader** all the time!

George: Come on. It's much more fun to do things together.

Betty: Maybe. But definitely not with you!

貝蒂：又是你，你要做什麼？

喬治：第五台在轉播比賽，我們叫披薩來吃吧。

貝蒂：你真是個很愛白吃白喝的人耶！

喬治：別這樣嘛，大家一起才好玩啊。

貝蒂：也許，但絕對不是跟你一起！

字彙／片語充電區 *Words and Phrases*

sponge 名 海綿；吃閒飯的人 / brazen 形 厚臉皮的 / contribution 名 貢獻
attach oneself to 依附 / in clover 安逸 / load the dice 採用不正當的手段

UNIT 045

deadbeat
準確的致命一擊？

🎧 045

 暖身猜猜看 *Warming Up*

Arthur: Dylan told me that Albert has become a **deadbeat**.

Katie: What happened? He was so talented back in school.

亞瑟：狄倫告訴我，亞伯特現在變成一個懶鬼了。

凱蒂：發生什麼事了？他以前在學校那麼有才華。

 原來是這個意思！

deadbeat 懶鬼；欠錢不還的人

　　deadbeat起源於美國南北戰爭（Civil War）時期，當時意指completely beaten（徹底被打倒），之後取其基本意涵「筋疲力竭、毫無用處」的意思，引申形容「不願意負責任、想依靠他人者」或「想躲避債務的人」。

 對話練習 *Let's Talk!*

Arthur: I've heard Albert is too proud to do low-paying jobs.

Katie: His ego caused him trouble back in school.

Arthur: It's the same thing now. He indulges himself in drinking.

Katie: What a pity!

Arthur: Yeah. He has turned from a promising young man into a **deadbeat**.

亞瑟：我聽說亞伯特太驕傲，不願意做低薪的工作。

凱蒂：在學校的時候，他的自負就給他帶來麻煩。

亞瑟：現在也是，他還沈迷於喝酒。

凱蒂：真是太令人感到遺憾了！

亞瑟：是啊，一個前途大好的年輕人就這樣變成了懶鬼。

字彙／片語充電區 *Words and Phrases*

debt 名 債務 / creditor 名 債權人 / deficit 名 赤字；不足額 / gloomy 形 憂鬱的
shrink from 躲避 / in arrears with 拖欠 / live up to one's potential 發揮潛能

UNIT 046
a mall rat
在購物中心發現老鼠？

🎧 046

 暖身猜猜看 *Warming Up*

Nina: Do you want to go shopping this weekend?
Mike: You're **a real mall rat**.

妮娜：你週末想去逛街嗎？
麥克：你真是個購物狂。

 原來是這個意思！

a mall rat 購物狂

　　rat指的是我們一般不喜歡的灰色大老鼠，但是這個慣用語可不是在形容商場中的老鼠，而是在比喻購物狂，形容他們流連於購物中心的時間，就彷彿是定居在商場裡的老鼠那麼多。

 對話練習 *Let's Talk!*

Linda: I think Janet has a crush on you.
Terry: She is fine, but not my type.
Linda: What do you mean? She is quite good-looking.
Terry: It's not about that. She's **a mall rat**, but I love being outdoors.
Linda: That's too bad. You guys would make a cute couple.

琳達：我覺得珍妮特在暗戀你。
泰瑞：她是很好，但不是我喜歡的類型。
琳達：什麼意思？她很漂亮耶。
泰瑞：不是外表的問題，她是個購物狂，但我喜歡戶外活動。
琳達：真可惜，不然你們會是很棒的一對情侶。

字彙／片語充電區 *Words and Phrases*

loiter 動 閒逛 / purchase 動 購買 / boutique 名 精品店 / accessory 名 配件
keep a budget 控制預算 / sell off 廉價出清(存貨) / rat fink (美/口)告密者

UNIT 047
a pack rat
把老鼠裝進箱子？

🎧 047

暖身猜猜看 Warming Up

Ruby: Your sister seems to be in a panic over moving next month.

Ian: Definitely. She's **a pack rat**. I bet she has tons of stuff to pack.

露比：你妹妹看起來很擔心下個月搬家的事。

伊恩：肯定的，她是個囤積狂，肯定有一堆東西要打包。

原來是這個意思！

a pack rat 習慣囤積東西的人

　　pack rat是北美洲的狐尾大林鼠，這種動物習慣將找到的東西拖回去，以便築巢時使用，或者將食物拖回巢穴儲存；用來比做人的話，則是比喻「為了紀念意義或不時之需等理由，囤積沒有用途與舊東西的人」。

對話練習 Let's Talk!

Ian: I suggest you get rid of some useless stuff.

Eve: I can't. Every item has a special value to me.

Ian: Even this tattered notebook?

Eve: It's my first notebook; the sketches are the marks of my youth.

Ian: You are such **a hopeless pack rat**.

伊恩：我建議你丟掉一些沒有用的東西。

伊芙：不行啦，每件東西對我都有特殊意義。

伊恩：這本破爛的筆記本也有意義？

伊芙：那是我的第一本筆記本，裡面的塗鴉是我青春的紀錄。

伊恩：你真是個無藥可救的囤積狂。

字彙／片語充電區 Words and Phrases

hoard 動 貯藏 / **perpetuate** 動 留存 / **disorderly** 形 雜亂的 / **arrange** 動 整理
stock up (為某種目的)儲備 / **tidy up** 整理；清理 / **sit on the fence** 猶豫不決

UNIT 048 windbag
裝滿風的袋子是風箱？

🎧 048

 暖身猜猜看 Warming Up

Kevin: Are we inviting Ivy to the tea party?

Helen: I'd prefer not to. She is a **windbag**.

凱文：我們要邀請艾薇來參加茶會嗎？

海倫：我寧可不要，她說話很沒內容。

 原來是這個意思！

windbag 講話無實質意義的人

　　windbag意同a bag of wind，字面上意思為「裝滿一袋的風」，想像如果一個人講起話來，都沒有實質內容，是不是就像裝滿一袋的風一樣，無實體而空洞呢？所以，這個慣用語就用來比喻「愛說話，但內容空洞的人」。

 **對話練習 Let's Talk!**

Tracy: Have you heard that Jane is opening up an art gallery?

Hugo: No. What type of art will she show?

Tracy: I think it's for lovers of modern art.

Hugo: Are you interested in going there?

Tracy: I don't think so. Jane is actually a **windbag**.

崔西：你聽說了嗎？珍辦了一個藝術展。

雨果：沒有，是關於什麼的？

崔西：我記得是為了熱愛現代藝術的人而舉辦的。

雨果：你有興趣去看嗎？

崔西：我應該不會去，珍講話沒什麼內容。

字彙／片語充電區 Words and Phrases

vacuous 形 空洞的；無聊的 / **frivolous** 形 瑣碎的 / **exhausting** 形 使人精疲力竭的 / **indulge in idle gossip** 說長道短 / **bend with the wind** 牆頭草 / **talk over** 討論

UNIT 049　showboat
性質像花車的船？

🎧 049

 暖身猜猜看 *Warming Up*

Nora: Did you know May bought an expensive outfit for the reunion?
Danny: Yeah. I just saw her. What a **showboat**!

諾拉：你知道梅為了聚餐買了一件昂貴的套裝嗎？
丹尼：我知道，我剛剛看到她，真是愛現！

 原來是這個意思！

showboat 愛賣弄的人

　　在美國的南方跟中西部，沿密西西比河及俄亥俄河的城鎮，有船隻以水上劇院的形態，為偏遠鄉鎮的人提供文化及娛樂節目，這樣的船隻即為showboat，這個詞彙後來就被引申為「愛表現、愛賣弄的人（像在做秀）」。

 對話練習　*Let's Talk!*

Jenny: Have you prepared for the seminar yet?
　Bob: Yes. I read through all the references.
Jenny: Brilliant! You should share your conclusions.
　Bob: Nah. I don't want to be mistaken for a **showboat**.
Jenny: Come on. They would love to hear your analyses.

珍妮：你有為研討會做準備了嗎？
鮑伯：有啊，我把參考文獻都讀了一遍。
珍妮：太棒了！你應該分享你的結論。
鮑伯：不了，我不想被誤會是個愛賣弄的人。
珍妮：拜託，大家會很樂意聽到你的分析的。

字彙/片語充電區 *Words and Phrases*

vanity 名 虛榮心；自負 / **bombastic** 形 誇大的；吹噓的 / **marvelous** 形 非凡的
head in the clouds 不切實際 / **stand out** 突出 / **keep a low profile** (做人)低調

UNIT 050

a third wheel
古早時候的三輪車？

🎧 050

暖身猜猜看 *Warming Up*

Lucy: Sorry. I have to baby-sit my brother tonight.

Tom: It's OK. You can bring **that third wheel** along.

露西：抱歉，我今晚得照顧我弟弟。

湯姆：沒關係，你可以帶著那個電燈泡一起來。

原來是這個意思！

a third wheel 情侶間的電燈泡

　　這個慣用語起源於十七世紀的馬車，四輪馬車會多準備一個輪胎，以防不時之需，稱為fifth wheel，當時也有兩輪的輕便馬車，third wheel的概念就是由此引申而來，取其「多餘的」概念，來比喻「打擾人約會的電燈泡」。

對話練習 *Let's Talk!*

Tom: I want to ask your brother to be my best man.

Lucy: My brother, Joe? The one who often joined us on our dates?

Tom: Yeah. Who else knows us better than him?

Lucy: Wow. He'd be thrilled.

Tom: Same here. Finally, he's not going to be **a third wheel** anymore.

湯姆：我想請你弟弟來做伴郎。

露西：我弟弟？經常跟著我們約會的喬嗎？

湯姆：是啊，還有誰比他更了解我們呢？

露西：哇，他會開心死的。

湯姆：我也是，他終於不會再當我們的電燈泡了。

字彙／片語充電區 *Words and Phrases*

intrude 動 打擾 / lovebirds 名 一對情侶 / accompany 動 陪同 / pout 動 板起臉

go on a date with sb. 約會 / behind the wheel 開車 / oil the wheels 使順利進行

UNIT 051
henpeck
憤怒的母雞在啄人？

🎧 051

暖身猜猜看 Warming Up

Robert: What happened to Julie and Mike?

Alice: Mike just couldn't stand her endless **henpecking**.

羅伯特：茱莉跟麥克怎麼了？
艾莉絲：麥克無法忍受她無止盡的叨念。

原來是這個意思！

henpeck 妻子或女友碎碎唸

　　hen為母雞，在俚語中可指女性，peck則是禽鳥類啄食的動作，兩者結合而成的henpeck是母雞啄食的模樣，後來被拿來比喻妻子或女朋友的叨念威逼，就像鳥類用尖嘴猛啄，令人感到厭煩，是相當生動的敘述。

對話練習 Let's Talk!

Cindy: Jeff and I are always arguing over the same issue.

Carl: You'd better try another way to communicate with him.

Cindy: Like what? I can't stay calm while reasoning with him.

Carl: You can at least try to stop **henpecking** him.

Cindy: I guess you are right. I'll try that next time.

辛蒂：傑夫跟我老是為了同樣的事情爭論不休。

卡爾：你最好換個方式跟他溝通。

辛蒂：例如？我沒辦法冷靜地跟他講道理。

卡爾：你至少可以試著別對他碎碎唸。

辛蒂：有道理，我下次會試試看。

字彙／片語充電區 Words and Phrases

nagging 形 嘮叨的；挑剔的 / **pointless** 形 無意義的 / **disagreement** 名 意見不合 / **as mad as a wet hen** 非常生氣 / **argue over** 為…爭辯 / **reason down** 說服

UNIT 052
put on airs
什麼樣的空氣能穿戴？

🎧 052

 暖身猜猜看 *Warming Up*

Danny: How are you and Emily getting along at work?

Cindy: I just can't stand the way she **puts on airs** anymore.

丹尼：你在工作上跟艾蜜莉處得還好嗎？

辛蒂：我實在無法忍受她那副高高在上的樣子。

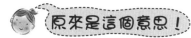 **原來是這個意思！**

put on airs 擺架子

　　這個慣用語起源於十八、十九世紀，描述有些做家務事的僕人，會擺高姿態來指使其他僕人；這裡的air，指的是一種高高在上、優越的神態，put on airs 就是「拿出高人一等、了不起的姿態」，意即我們常說的擺架子。

 **對話練習** *Let's Talk!*

Peter: I really love Ms. Jones's class. She is so knowledgeable!

Mary: And she is always willing to answer our questions.

Peter: Mr. Smith, on the other hand, always **puts on airs**.

Mary: He's a great scholar, but I don't think he enjoys teaching.

Peter: I wish he were a bit more like Ms. Jones.

彼德：我超愛瓊斯老師的課，她好博學多聞！

瑪莉：而且她很願意回答我們的問題。

彼德：史密斯老師就很愛擺架子了。

瑪莉：他是很優秀的學者，但我不覺得他喜歡教書。

彼德：真希望他能多像瓊斯老師一些。

字彙／片語充電區 *Words and Phrases*

haughty 形 高傲的 / snooty 形 自大的 / bossy 形 愛指揮他人的 / attitude 名 態度
look down on 輕視；瞧不起 / walk on air 得意洋洋 / beyond the limit 超出限度

UNIT 053

butter sb. up
往某人臉上砸派？

🎧 053

 暖身猜猜看 *Warming Up*

Lily: How did Grace get promoted so soon?

Mike: It's because she's very good at **buttering our boss up**.

莉莉：葛瑞絲怎麼這麼快就升職了？

麥克：因為她很會吹捧我們的老闆啊。

 原來是這個意思！

butter sb. up 吹捧；撒嬌

　　butter是奶油，在這個慣用語中當動詞用（塗奶油）。麵包塗上奶油後，口感與味道都會很好，這個慣用語用奶油這樣討人喜歡的味道，來形容圓滑的言語，即「以奶油般的言語討好或哄騙別人」。

 **對話練習** *Let's Talk!*

Jack: I am planning for a road-trip this summer.

Betty: The problem is, you don't have a car.

Jack: I can borrow one from my roommate.

Betty: You mean Rick?

Jack: Yeah. If I **butter him up**, he might lend it to me.

傑克：我在計劃今年夏天要駕車旅遊。

貝蒂：問題是，你又沒有車。

傑克：我可以和我的室友借車啊。

貝蒂：你是說瑞克嗎？

傑克：沒錯，如果我吹捧他幾句，他說不定就會把他的車借給我。

字彙/片語充電區 *Words and Phrases*

flattery 名 阿諛之詞；諂媚之舉 / **adulate** 動 諂媚；奉承 / **intention** 名 意圖；意向
lay it on thick (口)誇大地讚揚 / **rub sb. the right way** 討好某人 / **puff up** 吹捧

UNIT 054 cry wolf
一隻哭泣的狼？

🎧 054

 暖身猜猜看 *Warming Up*

Winnie: Britney says that she and Sam are breaking up.
Hunter: Don't buy that. She is **crying wolf** again.

溫妮：布蘭妮說她跟山姆要分手了。
杭特：不要相信，她又在瞎扯了。

 原來是這個意思！

cry wolf 謊稱

　　cry wolf的起緣來自於大家熟知的伊索寓言《狼來了》，一個牧羊的孩子只因為無聊，便大喊「狼來了」騙村民趕來；最後，當狼真的來時，牧羊的孩子無論怎麼求救，也沒人來幫忙。cry wolf就是以故事中的行為來比喻「騙人」。

 對話練習 *Let's Talk!*

Mindy: This case is massive. I need some help.

Nick: Stop **crying wolf**. You said the same thing last time.

Mindy: I'm not! The deadline is right around the corner.

Nick: I am sure you can finish it by yourself.

Mindy: Come on! I'll buy you dinner. Please help me.

明蒂：這個案子的工作量太大了，我需要幫忙。

尼克：別再騙人了，你上次也這麼說。

明蒂：我沒有騙人！截止日就快到了。

尼克：我相信你可以自己完成。

明蒂：拜託！我請你吃晚餐，拜託幫我。

字彙／片語充電區 *Words and Phrases*

fable 名 寓言 / perjury 名 背信棄義 / actual 形 事實上的 / commitment 名 承諾
false alarm 假警報；虛驚 / a white lie 善意的謊言 / string along 哄騙；追隨

UNIT 055 bring down the house 拆掉一棟房屋？

🎧 055

 暖身猜猜看 Warming Up

Merry: How was the show last night?

Kenny: It was brilliant! The performers **brought down the house**.

梅莉：昨晚的表演如何？

肯尼：太精采了！表演者們博得滿堂喝彩。

 原來是這個意思！

bring down the house 博得滿堂喝彩

　　這裡的house指的是劇院或劇場。十九世紀晚期，英國的喜劇演員會在觀眾對他們的笑話無動於衷時，自我嘲解地說：「鼓掌不要太大聲，會把劇院給震垮！」bring down the house即從此衍生，比喻熱烈的掌聲，足以震垮劇院。

 **對話練習** *Let's Talk!*

Karen: What inspired you to be an actor?

Johnny: Well, I have loved movies since my childhood.

Karen: Your performances always **bring down the house**.

Johnny: Thank you. I am just following my passion.

Karen: Your acting ability is beyond compare.

凱倫：是什麼啟發了你想要當演員的念頭呢？

強尼：我從小就非常喜愛電影。

凱倫：你的表演總是大獲好評呢。

強尼：謝謝你，我只是忠於熱情而已。

凱倫：你的演技實在是無人能敵。

字彙／片語充電區 *Words and Phrases*

hail 動 喝采／ ovation 名 熱烈鼓掌／ attainment 名 成就／ constantly 副 不斷地
take...to the next level 提升到更高的層次／ a feather in one's cap 值得嘉獎之事

UNIT 056 pull one's leg
扯人後腿？

🎧 056

暖身猜猜看 Warming Up

Sam: Mike told me we're making a presentation today!
Dora: He must be **pulling your leg**. Relax.

山姆：麥克告訴我，我們今天要報告！
朵拉：他一定是跟你開玩笑的，別緊張。

原來是這個意思！

pull one's leg 開玩笑

　　一百多年前，這個慣用語在蘇格蘭的詩歌中出現時，意思跟我們由中文直譯的意思相同，是扯後腿、出賣的負面意思；時至今日，其中負面的意涵已經被取代，pull one's leg 轉為「帶幽默的玩笑、善意地嘲弄」之意。

 對話練習 Let's Talk!

Hannah: Are you going to our university reunion?
George: Of course! It'll be nice to catch up.
Hannah: I miss those carefree days. We had lots of parties.
George: Yeah. And we were busy **pulling each other's leg**.
Hannah: Sure, we had so much fun then.

漢　娜：你會參加我們的大學同學會嗎？
葛瑞格：當然會！和大家敘舊肯定很棒。
漢　娜：我好懷念那段無憂無慮的時光，我們參加很多派對。
葛瑞格：是啊，還忙著整對方。
漢　娜：沒錯，那時候我們做了很多有趣的事。

字彙／片語充電區 Words and Phrases

jeering 形 嘲弄的 / hilarious 形 極好笑的 / humorous 形 幽默的 / laugh 動 笑
small talk 閒聊 / split one's sides 笑破肚皮 / make a mockery of 使成為徒勞

UNIT
057

drink like a fish
喝得像魚一樣是什麼樣？

🎧 057

 暖身猜猜看 *Warming Up*

Tom: Wow! This is a great party!

Fanny: Behave yourself. Don't **drink like a fish** this time.

湯姆：哇！這個派對真棒！

芬妮：節制一點，這次可別再狂飲酒了。

 原來是這個意思！

drink like a fish 牛飲；狂灌

　　這個慣用語於十七世紀時出現。魚與水的關係非常緊密，魚在水中呼吸時，嘴巴會不停地一張一合，所以後來人們就用drink like a fish來形容一個人不斷灌下飲料的模樣，特別是指酒精類的飲料。

 對話練習 *Let's Talk!*

Emma: You've stayed in your room for hours. What are you doing?

John: I'm inviting some friends over for my wine tasting party.

Emma: Are you going to invite Janet?

John: I wanted to, but I thought she doesn't drink.

Emma: She sure does. Last time we went to a bar, she **drank like a fish**!

艾瑪：你待在房間好幾個小時了，在做什麼？

約翰：我打算邀請一些朋友來我的品酒派對。

艾瑪：你會邀請珍妮特嗎？

約翰：我是想邀請她，可是我以為她不喝酒。

艾瑪：她喝得可多了，上回我們去酒吧，她可是狂飲呢！

字彙／片語充電區 *Words and Phrases*

beverage 名 飲料 / sober 動 清醒；冷靜 / tipsy 形 微醉的 / momentary 形 瞬間的 / tank up 喝大量的酒 / drink to sb. 向某人舉杯祝賀 / make merry 盡情歡樂、作樂

UNIT 058

in one's cups
玩遊樂場的咖啡杯？

🎧 058

 暖身猜猜看 Warming Up

Leo: Have you seen Ted? I need to verify this data with him.

Gina: It's not the right time to talk to him. He's **in his cups**.

里歐：你有看到泰德嗎？我得跟他確認數據。

吉娜：現在不方便跟他談這個，他正酩酊大醉呢。

 原來是這個意思！

in one's cups 醉醺醺地；酩酊大醉

　　在東正教的經典與羅馬人的記載中，都用過這樣的說法。和現今不同，cup 在當時指裝了酒精飲料的杯子，所以用in one's cup來比喻沈溺於杯中物的人們，這個慣用語沿用至今，意指喝醉的，意同drunk。

 **對話練習** *Let's Talk!*

Henry: Mr. Hammer decided to hand the company over to his son.

Bella: Seriously, I don't think it's a wise decision.

Henry: I agree. He is too frivolous.

Bella: He spends more time partying.

Henry: Let's just hope he won't keep staying **in his cups**.

亨利：漢默先生決定把公司移交給他兒子。

貝拉：說真的，我覺得這是不智之舉。

亨利：我也這麼認為，他兒子太輕浮了。

貝拉：他花很多時間在派對上。

亨利：我們就期望他別再繼續尋歡狂飲吧。

字彙／片語充電區 *Words and Phrases*

spree 名 嬉鬧；狂歡 / indulge 動 沈迷 / carousal 名 宴會；狂歡 / booze 名 酒會
wet one's whistle 喝酒 / drink a toast to 為⋯乾杯 / be on the bottle 是個酒鬼

UNIT 059 nature's call 熱愛大自然的心情？

🎧 059

 暖身猜猜看 *Warming Up*

Nora: Okay. Now let's go through the presentation slides.

Roy: Hold on a second. I feel **nature's call**. I'll be right back.

諾拉：那我們現在來複習一遍簡報內容。

羅伊：等一下，我內急，馬上就回來。

 原來是這個意思！

nature's call 上廁所

　　nature's call的字面解釋是自然的召喚；指因為自然的需求，必須停下手邊的事情或中途離席，可以用於指稱生理上的所有需求，但以「上廁所」為最主要的意思；使用時也會以Nature's calling!這樣的短句呈現。

 *Let's Talk!*

Mindy: How did your wedding rehearsal go?

Kent: Don't mention it. It was distressing.

Mindy: What happened?

Kent: My best man kept answering **nature's call**, which terribly teamed me up!

Mindy: Well, when a man has to go, he has to go.

明蒂：婚禮排演得怎麼樣了？

肯特：別提了，真是令人焦慮。

明蒂：怎麼了嗎？

肯特：我的伴郎不停跑廁所，我都快抓狂了！

明蒂：當一個人想要上廁所的時候，他就是得去啊。

字彙/片語充電區 *Words and Phrases*

lavatory 名 洗手間 / **hygiene** 名 衛生 / **tissue** 名 衛生紙 / **urgent** 形 急迫的
go back to nature 返璞歸真 / **come natural to sb.** 對某人來說輕而易舉

UNIT 060

toss one's cookies
扔餅乾的遊戲？

🎧 060

 暖身猜猜看 *Warming Up*

Glenn: I don't feel well. I **tossed my cookies** this morning.

Judy: God! You'd better take a day off and go see a doctor.

葛蘭：我不舒服，今天早上我還嘔吐了。

朱蒂：天啊！你今天最好請假去看醫生。

 原來是這個意思！

toss one's cookies 嘔吐

　　cookie（餅乾）是非常普遍的食物，在這個慣用語中作為一般食物的代稱，如果一個人將吃下去的食物都倒出來、傾瀉出來，就是把食物吐出來的意思，與vomit同義，類似的用法還有toss lunch、toss tacos。

 對話練習 *Let's Talk!*

Judy: I think you might have caught the flu.

Glenn: Probably. I've been to quite a lot of public places.

Judy: What are your symptoms?

Glenn: I **tossed my cookies** and had diarrhea.

Judy: Oh man! You should take a good rest today.

朱蒂：我想你可能染上流感了。

葛蘭：有可能，我最近去了滿多公眾場所。

朱蒂：你的症狀是什麼？

葛蘭：我有嘔吐，還拉肚子。

朱蒂：天啊！你今天最好還是好好休息。

字彙／片語充電區 *Words and Phrases*

puke 動 嘔吐 / pale 形 蒼白的；灰白的 / digestion 名 消化作用 / fever 名 發燒
be laid up 病倒；臥病在床 / run a fever 發燒 / not give a toss 毫不在乎

UNIT 061

blow this joint
吹某物品的接合處？

🎧 061

 暖身猜猜看 Warming Up

Chris: Relax. We won't be caught drinking.

Melissa: I think Mom's coming! Let's **blow this joint**!

克里斯：放輕鬆，不會有人發現我們偷喝酒的。

梅莉莎：我覺得媽媽來了，快撤啦！

 原來是這個意思！

blow this joint 離開這個地方

　　blow意指「吹」，而joint為「關節」，這個慣用語的意思常被誤會，其實joint在口語中也有「場所」之意，blow this joint就是「迅速離開某地」；注意joint在口語中也能指毒品，所以這個慣用語有時會被人暗稱「吸毒」。

 **對話練習** Let's Talk!

Rita: Are you sure it's OK to sneak into this abandoned house?

Simon: I have been here several times. Don't worry.

Rita: This place creeps me out.

Simon: You are just imagining things.

Rita: I heard a sound! I'm **blowing this joint**!

芮塔：你確定我們可以偷跑進這間廢棄的房子嗎？

賽門：我來過好幾次了，別擔心。

芮塔：這地方令我渾身發毛。

賽門：你只是在胡思亂想而已。

芮塔：我聽到聲音！我要閃了！

字彙／片語充電區 Words and Phrases

scamper 動 驚逃；奔跑 / blower 名 風箱；(口)吹牛家 / dreadful 形 令人恐懼的
blow one's cover 穿幫；洩底 / **cut and run** 急忙逃走 / **in hot water** 惹上大麻煩

UNIT 062　chicken out 把雞養在室外？

🎧 062

 暖身猜猜看 Warming Up

Karen: I heard Johnny just quit the research team.
Henry: Really? I can't believe he **chickened out**.

　凱倫：我聽說強尼剛剛退出研究小組了。
　亨利：真的嗎？真不敢相信他臨陣退縮了。

 原來是這個意思！

chicken out 臨陣退縮

　　在英文用語裡，雞有很多種說法，例如：公雞是rooster、母雞則是hen，而chicken指的是年紀較輕的小雞；後來被沿用來形容經驗不足的年輕人，因為怕犯錯而怯懦，chicken out則是比喻「因為害怕而臨陣脫逃」。

 對話練習 *Let's Talk!*

Amy: I heard that you got engaged.
Jack: I was, but we split up.
Amy: I am sorry to hear that. What happened?
Jack: It was my bad. I wasn't sure if I really wanted a family, so I **chickened out**.
Amy: Well, maybe it's better to find out sooner than later.

艾咪：我聽說你訂婚了。
傑克：曾經是，但我們分開了。
艾咪：我很遺憾，發生什麼事了嗎？
傑克：是我的錯，我不確定自己是否想成家，所以臨陣退縮了。
艾咪：也許早點發覺會比後來才發現好。

字彙／片語充電區 *Words and Phrases*

timidity 名 膽怯 / agitation 名 不安 / anxious 形 焦慮的 / surrender 動 放棄
cop out 逃避 / pull out 退出 / draw in one's horns 打退堂鼓 / strive for 爭取

UNIT 063 talk shop
在咖啡廳裡閒話家常？

🎧 063

 暖身猜猜看 Warming Up

Linda: Have you seen your brother?
Adam: I saw him and David **talking shop** in the backyard.

琳達：你有看到你哥哥嗎？
亞當：我看到他和大衛在後院談公事。

 原來是這個意思！

talk shop 談公事

　　這裡的shop並不只是店鋪的意思，而是引申其店鋪之意，用來指「和生意或事業相關的話題」，所以這個慣用語的意思就是「談公事」，通常用於出了公司後，還在談論公事的情況。

 **對話練習 Let's Talk!**

Billy: I saw Henry picking you up after work yesterday.
Rose: Yeah. We had dinner together.
Billy: I didn't know you guys are dating.
Rose: It was not a date. We **talked shop** over dinner.
Billy: Maybe you can have a real date next time.

比利：昨天我看到亨利下班後來接你。
蘿絲：是啊，我們約好一起吃晚餐。
比利：我都不知道你們在約會交往。
蘿絲：那才不是什麼約會，我們是為了談公事。
比利：也許你們下次可以來場真正的約會。

字彙／片語充電區 Words and Phrases

occupation 名 工作；職業 / partner 名 合夥人；股東 / tedious 形 冗長乏味的
fall into talk 攀談 / talk sb. into sth. 說服…做某事 / confer with sb. on sth. 商討

UNIT 064

bring home the bacon
買培根回家？

🎧 064

 暖身猜猜看 *Warming Up*

Daisy: Are you working overtime again? You work too hard.

Larry: Well, I have to **bring home the bacon**.

黛西：你又要加班嗎？你工作得太拼命了。

賴瑞：我得養家活口啊。

 原來是這個意思！

bring home the bacon 扶養家庭

　　早年的鄉村市集，流行一種遊戲，大家比賽抓住一隻抹了油的小豬，勝利者可以把豬帶回家。這個慣用語中的bacon指的就是那隻豬，引申bring home the bacon（帶回戰利品、生活物資）的原意之後，就有了養家活口之意。

 對話練習 *Let's Talk!*

Hank: Sometimes I wonder if this is the life I dreamed of.

Suzy: Well, you win some and lose some.

Hank: Don't you long for things you don't have sometimes?

Suzy: Of course I do. But I also need to face reality.

Hank: True. We all have to **bring home the bacon**.

漢克：有時候我會懷疑，這是否是我夢想中的人生。

蘇西：有得必有失囉。

漢克：對於自己沒有的東西，你難道都沒有渴望的時候嗎？

蘇西：當然有，但我也必須面對現實啊。

漢克：也是，我們都還得養家活口。

字彙／片語充電區 *Words and Phrases*

salary 名 薪資 / **subsidy** 名 津貼；補貼 / **expense** 名 支出 / **balanced** 形 平衡的
support one's family 養家活口 / **bring up** 培養；養育 / **make an overdraft** 透支

UNIT 065
jump ship
因為緊急情況跳船？

🎧 065

 暖身猜猜看 *Warming Up*

Nina: I really don't see the potential of this job.

Harry: Me, neither. Actually, I've thought about **jumping ship**.

妮娜：我真的看不到這份工作的前景。

哈利：我也是，說實話，我想過要離職。

 原來是這個意思！

jump ship 解約；離開工作或團體

　　當船員簽約到一艘船上工作，就必須一直待在那艘船上，直到約滿，船回到港口為止，已簽約的水手如果想提早離開，就得在靠近陸地的時候，跳船自行游上岸；因此，jump ship被用來比喻離職、解約或是脫離一個團體。

 對話練習 *Let's Talk!*

John: How's your volunteering going?

Dora: I **jumped ship** from that charity group already.

John: How come?

Dora: I found they only take an interest in building their image.

John: Well, that's inevitable in many foundations.

約翰：你的義工做得如何？

朵拉：我離開那個慈善團體了。

約翰：為什麼？

朵拉：我發現他們只對建立形象感興趣。

約翰：在很多基金會裡，這是無可避免的事。

字彙/片語充電區 *Words and Phrases*

vacate 動 撤出；辭職 / **relinquish** 動 放棄；交出 / **compact** 名 契約；合同
bow out 退出 / **walk out on** 離開；遺棄 / **earn one's stripes** 證明能勝任

UNIT 066　hit the road 因為氣憤而打馬路？

🎧 066

 暖身猜猜看 Warming Up

Paula: Can I sit here a bit longer? We've been walking for hours.
Ryan: Come on. We're almost there. Let's **hit the road**!

寶拉：我可以再坐一會兒嗎？我們走了好幾個小時了。
萊恩：拜託，我們就快到了耶，快出發吧！

 原來是這個意思！

hit the road 離開

　　這個慣用語起源於馬還是主要交通工具的時候，用來形容馬經過時所留下的「廢棄物」，起源較不衛生，後來取其「出發、動身」之意；要注意的是，這個慣用語的口氣相對強硬，建議只用於親近的朋友，否則可能會冒犯他人。

 **對話練習** Let's Talk!

Rick: Mandy! Are you ready?
Mandy: Not yet. Just give me ten minutes.
Rick: You mean "another" ten minutes? What took you so long?
Mandy: It's my hair. I must do something with my cowlick.
Rick: I've been waiting for that? Let's **hit the road**! Now!!

瑞克：曼蒂！你好了沒？
曼蒂：還沒，給我十分鐘。
瑞克：你是說「再」給你十分鐘吧？你到底在摸什麼？
曼蒂：是我的頭髮啦，我得把我翹起來的頭髮弄平。
瑞克：我就因為你的頭髮而等了這麼久？要出發了！現在、立刻！

字彙/片語充電區 Words and Phrases

destination 名 目的地 / **traffic** 名 交通 / **roadblock** 名 障礙物 / **roadster** 名 敞篷車
hit the trail 上路 / **take the road** 啟程 / **rush hour** 尖峰時間 / **snarl up** 交通堵塞

UNIT 067　hit the books 毆打書本的舉動？

🎧 067

 暖身猜猜看 *Warming Up*

Lisa: I haven't seen Adam the entire day.
Bob: He's **hitting the books** for the final exam in the library.

麗莎：我一整天都沒看到亞當耶。
鮑伯：他正為了期末考在圖書館用功。

 原來是這個意思！

hit the books 用功唸書

　　hit有許多解釋，包括打擊、解決、擊中等等，不管是哪一種解釋，當中都隱含「得分、完成」的意思；而hit the books則引申其「完成」之意，用來比喻集中注意力，埋首苦讀，解決書中難題的模樣。

 對話練習 *Let's Talk!*

John: How's your studying going?
Laura: I'm still **hitting the books** to catch up.
John: Do you need a hand?
Laura: Can I borrow your notes on taxation?
John: Sure. I will give them to you later when I swing by your room.

約翰：你書念得怎麼樣了？
蘿拉：我還在拼命唸書趕進度呢。
約翰：需要幫忙嗎？
蘿拉：我可以跟你借稅務那堂課的筆記嗎？
約翰：當然，我晚點經過你房間時拿給你。

字彙/片語充電區 *Words and Phrases*

peruse 動 細讀 / **review** 動 複習 / **correction** 名 訂正 / **bookworm** 名 書呆子
burn the midnight oil 熬夜 / **stay up** 不睡覺 / **plunge into** 貿然決定開始做某事

UNIT 068
pull up one's socks
為了整理儀容而拉襪子？

🎧 068

 暖身猜猜看 *Warming Up*

Danny: Mom, this is my school report card for this semester.
Mother: Well, it looks like you'd better **pull your socks up**.

丹尼：媽，這是我這學期的成績單。
母親：嗯，看起來你最好加緊努力。

 原來是這個意思！

pull up one's socks 打起精神；加緊努力

　　Pull up your socks!一般是用來提醒小孩子的話，特別是小男生，因為他們跑來跑去，襪子很容易滑到腳踝，這句對小孩子的叮嚀，後來就引申為「要對方打起精神，把自己整理好」或「提醒人加緊努力，不要落後」的意思。

 對話練習 *Let's Talk!*

Carl: Is everything all right? You looked exhausted.

Lily: I just wrapped up a major project.

Carl: Why don't you take a day off today?

Lily: Well, I need to **pull up my socks** for the upcoming event.

Carl: Oh, right. You are in charge of it.

卡爾：沒事吧？你看起來累壞了。
莉莉：我才完成一個大案子。
卡爾：你今天何不請一天假？
莉莉：這個嘛，為了接下來的活動，我必須打起精神。
卡爾：對喔，你是活動的負責人。

字彙/片語充電區 *Words and Phrases*

endeavor 動 努力 / encourage 動 鼓勵 / slacker 名 偷懶的人 / scrutiny 名 監督
in full force 盡全力；全部 / loosen up 放輕鬆 / trust sb. with sth. 託付；重用

UNIT 069 knuckle down 手關節朝下？

🎧 069

 暖身猜猜看 Warming Up

Hardy: Hi, Julie. What have you been up to?

Julie: I have been **knuckling down** for my new job.

哈帝：嗨，茉莉，最近都在忙些什麼？

茉莉：為了新工作而拼命努力囉。

 原來是這個意思！

knuckle down 賣命地認真工作

在彈珠的遊戲中，小孩子會跪在地上，將手背的指關節盡量貼近地面，以便瞄準彈珠；knuckle down便是由彈珠遊戲中，為了取勝而認真瞄準的動作引申而來，比喻「認真、努力地投入正事」。

 對話練習 Let's Talk!

Rita: Our performance was weak this season.

Mike: It's because several old hands have left.

Rita: I know. But this is business.

Mike: Right. We need to **knuckle down** from now on.

Rita: Let's go through the mistakes we have made.

芮塔：我們這一季的表現太差了。

麥克：這是因為有好幾位資深老手離開。

芮塔：我知道，但這是工作。

麥克：是啊，現在起我們得拼命努力了。

芮塔：我們來將過去犯的錯誤檢討一遍吧。

字彙／片語充電區 Words and Phrases

determine 動 決定 / keen 形 熱切的 / eager 形 渴望的 / strenuous 形 奮發的
apply oneself to 投身 / plug away 埋頭苦幹 / have the urge to 迫切要做某事

UNIT 070

raise the bar
大家一起把竿子舉高？

🎧 070

暖身猜猜看 Warming Up

Wendy: I can't believe Kent's team achieved their goal so soon.

Dylan: It seems we can **raise the bar** for the next season.

溫蒂：不敢相信肯特的團隊這麼快就達成目標。

狄倫：看來我們下一季可以提高整體的要求了。

原來是這個意思！

raise the bar 提高整體水平

　　這裡的bar指的是橫桿，特別是馬術比賽時，讓馬跳躍過去的跳桿障礙物，將跳桿升高，意思就是提高比賽的難度和標準，用來比喻「要求品質或整體表現的提升」；在別人表現好的時候，也可以用此慣用語來稱讚對方。

對話練習 Let's Talk!

Kent: The upcoming season is going to be stressful.

Sara: Why? Are they going to **raise the bar** on evaluation?

Kent: Exactly. But I believe we can do it.

Sara: Me, too. We have the strongest team here.

Kent: I am confident that we can achieve the highest sales.

肯特：下一季我們的壓力會很大。

莎拉：為什麼？他們打算提高評估的標準嗎？

肯特：沒錯，但我相信我們能做到。

莎拉：我也相信，我們有最強的團隊。

肯特：我有信心我們能締造最高的業績。

字彙／片語充電區 Words and Phrases

evaluate 動 評估；鑑定 / **advancement** 名 進展；提高 / **enhancement** 名 提高
set a higher standard 設立更高的標準 / **size up** 評估 / **raise a fort** 構築堡壘

UNIT 071 go Dutch
動身前往荷蘭？

🎧 071

 暖身猜猜看 *Warming Up*

Cindy: How was your date last night?

Nick: My date was cute. And she insisted on **going Dutch** for dinner.

辛蒂：你昨天的約會怎麼樣？

尼克：我的約會對象很可愛，付晚餐錢時，她還堅持各付各的。

 原來是這個意思！

go Dutch 各自付帳

　　十七世紀時，相鄰的荷蘭與英國交惡，於是英國人便衍生出許多批評荷蘭人的慣用語，Dutch meal就是其中之一，意思是主人請客，但是要客人掏腰包；引申至go Dutch，便用來比喻「一起吃飯，但是要各自付帳」的情境。

對話練習 *Let's Talk!*

Henry: How do you like the dinner?

Maggie: It's great. Everything is fresh and dainty.

Henry: I am glad you enjoyed it. Let me get the bill.

Maggie: Let's **go Dutch**.

Henry: No, this one is on me. How about you take me to dinner next weekend?

亨利：你喜歡這頓晚餐嗎？

梅姬：很喜歡，每道菜都很新鮮、精緻。

亨利：我很高興你喜歡，我來買單。

梅姬：我們各付各的吧。

亨利：不行，這頓算我的，不如下個週末換你請我吃晚餐吧？

字彙 / 片語充電區 *Words and Phrases*

apportion 動 分攤 / manner 名 舉止；態度 / decent 形 有禮的 / dainty 形 講究的
share the expenses (of) 分攤費用 / be on the house 店家請客 / pitch in 動 開動

UNIT 072

pay on the nail
買釘子付錢？

🎧 072

暖身猜猜看 *Warming Up*

Grace: I am sure this is the best price on the market.

Larry: I'd say if you gave me another 10% off, I would **pay on the nail**.

葛瑞絲：相信我，這是市場上最好的價格了。

賴　瑞：如果再降10%，我馬上結帳。

原來是這個意思！

pay on the nail 立即支付

　　這裡的nail指的並不是釘子，而是柱子，在古歐洲的交易市場和市集上，會用固定或是可搬移的柱子搭建平台，讓人在上面談好價錢，並且一手交錢、一手交貨；pay on the nail就是指談妥價錢後，馬上付帳。

對話練習 *Let's Talk!*

Grace: Mr. Baker wants another 10% off.

Howard: That would leave us with almost nothing.

Grace: Exactly. But he is our important client.

Howard: Maybe we can try offering another 5% off.

Grace: Alright. I hope he can agree to **pay on the nail**.

葛瑞絲：貝克先生要求再降10%。

霍華德：那我們幾乎就沒有利潤了。

葛瑞絲：就是啊，但他是我們很重要的客戶。

霍華德：我們也許可以試著再降5%給他。

葛瑞絲：好吧，希望他會同意成交。

字彙／片語充電區 *Words and Phrases*

payment 名 支付 / **discount** 名 折扣 / **depreciation** 名 跌價 / **rollback** 名 削減
on the spot 立即；當場 / **pay in cash** 現金支付 / **cost next to nothing** 幾乎不用錢

UNIT 073 bite the bullet 什麼情況要咬子彈？

🎧 073

 暖身猜猜看 Warming Up

Nick: I heard you are going to work with Greg for next case.

Vicky: Yes. I'll just **bite the bullet** and get it over with.

尼克：我聽說你下個案子要跟葛瑞格合作。

薇琪：是啊，我會咬緊牙關撐過去的。

 原來是這個意思！

bite the bullet 忍受令人不愉快的事情

　　這是源自於軍中的慣用語。以前因戰爭而受傷的軍人接受治療時，因為沒有麻醉劑，所以會被要求咬住一個彈殼，以防叫出聲音或是咬到自己，因此，bite the bullet便被用來比喻「咬緊牙關撐過痛苦」或「忍受辛苦的任務」。

 **對話練習** *Let's Talk!*

Will: You were under some kind of diet regimen, right?

Emma: Yeah. I went through a kind of fasting for a few days.

Will: That sounds difficult.

Emma: Yeah. I had to **bite the bullet** to survive the fasting.

Will: Well, I think I would try changing my diet first.

威爾：你有進行過某種養生的節食療法，對嗎？

艾瑪：是啊，我維持了幾天齋戒飲食。

威爾：那聽起來好困難。

艾瑪：沒錯，我可是咬緊牙關撐過去的。

威爾：嗯，我想我可能會先試著改變飲食習慣吧。

字彙/片語充電區 *Words and Phrases*

bitterness 名 痛苦 / **swallow** 動 忍受 / **repress** 動 抑制 / **fortitude** 名 剛毅
hang in 撐住；堅持 / **bear with** 忍受 / **take for better or worse** 概括承受

UNIT 074　skinny dip
要一個皮包骨泡澡？

🎧 074

 暖身猜猜看 *Warming Up*

Kathy: What do you remember the most from college?

Bert: I celebrated my birthday by **skinny dipping** once.

凱西：大學生涯中，你最難忘的一件事是什麼？

伯特：我有一次過生日，為了慶祝而去裸泳。

 原來是這個意思！

skinny dip 裸泳

　　skinny有「極瘦的、瘦成皮包骨」之意，但在這個慣用語中，是當作「皮膚的」解釋，dip指「沾取、浸泡」的動作，直接用皮膚去沾水，其實就是在形容人裸泳時，沒有穿衣物的狀態。

 **對話練習** *Let's Talk!*

Carl: The life abroad in the U.S. is really great.

Wendy: Sounds like you've already adapted to the foreign culture.

Carl: Not really. I still need time to get used to it.

Wendy: I've heard that school life there can be crazy sometimes.

Carl: You bet. My roommates even invited me to go **skinny dipping**!

卡爾：在美國留學的生活很棒。

溫蒂：聽起來你已經完全適應國外的文化了嘛。

卡爾：也不是，我還需要時間來適應。

溫蒂：我聽說那裡的校園生活有時很瘋狂。

卡爾：是真的，我室友還邀我一起去裸泳呢！

字彙／片語充電區 *Words and Phrases*

naked 形 裸體的 / **brave** 形 勇敢的 / **swimsuit** 名 泳裝 / **dipper** 名 長柄勺；汲器
swim with the tide 隨波逐流 / **be skin and bones** 瘦成皮包骨 / **skin a flint** 吝嗇

UNIT 075　have the heart to
很有心去做某件事？

🎧 075

暖身猜猜看 *Warming Up*

Vicky: Look! There's a child peddling flowers alone in the rain.

Jack: How can his parents **have the heart to** let him do it!

薇琪：你看！那裡有個小孩一個人在雨中賣花。

傑克：他的父母怎麼忍心讓他這樣做！

原來是這個意思！

have the heart to （通常用於否定句）忍心做

　　have the heart to表面上看起來有「有心或用心做」的意思，但其實它的意思正好相反；這句慣用語用於質問對方「怎麼捨得」或「怎麼忍心」，通常會與否定句組成not have the heart to，表達「不忍心」之意。

Vicky: I went to see the acrobatics yesterday.

Billy: How did you like it?

Vicky: I kept wondering what kind of training the kids had been through.

Billy: I wouldn't **have the heart to** allow my children to go through it.

Vicky: Honestly, I don't think I want to go to another one.

薇琪：我昨天去看了雜技表演。

比利：那你喜歡嗎？

薇琪：我一直在想，那些孩子都經歷了些什麼樣的訓練。

比利：我可不忍心讓我的小孩接受那樣的訓練。

薇琪：說實話，我不想再看那樣的表演了。

字彙／片語充電區 *Words and Phrases*

compassion 名 同情；憐憫 / conscience 名 良心；道義心 / oblivious 形 不在意的
show sympathy for 同情 / feel for 同情 / deal with 對待 / a cruel blow 沉痛打擊

UNIT 076
cut sb. dead
傷害致死的事件？

🎧 076

 暖身猜猜看 *Warming Up*

Cindy: I ran into Joyce and she just **cut me dead**.

Danny: Really? But she looked fine when I saw her.

辛蒂：我遇到喬伊絲，她完全不理我。

丹尼：真的嗎？但我遇到她的時候，她看起來很正常啊。

 原來是這個意思！

cut sb. dead 故意不理睬某人

　　十七世紀初期，有個英文說法cut sb.，其意思是「與某人斷交、杯葛某人」，在這個用法中，cut指的是社交上的傷害，即冷落的態度；到了十九世紀，人們加上dead來強調語氣，意指「絕對不理某人、徹底與某人絕交」。

 對話練習 *Let's Talk!*

Danny: Did something happen between you and Cindy?

Joyce: No. Why do you ask?

Danny: Cindy said you **cut her dead** this morning.

Joyce: Oh no! She misunderstood the whole situation.

Danny: I figured so. Well, you'd better explain it to her later.

丹　尼：你跟辛蒂之間發生了什麼事嗎？

喬伊絲：沒有啊，怎麼這麼問？

丹　尼：辛蒂說你今天早上故意不理她。

喬伊絲：天啊！她完全誤會了。

丹　尼：我就知道，你晚點最好和她解釋清楚。

字彙/片語充電區 *Words and Phrases*

rebuff 動 冷落 / despise 動 藐視 / friendship 名 友誼 / reconcile 動 使和好
break up with sb. 與某人絕交 / pay attention to 關心 / get sb. wrong 誤會某人

UNIT 077 smell a rat 聞到老鼠的氣味？

🎧 077

 暖身猜猜看 *Warming Up*

Kelly: Dad, I saw Rick and Dan running down to the basement.
Father: Hmm...I **smell a rat**. I'd better go check it out.

凱莉：爸，我看到瑞克和丹跑到地下室去了。
父親：嗯…不太對勁，我最好去看看。

 原來是這個意思！

smell a rat 懷疑；感到不對勁

　　這個慣用語是取材自貓咪靠嗅覺找出藏匿的老鼠，當嗅到什麼氣味時，牠們就會開始警戒，並準備行動；後來就將這個用法衍生至人的行為，比喻人如貓一般，靈敏地感覺到事情可疑、不對勁。

 對話練習 *Let's Talk!*

Gavin: The fabric supplier suddenly offered us another 15% discount.

Linda: I noticed that, too. We just received the catalogue.

Gavin: The price of those items has always been fixed.

Linda: I **smell a rat**. We should try to figure out what's up.

Gavin: I agree. Let's report this to Ms. Lin first.

蓋文：布料供應商突然額外給我們15%的折扣。

琳達：我也注意到了，我們剛拿到目錄。

蓋文：那類產品的價格通常都是固定的。

琳達：我覺得哪裡不對勁，我們應該試著去查清楚。

蓋文：我也這麼覺得，我們先上報這件事給林經理吧。

字彙／片語充電區 *Words and Phrases*

unusual 形 不平常的 / sense 動 感覺到 / perceive 動 注意到；領悟 / proof 名 證據
be aware of 察覺 / pull the wool over one's eyes 蒙騙 / an easy mark 易受騙者

UNIT 078 hit the sack
打麻袋等同於練拳擊？

🎧 078

 暖身猜猜看 Warming Up

Sally: Do you want to go out for pizza tonight?

Danny: Nah. I've had a long day. I am going to **hit the sack**.

莎莉：今晚要不要出去吃披薩？

丹尼：不了，我度過了漫長的一天，想去睡了。

 原來是這個意思！

hit the sack 上床睡覺

這個慣用語是從更早的hit the hay變化而來，二十世紀初期，許多生活較不富裕的人家，會用麻袋裝滿乾草或馬毛來當作床，在睡前，人們會拍打那個麻袋，以讓當中的稻草平均分布，所以hit the sack便用來指稱「上床睡覺」。

 對話練習 *Let's Talk!*

Cindy: What do you remember the most from your biking trip?

Harvey: I'd say all the people I encountered and their stories.

Cindy: Weren't you scared camping out in the field?

Harvey: Not at all. All I could think of was **hitting the sack**.

Cindy: Ha! You must have been dog-tired then.

辛蒂：你這一趟單車旅行中，最難忘的是什麼？

哈維：我想是過程中遇到的人，和他們的故事。

辛蒂：那你在野外紮營時，都不會害怕嗎？

哈維：一點都不會，我腦子裡唯一想的就是睡覺。

辛蒂：哈！你那時候肯定累翻了。

字彙/片語充電區 *Words and Phrases*

weariness 名 疲倦 / lethargic 形 愛睡的 / conscious 形 神智清醒的 / drain 動 耗盡

sleep tight 睡個好覺 / get a wink of sleep 小睡片刻 / be done in 精疲力竭

UNIT 079

rain check
雨天的時候要檢查什麼？

🎧 079

 暖身猜猜看 *Warming Up*

Carter: Would you like to go to dinner with me tomorrow?

Nicole: I'll be busy tomorrow. Can we take a **rain check**?

卡特：你明天要不要跟我一起用晚餐？

妮可：我明天會很忙，能改期嗎？

 原來是這個意思！

rain check 改到將來兌現的承諾

　　這個慣用語源自於體育比賽，在戶外舉辦的球賽，遇到下雨天時，會被迫改期，並且發給觀眾一張雨天票（rain check），讓他們下一次開賽時使用，後來rain check便被用來比喻「延期的承諾」或「留到下次的機會」。

 **對話練習** *Let's Talk!*

Karen: Have you seen your paycheck yet?

Allen: Not yet. Why?

Karen: They didn't give us the raise they promised.

Allen: I heard that they are giving us a **rain check**.

Karen: What?! They've pushed our raise back twice already!

凱倫：你看了你薪水的支票了嗎？

亞倫：還沒，怎麼了嗎？

凱倫：他們沒有照承諾給我們加薪。

亞倫：我聽別人說，上面說加薪的事要延期了。

凱倫：什麼？！他們已經改期兩次了耶！

字彙／片語充電區 *Words and Phrases*

suspend 動 懸掛；暫停 / **adjourn** 動 使中止 / **inoperative** 形 不活動的；無效的

push back 推遲 / **on hold** 暫停 / **put off** 延遲；拖延 / **break one's promise** 食言

UNIT 080

get one's goat
搶走別人的山羊？

🎧 080

 暖身猜猜看 *Warming Up*

Megan: What's going on between you and Eve?

Danny: I **got her goat** by telling the truth about her hairstyle.

梅根：你跟伊芙之間怎麼了？

丹尼：我老實說出對她髮型的想法，惹毛她了。

 原來是這個意思！

get one's goat 使人發怒

　　人們將山羊跟賽馬放養在一起，是因為山羊可以讓賽馬冷靜下來，這樣比賽時的表現會比較穩定；希望對方的馬輸時，會把山羊帶走，藉此害賽馬變得焦躁不安，因此get one's goat便被用來表達「使人生氣或焦躁不安」。

 對話練習 *Let's Talk!*

Ted: Is Zoe in the lounge? I need her to revise her article.

Cindy: I suggest talking to her another time.

Ted: Why is that?

Cindy: She is in a bad mood now. You'll probably **get her goat** at this point.

Ted: Not again! I guess I'll have to do it myself.

泰德：柔伊在休息室嗎？我需要她修改文章。

辛蒂：我勸你晚點再去找她。

泰德：為什麼？

辛蒂：她現在心情不好，你現在去八成會惹惱她。

泰德：別又來了！我猜我得自己修改文章了。

字彙／片語充電區 *Words and Phrases*

irksome 形 令人惱恨的 / **offend** 動 冒犯 / **contradict** 動 反駁 / **introspect** 動 內省

drive up the wall 使大怒 / **side with** 支持 / **as gentle as a lamb** 像綿羊般溫和

UNIT 081 burn up
什麼東西起火了？

🎧 081

 暖身猜猜看 Warming Up

Jack: I forgot to change my white shirt before playing soccer.

Nancy: Mom will **burn up** when she sees it.

傑克：踢足球前，我忘了換掉我的白襯衫。

南西：媽看到你這樣子會氣死的。

 原來是這個意思！

burn up 發火

　　burn up若由原文直譯，就是燒起來的意思，當用來形容人時，可不是在講人體自燃現象，而是在比喻「極端的氣憤」導致體溫升高，彷彿快燒起來似的；使用時常用It burns sb. up/sb. be burned up等。

 Let's Talk!

Mary: What are you looking for?

Jeff: I am looking for the bracelet my girlfriend gave me.

Mary: You lost it while playing soccer? But this field is huge!

Jeff: I have to find it. She is going to **burn up** if I lost it.

Mary: Alright. Let me help you then.

瑪莉：你在找什麼？

傑夫：我在找我女朋友送的手鍊。

瑪莉：你踢足球的時候弄丟了嗎？但是這個球場超大的耶！

傑夫：我必須找到才行，如果我弄丟了，她會氣炸的。

瑪莉：好吧，那我也來幫你找。

字彙／片語充電區 *Words and Phrases*

resentful 形 忿恨的 / rationality 名 合理性 / complaint 名 抱怨 / gaiety 名 高興

hold a grudge against sb. 對某人心懷怨恨 / haul sb. over the coals 嚴厲斥責

UNIT 082

fit to be tied
綁東西綁得剛剛好？

🎧 082

 暖身猜猜看 *Warming Up*

Alvin: I thought you were going out with Tim.

Lucy: I waited for him for two hours, and now I am **fit to be tied**!

亞文：你不是跟提姆出去嗎？

露西：我等了他兩個小時，我要氣瘋了！

原來是這個意思！

fit to be tied 氣得要命；氣炸了

　　fit to be tied最早起源於十九世紀，原本是用來比喻精神病患者的失控狀態，必須用皮帶將其綁住；後來轉而用來形容「生氣到近乎失控的狀態」，情緒激動到需要被綁住的程度，也就是「氣瘋了、氣炸了」。

 對話練習 *Let's Talk!*

Helen: My sister waited for you for two hours!

Larry: My car broke down on the way, and I left my cell phone at home.

Helen: She is totally **fit to be tied** now.

Larry: I can imagine. But that was truly an accident.

Helen: No matter what, you'd better apologize to her as soon as possible.

海倫：我姊等你等了兩個鐘頭耶！

賴瑞：我的車半路拋錨，我又把手機忘在家裡。

海倫：她現在可真是氣炸了。

賴瑞：我可以想像，但那真的是意外。

海倫：無論如何，你最好快點去向她道歉。

字彙／片語充電區 *Words and Phrases*

convulse 動 憤怒至顫抖 / fume 名 憤怒 / irascible 形 暴躁的 / temper 名 脾氣

get in one's hair 惹惱某人 / tick off 斥責 / give sb. a hard time 讓某人不好過

UNIT
083

have a fit
穿著合身的衣服？

🎧 083

暖身猜猜看 *Warming Up*

Tim: Have you told Mom that you flunked the exam?

Merry: Not yet. I am so scared that she might **have a fit**.

提姆：你告訴媽媽你考試不及格的事了嗎？

梅莉：還沒，我超怕她生氣的。

原來是這個意思！

have a fit 勃然大怒

這個慣用語於二十世紀出現，是由throw a fit演變而來；fit作為名詞時，有發病、昏厥、痙攣之意，用這些情況去比喻激動的情緒，即「要氣死了」的意思；若要表達「把某人氣死」則可用give sb. a fit。

對話練習 *Let's Talk!*

Scott: That singer's agent just called and wants some changes.

Mia: Was it about the photo for the magazine cover?

Scott: Yes. Her boss wants her to look slimmer and younger.

Mia: But I already submitted the photo yesterday.

Scott: Well, that woman's boss is going to **have a fit**.

史考特：那個歌手的經紀人打來要求修片。

米　亞：你是說那張做雜誌封面的照片嗎？

史考特：是啊，她的老闆希望她的照片看起來更瘦、更年輕。

米　亞：但我昨天就把照片送出去了。

史考特：看來那個女歌手的老闆要氣炸了。

字彙／片語充電區 *Words and Phrases*

sentimental 形 感情用事的 / furious 形 暴怒的 / pacify 動 撫慰 / quarrel 名 爭吵
blow one's top 勃然大怒 / lose nerve 驚慌失措 / come to a deadlock 僵持不下

UNIT 084

see red
看見紅色有什麼特別？

🎧 084

 暖身猜猜看 *Warming Up*

Andy: What's wrong with you and Carl?

Julie: That snob just makes me **see red**!

安迪：你和卡爾之間是怎麼一回事？
茱莉：那個諂媚的勢利鬼真讓我抓狂！

 原來是這個意思！

see red 大怒

　　普遍認為這個慣用語源自於鬥牛運動，鬥牛士揮舞著紅布以激怒鬥牛，因而藉此形容一個人被激怒、發火的情況，就像牛看到紅布而生氣；另一個起源是美國早期的慣用語see things red，以生氣時血壓升高等生理現象來比喻生氣。

 **對話練習** *Let's Talk!*

Martin: I've read a book about moral practice.

Tina: I didn't know you are a religious person.

Martin: Actually, it's more for self-development.

Tina: Do you find it applicable for you?

Martin: Well, yeah. I don't **see red** that often anymore.

馬丁：我閱讀了一本關於修行的書。

蒂娜：我都不知道你有宗教信仰。

馬丁：其實，這本書的內容和自我成長比較有關。

蒂娜：那你覺得對你有用嗎？

馬丁：有啊，我沒那麼易怒了。

字彙 / 片語充電區 *Words and Phrases*

severely 副 嚴厲地 / forbear 動 克制 / reddish 形 淡紅的 / boaster 名 自誇的人
out of control 不受控制 / be on the level 誠實的；真誠的 / in the red 虧損；負債

UNIT 085

bite one's head off
把某人的頭咬掉？

🎧 085

 暖身猜猜看 *Warming Up*

Nick: I accidentally answered Lucy's cell phone.

Mother: She must have **bitten your head off**.

尼克：我不小心接了露西的手機來電。

母親：她肯定把你臭罵了一頓吧。

 原來是這個意思！

bite one's head off 怒斥某人

　　當一個人的語氣或態度，像是可以把對方的頭咬掉的時候，即是比喻憤怒又兇狠的說話方式，意即「斥責或怒罵」；另一個慣用語 eat one's head off 雖然可以依照情境理解成相同的意思，但多半是用來形容「一個人吃得非常多」。

 對話練習 *Let's Talk!*

Irene: Hank is your new partner, right?

George: Don't even mention his name. I just **bit his head off** this morning.

Irene: That's unusual for you. What happened?

George: I just had enough. He's been so demanding.

Irene: Calm down. Let me buy you a drink after work.

艾琳：漢克是你的新搭檔，對嗎？

喬治：別提到他，我今天早上才把他痛罵了一頓。

艾琳：你會這樣還真不尋常，怎麼了嗎？

喬治：我真是受夠他了，一直頤指氣使的。

艾琳：冷靜點，今天下班後我請你喝一杯吧。

字彙／片語充電區 *Words and Phrases*

scold 動 斥責 / reprimand 動 訓斥 / delirious 形 亂說話的 / impatient 形 急躁的
jump down one's throat 氣得大吼 / lash out at sb. 猛烈抨擊某人 / chip in 插話

UNIT 086
eat crow
吃下公雞的叫聲？

🎧 086

暖身猜猜看 *Warming Up*

Peter: Greg told me he made a mistake and gave the wrong data to the client.

Fanny: Yes. And now the client is making him **eat crow**.

彼德：葛瑞格和我說他出了錯，拿給客戶錯的數據。

芬妮：沒錯，現在那名客戶要他吃不完兜著走。

原來是這個意思！

eat crow 忍氣吞聲

　　第二次美國獨立戰爭後期，一名美國軍人越河打獵，槍聲引來一名英國軍人，他逼對方吃一口獵到的烏鴉，以示警告；後來美國軍人又強迫英國軍人吃掉剩下的烏鴉；eat crow後來就用來比喻「以被羞辱的方式承擔錯誤」。

對話練習 *Let's Talk!*

Cathy: You are a really sincere and supportive leader.

Jack: Actually, I have learned a lot from my personal experience.

Cathy: How so?

Jack: I had a tough manager before. He even made me **eat crow** for my mistakes.

Cathy: So that made you become a great leader.

凱西：你真是個誠懇又幫忙的領導者。

傑克：其實，我從自身的經驗學到很多。

凱西：怎麼說？

傑克：我之前的經理非常難搞，我還曾經為了自己犯的錯忍辱賠罪。

凱西：所以這讓你成為一個優秀的領導者。

字彙/片語充電區 *Words and Phrases*

succumb 動 屈服 / acquiesce 動 默認 / silence 名 沉默 / affront 動 公開侮辱

eat dirt 忍氣吞聲 / swallow one's pride 忍辱負重 / eat one's word 收回說過的話

UNIT 087

make one's hair stand on end
氣到怒髮衝冠的模樣？

🎧 087

 暖身猜猜看 *Warming Up*

Sam: Do you want to go check that lake cabin out?

Carol: No way. That area **makes my hair stand on end**.

山姆：你想不想去看看那間湖濱小屋？

卡蘿：才不要，那一帶讓我不寒而慄。

 原來是這個意思！

make one's hair stand on end 令人毛骨悚然

　　hair指頭髮，光看這個慣用語，會以為是在形容頭髮的狀態，其實，這裡的hair指的是身上的汗毛，end則為髮根，由原文直譯就是「令人寒毛直豎」，用來比喻人因為恐懼或驚嚇，身上汗毛都豎立起來的樣子。

 **對話練習** *Let's Talk!*

Henry: You're bold to take possession of that old house.

Sally: Why is that?

Henry: It's been abandoned for so long!

Sally: Yeah. It kind of **makes my hair stand on end**. But I got it for a really good price.

Henry: Well, good luck. I'm sure everything will be fine.

亨利：敢買下那棟老房子，你真勇敢。

莎莉：為什麼這麼說？

亨利：它已經荒廢很久了！

莎莉：的確，那房子是有點令我毛骨悚然，但我用非常便宜的價格就買到了。

亨利：好吧，祝你好運，我相信一切都會很順利的。

字彙/片語充電區 *Words and Phrases*

spooky 形 詭譎的；毛骨悚然的 / horrendous 形 可怕的 / cowardly 副 膽小地
scare sb. to death 嚇死 / curdle the blood 毛骨悚然 / shake in one's boots 發抖

UNIT 088 give (sb.) goose bumps
像鵝般地猛烈一撞？

🎧 088

 暖身猜猜看 *Warming Up*

Bill: What is that sound? It really **gives me goose bumps**.

Cindy: Mr. Lee's kid has been learning to play violin recently.

比爾：那是什麼聲音？真是讓我起雞皮疙瘩。

辛蒂：李先生的小孩最近開始學小提琴。

 **原來是這個意思！**

give (sb.) goose bumps 使起雞皮疙瘩

　　goose bumps也可以寫成goosebumps/goose pimples，是指鵝皮膚上毛細孔所造成的小疙瘩，拿來形容人時，就是指人在感到不舒服或恐懼時會有的生理現象（起雞皮疙瘩），若主詞是人，可説sb. get goose bumps。

 **對話練習** *Let's Talk!*

Nick: It's pouring out there, and it has turned so chilly.

Alice: What terrible weather for visiting clients.

Nick: What else can we do? We'd better get going now.

Alice: Hey, you are shaking!

Nick: I'll get my coat. The cold air is **giving me goose bumps**.

尼　克：外面在下大雨，天氣也變得好冷。

愛麗絲：真是個不適合拜訪客戶的壞天氣。

尼　克：我們能怎麼辦呢？還是趕緊出發吧。

愛麗絲：天啊，你在發抖耶！

尼　克：我要去拿外套，這冷空氣真是讓我直起雞皮疙瘩。

字彙/片語充電區 *Words and Phrases*

unpleasant 形 討厭的 / mysterious 形 神秘的；詭祕的 / antipathy 名 反感；厭惡
cold creeps 冷顫 / tremble with fear 不寒而慄 / entertain sb. with sth. 使愉悦

UNIT 089　full of beans
裝滿豆子的罐頭？

🎧 089

暖身猜猜看 Warming Up

Rose: Did you sleep well last night?

Sam: Definitely. Now I am **full of beans**!

蘿絲：你昨晚睡得好嗎？

山姆：很好，我現在精神充沛呢！

原來是這個意思！

full of beans 精神飽滿

　　早期被飼養的馬，都是以豆子作為食料，當馬被餵飽，精神就飽滿，體力也充足，因此，full of beans才被用來比喻「活力充沛、精神飽滿」的狀態；同義的慣用語還有full of prunes（梅乾）。

Jenny: I heard you caught a cold last week.

Tom: I had a fever and my entire body was sore.

Jenny: That's quite serious. Are you feeling better now?

Tom: Much better. I slept through the entire weekend.

Jenny: Take care. I hope you will be **full of beans** again soon.

珍妮：聽說你上週感冒了。

湯姆：我發燒，還全身痠痛。

珍妮：還滿嚴重的，那你現在有比較好了嗎？

湯姆：好多了，我整個週末都在睡覺休息。

珍妮：保重，希望你很快又是活蹦亂跳的。

字彙／片語充電區 Words and Phrases

vivid 形 有生氣的；活潑的 / **vitality** 名 活力；生氣 / **industrious** 形 勤勉的；勤勞的
in high spirits 精力充沛 / **be all set** 準備好 / **get-up-and-go** 進取的；衝勁十足的

UNIT 090　get cold feet
冷到發抖、雙腳冰冷？

🎧 090

 暖身猜猜看 Warming Up

Glenn: So, did you go out with Bart last night?

Kelly: No. I **got cold feet** since I don't know him well.

葛蘭：結果呢？你昨晚跟巴特約會了嗎？

凱莉：沒有，我臨陣退縮，因為我不怎麼認識他。

 原來是這個意思！

get cold feet 臨陣退縮

　　get cold feet最早起源於十九世紀的小說。當人把腳探進冰冷的水裡時，會反射性地縮起腳或是捲起腳趾頭，這種模樣和做事臨陣退縮的樣子很相似，所以被拿來形容人失去勇氣而退縮的行為。

 *Let's Talk!*

Anna: What positions have you been applying for?

Paul: I've applied to be a research assistant.

Anna: I thought you want to work in a lab.

Paul: I filled out the application form but **got cold feet**.

Anna: Why? You've worked so hard.

安娜：你申請了哪些職位？

保羅：我申請了研究助理的職位。

安娜：我以為你想到實驗室工作耶。

保羅：我填了申請表，但是後來又退縮了。

安娜：為什麼？你都那麼努力了。

字彙/片語充電區 *Words and Phrases*

hesitate 動 躊躇；猶豫 / uneasy 形 心神不安的 / apprehension 名 恐懼；憂慮
back out 退出；取消 / make up one's mind 下定決心 / keep a promise 履行諾言

UNIT 091 for crying out loud 大聲哭出來？

🎧 091

 暖身猜猜看 Warming Up

Kent: I can't take the trash out. The World Cup is about to start.

Mary: Can't you just help me out once **for crying out loud**?

肯特：我不能去丟垃圾，世界盃要開始了。

瑪莉：拜託你好不好，就不能幫我一次忙嗎？

 原來是這個意思！

for crying out loud 拜託（你）好不好？

　　美式口語中，會以For Christ's sake!或For God's sake!來表達「你饒了我吧！」、「看在老天的份上！」等情緒性的用語；然而在基督教的信仰中，一般不能直呼上帝或基督的名號，因此便有人用For crying out loud!來取代。

 *Let's Talk!*

Hank: What are our neighbors doing? It's 11 p.m. already!

Anna: They are having a crazy party.

Hank: **For crying out loud**! I need to focus on my studying now.

Anna: Calm down. I will go over and reason with them.

Hank: Maybe I should go do that.

漢克：我們的鄰居在做什麼？已經晚上十一點了耶！

安娜：他們正在開狂熱派對。

漢克：老天爺！我現在必須專心在我的研究上。

安娜：冷靜點，我會過去跟他們反應的。

漢克：也許應該由我過去跟他們說。

字彙／片語充電區 *Words and Phrases*

utter 動 表達 / convey 動 表達 / unbearable 形 無法忍受的 / blurt 動 脫口而出

do sb. a favor 幫…的忙 / cry out for sth. 要求 / cry in one's beer 難過地可憐自己

UNIT 092

Over my dead body!
越過身體的雜技動作？

🎧 092

 暖身猜猜看 *Warming Up*

Bella: Can I borrow your new camera?

Dylan: **Over my dead body!**

貝拉：你的新相機可以借我嗎？

狄倫：門兒都沒有！

 原來是這個意思！

Over my dead body! 門兒都沒有！

在日常對話中，當想要強烈否定對方時，可以說Over my dead body!（跨過我的屍體），義同that can only happen if I'm dead/but you have to kill me first，直譯為「等我死了再說！」，多半為開玩笑的誇張表達。

 **對話練習** *Let's Talk!*

Father: Your prom is next Friday, right?

Emma: Yeah. Danny asked me if I could be his partner.

Father: Have I met Danny before?

Emma: I think so. He came to my birthday party last month.

Father: Oh, that Danny. He's such a strange boy, so he can date you **over my dead body**.

父親：你的畢業舞會是下個星期五，對吧？

艾瑪：是啊，丹尼問我能不能做他的舞伴。

父親：我有見過丹尼嗎？

艾瑪：應該有吧，他上個月有來參加我的生日派對。

父親：喔，那個丹尼，那男孩怪裡怪氣的，他想跟你約會，門兒都沒有。。

字彙／片語充電區 *Words and Phrases*

veto 名 反對 / **resolute** 形 堅決的 / **response** 名 回覆 / **renounce** 動 聲明放棄
Forget it! 算了吧！ / **Not on your life.** 這輩子都不可能。 / **at no time** 永遠不會

UNIT 093

with all due respect
誇獎人很有禮貌？

🎧 093

 暖身猜猜看 Warming Up

Harper: The final paper should be turned in next week.

Sandy: **With all due respect**, sir, you already said it was due in two weeks.

哈波：期末報告要在下星期繳交。

仙蒂：恕我直言，教授，您之前說的是兩週後交。

 原來是這個意思！

with all due respect 恕我直言

　　due在此處指「應當的」，這個慣用語字面上的意思為「秉持著尊敬」，但在實際使用時，是因為接下來講的話或許會冒犯他人，才會用這句慣用語；須注意的是，有些人會把這句看作是你在污辱他的智商，使用時請多加小心。

 Let's Talk!

Rita: Are we supposed to complete the field research within a week?

Larry: Yes. And we need to come up with a proposal in that time as well.

Rita: **With all due respect**, that's not nearly enough time.

Larry: I understand how you feel, but we have to accept the terms.

Rita: We can at least ask for a bit more time.

芮塔：我們必須在一週內完成市調嗎？

賴瑞：沒錯，而且還必須提出一個計畫。

芮塔：恕我直言，給的時間根本就不夠。

賴瑞：我理解你的心情，但我們必須接受這樣的條件。

芮塔：那我們至少可以要求多一點的時間吧。

字彙／片語充電區 Words and Phrases

esteem 名 尊敬；尊重 / courtesy 名 禮貌 / respectful 形 恭敬的 / direct 形 直接的
No offence. 恕我直言 / show respect for 尊敬 / come clean about 從實招來

UNIT 094

be taken in
東西被拿到哪裡去了？

🎧 094

暖身猜猜看 *Warming Up*

Maggie: Do you know the reason why Paul quit?

Warner: He **was taken in** by a client and it cost a lot.

梅姬：你知道保羅辭職的原因嗎？

華納：他被一個客戶騙了，虧損了一大筆錢。

原來是這個意思！

be taken in 受騙；上當

　　take有許多用法及解釋，衍生出的慣用語take in也有幾種不同的意思（收容；改小衣服；理解…等）；此處的take為常見的俚語用法，意指「欺騙」，be taken in則指「被欺騙」，意同be deceived。

Let's Talk!

Joey: I **was taken in** by the advertisement!

Lily: If you don't like the fitness machine, can you return it?

Joey: What really drives me nuts is that this is not refundable!

Lily: All right. Cool off. Let me try to sell it on-line.

Joey: Really? You are my savior!

喬伊：我被廣告騙了！

莉莉：如果你不喜歡那台健身器材，可以退貨嗎？

喬伊：真正讓我抓狂的是，這台機器不接受退貨！

莉莉：好啦，冷靜點，讓我試著在網路上賣掉。

喬伊：真的嗎？你真是我的救星！

字彙/片語充電區 *Words and Phrases*

dupe 名 易受騙者 / circumvent 動 陷害 / exaggerate 動 誇大 / advantage 名 好處
be born yesterday 無知的 / expose a fraud 拆穿騙局 / on the up and up 光明磊落

UNIT 095
red tape
紅色膠帶與文具有關？

🎧 095

 暖身猜猜看 *Warming Up*

Mindy: When are you going to renovate the shop?

Owen: Well, we need to go through lots of **red tape** first.

明蒂：你什麼時候要翻修店鋪？

歐文：我們還得先處理繁雜的手續才行。

 原來是這個意思！

red tape 官僚的作業流程

　　幾世紀以來，英國的律師和官員，都是以紅色的書帶綁住一疊疊的文件，因而狄更斯在他的作品中，以red tape來諷喻死板苛刻的法規和流程，沿用至今，這個詞彙便被用來形容官僚體系的作業流程。

 *Let's Talk!*

Rachel: How was your vacation?

Paul: It was great. My wife and I just fell in love with the island.

Rachel: Then why don't you invest in a villa there?

Paul: We thought about it, but the **red tape** is crazy.

Rachel: That's too bad. If you bought a villa, I could visit you.

瑞秋：你的假期如何？

保羅：很棒，我太太跟我都愛上了那座島。

瑞秋：那你們何不在那裡投資一間渡假別墅呢？

保羅：我們有想過，但申請的流程太繁複了。

瑞秋：真可惜，如果你買下渡假別墅的話，我就可以去參觀了。

字彙／片語充電區 *Words and Phrases*

bureaucracy 名 官僚政治 / authority 名 官方；當局 / solemnity 名 莊嚴；嚴肅

fawn on 巴結 / bring to light 揭發 / go along with 附和 / in league with 聯合

UNIT 096

cream of the crop
在作物上塗奶油？

🎧 096

 暖身猜猜看 *Warming Up*

Bella: I must work harder if I want to join that company.

Kent: Yeah. They only hire those who are the **cream of the crop**.

貝拉：如果想要加入那家公司，我得更努力。

肯特：是啊，他們只聘請最頂尖的人。

 原來是這個意思！

cream of the crop 最好的（人事物）

　　這個慣用語於十六世紀時出現，用來形容最優質的選擇，在此之前，cream就常被拿來比喻「最好的部分」，這是因為cream被認為是牛奶中的精華；這個慣用語也可以用來形容收成時，品質最好的作物，但這個用法較少見。

 對話練習 *Let's Talk!*

John: Wow! This laptop is on sale!

Cindy: Didn't I mention it's the seasonal sale period?

John: You don't understand. This company seldom reduces their prices.

Cindy: I guess even the **cream of the crop** needs a sales promotion sometimes.

John: That's true.

約翰：哇！這台筆記型電腦在特價耶！

辛蒂：我沒跟你說現在是換季大拍賣嗎？

約翰：你不懂，這家公司的產品幾乎不降價的。

辛蒂：就算是表現最好的龍頭公司有時候也需要促銷活動吧。

約翰：這倒是。

字彙/片語充電區 *Words and Phrases*

superiority 名 優越 / **idealize** 動 理想化 / **distillation** 名 精華 / **blemish** 名 瑕疵
the best of all 最好的 / **better shop around** 貨比三家 / **a knock-off** 仿名牌製品

UNIT 097　showstopper 中斷演出的人？

🎧 097

 暖身猜猜看 *Warming Up*

Arthur: The fundraising dinner last night was a success.

Lucy: Yeah, the children's chorus was the **showstopper**.

亞瑟：昨晚的募款餐會真是太成功了。

露西：是啊，兒童合唱團是整場活動的高潮。

 原來是這個意思！

showstopper 表演中最精彩的部分

　　這個慣用語光看字面，會以為是某個中斷表演的人吧？其實，showstopper描述的是，一個表演者的演出博得滿堂喝采，觀眾的掌聲實在太過熱烈，以至於中斷了演出的盛況，後來被用來形容「表演中的精華橋段」。

 *Let's Talk!*

Kelly: Did you attend the annual party last night?

Elton: Yes, it was great. Weren't you there?

Kelly: Our crew was hosting an event, so we all missed it.

Elton: It's a pity! The founder's speech was the **showstopper**.

Kelly: I hope somebody recorded it.

凱　莉：你有參加昨晚的年度晚會嗎？

艾爾頓：有啊，晚會很棒，你沒有去嗎？

凱　莉：我們的團隊剛好在主持一個活動，所以都沒去。

艾爾頓：太可惜了！創辦人的演講成了整晚的焦點。

凱　莉：真希望有人把演講錄下來。

字彙／片語充電區 *Words and Phrases*

enthusiastic 形 熱烈的 / applaud 動 向…鼓掌 / impressive 形 令人印象深刻的
steal the show 搶盡風頭 / pump up 加油；打氣 / beat sb. by miles 遠遠勝過某人

UNIT 098

silver bullet
這就是「銀彈攻勢」？

🎧 098

暖身猜猜看 *Warming Up*

Jill: Our landlord wants us out by the end of this month!

Sam: This is ridiculous. We really need a **silver bullet**.

吉兒：房東要我們月底前搬出去！

山姆：這太扯了，我們需要能解決這件事的辦法。

原來是這個意思！

silver bullet 簡單又有效的解決方式

　　古老的西方世界認為銀有神奇的力量，當時人們相信只有銀製的子彈可以殺死狼人等怪物或惡靈，十九世紀出版的許多科幻小說，都有提到這個概念；直到二十世紀，silver bullet才被用來比喻「能解決大麻煩的簡單方法」。

對話練習 *Let's Talk!*

John: The financial report shows that we are over budget.

Emma: Are you sure? We can't get any more funds.

John: Positive. We'd better find a **silver bullet**.

Emma: How about cutting down on PR expenses?

John: We can also try doing marketing through other channels.

約翰：財務報告顯示，我們超出預算了。

艾瑪：你確定嗎？我們沒有更多資金可申請了。

約翰：我確定，我們必須想個好辦法解決。

艾瑪：降低公關支出怎麼樣？

約翰：我們也可以試著用其他的管道做行銷。

字彙／片語充電區 *Words and Phrases*

quandary 名 窘境 / effective 形 有效的 / intimation 名 暗示 / silverware 名 銀器
a quick fix 應急 / know the ropes 瞭解內情 / roll with the punches 從容應對

UNIT 099

a capital idea
毫無創意的基本想法？

🎧 099

 暖身猜猜看 Warming Up

Allen: Coming up with a proposal is difficult.

Rose: You'd better have **a capital idea**.

亞倫：要想出求婚的方式真困難。

蘿絲：你最好有個絕妙的主意。

 原來是這個意思！

a capital idea 好主意

　　capital有「基本的、資本的」等意思，所以我們容易誤解這個慣用語的意思，其實，capital在口語中還能指「一流的、最好的」，因此，a capital idea即是指「絕佳妙計、好主意」。

 Let's Talk!

Nina: Let's brainstorm for the new marketing project.

Eddy: I am thinking of using an advertising vehicle.

Nina: You mean like a loudspeaker van?

Eddy: No. What I'm thinking is more like a mobile catwalk.

Nina: That sounds like **a capital idea**!

妮娜：我們來為新的行銷企劃腦力激盪一下。

艾迪：我想採用宣傳車的概念。

妮娜：你是說那種裝有擴音器的箱型車嗎？

艾迪：不是，我在想的比較像行動伸展台。

妮娜：聽起來是個很棒的主意！

字彙／片語充電區 Words and Phrases

conceptualize 動 使概念化 / superlative 形 最高的；最好的 / originality 名 新穎

conjure up 想起 / second to none 首屈一指 / back up one's idea 支持某人想法

UNIT 100

familiar talk
之前聊過的熟悉話題？

🎧 100

 暖身猜猜看 *Warming Up*

Colin: Do you want to have a drink with the others after work?

Kelly: No. I can't handle **familiar talk** after a long day.

科林：你下班後要跟大家去喝一杯嗎？

凱莉：不了，在辛苦了一天後，我沒精神應付無趣的閒談。

 原來是這個意思！

familiar talk 平庸的、了無新意的談話內容

　　familiar意指「熟悉的」，與talk結合之後，很容易讓人誤解為「曾經聊過，所以熟悉的話題」；試想一下，讓你覺得了無新意的談話，是不是聽來聽去都是那些呢？這個慣用語的意思，正是「讓人感到無趣的談話內容」。

 **對話練習** *Let's Talk!*

Jack: How was your dinner last night?

Lucy: Nothing new. Everyone was only interested in **familiar talk**.

Jack: So your gathering turned into a bragging competition?

Lucy: Yeah. I just hate to see that.

Jack: Me, too. Never mind, you still have some real friends.

傑克：你昨天晚上的聚餐怎麼樣？

露西：沒什麼特別的，大家都只想閒扯。

傑克：所以聚餐變成吹牛大會了？

露西：是啊，我真的很討厭那樣。

傑克：我也不喜歡，別在意，你還是有知心好友。

字彙／片語充電區 *Words and Phrases*

content 名 內容 / hearsay 名 傳聞 / mediocre 形 二流的 / throng 名 一大群人
be devoid of content 空洞無物 / give vent to 發洩 / of poor quality 劣質的

UNIT 101　fishy 一股魚腥味？

🎧 101

 暖身猜猜看 Warming Up

Rena: Jack said he drove Tina home out of politeness.

Carl: I am sure I smell something **fishy**.

芮娜：傑克說他送蒂娜回家只是出於禮貌。

卡爾：我怎麼覺得事有蹊蹺。

 原來是這個意思！

fishy 可疑的

　　fishy字面上的解釋是「像魚一樣的」，魚的滑溜感和掩蓋不住的腥味，這是此慣用語原本的意思。一般來說，魚腥味與新鮮度不夠有關（開始變質），所以後來衍生出「不可靠、掌握不住及隱約嗅到什麼氣味的意象」。

 對話練習 Let's Talk!

Sunny: Who do you think will be the new vice president?

George: I'd bet on Will because I found Peter a bit slippery.

Sunny: What made you think so?

George: I walked in on his dinner with our supplier once.

Sunny: There could be something **fishy** between them.

桑妮：你覺得誰會當選新任的副總？

喬治：我寧可賭威爾，因為彼德有點靠不住。

桑妮：你為什麼會這麼覺得？

喬治：我曾經撞見他跟我們的供應商在一起用晚餐。

桑妮：他們之間很可疑喔。

字彙／片語充電區 Words and Phrases

equivocal 形 模稜兩可的 / peculiar 形 罕見的；奇怪的 / implausible 形 難以置信的
have a bee in one's bonnet 胡思亂想 / put a bug in one's ear 事先給某人消息

UNIT 102　a dime a dozen
一打物品只賣一角？

🎧 102

暖身猜猜看 *Warming Up*

Susan: I went to the shopping mall. They are having a seasonal sale!

Kent: Those kinds of sales are **a dime a dozen**.

蘇珊：我去了購物中心，現在正在舉辦換季大拍賣呢！

肯特：那類的拍賣太常見，都不稀奇了。

原來是這個意思！

a dime a dozen 常見而不稀奇的

　　美國於1796年發行以「角」為單位的貨幣，這個慣用語被認為於十九世紀出現，其用法與dime本身的價值有關，因為大量製作與流通，所以就算蒐集也沒有價值，由此發展出這個慣用語，表示「不值錢、沒價值的（東西）」。

對話練習 *Let's Talk!*

Nick: Trading is not that profitable these days.

Betty: Price has become the only thing that matters to buyers.

Nick: As a result, you can hardly find any good quality goods.

Betty: It's frustrating.

Nick: Yeah. The prices they want to pay are good for **a dime a dozen** items only.

尼克：現在貿易不好賺了。

貝蒂：售價已經變成買家唯一在乎的事情。

尼克：結果，就幾乎找不到什麼精品了。

貝蒂：這滿令人沮喪的。

尼克：是啊，他們出的價錢都只能買些不值錢的東西而已。

字彙／片語充電區 *Words and Phrases*

bargain 名 交易 / **profit** 名 利潤 / **superfluous** 形 過剩的 / **inevitable** 形 必然的
think little of 認為…沒價值 / **a back number** 過期的刊物 / **in the black** 有收益

UNIT 103　quick-and-dirty 又快又髒的東西？

🎧 103

 暖身猜猜看 Warming Up

Eddy: This is an old van that needs some touchup.

Nora: I am going to sell it, so a **quick-and-dirty** job will do.

艾迪：這台廂型車很老舊了，需要修理。

諾拉：我打算賣了這台車，所以只要粗略修一下就好。

 原來是這個意思！

quick-and-dirty 快但粗劣的；應急的

　　quick-and-dirty最早用來形容餐廳，供餐快速、價格便宜但是衛生條件不好，只要能吃飽就可以了；引申其意至事物上，形容因為時間或其他壓力，無法將一件事做完善，只能「講求快速而隨便應付」，通常隱喻後續會有問題。

 **對話練習** *Let's Talk!*

Judy: How's your term paper going?

Hank: Not good at all. I went off topic.

Judy: Don't tell me you're going to rewrite the whole thing.

Hank: Yes, I am. I have to wrap it up **quick-and-dirty**.

Judy: Yeah. The due date is less than a week from now.

茱蒂：你的期末報告怎麼樣了？

漢克：一點都不好，我離題了。

茱蒂：別告訴我你打算全部重寫。

漢克：我的確得重寫，只能先不顧品質，盡快做完了。

茱蒂：也是，離繳交日只剩不到一週了。

字彙／片語充電區 *Words and Phrases*

perfunctory 形 敷衍的 / **hasty** 形 匆忙的 / **skeleton** 名 概略 / **exquisite** 形 精緻的
meet an urgent need 應急 / **be fussy about** 挑剔的 / **be particular about** 講究

UNIT 104　a dead ringer
一個壞掉的門鈴？

🎧 104

 暖身猜猜看 *Warming Up*

Collin: I ran into **a dead ringer** for Tina yesterday!

Polly: Oh, that was her twin sister.

科林：我昨天看到一個和蒂娜長得一模一樣的人！

波莉：喔，那是她的雙胞胎妹妹啦。

 原來是這個意思！

a dead ringer 極為相似的人或物

　　dead除了死亡之外，還有「非常的、絕對的、完全的」之意，常用來加強語氣；ringer的起源則來自於賽馬文化，指的是和參賽馬匹長相一模一樣的備用馬，後來被用來比喻幾乎完全相同的人或物。

 **對話練習** *Let's Talk!*

Kyle: I heard that your new car is arriving today. Can I see it?

Amy: Sure. But you'll probably be turned off.

Kyle: Why is that?

Amy: Because it's simply **a dead ringer** for my old car.

Kyle: Wow. You really love that model, don't you?

凱爾：我聽說你的新車今天會到，我可以看看嗎？

艾咪：可以啊，不過你恐怕會失望。

凱爾：為什麼？

艾咪：因為它跟我的舊車是一模一樣的。

凱爾：哇，你肯定很愛那個款式的車吧？

字彙／片語充電區 *Words and Phrases*

duplicate 形 完全一樣的 / reproduction 名 繁殖；複製品 / appearance 名 外表
a spitting image 極相似的人 / **knock sb. dead** 讓人刮目相看 / **look into** 深入觀察

117

UNIT 105 jump the shark 往鯊魚的嘴裡跳？

🎧 105

暖身猜猜看 *Warming Up*

Anna: Are you still watching the eight-o'clock show?

Carter: No, it's starting to **jump the shark**.

安娜：你還在看那齣八點檔嗎？

卡特：沒耶，那齣劇已經開始失去吸引力了。

原來是這個意思！

jump the shark （電視節目）失去吸引力

　　1977年美國電視連續劇《Happy Days》在收視率開始走下坡的時候，安排男主角滑水跳過迎面游來的鯊魚，爾後觀眾即以jump the shark來形容為了挽回觀眾的新鮮感，電視劇中開始出現與劇情無關的噱頭跟花招。

對話練習 *Let's Talk!*

Penny: I am going to watch a DVD tonight.

Kevin: I thought you were a big fan of that TV series called "My Life Story".

Penny: It has started to **jump the shark**.

Kevin: They have probably run out of ideas.

Penny: For sure! The lead has been almost killed twice already for heaven's sake!

潘妮：我今天晚上要看DVD。

凱文：我以為你是《我的人生故事》那齣連續劇的忠實粉絲。

潘妮：那齣劇已經開始亂演，沒什麼吸引人的了。

凱文：他們大概想不出新點子了吧。

潘妮：肯定如此！主角都差點死兩次了，真是拜託喔！

字彙／片語充電區 *Words and Phrases*

gimmick 名 噱頭 / **ludicrous** 形 滑稽的 / **attraction** 名 吸引 / **synopsis** 名 概要

wear out 耗盡；用盡 / **feeling of freshness** 新鮮感 / **jump the battery** 充電

UNIT 106　dog-and-pony show
狗與小馬的馬戲團秀？

🎧 106

 暖身猜猜看 Warming Up

David: Look at the bouquet of roses. Tim is sweet.

Lucy: It's his **dog-and-pony show** after I caught him cheating.

大衛：看那一大束玫瑰花，提姆真貼心。

露西：那是他被我抓到偷吃，才要的爛把戲。

 原來是這個意思！

dog-and-pony show 用很陽春的方法來獲得認同（負面）

　　早期的美國有很多家庭式的馬戲團，由於負擔不起大型的動物和特技演員，就只有小狗和小馬；dog-and-pony show這個慣用語衍生至今，帶有輕蔑、鄙視的語氣，表示費盡心機、過度包裝的訊息或表演。

 **對話練習** *Let's Talk!*

Bonnie: Your community holds events almost every weekend!

Kevin: Sometimes I get tired of all the **dog-and-pony shows**.

Bonnie: Really? I thought you loved Halloween parties.

Kevin: That one is fun, but the best-garden competition?

Bonnie: I see. They try too hard to impress the neighborhood.

邦妮：你的社區幾乎每個週末都有活動耶！

凱文：有時候我對那些陽春的活動感到很厭煩。

邦妮：是嗎？我以為你很喜歡萬聖節派對。

凱文：萬聖節派對是很好玩，但是最佳花園選拔賽？

邦妮：原來如此，他們過度積極地想給社區留下好印象。

字彙/片語充電區 *Words and Phrases*

enact 動 上演 / parody 名 拙劣的模仿 / contempt 名 輕視 / sarcasm 名 挖苦

put on a show 做戲 / **a storm in a teacup** 小題大作 / **act as if** 假裝；若無其事

UNIT 107

face the music
與音樂面對面？

🎧 107

 暖身猜猜看 Warming Up

Helen: Tom should have reported the problem to Mr. Lee.

Gary: Yeah. Now it's time for him to **face the music**.

海倫：湯姆應該要把這個問題上報給李經理的。

蓋瑞：是啊，現在他得承擔後果了。

 原來是這個意思！

face the music 面對困難；承擔後果

　　face the music的出處有兩種說法，一指劇場的樂團和演員，必須面對不賞臉的觀眾；另一說法來自軍隊，被撤職的軍人，在不光彩的那一刻，有樂隊的伴奏；無論如何，這個慣用語都是指「不光彩的時刻」或「艱難的場面」。

 **對話練習** Let's Talk!

Bert: Did you watch the news last night?

Gina: You mean the story about the famous food chain owner?

Bert: Yes. I can't believe he got sent to prison.

Gina: Who knows how many poisons he had been feeding us?

Bert: Well, now he has to **face the music**.

伯特：你看了昨晚的新聞了嗎？

吉娜：你是說那個有名的食品連鎖店老闆的新聞嗎？

伯特：是啊，不敢相信他竟然被關進牢裡了。

吉娜：誰知道他給我們吃下了多少的毒？

伯特：是啊，現在他得自食惡果了。

字彙／片語充電區 Words and Phrases

tolerate 動 容忍 / dilemma 名 困境 / consequence 名 後果 / accustom 動 習慣於
face up to 勇敢面對；正視 / pay the piper 自食其果 / swallow the pill 吞下苦果

UNIT 108　out to lunch
午休時間外出用餐？

🎧 108

 暖身猜猜看 *Warming Up*

Cathy: Sam said that our department will be reduced in size.

Jerry: Don't buy that. He is **out to lunch**!

凱西：山姆說我們的部門要裁員。

傑瑞：別相信他說的，他發瘋了！

 原來是這個意思！

out to lunch 放空；心不在焉；瘋了

　　字面上是指某人去午餐了，實際上是比喻心不在焉（distracted）的狀態，或是精神狀態上的瘋癲（crazy/stupid）；在適當的對話情境之下，也可以表示某人去用餐，如果擔心聽者誤會的話，不妨使用be at lunch。

 對話練習　*Let's Talk!*

Mary: Have you heard any of the words I have been saying to you?

Danny: What? Sorry. I was **out to lunch** for a few moments.

Mary: What's going on with you? You've been so absent-minded recently.

Danny: I've been staying up late working on a project.

Mary: No wonder your performance these days has been quite poor.

瑪莉：你有沒有聽到我跟你說的話啊？

丹尼：什麼？抱歉，我恍神了一下。

瑪莉：怎麼回事？你最近很心不在焉。

丹尼：我最近都在熬夜趕一個案子。

瑪莉：難怪最近你的表現很差。

字彙/片語充電區 *Words and Phrases*

abstracted 形 出神的；發呆的 / heedless 形 不留神的 / preoccupied 形 入神的
have one's head in the clouds 做白日夢 / be lost in thought 出神；陷入沈思

UNIT 109 in the dark
身處無燈光的黑暗當中？

🎧 109

 暖身猜猜看 *Warming Up*

Carter: Our company is going to lay off some personnel.

Emily: Really? I am completely **in the dark** about that.

卡　特：我們公司要裁員了。
艾蜜莉：真的嗎？我完全不知道這件事。

 原來是這個意思！

in the dark 一無所知

　　這個慣用語的字面意思是「在黑暗中」，以什麼都看不到來比喻一無所知的狀態；be in the dark 指處於無知的狀態（靜態描述），keep sb. in the dark 則是隱瞞、不告知某人（動作行為），搭配的動詞不同，意思也不一樣。

 **對話練習** *Let's Talk!*

Mike: Cindy's birthday is coming. Have you bought a gift yet?

Daisy: Let's give her a surprise. She would love it.

Mike: Cool. How about taking her to Molly's Diner?

Daisy: You take her there, and we'll wait inside.

Mike: Okay. Remember to keep her **in the dark**!

麥克：辛蒂的生日要到了，你買禮物了嗎？

黛西：我們給她個驚喜吧，她會很喜歡的。

麥克：酷，帶她去《莫莉的餐點》用餐怎麼樣？

黛西：你帶她去，我們會在那裡等你們。

麥克：好，記得別讓她發現喔！

字彙／片語充電區 *Words and Phrases*

aware 形 知道的；察覺的 / circumstance 名 情況 / darkened 形 無燈光的
pull the wool over one's eyes 隱瞞某人 / be unaware of 沒有意識到的

UNIT 110 see eye to eye 兩人對視的情景？

🎧 110

暖身猜猜看 *Warming Up*

Dora: I'm glad that we have the chance to work on the project together.

Nick: Me, too. We often **see eye to eye** on ideas.

朵拉：我很高興有機會跟你一起執行這份企劃。

尼克：我也是，我們對事情的想法經常都一樣。

原來是這個意思！

see eye to eye 完全同意

　　這個慣用語源自《聖經：以薩亞書52:8》，在聖經當中，see eye to eye 的確有面對面、互相對視之意，但後來漸漸引申出「所見一致」與「意見相同」的用法。當後面要點名「針對某件事情」的看法時，請用介系詞on。

對話練習 *Let's Talk!*

Henry: Did you know that Josh and Dan are in charge of our next project?

Fanny: Really? Whose idea was that?

Henry: I heard that is a demand made by the client.

Fanny: He obviously doesn't know our team very well.

Henry: Yeah. They don't **see eye to eye** on most issues.

亨利：你知道賈許跟丹要一起負責下個企劃嗎？

芬妮：真的嗎？這是誰的想法啊？

亨利：聽說是客戶的要求。

芬妮：他顯然不怎麼了解我們的團隊。

亨利：是啊，他們兩個對大多數的事情都沒有共識。

字彙/片語充電區 *Words and Phrases*

consensus 名 一致 / acquiesce 動 默認；默許 / reconsider 動 重新考慮

on the same wavelength 相互理解 / shift one's ground 改變某人的立場

UNIT 111　eat one's words
某人食言而肥？

🎧 111

暖身猜猜看 Warming Up

Sara: I can't believe it. I bet your team would lose.
Joey: Now you have to **eat your words**!

莎拉：真不敢相信，我本來斷言你們隊會輸的。
喬伊：現在你得收回你的話啦！

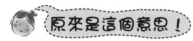
原來是這個意思！

eat one's words 收回前言

　　這個慣用語的起源相當久遠，在莎士比亞時期就出現這個用法。這裡的 words不單指單字，而是某人說出口的話，eat one's words的意象是因為言論從某人口中出來，所以要他自己吃下去，即「收回前言」。

對話練習 Let's Talk!

Sara: I can't believe that our team lost the game to Joey's!

Roy: Yeah. Everyone thought that we could beat a young team.

Sara: I guess experience is not enough.

Roy: Right. We underestimated our competitor.

Sara: Now I have to **eat my words**.

莎拉：不敢相信我們竟然會輸給喬伊的隊伍！

羅伊：是啊，大家都認為我們能擊敗成軍不久的新球隊。

莎拉：看來只有經驗是不夠的。

羅伊：的確，我們低估了對手的能耐。

莎拉：現在我得收回前言了。

字彙／片語充電區 Words and Phrases

outcome 名 結果 / regret 動 懊悔 / astonishing 形 令人驚訝的 / belittle 動 輕視
call off 取消；使停止 / go back on one's word 違背諾言 / weasel out 推諉責任

124

UNIT 112

in a nutshell
在果殼當中？

🎧 112

暖身猜猜看 *Warming Up*

Bob: So, what is your proposal for this case?

Amy: **In a nutshell**, we should buy ABC company.

鮑伯：那麼，你對這件案子的提案是什麼？

艾咪：簡而言之，我們應該收購ABC公司。

原來是這個意思！

in a nutshell 簡而言之

　　in a nutshell的起源，來自於古羅馬作家普林尼對荷馬史詩《伊里亞德》（Iliad）的敘述文，被印製成極小的篇幅，小到可以塞進一個果核裡；後來這個說法就被用來比喻「長話短說」、「簡而言之」。

對話練習 *Let's Talk!*

Julie: I'm still discussing the offer with the new firm.

Dean: What do you mean?

Julie: **In a nutshell**, we disagree over my salary.

Dean: That's not good. How badly do you want this job?

Julie: I don't want it badly enough to accept a low paycheck.

茱莉：我還在跟新公司談。

迪恩：什麼意思？

茱莉：簡單的說，我們在薪資上談不攏。

迪恩：這很不妙，你有多想要這份工作？

茱莉：沒有想要到能接受一份低薪。

字彙／片語充電區 *Words and Phrases*

complex 形 複雜的 / conclusion 名 結論 / mediate 動 調停 / apparent 形 明顯的
hammer out a deal 爭出結論 / bring to terms 使接受條件 / put across 表達；傳達

UNIT 113　You can say that again.
拜託對方再說一次？

🎧 113

 暖身猜猜看 *Warming Up*

Mary: Thank God that nobody got hurt in the fire.
Dylan: **You can say that again.**

瑪莉：謝天謝地，沒人因火災受傷。
狄倫：可不是。

 原來是這個意思！

You can say that again. 說的好。

　　聽到對方和你這麼說的時候，可不要重複剛剛的話，他的意思其實等同於 I totally agree with you!（我完全同意你說的話。）翻譯的時候，有「說得好！」、「可不是嗎！」、「就是說啊！」等略為不同的翻法。

 *Let's Talk!*

Greg: How was the mental health seminar?

Karen: It was informative. We learned different ways to help ourselves.

Greg: It's always great to learn something helpful.

Karen: **You can say that again!**

Greg: Can you let me know about these kinds of seminars in advance next time?

葛瑞格：那個心靈健康的講座如何？
凱　倫：內容很充實，我們學到各種幫助自己的方法。
葛瑞格：能學到有所助益的內容很棒。
凱　倫：就是說啊！
葛瑞格：你下次可不可以事先告訴我這類型的講座資訊啊？

字彙／片語充電區 *Words and Phrases*

standpoint 名 立場 / negotiate 動 交涉 / reception 名 反應 / convention 名 會議
approve of 認同 / Anything you say. 悉聽尊便。 / talk nonsense 胡說八道

UNIT 114   I'll say!
我一定會把想法說出來？

🎧 114

 暖身猜猜看 *Warming Up*

Bill: This science fiction movie is awesome!

Amy: **I'll say!** It has a plot that is one of a kind.

比爾：這部科幻片拍得真棒！

艾咪：可不是！劇情真的很獨特。

 原來是這個意思！

I'll say! 可不是嗎！

I'll say! 適用於「強烈同意他人言論」的情境中，意同You are definitely/ absolutely right. 語氣相當強烈，翻譯時有「沒錯！」、「對極了！」、「就是說！」等意思，須注意的是，對於部分人來說，這是個較為過時的用法。

 *Let's Talk!*

Eddy: Let's make plans for our summer vacation.

Lily: Sure. What do you have in mind?

Eddy: I think we should take a backpacking trip to Cambodia.

Lily: Sounds great. It's a beautiful country.

Eddy: **I'll say!** I'm so interested in its historical sites.

艾迪：我們來計劃一下暑假吧。

莉莉：好啊，你有什麼建議嗎？

艾迪：我覺得我們應該到束埔寨，來趟背包客之旅。

莉莉：聽起來很棒，那裡很美。

艾迪：就是說！我對那裡的古蹟很有興趣呢。

字彙／片語充電區 *Words and Phrases*

fabulous 形 極好的；驚人的 / **magnificent** 形 壯麗的；宏偉的 / **describe** 動 形容
stand to reason 理所當然 / **No comment.** 不予置評。 / **I can't tell.** 我不知道。

UNIT 115

You said it!
提醒他人「這是你說的喔」？

🎧 115

 暖身猜猜看 *Warming Up*

Julie: That huge house Sandy bought is incredible.
Carl: **You said it!** She saved for it for years.

茱莉：仙蒂買的那棟大房子真是驚人。
卡爾：沒錯！為了這個，她存了好幾年的錢。

 原來是這個意思！

You said it! 你說的對！

　　理解You said it!時，可別從字面猜意思，以為是「提醒對方」或給對方決定權的「你說了算」，這個慣用語和You can say that again.的意思相同，用於「強烈贊同對方」的情境當中，表示「說得好！」。

 *Let's Talk!*

Nina: I've been thinking about studying abroad for years.

Billy: That's nice. Have you applied to any schools yet?

Nina: I did. And I just got admitted into one of them.

Billy: Congratulations! Now you can plan for your future.

Nina: **You said it!**

妮娜：我想出國唸書想了好幾年了。

比利：那很好啊，你有申請任何一所學校了嗎？

妮娜：申請了，而且其中一所學校已經確定錄取我了。

比利：恭喜你！現在你可以為了你的將來做打算了。

妮娜：你說的對！

字彙／片語充電區 *Words and Phrases*

absolutely 副 (口)完全對 / **conversation** 名 對話 / **acceptance** 名 接受；贊同
You're telling me. 這還用說。 / **concur with** 一致；認同 / **not exactly** 不完全

UNIT 116 What a shame. 真令人感到羞恥？

🎧 116

暖身猜猜看 *Warming Up*

Bob: I was so tired that I fell asleep on the tour bus.

Kelly: **What a shame!** The scenery was beautiful.

鮑伯：我太累了，在遊覽車上的時間都在睡覺。

凱莉：好可惜！風景很美耶。

原來是這個意思！

What a shame. 多可惜；真遺憾。

　　shame除了常用到的「羞恥」這個解釋以外，還有「遺憾」的意思，這句實用的慣用語所表達的意思即為「真遺憾啊！」、「真可惜啊！」意同That's too bad.但語氣更強烈，也可以用What a pity!取代。

對話練習 *Let's Talk!*

Blake: Did you enjoy the trip to Paris?

Cindy: How could I not? I loved the museums and cafés there.

Blake: Did you go to the Eiffel Tower?

Cindy: No, I missed it. I didn't have enough time.

Blake: **What a shame!**

布雷克：你的巴黎之行好玩嗎？

辛　蒂：怎麼可能不好玩？我愛死那裡的博物館跟咖啡館了。

布雷克：那你有去艾菲爾鐵塔嗎？

辛　蒂：沒有，時間不夠。

布雷克：真可惜！

字彙／片語充電區 *Words and Phrases*

unfortunate 形 可惜的；可嘆的 / complement 動 補足 / afterwards 副 後來
a bad patch 倒楣的時期 / bring shame on 使蒙羞 / in the lap of fortune 走運

UNIT 117 You don't say!
一個字都不讓對方說？

🎧 117

 暖身猜猜看 *Warming Up*

Carter: Taking care of a baby is a lot of work.

Judy: **You don't say!** Your mother has been a great help.

卡特：照顧嬰兒真令人手忙腳亂。

茱蒂：可不是！你母親真是幫了大忙。

原來是這個意思！

You don't say! 不會吧！那還用說！

　　You don't say!是You don't say so.的簡化講法，表示「不會吧！」、「那還用說！」；使用時帶有「驚訝」之感（也許是因為第一次聽到），須注意的是，依照情境與說話語氣的不同，這個慣用語可能帶有諷刺意味。

 對話練習 *Let's Talk!*

Emma: Did you receive Gina's mail?

Earl: What's it about? I haven't checked my mail-box this week.

Emma: It's about her wedding with John next month.

Earl: **You don't say!** I thought they broke up two months ago.

Emma: Apparently, they made up after that.

艾瑪：你有收到吉娜的信嗎？

厄爾：信上的內容是什麼？我這禮拜都沒看信箱。

艾瑪：是關於她與約翰下個月的婚禮。

厄爾：不是吧！他們不是兩個月前分手了嗎？

艾瑪：很顯然，他們在那之後又復合了。

字彙／片語充電區 *Words and Phrases*

interjection 名 感嘆語 / exclamation 名 感嘆；叫喊 / colloquial 形 口語的
consent to 同意 / say for oneself 為自己找藉口 / give credit to 相信；信任

UNIT 118　It's a long shot.
射擊的靶子擺得太遠？

🎧 118

暖身猜猜看 *Warming Up*

Debby: I just sent my resume to a top fashion company.

Nick: Me, too. **It's a long shot** but worth trying.

黛比：我把履歷寄給一間頂尖的時裝公司了。

尼克：我也是，雖然機會不大，但值得一試。

原來是這個意思！

It's a long shot. 機率不大。

　　a long shot其實不一定起源於射擊；這個說法最早出現於英國的賽車，用於「大膽押注」的情況，有一種說法認為它是由更早的not by a long chalk而來（意指機會不大），使用chalk是因為酒館裡的小遊戲是用粉筆記錄的。

Jack: Have you applied for a promotion yet?

Molly: Yeah, I sent out the application for manager.

Jack: You are applying to be a manager already?

Molly: Although **it's a long shot**, I still want to give it a try.

Jack: Good luck. After all, you've worked so hard.

傑克：你提出升職的申請了嗎？

莫莉：嗯，我申請了經理的職位。

傑克：你已經在申請經理的職位了？

莫莉：雖然機會不大，我還是想試試看。

傑克：祝你好運，畢竟你一直都很努力。

字彙／片語充電區 *Words and Phrases*

probability 名 機率 / **fluke** 名 (口)僥倖 / **hazard** 名 冒險 / **contingency** 名 偶然
on the off chance 不太可能 / **one in a million** 萬中選一 / **a fair shake** 均等機會

UNIT 119 Speak for yourself.
為了你自己而發聲？

🎧 119

暖身猜猜看 Warming Up

Kent: I don't think we should invite Jill to go hiking with us.

Jenny: **Speak for yourself.** I really like Jill.

肯特：我覺得我們不應該邀請吉兒和我們去健行。

珍妮：那只是你的想法，我很喜歡吉兒。

原來是這個意思！

Speak for yourself. 那只是你個人的想法。

　　Speak for yourself.直譯的意思為「為你自己說話」或「說的是你自己吧」，是個很容易被誤解的慣用語；在口語對話中，說這句話的人所要表達的是他的「不贊同」，意思為「那只是你個人的想法！」。

Erica: These historical buildings are beautiful.

Henry: How so? I find them old and shaky.

Erica: They are not. Look at the delicate carvings!

Henry: Well, I'm sure you would agree that these blocks should be repaired.

Erica: **Speak for yourself!**

愛芮卡：這些歷史建築好美。

亨　利：怎麼說？我只覺得它們又舊又破。

愛芮卡：它們才不破舊，看看這些精細的雕刻！

亨　利：我相信你也同意這幾個街區需要美化一下。

愛芮卡：這只是你個人的看法而已！

字彙／片語充電區 Words and Phrases

individual 形 個人的；個別的 / opinion 名 想法；意見 / distinct 形 有區別的
speak out 大聲說出來 / speak ill of sb. 說某人壞話 / draw a conclusion 下結論

UNIT 120

a watering hole
在哪裡挖的水井？

🎧 120

暖身猜猜看 *Warming Up*

Nick: Care to join us at **the watering hole** on the corner?
Julie: Sure. I want to find out why you guys go there so often.

尼克：要不要跟我們一起去街角的酒吧？
茱莉：當然好，我想知道你們為何那麼常去。

原來是這個意思！

a watering hole 酒吧

　　在正規用語中，a watering hole指的是野外的小水塘，各種動物都會聚集在水塘飲水；作為口語化用法時，引申用來描述一間小酒館或小酒吧，裡面聚集各色各樣的人們，成為熱鬧的社交場所。

對話練習 *Let's Talk!*

Julie: This is not the kind of bar I imagined.
Nick: I told you! It used to be **a watering hole** for actors.
Julie: I can see that from those old photos on the walls.
Nick: Nowadays, it's still packed with artists and musicians.
Julie: No wonder you come here almost every day.

茱莉：這和我想像的酒吧完全不一樣耶。
尼克：就跟你說了！這裡曾經是演員聚集的酒吧。
茱莉：從牆上那些舊相片就看得出來。
尼克：現在這裡依然有許多藝術家跟音樂家出沒。
茱莉：難怪你們幾乎每天都到這裡來。

字彙/片語充電區 *Words and Phrases*

alehouse 名 酒館 / The Rathskeller 名 地下室的酒吧 / bartender 名 酒保
a stomping ground 聚會所 / bend one's elbow 喝酒；縱飲 / bet against 打賭

UNIT 121

a tea shop
賣茶葉的店家？

🎧 121

 暖身猜猜看 *Warming Up*

Kevin: Let's find something to eat. I am starving!

Lucy: Oh! There is **a tea shop** ahead. Let's go.

凱文：我們找點吃的吧，我快餓死了！

露西：喔！前面有間小吃店，走吧。

 原來是這個意思！

a tea shop 茶館；小吃店

　　十八世紀的英國有一些喝茶的小店（也稱tea room），供應熱茶的同時，會附上簡單的小點心，沿用至今，tea shop便用來指稱提供茶點或輕食，可以坐坐的小店；甚至與泡茶有關的器具都會在店內販售，可不只有茶葉喔！

 **對話練習** *Let's Talk!*

Dylan: Did you watch the interview of that famous chef?

Bella: Yeah! He is a legend.

Dylan: He started his career at **that tea shop** down the street.

Bella: Right. We walk past it every day.

Dylan: This kind of story always enlightens me.

狄倫：你有看那個名廚的專訪嗎？

貝拉：有啊！他真是個傳奇人物。

狄倫：街尾那間小吃鋪就是他的發跡處。

貝拉：是啊，我們每天都會路過呢。

狄倫：這類的故事總是帶給我很多啟發。

字彙／片語充電區 *Words and Phrases*

deli 名 熟食店 / bistro 名 小餐館 / pastime 名 消遣 / refreshments 名 茶點
a coffee bar 咖啡館 / tea cloth 吃茶點的小臺布 / all-you-can-eat 吃到飽的

UNIT 122 roadside business
路邊的生意就是路邊攤？

🎧 122

暖身猜猜看 *Warming Up*

William: I heard that Joe is doing some type of **roadside business**.

Dana: Yeah. He is running a drive-in-theater.

威廉：聽說喬在從事某種免下車服務的生意。

黛娜：是啊，他在經營一家露天電影院。

原來是這個意思！

roadside business 汽車飯店；汽車旅館；汽車電影院

在美國絕大多數的地方，都是以私人車輛作為交通工具，因此roadside business（沿著道路開設的生意）即是為了方便駕駛人而設立的店家，例如：得來速、坐在車上即可看戲的露天電影院、汽車旅館、隧道式洗車站等等。

對話練習 *Let's Talk!*

Hannah: I'm looking for a topic for my research on unique industries.

Kenneth: What about **roadside business**?

Hannah: You mean a gas station or a drive-through?

Kenneth: Not just that! There're even some types designed for travelers.

Hannah: I didn't know that. I guess I just found my topic.

漢　娜：我在找關於獨特產業的研究題目。

肯尼斯：免下車服務的產業怎麼樣？

漢　娜：你是說加油站跟得來速嗎？

肯尼斯：不只那些啦！有些甚至是針對遊客所設計的。

漢　娜：我都不知道，我想我找到好題目了。

字彙/片語充電區 *Words and Phrases*

roadhouse 名 旅館；酒店 / **stopover** 名 中途停留 / **roadblock** 名 路障；障礙物

a crash pad 臨時住所 / **in the open air** 露天 / **a road hog** (美/口) 莽撞的駕駛員

UNIT 123 service station 顧客服務中心？

🎧 123

 暖身猜猜看 *Warming Up*

Sally: Could you give me a lift home?

Eddy: Sure, but I need to swing by the **service station** first.

莎莉：你可以順道載我回家嗎？

艾迪：好啊，不過我得先去一下加油站。

 **原來是這個意思！**

service station 加油站

　　既然加油站的説法有gas station，為什麼還要用這個容易讓人誤解的慣用語呢？這是因為美國的加油站大多附設商店以及汽機車的維修站，提供打氣、換油、更換零件等服務，不單只是加油，所以才有service station這樣的説法。

 **對話練習** *Let's Talk!*

Danny: Do you want to join us on a weekend trip?

Amy: Where are you guys heading?

Danny: We are driving down south.

Amy: Well, my car broke down, so I had it towed to a **service station** a few days ago.

Danny: I told you before to check that old engine!

丹尼：你這週末要不要跟我們一起去旅行？

艾咪：你們要去哪？

丹尼：我們要開車往南方走。

艾咪：喔，我的車子故障，所以前幾天被拖去送修了。

丹尼：所以我之前就叫你去檢查那顆舊引擎啊！

字彙/片語充電區 *Words and Phrases*

mobile 名 汽車 / gasoline 名 汽油 / mechanic 名 機械工 / upkeep 名 保養；維修
patch sth. up 快速修理 / grease monkey 機械修理工 / at one's service 提供服務

UNIT 124　restroom
公共場所的休息室？

🎧124

暖身猜猜看 Warming Up

Nancy: I really need to answer the call of nature.

Mike: Okay. Let's find you a **restroom**.

南西：我真的必須跑個廁所。

麥克：好吧，我們先找洗手間。

原來是這個意思！

restroom 廁所；洗手間

　　英文裡與「廁所」有關的單字很多，其中restroom可能是語意最模糊的一個，起源於美國，這裡的rest有「重新整理好；恢復（refresh oneself）」之意，強調洗手間讓人回復良好狀態、整理自己儀容的功能。

對話練習 Let's Talk!

Sam: How do you like this tour so far?

Lily: I enjoy all the sights, but I wish we had more toilet breaks.

Sam: Yeah, they haven't taken that many.

Lily: Oh, there's a **restroom** over there. See you in a few minutes.

Sam: Maybe you shouldn't drink so much water.

山姆：你還喜歡這趟旅程嗎？

莉莉：我很喜歡參觀的景點，但真希望能有更多的如廁機會。

山姆：這倒是，上廁所的時間確實不多。

莉莉：喔，前面有廁所，等會兒再碰頭吧。

山姆：也許你不應該喝那麼多水。

字彙／片語充電區 Words and Phrases

latrine 名 公共廁所 / sanitary 形 衛生的 / toiletry 名 盥洗用品 / sauna 名 桑拿浴
fresh up 盥洗 / put on makeup 化妝 / hold one's water 憋尿 / take a break 小憩

UNIT 125　dressing room 購物時的更衣室？

🎧 125

 暖身猜猜看 Warming Up

Betty: Have you seen my hair band?
Porter: Maybe you left it in the **dressing room**.

貝蒂：你有看到我的髮圈嗎？
波特：你可能忘在更衣室裡了。

 原來是這個意思！

dressing room 更衣室；化妝室

　　dressing room光看字面可以推知與衣服有關，即中文的「更衣室」，但這其實很容易讓人誤解；這個慣用語所指的是上台前，表演者們更衣、化妝的房間，也指球員上場前的更衣間，現在也用來稱呼家中可整裝與化妝的小房間。

 **對話練習 Let's Talk!**

Lucy: How was your tour to the historical theater?
Nick: It was great. You can't imagine how complicated the building is.
Lucy: Did you explore the backstage?
Nick: Yeah. We also got to visit the **dressing rooms**.
Lucy: What an experience! I should visit there some time.

露西：那間歷史戲院的導覽好玩嗎？
尼克：很棒，你無法想像那棟建築的設計有多複雜。
露西：那你們有參觀後台嗎？
尼克：有啊，我們還看了後台的更衣間。
露西：真棒的體驗！我應該找個時間去參觀。

字彙／片語充電區 Words and Phrases

chiffonier 名 帶鏡五斗櫃 / wardrobe 名 衣櫥；衣帽室 / design 名 設計；圖樣
a fitting room 試衣間 / try on 試穿 / free trial 試用(期) / free of charge 免費

UNIT 126
nosebleed section
和流鼻血有關的地方？

🎧 126

暖身猜猜看 *Warming Up*

Anna: I was only able to get seats in the **nosebleed section**.
Hank: That's alright. The game will be exciting anyway!

安娜：我只買到最外區的座位。
漢克：沒關係啦，比賽的氣氛一定會令人很亢奮的！

原來是這個意思！

nosebleed section 看球賽或表演時，最上面最遠的位置

　　這裡的流鼻血，是誇張的描述，指在大型球場或劇院裡，廉價區座位的高度高到足以引發高山症，令人流鼻血；因此，nosebleed section就是指比賽或表演場所中，高度最高、離球場或舞台最遠的位子。

對話練習 *Let's Talk!*

Dana: Guess what? I got us two tickets to the concert tomorrow!

Jack: Wow! I thought all the seats were sold out a month ago.

Dana: It took me quite some time to find these.

Jack: Thank you! You must have tried very hard.

Dana: Yeah. But we are sitting in the **nosebleed section**.

黛娜：猜怎麼著？我買到兩張明天演唱會的票囉！

傑克：哇！座位不是一個月前都賣光了嗎？

黛娜：我花了很多時間才買到這兩張票。

傑克：謝謝！你一定找得很辛苦。

黛娜：是啊，不過，我們是坐在很後面的位子。

字彙／片語充電區 *Words and Phrases*

aisle 名 通道 / bleachers 名 露天看台 / occupied 形 已占用的 / ambience 名 氣氛
a bargain price 廉價 / the floor section 搖滾區 / beat the band 竭盡全力的

UNIT 127 hole-in-the-wall
牆上開了一個洞？

🎧 127

 暖身猜猜看 *Warming Up*

Mandy: When can we go and visit your new apartment?
Simon: Anytime! But it is just a **hole-in-the-wall**.

曼蒂：我們什麼時候可以去參觀你的新家啊？
賽門：隨時歡迎！不過我家很小也不起眼。

 原來是這個意思！

hole-in-the-wall 小而不起眼的地方

　　(a) hole-in-the-wall的直譯，即是牆上的坑洞，這句慣用語被用來描述一個小而不起眼的地方，通常指的是鄉間或美國南方地區的簡陋酒館、餐室或設備老舊的旅店；而在英式英語中，則是指提款機。

 *Let's Talk!*

Danny: Okay, here's the restaurant I recommend.
Claire: Are you sure this is the place?
Danny: This is it! This **hole-in-the-wall** is a classy restaurant.
Claire: Really? It looks so old and shabby!
Danny: You'll be surprised. They have the best Italian cuisine!

丹　尼：到了，這就是我推薦的餐館。
克萊兒：你確定是這裡嗎？
丹　尼：就是這裡！這個小地方可是間別緻的餐館。
克萊兒：真的嗎？它看起來又老又破的。
丹　尼：你會大吃一驚的，他們有最美味的義大利料理！

字彙/片語充電區 *Words and Phrases*

residence 名 住所 / district 名 行政區 / habitat 名 棲息地 / significant 形 顯著的
a rooming house 出租雅房 / drop by 順道拜訪；順便 / on a shoestring 花很少錢

UNIT 128 corner office
位於角落的辦公室？

🎧 128

 暖身猜猜看 *Warming Up*

Bill: I've heard that you are moving to the **corner office**.

Lisa: Yes. I will need to work even harder now.

比爾：聽說你升遷到專屬辦公室了。

麗莎：是啊，現在我得更努力工作才行。

 原來是這個意思！

corner office 主管級的高級辦公室

　　高級辦公大樓的角落房間，不但空間方正寬敞，更有兩面對外的景觀窗，這樣的辦公環境，自然是給重要的主管或高階經理人，因此，corner office指的便是給重要人物所使用的高級辦公室。

 *Let's Talk!*

Nora: Did you know Lisa is moving to the **corner office**?

Hans: I do. Let's do something to celebrate her promotion.

Nora: Cool. How about going to the bar tonight?

Hans: Nah. That's too cheesy. I prefer something special.

Nora: I got it! Let's hold a surprise party after work.

諾拉：你知道麗莎升遷，要搬到專屬辦公室了嗎？

漢斯：我知道，我們來做點什麼慶祝她升遷吧。

諾拉：好耶，今晚去酒吧怎麼樣？

漢斯：不，那太老套了，我想做點特別的。

諾拉：我想到了！我們在下班後辦個驚喜派對吧。

字彙/片語充電區 *Words and Phrases*

liability 名 傾向；責任 / **subordinate** 名 部屬 / **degradation** 名 降級；下降
take on an additional shift 加班 / **Every dog has his day.** 風水輪流轉。

UNIT 129

black tea
黑色的茶？

🎧 129

 暖身猜猜看 *Warming Up*

Tina: Would you like to have milk tea or herbal tea?

Rick: No, **black tea** is fine. Thanks.

蒂娜：你想喝奶茶或草本茶嗎？

瑞克：不用，紅茶就可以了，謝謝。

 原來是這個意思！

black tea 紅茶

　　green tea在英文中是綠茶，所以black tea很容易被誤解為黑色的茶，其實這個慣用語所指的是「紅茶」。當茶葉發酵後，茶葉會從綠色轉變成黑色，因此black tea是取名自葉子的顏色，指的是泡起來呈紅褐色的熟茶。

 **對話練習** *Let's Talk!*

Walter: I've never been to a teahouse like this before.

Merry: I know. You are a coffee person.

Walter: What should I order? Asian teas are all green, right?

Merry: Not really. They also have some really good **black tea**.

Walter: Great! I will have that then.

華特：我從沒來過類似這樣子的茶館。

梅莉：我知道，你都喝咖啡。

華特：我該點什麼？亞洲產的都是綠茶吧？

梅莉：不一定，他們也有很棒的紅茶。

華特：太好了！那我要點那個。

字彙 / 片語充電區 *Words and Phrases*

brew 動 泡；煮 / teapot 名 茶壺 / aroma 名 香氣；芳香 / insomnia 名 (醫)失眠
a tea bag 茶包 / not one's cup of tea 不合某人胃口 / feel at ease 感到自在、舒適

UNIT 130

sweet water
甜甜的糖水？

🎧 130

 暖身猜猜看 Warming Up

Harry: Gosh! It's so hot! Can I have something to drink?

Vicky: Here, have a glass of **sweet water**.

哈利：天啊，天氣好熱！可以給我點喝的嗎？

薇琪：哪，喝杯白開水吧。

 原來是這個意思！

sweet water 淡水；白開水

　　光由字面上看，這個慣用語應該是甜甜的糖水或是甜湯，但這裡的sweet water是跟又苦又鹹的海水（salt water）做對比，指淨化過或過濾過的水，是甘甜、可飲用的「淡水或白開水」。

 **對話練習** *Let's Talk!*

Mary: Here's the blueprint for the villa and the map of the island.

Paul: The layout seems spacious and comfortable.

Mary: Have you noticed there is another small island nearby?

Paul: Yes. Can I have a glass of **sweet water**?

Mary: Sure. I'll get you a glass right away.

瑪莉：這是度假屋的設計圖，還有島嶼的地圖。

保羅：這個規劃看來很寬敞跟舒適。

瑪莉：你有注意到鄰近的另一座小島嗎？

保羅：有，可以給我一杯白開水嗎？

瑪莉：當然，我馬上就拿給你。

字彙/片語充電區 *Words and Phrases*

aquatic 形 水生的 / gulf 名 海灣 / watertight 形 不透水的 / reservoir 名 水庫
water down 稀釋 / well over 流出；氾濫 / water under the bridge 過去的事

UNIT 131 coffee cake 咖啡口味的蛋糕？

🎧 131

 暖身猜猜看 *Warming Up*

Bob: I'd like to have some hot coffee, please.

Clerk: Would you like to make it a set with some **coffee cake**?

鮑伯：請給我熱咖啡。

店員：您要不要搭配蛋糕成套餐呢？

 原來是這個意思！

coffee cake 配咖啡吃的蛋糕

在美國文化中，麵包店（bakery）裡賣的種類很單純，不像我們這裡有那麼多口味，所以，他們所謂的coffee cake就只是「可以搭配咖啡的甜點」，真的要講咖啡口味的蛋糕，要用coffee-flavored cake。

 **對話練習** *Let's Talk!*

Sam: This is the café I've always wanted to take you to.

Lily: It seems pretty nice and cozy.

Sam: You will find it more impressive when you try their coffee set.

Lily: You know I am not a big fan of coffee.

Sam: But you will definitely love their homemade **coffee cake**.

山姆：這就是我一直想帶你來的咖啡館。

莉莉：看起來滿漂亮、舒服的。

山姆：等你嚐過他們的咖啡套餐，你的印象會更深刻。

莉莉：你知道我不怎麼愛喝咖啡。

山姆：但你一定會愛上他們的手工蛋糕。

字彙／片語充電區 *Words and Phrases*

loaf 名 一條麵包 / **pancake** 名 鬆餅 / **dainty** 形 美味的 / **flavor** 名 味道；香料
a piece of cake 易如反掌 / **a slice of the cake** 分得的利益 / **bolt down** 狼吞虎嚥

UNIT 132
love apple
愛心的蘋果是突變嗎？

🎧 132

暖身猜猜看 *Warming Up*

John: Do you need any help with the party this evening?

Kelly: Can you buy some **love apples** for the salad?

約翰：你需要人幫忙準備今晚的派對嗎？

凱莉：你可以幫忙買沙拉要用的番茄嗎？

原來是這個意思！

love apple 番茄

　　love apple是法式浪漫的產物，法文的番茄叫pomme d'amour，翻譯成英文就是「愛的蘋果」，這算是外來語的直接翻譯；另一個起源是羅馬時期，當時番茄被教會認為是失樂園的那顆禁忌之果，因而被視為惡魔的水果。

對話練習 *Let's Talk!*

Helen: I heard that you've spent a lot of time in your garden.

Jeff: That's right. Do you want to take a look?

Helen: This is amazing! You have a great collection of plants.

Jeff: You'd be surprised to know how many plants are here.

Helen: They all look great. You even grow **love apples**!

海倫：聽說你花很多時間在你照顧的花園。

傑夫：沒錯，要不要看看？

海倫：真厲害！你種的植物好多。

傑夫：如果知道裡面有多少植物，你會更驚訝。

海倫：他們看起都很漂亮，你還種了番茄耶！

字彙/片語充電區 *Words and Phrases*

vegetable 名 蔬菜 / ingredient 名 食材 / peel 動 削皮 / herbaceous 形 草本的
a wax apple 蓮霧 / apples and oranges 無法比較的東西 / scrub sponge 菜瓜布

UNIT 133
cold cash
賺不得的黑心錢？

🎧 133

暖身猜猜看 *Warming Up*

Jenny: Why don't we get the camping equipment from that shop?

Mark: Because they accept **cold cash** only.

珍妮：我們為什麼不在那家店買露營裝備？

馬克：因為他們只收現金。

原來是這個意思！

cold cash 現金

　　在以前的銀行或財經術語中，人們會用hard cash來稱呼錢（因為以前的錢是用金屬製作的），後來才出現cold cash的用法，cold用來形容這些財物的質感，指不同於支票，能立即交易的現金。

對話練習 *Let's Talk!*

Bill: I can't go to the hot springs with you. I am saving up.

Emma: For what? You don't spend much money.

Bill: I really want a handmade clock, and I am 1,200 bucks short.

Emma: Why don't you use a credit card?

Bill: I wish I could, but only **cold cash** works in that store.

比爾：我沒辦法和你去泡溫泉，我在存錢。

艾瑪：要幹嘛？你平時又不怎麼花錢。

比爾：我很想要一個手工鐘，還差一千兩百塊。

艾瑪：你為什麼不用信用卡呢？

比爾：我也想，但那間店只做全額現金交易。

字彙／片語充電區 *Words and Phrases*

cabbage 名 (美/俚)紙鈔 / **bankroll** 名 資金 / **receipt** 名 收據 / **cashier** 名 出納員
pay in cash 以現金付款 / **cash in on sth.** 謀取利益 / **chicken feed** 少額零錢

UNIT 134

dead presidents
過世的總統？

🎧 134

暖身猜猜看 *Warming Up*

Nicole: Did Joe find a new job in a bank?

Kevin: Yeah. He's working with **dead presidents** every day.

妮可：喬的新工作是在銀行嗎？

凱文：是啊，他每天都和鈔票共事。

原來是這個意思！

dead presidents 美鈔

　　這個怎麼看都是「過世總統」的慣用語，為什麼會與美鈔扯上關係呢？這是因為美鈔上都印有歷屆的總統頭像，然而只有已過世的，才會被製作成肖像，因此在對話中，要小心判斷對方指的是鈔票，還是真的已故總統。

對話練習　*Let's Talk!*

Sally: How did your job interview go?

Kenny: Well, I got the position, but I'm not thrilled about it.

Sally: What's wrong?

Kenny: I just wish they would offer a decent salary.

Sally: Who doesn't? But almost every company is short of **dead presidents** now.

莎莉：你工作的面試如何？

肯尼：我被錄用了，但我沒有很興奮。

莎莉：怎麼了嗎？

肯尼：我只是希望他們提供的薪水能好一點。

莎莉：誰不是呢？但現在幾乎所有的公司都缺錢。

字彙／片語充電區 *Words and Phrases*

currency 名 貨幣 / **fiscal** 形 財政的；會計的 / **monetary** 形 貨幣的 / **bond** 名 債券
legal tender 法定貨幣 / **bite the dust** 獻身而死亡 / **preside over** 管轄；指揮

UNIT 135　seed money 存錢去買種子？

🎧 135

暖身猜猜看 *Warming Up*

Anna: Jeff mentioned a business opportunity to me.

John: Don't bother. His idea wasted all my **seed money** last year.

安娜：傑夫和我提到一個生意上的機會。

約翰：不要理他，去年他的想法害我損失了所有的創業資金。

原來是這個意思！

seed money 創業基金

　　這個慣用語其實是指「創業用的資本」，因為是為了事業起步而投入的金額，所以用seed（種子）這個單字；所謂的seed money，其來源通常來自於親朋好友或創業者自身，將小筆的金額聚積在一起的創業資本。

對話練習　*Let's Talk!*

Mike: What are you writing?

Vicky: I am working on my business plan for opening a flower shop.

Mike: Sounds interesting. You've always liked flowers.

Vicky: Yeah. I am still saving up some **seed money**.

Mike: Let me know if you need help. Good luck!

麥克：你在寫什麼？

薇琪：寫我要開花店的創業企劃書。

麥克：聽起來很有趣，你一直都很喜愛花卉。

薇琪：是啊，我還在存創業基金。

麥克：需要幫忙的話，就告訴我一聲，祝你好運！

字彙／片語充電區 *Words and Phrases*

asset 名 資本；財產 / **equity** 名 抵押資產的淨值 / **possession** 名 所有物；財產
nest egg 儲蓄金；養老金 / **start a business** 創業 / **flights of fancy** 異想天開

UNIT 136
a Greek gift
一份希臘製的禮物？

🎧 136

暖身猜猜看 *Warming Up*

Sara: May just sent me a gift. I thought she hated me.

Joey: If I were you, I wouldn't accept **a possible Greek gift**.

莎拉：梅剛剛送我一份禮物，我還以為她討厭我。

喬伊：如果我是你，就不會收下這份意圖不明的禮物。

原來是這個意思！

a Greek gift 害人的禮品

　　這個慣用語起源於特洛伊戰爭，希臘人製作木馬放在特洛伊的城門，特洛伊人民以為對方已退兵，沒有發現希臘士兵藏在木馬中，當晚希臘士兵們偷襲，大敗特洛伊，後來這個慣用語就用以表示「害人或圖謀不軌的禮物」。

對話練習 *Let's Talk!*

Jim: Congratulations on your promotion!

Amy: Thanks. In fact, it's **a Greek gift**. I am not happy at all.

Jim: How come?

Amy: Well, I've always been a project developer, and now I'm the marketing manager.

Jim: That's challenging. You'll be responsible for improving sales.

吉姆：恭喜你升職！

艾咪：謝謝，但這其實會害慘我，完全高興不起來。

吉姆：為什麼這麼說？

艾咪：我一直都是負責企劃開發的，現在竟然要做行銷部的經理。

吉姆：這很有挑戰性，你得承擔提高業績的責任了。

字彙／片語充電區 *Words and Phrases*

entice 動 誘使 / embroil 動 使混亂 / strategy 名 策略 / thwart 動 阻撓；使挫折
a snake in the grass 隱藏的危險 / box in 阻礙；進退維谷 / set up 陷害；設圈套

UNIT 137

hand-me-down
把東西傳給我？

🎧137

 暖身猜猜看 *Warming Up*

Nina: That sweater looks good on you!

Andy: Thanks. This is an old **hand-me-down** from my brother.

妮娜：你穿的毛衣很好看喔！

安迪：謝了，這是我哥哥給我的舊毛衣。

 原來是這個意思！

hand-me-down 送人的舊東西或衣物

　　hand-me-down是動詞用語（hand down）所轉化成的名詞，字面意思為「交接給我、傳承給我」，後來用以比喻傳承的物件或二手物品；要注意的是，這個慣用語也可能用來形容東西的品質差或老舊（負面意味）。

 對話練習 *Let's Talk!*

Lucy: Did you hear James's marketing proposal?

Kevin: Yeah. It sounded so familiar.

Lucy: He used a **hand-me-down** idea from our previous project!

Kevin: If the manager is okay with it, we have nothing to complain about.

Lucy: It bothers me that he doesn't find it embarrassing.

露西：你有聽到詹姆士的行銷提案嗎？

凱文：有啊，很耳熟。

露西：他竟然沿用我們之前提案的舊創意！

凱文：如果經理不介意，我們也沒什麼好抱怨的。

露西：讓我受不了的是，他都不覺得不好意思耶。

字彙／片語充電區 *Words and Phrases*

bestow 動 贈與／relinquish 動 放棄／outdated 形 舊式的／durable 形 耐用的
second-hand 二手的；中古的／hand over 移交；交出／pass down 傳承；傳下去

UNIT 138 monkey suit
猴子造型的服裝？

🎧 138

 暖身猜猜看 *Warming Up*

Bob: Since it's my boss's party, I'll put on my **monkey suit**.

Sally: Ha! Enjoy your evening anyway.

鮑伯：既然是老闆的舞會，就得穿上我的行頭。
莎莉：哈！無論如何，盡興一點吧。

 原來是這個意思！

monkey suit 男性禮服、制服

當街頭藝人或馬戲團裡的猴子要表演時，都會換上像小西裝那樣的表演戲服，因此，monkey suit就被用來比喻男性為了工作、應酬或是表現自己等目的，必須穿上的制服或禮服。

 對話練習 *Let's Talk!*

Kent: Can I cancel our date tonight? I'm heading to the tailor's.

Helen: The tailor's? For what?

Kent: I need to have a tuxedo made. It's for the annual ball.

Helen: Wow! A formal ball sounds fun.

Kent: It is. But preparing a **monkey suit** is expensive!

肯特：我可以取消今晚的約會嗎？我要去裁縫店。
海倫：裁縫店？要做什麼？
肯特：我得訂做一套晚禮服，年度晚宴上要穿的。
海倫：哇！正式的晚宴聽起來很好玩。
肯特：是很棒，但是準備禮服很昂貴！

字彙/片語充電區 *Words and Phrases*

attire 名 服裝；盛裝 / **tuxedo** 名 (男)無尾禮服上衣 / **ceremony** 名 典禮；儀式
one's best bib and tucker 最好的衣服 / **suit yourself** 請便 / **out of fashion** 過時的

151

UNIT 139 French chalk 法國產的粉筆？

🎧 139

暖身猜猜看 Warming Up

Tim: Can you dry clean this suit? It has two stains here.
Laura: Okay. Let me mark it with **French chalk** first.

提姆：你可以乾洗這件西裝嗎？這裡有兩處污漬。
蘿拉：好，我先用滑石粉做個記號。

原來是這個意思！

French chalk 滑石粉

　　chalk是粉筆的意思，不過French chalk並非法國製的粉筆，而是指滑石粉、爽身粉（talc），要注意的是，雖然中文翻譯看不出來，但這個慣用語特別指裁縫或乾洗店為了修改或去除污漬，而在布料上作記號的工具。

對話練習 Let's Talk!

Julian: This tuxedo is too loose. Can you fix it for me?
Jenny: Sure. Let me mark the places needed to be fixed.
Julian: Oh! Are you marking on it directly?
Jenny: Don't worry. It's just **French chalk**. It can be rinsed off easily.
Julian: Oh, I see. I was worried it might stain the suit.

朱利安：這件晚禮服太鬆了，可以幫我改嗎？
珍　妮：沒問題，我來標記一下需要改的地方。
朱利安：噢！你就直接在上面做記號啊？
珍　妮：別擔心，這是滑石粉，很容易洗掉的。
朱利安：原來如此，我剛剛還擔心我的晚禮服被弄髒了呢。

字彙／片語充電區 Words and Phrases

grain 動 使成粒狀 / grit 名 沙礫 / powder 名 粉末 / marker 名 做記號的人或物
powder blue 淺灰藍色 / a powder puff (化妝用的)粉撲 / baby powder 爽身粉

UNIT 140 dead tree
枯死的樹木？

🎧 140

暖身猜猜看 *Warming Up*

Henry: Have you gotten that book I mentioned last time?

Jenny: Yes. I got a **dead tree** edition last week.

亨利：你有買到我上回提到的那本書嗎？

珍妮：有啊，我上禮拜買了印刷版。

原來是這個意思！

dead tree 印刷出版物

　　這個慣用語其實是藉由「樹木」的概念強調與數位品（digital edition）相對的印刷品。紙張取材自樹木，因此 dead tree 強調的是印刷品所浪費的天然資源，並且暗指比起電子產品，印刷品所呈現的效果較為單調、死板。

對話練習 *Let's Talk!*

Paula: How are we supposed to sort out all the data within a week?

Harry: I don't know, but we have to.

Paula: All right. I can start with an online library tonight.

Harry: Well, all the references are available in **dead tree** editions only.

Paula: You are kidding me! So we must lock ourselves up in the archives.

寶拉：我們怎麼可能在一週內整理完所有的數據？

哈利：我不知道，但我們就是得完成。

寶拉：好吧，我今晚可以先使用圖書館的線上資料。

哈利：嗯，所有的參考文獻都只有印刷版本。

寶拉：開玩笑的吧！那我們都得關在檔案室裡了。

字彙／片語充電區 *Words and Phrases*

publisher 名 出版社 / resource 名 資源 / compile 動 彙編 / process 名 程序
a dull book 沉悶的書 / look sth. up 查詢 / bark up the wrong tree 弄錯目標

UNIT 141 packing peanuts 打包花生？

🎧 141

暖身猜猜看 *Warming Up*

Neil: Have you mailed the Christmas gift?

Linda: Not yet. I need some **packing peanuts** to fill the box.

尼爾：你寄出聖誕禮物了嗎？

琳達：還沒，我需要保麗龍球來塞箱子。

原來是這個意思！

packing peanuts 寄包裹時裝在箱子裡的保麗龍球

　　美語經常用物品來代表某物的體積、觸感、形狀等等，這裡的peanut指的就是形狀及大小都跟花生差不多的保麗龍填充物，也可以稱作foam peanuts，在對話中聽到時，可別以為對方要打包花生喔！

Jenny: Do you need any help with moving or packing?

Dylan: I have no idea how to transport that chandelier.

Jenny: It's huge! Are you going to carry it by yourself?

Dylan: I am not sure. I think I should pack it with **packing peanuts** first.

Jenny: You'd better call a shipping company. They'll deliver it safely.

珍妮：你需要幫忙搬家或打包嗎？

狄倫：我實在不知道該怎麼搬那盞水晶燈。

珍妮：好大一盞！你打算自己搬過去嗎？

狄倫：我也不知道，我想我應該先用防撞泡棉球包裝好。

珍妮：你最好請搬運公司幫忙，他們會安全地運送你的水晶燈。

字彙／片語充電區 *Words and Phrases*

wadding 名 填棉 / **replenishment** 名 填裝 / **fragile** 形 易碎的 / **transport** 動 運送
be filled to the brim 塞滿 / **air-tight wrapping** 密封包裝 / **pack a punch** 極有效

UNIT 142
black art(s)
黑色藝術很獨特嗎？

🎧 142

 暖身猜猜看 *Warming Up*

Bill: That dinner show was really interesting.

Nancy: You bet! I especially love a **black art** show.

比爾：那場晚餐秀實在很有趣。

南西：沒錯！我特別喜歡魔術秀。

 原來是這個意思！

black art(s) 魔術

　　black art並非黑色藝術的意思，事實上，這裡的art跟藝術無關，比較傾向於「詭計、技術、技藝」的解釋。最早的時候，black art與black magic的意思相同，指「巫術」，後來就用來形容一般人會感到神奇的魔術或幻術。

 對話練習 *Let's Talk!*

Louis: I am tired of constantly working so hard.

Jenny: What happened? I thought joining this company was your dream.

Louis: It was, but then everything went sour.

Jenny: Gee. Maybe someone has cursed you by using the **black arts** on you.

Louis: I can almost buy that.

路易士：我已經厭倦這種疲於工作的日子了。

珍　妮：怎麼回事？我以為你的夢想就是加入這間公司耶。

路易士：曾經是，但現在一切都變調了。

珍　妮：天啊，該不會是有人對你下咒了吧。

路易士：我幾乎要這麼相信了。

字彙／片語充電區 *Words and Phrases*

magician 名 魔術師 / disguise 動 假裝；掩飾 / allurement 名 誘惑；吸引

sleight of hand 巧妙的手法 / be bug-eyed 目瞪口呆 / expose to 揭露；揭發

UNIT 143 smoke and mirrors
煙和鏡子與遊樂設施有關？

🎧 143

暖身猜猜看 Warming Up

Sam: Did you read the news about the government scandal?

Sara: I did. The entire report is nothing but **smoke and mirrors**!

山姆：你看到關於政府醜聞的新聞了嗎？

莎拉：看了，整篇報導都只是在粉飾太平！

原來是這個意思！

smoke and mirrors 障眼法

　　這個慣用語源自於舞台表演，表演者在舞台上，會使用鏡子跟煙霧，以製造足以混淆觀眾的幻象，讓表演變得精采，從此義衍生而出的抽象意義，就是我們所說的「障眼法」，即利用經過包裝與美化的事實，來欺瞞大眾。

Ginny: Have you found out anything about the black-mail attempt?

Taylor: It was aimed at John, but none of the accusations are true.

Ginny: Are you sure about that?

Taylor: Positive. I've investigated it thoroughly.

Ginny: I see. It was just all **smoke and mirrors** after all.

吉妮：你查到那封黑函的目的為何了嗎？

泰勒：黑函的內容針對約翰，但所有的指控都不是事實。

吉妮：你確定嗎？

泰勒：確定，我徹底調查過了。

吉妮：我理解了，黑函的內容全都是煙霧彈而已。

字彙／片語充電區 Words and Phrases

sleight 名 巧計 / deception 名 欺騙 / conceal 動 隱瞞 / hypocrisy 名 偽善；虛偽
beguile sb. of sth. 騙取 / sail under false colors 冒充 / a smoke alarm 警報器

UNIT 144　horse sense
馬的知識是什麼？

🎧 144

暖身猜猜看 *Warming Up*

Terry: Do you really believe Henry's explanation?

Lily: I have too much **horse sense** to believe his words.

泰瑞：你真的相信亨利的解釋嗎？

莉莉：我的常識足以讓我不去相信那些鬼話。

原來是這個意思！

horse sense 常識

　　從其他英文慣用語來看，以馬為比喻的事物，和其他動物相比，通常隱含了「不聰明、不精緻」的意思，horse sense一開始也是如此。馬對於事物的應變比較基礎，也容易控制，所以後來便被拿來比喻「一般的知識、常識」。

Let's Talk!

Hank: Are you sure you can handle twenty days on the sea?	漢克：你確定你受得了二十天的海上生活嗎？
Amy: Of course! I'm professionally trained.	艾咪：那當然！我都受過專業訓練了。
Hank: A lot of victims were professionally trained.	漢克：有很多遇難者都是受過專業訓練的。
Amy: Don't worry. The two old hands going with me are equipped with good **horse sense**.	艾咪：別擔心，和我一起去的那兩位老手的常識豐富。
Hank: Okay, if you say so.	漢克：好吧，既然你這麼說的話。

字彙／片語充電區 *Words and Phrases*

general 形 普遍的 / knowledge 名 知識 / judgment 名 判斷力 / acumen 名 敏銳
make sense 合理 / with good reasoning 條理分明 / distinguish from 區別

UNIT 145

crash course
帶給人衝擊性的課程？

🎧 145

 暖身猜猜看 *Warming Up*

Ian: How come I haven't seen Gina around lately?

Nancy: She is taking a **crash course** in cooking.

伊恩：最近怎麼都沒有見到吉娜？

南西：她最近在上烹飪速成班。

 原來是這個意思！

crash course 速成課程

　　單看字面的意思，可能會不懂衝擊課、破壞課到底是指什麼，其實，這裡的 crash 意指「應急的、快速的」，因此 crash course 指的就是短時間內，傳授大量基礎的速成課（通常是在較為緊急的情況下所上的課程）。

 對話練習 *Let's Talk!*

Daisy: Have you planned your family trip this year?

Scott: Yes. We are going on a backpacking trip in Spain.

Daisy: Nice! Will it be your first time there?

Scott: It will. I am actually taking a **crash course** in Spanish now.

Daisy: Great. You will need that.

黛　西：你計劃好今年的家庭旅遊了嗎？

史考特：當然，我們要去西班牙來一趟自助的背包旅行。

黛　西：真棒！這是你第一次去嗎？

史考特：沒錯，其實我正在上西班牙文的速成班。

黛　西：那很好，你會用得上的。

字彙／片語充電區 *Words and Phrases*

elective 名 (美)選修課程 / intensive 形 密集的；加強的 / essence 名 本質；實質
sign up 報名登記 / a required course 必修課 / teach by correspondence 函授

UNIT 146　sound bite
咬住聲音是指不出聲嗎？

🎧 146

 暖身猜猜看 *Warming Up*

Mark: The election season is really annoying.

Sally: Yeah. The repetitious **sound bites** are driving me nuts.

馬克：選舉期真的很惱人。

莎莉：是啊，那些一再重複的新聞插播快把我逼瘋了。

 原來是這個意思！

sound bite 新聞用的摘錄語句、插播

　　sound bite最早出現於1980年，報導選舉活動的新聞裡；當時的訊息流通管道，以收音機和報紙為主，而sound bite指的是被節錄下來的一句話，適合被反覆播放以宣傳政見，沿用至今，可以用來形容各方面的宣傳口號或標語。

 對話練習 *Let's Talk!*

Hank: Guess what? I am working at a news channel now.

Mary: That's great! You've always wanted to be a journalist.

Hank: Well, I am actually working behind the scenes.

Mary: Oh. I thought you enjoy interviewing people face to face.

Hank: I do. But I am an editor and just deal with **sound bites** for now.

漢克：告訴你，我目前在新聞電視台工作。

瑪莉：那很棒啊！你一直都想當記者。

漢克：我負責的其實是幕後工作。

瑪莉：喔，我以為你喜歡面對面地訪問他人。

漢克：我是很喜歡，不過，目前我是負責焦點新聞的編輯。

字彙/片語充電區 *Words and Phrases*

slogan 名 口號；標語 / publicize 動 宣傳 / broadcast 動 播送 / blurb 名 大肆宣傳
spot news 最新消息 / inside dope 內幕消息 / bring sb. up to date 提供最新消息

UNIT 147
behind bars
在酒吧的後方？

🎧 147

 暖身猜猜看 *Warming Up*

Nancy: Have you heard from Danny recently?

Kent: Didn't you know that he is **behind bars**?

南西：你有丹尼的消息嗎？
肯特：你不知道他去坐牢了嗎？

 原來是這個意思！

behind bars 坐牢

　　監獄的牢房都是用金屬欄杆（bar）作成的，被關在欄杆後指的就是「被監禁、坐牢」，這個慣用語也不只用於坐牢，當感覺被困在某種情況下時，也可以使用這個說法；另外要注意的是，這個用法較常見於報章雜誌。

 對話練習 *Let's Talk!*

Anna: Have you found an apartment you are interested in?

Mike: Actually, I am considering a neighborhood six blocks away.

Anna: But you said it's not safe enough there.

Mike: It is much better now since the gangsters were put **behind bars**.

Anna: That's great! That area is quite convenient.

安娜：你找到中意的公寓了嗎？
麥克：老實說，我正在考慮六個路口外的街區。
安娜：但你說過那附近不夠安全。
麥克：自從流氓被關起來後，那裡已經好很多了。
安娜：那真棒！那個街區相當方便。

字彙／片語充電區 *Words and Phrases*

detention 名 拘留；滯留 / imprison 動 關押 / criminal 名 罪犯 / captive 名 囚徒
be in jail 坐牢 / serve one's time 服刑 / under arrest 被捕 / break the law 犯法

UNIT 148
Molotov cocktail
某種品牌的雞尾酒？

🎧 148

暖身猜猜看 *Warming Up*

Amy: I'm canceling my trip. The protests have turned violent.

Tom: I heard they attacked the embassy with **Molotov cocktails**!

艾咪：我要取消旅遊行程，那些抗議行動變得很激烈。

湯姆：我聽說他們用汽油彈攻擊大使館！

原來是這個意思！

Molotov cocktail 汽油彈

　　1939年蘇聯與芬蘭爆發冬季戰爭，Molotov是當時的外交部長，當蘇聯轟炸機投炸彈時，他辯稱投擲的是麵包籃（Molotov bread baskets），而後芬蘭人反擊時所用的汽油彈，則戲稱為Molotov雞尾酒，用來招待蘇聯的坦克車。

對話練習 *Let's Talk!*

Vicky: Have you decided on your topic yet? I'm stuck.

Hank: Yeah. I've decided to write about weapons of war.

Vicky: That sounds different.

Hank: I mentioned **Molotov cocktails** in the Winter War and the atom bomb.

Vicky: Cool! You can talk about their roles in history.

薇琪：你決定主題了嗎？我卡住了。

漢克：嗯，我決定寫關於戰爭武器的文章。

薇琪：聽起來滿不一樣的。

漢克：我提到冬季戰爭中的用到的汽油彈，還有原子彈。

薇琪：酷！你可以論述那些武器在歷史上所扮演的角色。

字彙/片語充電區 *Words and Phrases*

missile 名 飛彈 / **fulminate** 動 引爆 / **rebellious** 形 造反的 / **casualty** 名 傷亡人員
blow up 爆炸 / **rock the boat** 製造麻煩；搗亂 / **The fat is in the fire.** 火上加油。

UNIT 149
the handwriting on the wall
在牆上的塗鴉？

🎧 149

 暖身猜猜看 *Warming Up*

Anna: Have you received a notice from HR?

Bob: Not yet, but I can already read **the handwriting on the wall**.

安娜：你有收到人力資源部的通知嗎？

鮑伯：還沒，但我已經能感覺出這不是個好兆頭了。

 原來是這個意思！

the handwriting on the wall 警告

　　這個慣用語源自於《聖經：但以理書 5:5-31》，先知解讀了王宮牆上的文字，告訴國王這些文字預示了即將亡國的警告；到十八世紀時，這個慣用語就被用來比喻「即將到來的危險或災難」，即惡兆、警訊。

 **對話練習** *Let's Talk!*

Billy: Why are you looking for a new job?

Fanny: My company has been in the red recently.

Billy: I think a lot of companies are facing this situation now.

Fanny: The problem is, they keep ignoring **the handwriting on the wall**.

Billy: I see. Sorry to hear that.

比利：你為什麼要找新工作？

芬妮：我們公司最近虧很多錢。

比利：現在很多公司都面臨同樣的問題。

芬妮：問題是，我們公司的人不願意正視警訊。

比利：原來如此，很遺憾聽到這樣的消息。

字彙／片語充電區 *Words and Phrases*

omen 名 預兆 / **ominous** 形 不祥的 / **admonish** 動 警告 / **exemplary** 形 懲戒性的 / **a straw in the wind** 預兆 / **put a bug in one's ear** 事先警告 / **beat the air** 徒勞

UNIT 150 a heads-up 把頭抬起來？

🎧 150

暖身猜猜看 Warming Up

Parker: Jimmy gave us **a heads-up** about the next project.
Nina: Oh, what did he say about it?

帕克：關於下一份企劃，吉米給了我們警告。
妮娜：喔？那他說了什麼？

原來是這個意思！

a heads-up 警告；警示

　　這個慣用語是從更早以前的用法所引申而來的，當時的Heads up.等同於 Watch out.（小心、注意）常見於棒球或美式足球中，後來就以人抬頭注意情況的意思來形容一個消息或是警告，讓人集中注意力。

對話練習 Let's Talk!

Nick: Have you noticed that our sales have been dropping badly?

Dora: Is it because of the slow season?

Nick: No, I'm referring to the data from previous years.

Dora: Are you going to give **a heads-up** to the department head?

Nick: I will. We have to increase sales, or some of us might be laid off.

尼克：你有注意到我們的業績下滑得很厲害嗎？
朵拉：是因為淡季的關係嗎？
尼克：不是，我正在比對前幾年的數據了。
朵拉：你要不要提醒一下部門主管？
尼克：我會的，我們必須提高業績，不然可能有人會被裁掉。

字彙/片語充電區 Words and Phrases

vigilant 形 警戒的 / **dictate** 動 命令 / **cautious** 形 謹慎的 / **attention** 名 注意
take the rein 支配 / **ride herd on** 照看；監管 / **in the saddle** 處於控制地位

UNIT 151
the Big Apple
一顆巨無霸蘋果？

🎧 151

 暖身猜猜看 *Warming Up*

Phil: I moved to New York three months ago.

Amy: Life must be quite exciting in **the Big Apple**, right?

菲爾：我三個月前搬去紐約。

艾咪：紐約的生活一定很令人興奮吧？

 原來是這個意思！

the Big Apple 紐約

六〇年代起，爵士歌手引用西文的Apple orchard描述市中心最熱鬧的地方，到了七〇年代，the Big Apple被寫成吸引觀光客的標語，這裡的big指「受歡迎的、美好的」，因此紐約就以the Big Apple的名號聞名世界。

 對話練習 *Let's Talk!*

Wade: What's your plan for New Year's Eve?

Mandy: I will join the count down at Times Square for sure.

Wade: Looks like the whole world will gather in **the Big Apple**.

Mandy: I know! But since I'm moving back to Asia next year, I can't miss it.

Wade: That's right. Enjoy your holiday then.

韋德：跨年夜你有什麼計畫？

曼蒂：我一定要去時代廣場倒數。

韋德：看起來全世界的人都會擠到紐約。

曼蒂：是啊！不過我明年就要搬回亞洲，所以這次絕對不能錯過。

韋德：這倒是，好好享受你的假期吧。

字彙／片語充電區 *Words and Phrases*

capital 名 首都 / metropolis 名 首府 / municipal 形 市的 / prosperous 形 繁榮的
live in fat city 生活優渥 / a city slicker 時髦老練的都市人 / bustle around 極忙碌

UNIT 152 French windows
法國設計的窗戶？

🎧 152

暖身猜猜看 *Warming Up*

Jack: How do you like the apartment?

Nancy: I just love the beautiful **French windows**!

傑克：你喜歡那間公寓嗎？

南西：我愛死那扇落地窗了！

原來是這個意思！

French windows 落地窗

　　French windows（也稱French doors）於十七世紀起源於法國，受到文藝復興時期的啟發，加上當時的創新，開始出現具備窗戶功能的落地窗，但這些窗戶其實是門，可以通往陽台或屋頂的露台。

對話練習 *Let's Talk!*

Karen: I saw the ad that this apartment is for rent.

George: That's right. Would you like to take a look?

Karen: I'd love to. Thank you.

George: You must check out the view behind those **French windows**.

Karen: It's facing the botanical garden. The scenery is gorgeous!

凱倫：我看到廣告說這間公寓要出租。

喬治：沒錯，你要不要看一看？

凱倫：好啊，謝謝。

喬治：你一定要看一下落地窗外的景觀。

凱倫：這裡面對植物園，景色實在太美了！

字彙／片語充電區 *Words and Phrases*

dormer 名 屋頂窗 / **fanlight** 名 扇形窗 / **curtain** 名 窗簾 / **aperture** 名 孔；縫隙
window shopping 純逛街 / **the window seat** 靠窗座位 / **walk on air** 非常高興

UNIT 153 Chinese dragon
生於中國的龍？

🎧 153

 暖身猜猜看 *Warming Up*

Julie: The clothing of the Qing dynasty was so delicate!

Allen: Yeah. The **Chinese dragon** pattern looks complicated.

茱莉：清朝的服裝好精細喔！

亞倫：是啊，麒麟的圖騰看起來真複雜

 原來是這個意思！

Chinese dragon 麒麟

　　從字面上看，Chinese dragon會讓人以為是龍，但這個慣用語其實是指麒麟。西方人最初接觸到中國圖騰時，麒麟是經常出現的紋樣，為了讓西方人能理解這是我們的神獸（傳說中的神物），才使用他們所能理解的dragon。

 對話練習 *Let's Talk!*

George: I'll show you a significant historical garden this afternoon.

Dana: What makes it so special?

George: It's one of the biggest gardens left nowadays.

Dana: I know that one! They have **Chinese dragon** patterns along the corridor.

George: Yeah. And the construction layout is amazing.

喬治：今天下午，我要帶你去參觀一座了不起的歷史園林。

黛娜：這座園林有什麼特別的嗎？

喬治：它是現存大型園林中的其中一座。

黛娜：我知道這座！它的迴廊上有麒麟的圖騰。

喬治：是啊，而且建築設計令人嘆為觀止。

字彙/片語充電區 *Words and Phrases*

Oriental 形 亞洲的 / **creature** 名 生物 / **mythology** 名 神話 / **legendary** 形 傳說的 **a tall story** 難以置信的事 / **buy one's story** 相信…的話 / **under one's nose** 眼前

UNIT 154　pie hole
派上的一個洞？

🎧 154

 暖身猜猜看 Warming Up

Josh: Why are we having fried noodles for dinner again?

Lucy: Just eat your dinner and shut your **pie hole**!

賈許：怎麼晚餐又是吃炒麵啊？

露西：好好吃你的晚餐，把嘴巴閉上！

 **原來是這個意思！**

pie hole 嘴巴

　　pie hole源自於英式用語cake hole，從他們用「送入蛋糕的洞」來形容嘴巴，就能得知蛋糕點心類在英式生活中的重要性；至八○年代，美國依照自己的文化，將這個用語改成pie hole，開始盛行。

 **對話練習** *Let's Talk!*

Matt: You won't believe what came out of Daniel's **pie hole**!

Peggy: I wasn't at the meeting. What did he say?

Matt: He went out of his mind and scolded our manager.

Peggy: No, he didn't!

Matt: Yes, he did. What's wrong with him?

麥特：你不會相信竟然從丹尼爾口中聽到那些話！

佩姬：我沒去開會，他說了什麼？

麥特：他整個抓狂，大罵我們的經理。

佩姬：不會吧！

麥特：他就是罵了，到底發生了什麼事啊？

字彙／片語充電區 *Words and Phrases*

cavity 名 洞穴；腔 / chew 動 咀嚼 / digestion 名 消化 / spout 名 噴口；噴嘴
put one's foot in one's mouth 說錯話 / whet one's appetite 助長慾望(做某事)

UNIT 155 · a black eye
熬夜造成的黑眼圈？

🎧 155

 暖身猜猜看 *Warming Up*

Mindy: Wow! That hit must have hurt a lot.

Allen: Are my **black eyes** that obvious?

明蒂：哇！那一拳肯定很痛。

亞倫：我眼睛的瘀青就那麼明顯嗎？

 原來是這個意思！

a black eye 眼睛瘀青；汙點

　　a black eye是指「被打得瘀青所造成的黑眼圈」，如果要講睡眠不足造成的黑眼圈，請用dark circles；另外，由於眼睛周圍的瘀青很明顯，因此a black eye也被用來比喻不名譽的事。

 **對話練習** *Let's Talk!*

Jenny: Do you think Howard can serve another term as state governor?

Kevin: I don't know. He has to win back people's trust.

Jenny: Are you talking about the homeless issue?

Kevin: Yes. The growing number of homeless folks is **a black eye** for him.

Jenny: That's true.

珍妮：你認為霍華德能順利連任州長嗎？

凱文：不知道，他必須贏回人民的信任。

珍妮：你是指遊民問題嗎？

凱文：是啊，遊民人數的暴漲是他的汙點。

珍妮：這倒是。

字彙／片語充電區 *Words and Phrases*

bruise 名 瘀青 / injury 名 傷害 / diffuse 動 擴散；散布 / prickle 動 刺痛；戳；扎
red-eye flight 夜間航班 / look sb. in the eye 直視 / hit the bull's eye 達成目標

UNIT 156

have pink eye
眼睛布滿紅血絲？

🎧 156

 暖身猜猜看 *Warming Up*

Gina: I **have pink eye**. My eyes are red.

Larry: It must be from the swimming pool you swam in last week.

吉娜：我得了結膜炎，眼睛都紅紅的。

賴瑞：一定是你上週去的那個游泳池造成的。

 原來是這個意思！

have pink eye 得結膜炎

　　pink常與「健康」有關，例如in the pink是「身體健康」的意思，但此處的pink eye為結膜炎（conjunctivitis）的俚語用法，當人的眼睛感染發炎時，會變得紅紅的，可不要誤以為是單純的紅血絲或眼紅喔！

 對話練習 *Let's Talk!*

Larry: How did you like the hotel you stayed at?

Vicky: It's convenient and spacious. However, I think it has a hygiene problem.

Larry: What do you mean?

Vicky: I **had pink eye** there. I think it was because of the towels.

Larry: Oh! Did you tell the hotel staff?

賴瑞：你喜歡你住的飯店嗎？

薇琪：那裡很方便，也很寬敞，但是我覺得衛生有問題。

賴瑞：怎麼說？

薇琪：我在那裡感染了結膜炎，我懷疑是毛巾不夠乾淨。

賴瑞：喔！你有跟飯店人員說這件事嗎？

字彙／片語充電區 *Words and Phrases*

perception 名 感知 / contagious 形 感染的 / bandage 名 繃帶 / bacteria 名 細菌
stare at 盯著看 / private eye (口)私家偵探 / eye candy 華而不實的東西；花瓶

UNIT 157　be all ears
許多耳朵是指聽眾很多？

🎧 157

暖身猜猜看 Warming Up

Bella: Are you going to Lydia's party this weekend?

Lauren: Tell me who else is going? I **am all ears**.

貝拉：你週末會去莉蒂雅的派對嗎？

勞倫：告訴我還有誰會去？我豎著耳朵聽呢！

原來是這個意思！

be all ears 全神貫注地聆聽

　　這是個充滿想像力的慣用語，當人完全不想錯過聽到的一字一句時，會希望全身上下都是耳朵，聽得清清楚楚，以免錯過任何訊息，這個慣用語就是利用這樣的想像，去描述某人「全神貫注地聆聽」的模樣。

對話練習 Let's Talk!

Ann: Luke and I were assigned to take care of Mrs. Brown.

Dan: Seriously? She is indeed the toughest client.

Ann: Oh no! So the gossip is true. We are doomed!

Dan: Don't worry. I happen to know some good tips for dealing with her.

Ann: Thank God! Please help us. I **am all ears**!

安：我跟路克被指派負責布朗太太的案子。

丹：真的假的？她可是最難搞的客戶。

安：天啊！所以那八卦是真的，我們死定了！

丹：別擔心，我正好知道搞定她的訣竅。

安：謝天謝地！快幫幫我們，我都聽你的！

字彙/片語充電區 Words and Phrases

circumspect 形 慎重的；謹慎的 / absent 形 心不在焉的 / acoustic 形 聽覺的
hang on every word 仔細聽 / **on the lookout** 密切注意 / **on one's toe** 警覺

UNIT 158

beat one's brains out
狠狠地揍某人？

🎧 158

 暖身猜猜看 *Warming Up*

Linda: How come Andy is not joining us for dinner?
Danny: He is **beating his brains out** for the upcoming exam.

> 琳達：安迪怎麼不來吃晚餐？
> 丹尼：他正為了快到來的考試絞盡腦汁。

 原來是這個意思！

beat one's brains out 絞盡腦汁

　　這個慣用語可不是在講要打爆某人的頭，而是形容一個人費盡心神去思索，用力到腦都快擠出來了，也就是絞盡腦汁的意思；另外，想描述自己「太用力思考，以至於腦袋累了」，可以說 My brain is fried。

 對話練習 *Let's Talk!*

Eva: Why have you been walking up and down the entire morning?

Nick: I am **beating my brains out** trying to memorize the VIP list.

Eva: You have to remember all the details about them, don't you?

Nick: Yeah. Tomorrow night is the VIP banquet, and I'm in charge of it.

Eva: Wow! Would you like to have a cup of coffee first?

> 伊娃：你為什麼整個早上都在走來走去？
> 尼克：我正在用盡腦力試圖背起這份貴賓名單。
> 伊娃：你必須記得貴賓的所有資訊吧？
> 尼克：是啊，明晚是招待貴賓的宴會，我是負責人。
> 伊娃：哇！那你要不要先來杯咖啡？

字彙／片語充電區 *Words and Phrases*

diligent 形 費盡心血的 / **industrious** 形 勤奮的；勤勞的 / **ponder** 動 仔細考慮
rack one's brain 絞盡腦汁 / **an uphill task** 艱鉅的工作 / **on the go** 活躍；忙碌

UNIT 159　as fit as a fiddle
身材像小提琴般？

🎧 159

 暖身猜猜看 *Warming Up*

Bob: Are you sure you can go fishing with us? How's your cold?

Jill: Of course. I am **as fit as a fiddle** now!

鮑伯：你確定可以跟我們去釣魚嗎？感冒怎麼樣了？

吉兒：當然可以，我現在健康得很呢！

 原來是這個意思！

as fit as a fiddle 十分健康

　　這個慣用語出現於十七世紀，其中fit和現代普遍理解的健身或健美不同，為「適合、恰當」之意，as fit as a fiddle在當時是形容一個調好音的小提琴能演奏出優美的音樂，之後用來比喻人「健康」或「精神狀態良好」。

 *Let's Talk!*

Daniel: I went to visit my grandparents last weekend.

Karen: Wow! You must be very close.

Daniel: Yeah. I used to spend most of my summer vacations with them.

Karen: That was very sweet of you. They must have been thrilled to see you again.

Daniel: Well, it was so nice to see that they are still **as fit as a fiddle**.

丹尼爾：我上週末去看我的祖父母。

凱　倫：哇！你們的關係一定很親密。

丹尼爾：是啊，我以前暑假的大半時間都是跟他們一起過的。

凱　倫：你真貼心，他們一定很高興再見到你。

丹尼爾：嗯，看到他們身體還很硬朗真好。

字彙/片語充電區 *Words and Phrases*

fitness 名 健康 / **robust** 形 強健的 / **husky** 形 高大健壯的 / **vigorous** 形 精力充沛的
in good condition 狀態良好 / **alive and kicking** 生氣勃勃 / **pale as a ghost** 慘白

UNIT 160

go to pieces
物品被撕成碎片？

🎧 160

暖身猜猜看 *Warming Up*

Rod: Have you checked out Mary? How is she doing?

Lily: She just **went to pieces** when she learned of Tom's accident.

羅德：你去看瑪莉了嗎？她還好嗎？

莉莉：在得知湯姆發生意外後，她完全崩潰了。

原來是這個意思！

go to pieces 發狂；身心崩潰

　　這裡的go to不是去哪裡的意思，而必須解釋為「變成、成為」之意，字面上的翻譯為「變成碎片」，實際意思同fall apart，形容「人受到刺激後情緒崩潰」或是「精神狀態無法維持完整」。

對話練習 *Let's Talk!*

Kent: Would you like to join us to volunteer at the animal shelter?

Fanny: I don't think so.

Kent: Why not? You've always loved animals.

Fanny: I am afraid I might **go to pieces** when they euthanize the animals.

Kent: I felt that way at first, too. But you'll learn a lot.

肯特：要不要跟我們一起去動物收容所做義工？

芬妮：我想不要了吧。

肯特：為什麼？你一直都很喜歡動物的。

芬妮：我怕他們讓動物安樂死的時候，我會受不了。

肯特：我一開始也那麼覺得，不過你會學到很多。

字彙／片語充電區 *Words and Phrases*

shatter 動 粉碎 / succumb 動 屈服 / sorrowful 形 悲傷的 / spirit 名 精神；心靈

fall apart 崩潰；瓦解 / go mad 發瘋；失去理智 / as cool as a cucumber 鎮定自若

UNIT 161　under the weather
在大太陽或暴風雨底下？

🎧 161

 暖身猜猜看 *Warming Up*

Nick: I haven't seen Karen for a few days.

Daisy: She has been **under the weather** for some days.

尼克：好多天沒看到凱倫了。

黛西：她已經身體不適好幾天了。

 原來是這個意思！

under the weather 身體不舒服

　　這個慣用語源自航海生活，當天候不佳、海象不穩時，暈船的船員會到甲板下休息，因此under the weather便被用來形容人「不舒服」或「酒醉後的不適」；另一個慣用語under the influence則指「酒醉」，不要弄混了。

 *Let's Talk!*

Betty: Did you talk to Hank about your proposal last night?

Bill: I did, but I don't think our conversation was very productive.

Betty: What do you mean?

Bill: I talked to him and then realized he was pretty **under the weather**.

Betty: I see. You'd better make an appointment again.

貝蒂：你昨晚有跟漢克談你的提案了嗎？

比爾：是有，不過我不認為談了有用。

貝蒂：什麼意思？

比爾：我和他說了提案之後，才發現他身體很不舒服。

貝蒂：原來如此，你最好再和他約個時間。

字彙/片語充電區 *Words and Phrases*

ailing 形 生病的 / fever 名 發燒 / enfeebled 形 衰弱的 / discomfort 名 不舒服
out of sorts 不舒服 / run down 過勞 / be sick as a dog 重病 / brace up 打起精神

UNIT 162 set (sb.) back on one's feet 某人決心靠自己？

🎧 162

暖身猜猜看 *Warming Up*

Karen: Is Robert getting better now?
Lenny: Yeah. We tried our best to **set him back on his feet.**

凱倫：羅伯特現在好多了嗎？
蘭尼：好多了，我們很努力地幫助他復原。

原來是這個意思！

set (sb.) back on one's feet 復原

　　這個慣用語從字面上看，很容易聯想到靠自己站起來的意思，其實這是引申自 on one's feet 的用法；on one's feet 可以理解成自立自強、重新站起來，這個慣用語就是將此用法衍生至抽象概念，指「幫助某人復原至較好的狀態」。

對話練習 *Let's Talk!*

Nancy: It's good to take a few days off to be with my family.

Gary: But the consequence is to have tons of work to catch up with.

Nancy: Don't remind me of that! I am not ready for that yet.

Gary: You'd better **set yourself back on your feet.**

Nancy: I know. What a life!

南西：能夠休幾天假陪家人的感覺真好。

蓋瑞：但代價就是有堆積如山的工作要趕完。

南西：別提醒我這件事！我還沒準備好面對那些。

蓋瑞：你最好快點振作起來。

南西：我知道，這就是人生啊！

字彙/片語充電區 *Words and Phrases*

remedy 動 治療；醫治 / curative 形 治病的 / hospitalize 動 使住院 / urge 動 激勵
get back in shape 恢復健康 / throw up 嘔吐 / be strong as a horse 身體強壯

UNIT 163

sleep with the fishes
和魚睡在一起與游泳有關嗎？

🎧 163

 暖身猜猜看 *Warming Up*

Bonnie: I heard that Ken just messed up that gangster's case!

Henry: Oh no! I fear Ken will be **sleeping with the fishes** soon.

邦妮：聽說肯搞砸了那個流氓的案子！

亨利：不是吧！我擔心肯要死定了。

 原來是這個意思！

sleep with the fishes 死亡

　　經典名片《教父》曾引用這個慣用語："It means Luca Brasi sleeps with the fishes."意指按黑道的刑罰，把人扔下海餵魚，藉此表示「死亡」，後來也用來比喻抽象的「死定了」。

對話練習 *Let's Talk!*

Luke: This report is going to exhaust me.

Jenny: Do you know that there are only two more days left?

Luke: I know. The interview took me too much time.

Jenny: If you blow the presentation, you will be **sleeping with the fishes**.

Luke: Ha. I think you've seen too many gangster movies, Jenny.

路克：這份報告真的會把我累死。

珍妮：你應該知道只剩兩天了吧？

路克：我知道，訪談花了我太多時間。

珍妮：如果你搞砸簡報，你就死定了。

路克：哈，我想是你看太多黑道電影了吧，珍妮。

字彙／片語充電區 *Words and Phrases*

deceased 名 死者 / **inert** 形 無生命的；呆滯的 / **shock** 名 (醫)休克 / **revive** 動 復甦
buy the farm 死亡 / **pass away** 過世 / **push up daisies** 入土 / **off color** 氣色差

UNIT 164 in one's birthday suit
穿著生日宴會裝？

🎧 164

 暖身猜猜看 Warming Up

Betty: Can you get the door? I'm **in my birthday suit**.

Will: Oh! Okay, I'll get it.

貝蒂：你可以去開門嗎？我沒穿衣服。

威爾：喔！好，我去應門。

 原來是這個意思！

in one's birthday suit 赤身裸體

　　包含著suit（衣服）的這個詞，怎麼看都是某套服裝吧？這個慣用語的重點其實在birthday suit，人在出生時，身上穿的是什麼？當然是什麼都沒穿囉，因此，所謂「穿著出生的衣物」就是赤身裸體、一絲不掛。

 **對話練習** *Let's Talk!*

Tina: Would you like to go to a Japanese hot spring?

Sam: Well, I don't feel like it.

Tina: Why not? It's really comfortable and healing.

Sam: I can't enjoy bathing **in my birthday suit** in front of strangers.

Tina: Come on! It'll be too comfortable for you to sense any embarrassment.

蒂娜：要不要去泡日式溫泉？

山姆：不是很想耶。

蒂娜：為什麼？那很舒服又有療效耶。

山姆：我沒辦法在陌生人面前一絲不掛地泡澡。

蒂娜：拜託！泡湯的效果舒服到足以讓你忘記尷尬的。

字彙／片語充電區 *Words and Phrases*

denude 動 使裸露 / **disrobe** 動 脫衣服 / **nudity** 名 赤裸 / **apparel** 名 服裝；衣著
without a stitch 一絲不掛 / **in the raw** 未加工 / **beat the pants off sb.** 大敗某人

UNIT 165 I have never slept better. 我從來沒睡好覺？

🎧 165

 暖身猜猜看 *Warming Up*

Cindy: Did you rest well last night? It's our big day today.
Kenny: Sure! **I have never slept better.**

辛蒂：昨晚睡得好嗎？今天可是我們的大日子喔。
肯尼：當然，睡得好極了。

 原來是這個意思！

I have never slept better. 我睡得很好

　　這句慣用語在解讀時，要注意better，許多誤解此句英文的人，都是將之理解成well，所以誤解為「我沒有睡好。」其實這句話真正的意思是「我沒有睡得比這更好的了。」意即「我睡得好極了。」

 *Let's Talk!*

Jeff: Are you enjoying our trip so far?
Helen: I must admit how tiring traveling is for me.
Jeff: I thought this is your dream trip.
Helen: It is. But I didn't know we would have to walk so much!
Jeff: I know. **I have never slept better** last night.

傑夫：你還滿意我們的旅程嗎？
海倫：不得不承認，旅行對我來說很累人。
傑夫：這不是你的夢想之旅嗎？
海倫：這是啊，但我沒想到我們得走那麼多路！
傑夫：這倒是，我昨晚睡得可好了。

字彙/片語充電區 *Words and Phrases*

relaxation 名 放鬆 / sleepyhead 名 貪睡者 / recover 動 恢復 / stamina 名 精力
sleep in 睡懶覺；睡遲了 / not sleep a wink 完全睡不著 / sleep on it 思考(某事)

UNIT 166

a close call
關係親密的人打電話來？

🎧 166

暖身猜猜看 *Warming Up*

Andy: I thought you wouldn't make it!

Helen: That was **a close call**. I almost missed the exam.

安迪：我以為你來不及了！

海倫：真的是好險，我差點就錯過考試了。

原來是這個意思！

a close call 千鈞一髮

　　close call源自於十九世紀，這裡的call指的是「裁判的判決」。在運動場上，當雙方勢均力敵、勝負難以分辨時，裁判剎那間的決定就能定輸贏，因此，人們就用這個慣用語來形容「驚險、千鈞一髮的時刻」。

對話練習 *Let's Talk!*

Carl: Taking a ski trip can be dangerous sometimes.

Judy: What do you mean? What happened on your ski trip?

Carl: I didn't check the route carefully, so I almost fell off a cliff.

Judy: Thank God you are safe!

Carl: Yeah. That was **a close call**. I almost didn't make it back.

卡爾：滑雪有時候會是件很危險的事。

茱蒂：什麼意思？你去滑雪的時候怎麼了嗎？

卡爾：我沒有仔細勘查路徑，差點就摔出懸崖。

茱蒂：謝天謝地！你平安回來了。

卡爾：是啊，實在太驚險，差點就回不來了。

字彙／片語充電區 *Words and Phrases*

cliffhanger 名 扣人心弦 / **bewilderment** 名 混亂；迷惑 / **crux** 名 緊要關頭；關鍵
a close shave 萬幸 / **when the chips are down** 最後關頭 / **out on a limb** 涉險

UNIT 167　at the eleventh hour
在十一點鐘的時候？

🎧 167

 暖身猜猜看 Warming Up

Sandy: What are you doing here? I thought you went on vacation.

Will: My boss changed his schedule **at the eleventh hour**.

仙蒂：你怎麼在這裡？我以為你去渡假了。

威爾：我老闆臨時變更了行程。

 原來是這個意思！

at the eleventh hour 在最後一刻

　　這個慣用語源自《聖經》馬太福音二十章第一到十六節，說的是在十二小時的工時中，在最後第十一個小時被僱用的工人，領的薪資跟從第一個鐘頭就開始工作的工人，竟然是一樣的，用來比喻「最後一刻」。

 對話練習 Let's Talk!

Lily: God, I didn't sleep much last night.

Roy: Don't tell me you went to party on a Tuesday night.

Lily: Not at all! I was finishing up the marketing report.

Roy: That's right! It's due today.

Lily: Yeah. I got it done **at the eleventh hour**.

莉莉：天啊，我昨晚根本沒怎麼睡。

羅伊：別告訴我你週二晚上還去跑趴。

莉莉：才不是呢！我在趕行銷學的報告。

羅伊：對喔！今天是繳交期限的最後一天。

莉莉：是啊，我趕在最後一刻寫完的。

字彙／片語充電區 Words and Phrases

tardy 形 遲到的 / **dilatory** 形 拖延的 / **delay** 動 耽擱；使延期 / **constant** 形 持續的 / **under the wire** 及時完成 / **in the nick of time** 及時 / **drag one's feet** 拖拖拉拉

by a hair's breadth
一根頭髮的寬度？

UNIT 168

🎧 168

暖身猜猜看 *Warming Up*

Linda: Did you see the news about the huge car accident?

Bob: Actually, I was there. I missed it **by a hair's breadth**.

琳達：你看了那場大車禍的新聞報導嗎？

鮑伯：其實我就在現場，差一點就無法脫身了。

原來是這個意思！

by a hair's breadth 差一點；死裡逃生

　　breadth是寬幅的意思，從字面上看by a hair's breadth是比喻僅有一根頭髮的距離，用來形容極其驚險、一息之差；甚或僥倖的情況和心情，也可以用within a hair's breadth描述。

對話練習 *Let's Talk!*

Julie: I thought we were going to miss the flight!

Kevin: We are so lucky to have made it **by a hair's breadth**.

Julie: Thanks to the taxi driver. He took a shortcut for us.

Kevin: Hope we didn't get him any ticket.

Julie: Yeah, he ran two red lights on the way.

茱莉：我以為我們趕不上班機！

凱文：我們能千鈞一髮地趕上實在太幸運了。

茱莉：多虧了計程車司機，他為了我們抄捷徑。

凱文：希望我們沒害他被開罰單。

茱莉：是啊，他一路上闖了兩個紅燈呢。

字彙／片語充電區 *Words and Phrases*

incidental 形 偶然的；意料之外的 / coincidence 名 巧合 / thrilling 形 毛骨悚然的
by a fluke 僥倖 / **climb the walls** 極為焦慮；緊張擔憂 / **play it by ear** 隨機應變

UNIT 169 a red letter day
收到紅色信封的一天？

🎧 169

 暖身猜猜看 Warming Up

June: Today is **a red letter day** for us!

George: I know. It is our 10th anniversary.

瓊恩：今天是我們的大日子喔！

喬治：我知道，今天是我們的十週年紀念日。

 原來是這個意思！

a red letter day 重要的日子

　　a red letter day指的是「重要到會在日曆上以紅筆註記的日子」，起源自以前會在日曆上用紅字註記教會的節慶。然而，當單獨使用red（紅色的）這個形容詞時，要小心它所代表的負面意涵，例如：財務赤字（in the red）。

 **對話練習** *Let's Talk!*

George: I am going to call it a day.

Lucy: It's rare to see you getting off on time.

George: Today is **a red letter day**. It's June 12 and my 10th wedding anniversary.

Lucy: Wow! Have you planned anything special with your wife?

George: Of course! I have booked a table at Robuchon.

喬治：我要下班了。

露西：難得看到你準時下班。

喬治：今天是個大日子，六月十二日，是我的結婚十週年紀念日。

露西：哇！你有要跟你太太做什麼特別的慶祝嗎？

喬治：當然有！我已經在侯布雄訂好位子了。

字彙／片語充電區 *Words and Phrases*

calendar 名 日曆；曆法 / jubilee 名 25或50週年紀念日 / ceremony 名 典禮；儀式
paint the town red 跑遍每間酒吧；狂歡 / **call it a day** 收工 / **to the letter** 精準的

UNIT 170 Indian summer 印度的夏季？

🎧 170

 暖身猜猜看 *Warming Up*

Holy: We'll finally have an **Indian summer** starting this weekend.

Tim: Yeah. I am going to take my kids camping.

荷莉：這週末開始，氣溫終於要開始回暖了。

提姆：是啊，我想帶我的小孩去露營。

 原來是這個意思！

Indian summer 冬日回暖；愉快寧靜的晚年

　　這裡的Indian指的是北美的印第安人，而summer則是入秋後氣溫突然回升的幾天，緊接著又回復寒冷的天候；除了冬天裡突然回暖的那幾天，也藉由「回暖」的意象比喻晚年愉悅的生活。

 對話練習 *Let's Talk!*

Laura: My family and I went to visit my grandfather last week.

Harry: I remember you said he lives alone.

Laura: Yes. He bought a house by the lake and lives there.

Harry: Your grandfather is really something!

Laura: We are blessed that he is enjoying an **Indian summer** late in life.

蘿拉：我和家人上週去探望我的祖父。

哈利：我記得你說他一個人住？

蘿拉：沒錯，他在湖邊買了一間房子，住在那裡。

哈利：你的祖父真了不起！

蘿拉：看到他能安享晚年，我們都很高興。

字彙/片語充電區 *Words and Phrases*

retirement 名 退休 / tranquil 形 安寧的 / garner 動 儲入穀倉 / reap 動 收割
dog days 大熱天 / come rain or shine 無論如何 / chase rainbows 徒勞

UNIT 171

around the clock
在時鐘的附近？

🎧 171

暖身猜猜看 *Warming Up*

Jason: Sam has been working **around the clock** for four days.

Nina: My goodness! He needs a good rest.

傑森：山姆沒日沒夜地工作了四天。

妮娜：天啊！他需要好好休息一下。

原來是這個意思！

around the clock 一整天24小時

　　光看字面上的意思，可能會以為指的是在時鐘附近，其實這個慣用語是利用時鐘不斷在轉的情況，來形容「連續不斷、從白天到夜晚的24小時」，常用來形容人日以繼夜忙碌的情形，也可以寫成round the clock。

對話練習 *Let's Talk!*

Jack: Are you sure Tom is capable of being the project leader?

Dana: Yes. He is well experienced in conducting projects.

Jack: But he'll need to supervise a group of new hands.

Dana: I am sure he can handle the case.

Jack: Alright. They had better work **around the clock** from now on.

傑克：你確定湯姆能勝任企劃領導人的工作嗎？

黛娜：是的，他在指導企劃這方面很有經驗。

傑克：但他需要指導一群新手。

黛娜：我相信他可以處理。

傑克：好吧，他們最好從現在開始就日以繼夜地努力。

字彙／片語充電區 *Words and Phrases*

ceaseless 形 不間斷的 / weary 形 疲倦的 / schedule 名 日程 / emergent 形 緊急的
day and night 日夜 / get one's beauty sleep 美容覺 / at the drop of a hat 即刻

UNIT 172
in/on the hot seat
急得像熱鍋上的螞蟻？

🎧 172

暖身猜猜看 *Warming Up*

Anna: I've been **on the hot seat** listening to Ms. Lee's complaints.

Billy: Gee! Let me buy you a drink after work.

安娜：我剛剛一直很痛苦地在聽李小姐抱怨。

比利：天啊！下班後我請你喝一杯。

原來是這個意思！

in/on the hot seat 處於尷尬的情況中

　　hot seat這個用法，有兩個起源，一說是指處以死刑用的電椅；另一個則是指警察辦案時，用大燈直射犯人的拷問方式，從這兩種起源衍生，hot seat後來就被用來比喻「坐立難安、深陷危機的處境」。

Let's Talk!

Noah: I heard you are going to negotiate with the residents.

Linda: Yeah, I was assigned to settle the compensation deal.

Noah: You know if the negotiation breaks down, you'll be **in the hot seat**.

Linda: I know. But I don't have a choice.

Noah: Well, wish you luck!

諾亞：聽說你要去跟住戶談判。

琳達：是啊，我被指派去談妥賠償金。

諾亞：你知道如果談判破裂，你的處境會很尷尬吧？

琳達：我知道，但我沒其他選擇啊。

諾亞：祝你好運！

字彙 / 片語充電區 *Words and Phrases*

embarrass 動 困窘 / unfavorable 形 不利的 / torment 動 煩擾 / dispute 名 糾紛
walk a tightrope 兼顧 / a flea in one's ear 尖銳的指責 / put a damper on 潑冷水

UNIT 173　in the doghouse
在狗屋裡面？

🎧 173

 暖身猜猜看 *Warming Up*

Danny: I must deposit the check today or I'll be **in the doghouse**.
Donna: Oh! You've got fifteen minutes only. You'd better run now.

　丹尼：我得在今天存這張支票，不然麻煩就大了。
　唐娜：喔！只剩十五分鐘，你最好用跑的。

 原來是這個意思！

in the doghouse 深陷麻煩

　　國外的狗屋，大多放在戶外的院子裡，多數的情況下，狗都可以自由進出家裡，但當牠犯錯被處罰時，就會被送進狗屋面壁思過；因此，in the doghouse 就用來比喻「做錯事而暫時失寵」或是「惹上麻煩」。

 對話練習　*Let's Talk!*

Emma: How come Frank is not coming for the game?
　Mike: He forgot his wife's birthday, so he's now **in the doghouse**.
Emma: Ha! No wonder he is grounded.
　Mike: Don't mention this when you see him tomorrow.
Emma: Alright. I'll try not to tease him.

艾瑪：法蘭克怎麼沒來看球賽？
麥克：他忘了他太太的生日，現在被列管。
艾瑪：哈！難怪他被禁足了。
麥克：你明天看到他的時候，可別提這件事。
艾瑪：好吧，我盡量不取笑他就是了。

字彙 / 片語充電區 *Words and Phrases*

troublesome 形 麻煩的 / **solve** 動 解決 / **incident** 名 事件 / **deadlock** 名 僵局
appeal to 求助於；訴諸 / **a dog chance** 渺茫的希望 / **put on the dog** 擺排場

UNIT 174
get into hot water
洗澡水接得太燙了？

🎧 174

暖身猜猜看 *Warming Up*

Bill: If Jack keeps **getting into hot water**, he will lose his job.

Linda: Yeah. We'd better talk to him.

比爾：如果傑克再一直惹麻煩，會丟了工作的。

琳達：是啊，我們最好和他談談。

原來是這個意思！

get into hot water 惹麻煩

　　get into hot water是一個非常古老的慣用語，源自於早期的日常生活，當時的熱水可不像現代這麼方便，能隨意調整溫度，而是煮出來的滾燙開水，被潑到或掉進去就很嚴重，因此後來便藉hot water比喻麻煩、困境。

對話練習 *Let's Talk!*

Anna: Do you want to join the welfare committee?

Roy: No. I don't want to **get into hot water**.

Anna: What do you mean by that?

Roy: Why would I want extra work and to fight against the company?

Anna: Okay. I'll tell our boss that you have rejected his recommendation.

安娜：你想加入福利委員會嗎？

羅伊：不會，我不想惹麻煩。

安娜：什麼意思？

羅伊：我為什麼會想要攬下跟公司對抗的工作呢？

安娜：好吧，那我只好告訴老闆，你拒絕他的推薦了。

字彙/片語充電區 *Words and Phrases*

imminent 形 逼近的 / quandary 名 困惑 / bother 動 煩擾；打擾 / hinder 動 阻礙
in a pickle 處境艱難 / a hot potato 難對付的人(或事物) / a hard nut to crack 難題

UNIT 175　rapid-fire
快速蔓延的火苗？

🎧 175

暖身猜猜看 *Warming Up*

Will: Did you talk to the manager about your holidays?

Karen: Well, her **rapid-fire** talk gave me no chance to mention it.

威爾：你跟經理談了你的休假了嗎？

凱倫：她講話像連珠炮似地不間斷，我根本沒機會開口。

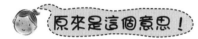

原來是這個意思！

rapid-fire 一連串的

　　在軍事用語中，rapid fire是指快慢交替、連續發射的小型武器，當這種武器的意思衍生至生活用語時，即代表「連續的、一連串的」之意；若用來形容談話，則指人說話不間斷，一句接著一句（連珠炮）。

對話練習　*Let's Talk!*

Kent: Oh God! The press conference was a disaster.

Nina: What? How come?

Kent: Well, I was drowned out by the journalists' **rapid-fire** questions.

Nina: But you did introduce our new product, didn't you?

Kent: Yeah, as best I could. I hope they got the point.

肯特：天啊！記者會真是一場災難。

妮娜：什麼？怎麼會？

肯特：我完全被記者連珠炮似的提問給淹沒了。

妮娜：但你有介紹我們的新產品吧？

肯特：是有盡我所能地介紹，希望他們有抓到重點。

字彙／片語充電區 *Words and Phrases*

succession 名 連續／**interrupt** 動 打斷／**brisk** 形 活潑的／**nimble** 形 機智的
run the show 掌控；稱霸／**make a point of** 強調／**quick as a wink** 一閃即逝

UNIT 176
shake a leg
抖腿的壞習慣？

🎧 176

暖身猜猜看 *Warming Up*

Joey: Hello? I am sorry. I am on my way to the theater now.

Vicky: You'd better **shake a leg** or we'll miss the first act.

喬伊：喂？抱歉，我在趕去戲院的路上了。

薇琪：你最好快點，不然我們會錯過第一幕。

原來是這個意思！

shake a leg 趕快；跳舞

　　shake a leg可不是抖腿的意思，根據十九世紀中葉的紀錄，這個慣用語指的是跳舞，這當然是因為跳舞時，腿部會隨著音樂舞動的關係；直到1904年，《紐約雜誌》將這個慣用語解釋為「趕快」，才衍生出不同的意思。

對話練習 *Let's Talk!*

Cindy: Do you want to go to a bar tomorrow?

Luke: Sure! Let's ask Daniel, too.

Cindy: Great idea! He loves music so much.

Luke: I know. It's time for him to **shake a leg**.

Cindy: He just can't help it whenever there is music.

辛蒂：你明天要不要去酒吧？

路克：當然好！我們找丹尼爾一起去吧。

辛蒂：好主意！他超愛音樂。

路克：我知道，他又有機會舞動一番了。

辛蒂：只要有音樂，他就無法抗拒。

字彙／片語充電區 *Words and Phrases*

rhythmic 形 有節奏的 / **recreation** 名 娛樂 / **joyful** 形 高興的 / **ballet** 名 芭蕾
have a leg to stand on 證明；有支持的論點 / **give sb. a leg up** 幫某人度過難關

Part **2**

這些講法，原來應該這樣說！
～中式英文狂NG？英文其實要這樣說。

常聽別人說「中文說法沒有完全對應的英文」？

所以，你也和其他人一樣，放棄中文的生動用語嗎？

其實，這些詞彙不是沒有，只是從來沒人教給你。

「頭腦簡單，四肢發達」有得說，

「舌燦蓮花」的口才用簡單字就能表達，

「拼命三郎」的人格特質老外也聽得懂，

不想再講饒口英文，或深受中式英語荼毒的你，

千萬不要錯過本章內容，中文也能用英文簡單說！

 學習POINT！

> 甩開中式英文，將妙趣橫生的中文轉為活潑生動
> 的英文，展現讓老外大吃一驚的英文實力！

UNIT 177　一個「喜怒形於色」的人，就是很會給人color瞧？

🎧 177

 暖身猜猜看 *Warming Up*

情境：你和朋友在討論某位同事喜怒形於色，這時應該怎麼說？

(　) Bill is one of those guys who wears his heart on his _____.

　　(A) shoulder　　　　(B) face　　　　(C) sleeve

正確解答：(C) 比爾是個會把感受表現在臉上的人。

 原來應該這樣說！

wear one's heart on one's sleeve 喜怒形於色

　　從字面上來看，這個慣用語是指將心穿在袖子上，也就是將心思顯露在外的意思。早期的西方社會有個習俗，會將女性的緞帶別在愛人的袖子上，所以產生這樣的說法，wear可以用have或pin取代。

 對話練習　*Let's Talk!*

Allen: If you need Jerry's help, ask him now. He's in a good mood.

Betsy: How can you tell?

Allen: It's easy. He **wears his heart on his sleeve**.

Betsy: So it's easy to get along with him, right?

Allen: I wouldn't say so. He has an unpredictable temper.

亞倫：如果你想找傑瑞幫忙，現在快去，他心情很好。

貝西：你怎麼知道？

亞倫：很容易啊，他的表情都寫在臉上。

貝西：那他應該很好相處吧？

亞倫：我不會說他是個好相處的人，他的脾氣說變就變。

字彙／片語充電區 *Words and Phrases*

manifest 形 顯然的 / obscure 形 含糊不清的；朦朧的 / sentiment 名 心情；情緒
written all over one's face 心思全寫在某人的臉上 / an open book 毫無隱瞞的人

UNIT 178 「頭腦簡單，四肢發達」，可以說without brain？

🎧 178

 暖身猜猜看 Warming Up

情境：你想強調某運動員不僅會打球，頭腦也好，這時應該怎麼說？

( ) That athlete is not just all _____ and no brains.

  (A) brawn   (B) power   (C) limbs

正確解答：(A) 那名運動員不僅球打得好，頭腦也好。

 原來應該這樣說！

all brawn and no brains 頭腦簡單，四肢發達

  理解這個慣用語的關鍵在brawn這個字，意思是「發達的肌肉」或「力氣」，這個字和brain只差一個字母，所以很容易記憶；英文俚語中常出現這樣的情形，用兩個字形很像但意思完全不同的單字來對比。

 對話練習 *Let's Talk!*

Emily: The game was awesome! I'm in love with Johnson.	艾蜜莉：比賽真精彩！我愛上強森了。
Carl: But I think he is **all brawn and no brains**.	卡　爾：但我覺得他是個頭腦簡單，四肢發達的人。
Emily: Is that right? Who do you like then?	艾蜜莉：是嗎？那你喜歡誰？
Carl: I like Matthew. He is really a great player, and he's intelligent, too.	卡　爾：我喜歡馬修，他真的是個很棒的球員，而且又聰明。
Emily: That's true. But I don't really appreciate his cockiness.	艾蜜莉：是沒錯，但我不喜歡他的自大。

字彙/片語充電區 *Words and Phrases*

muscular 形 肌肉發達的 / **macho** 名 強壯的男子 / **brainpower** 名 腦力
be slow on uptake 不聰明；理解力很差 / **a bright spark** 聰明又熱情的人

UNIT 179　說人「鐵石心腸」，就用rock比喻？

🎧 179

 暖身猜猜看 Warming Up

情境：你認為某人心腸很硬，不會參加公益活動，這時應該怎麼說？

(　　) I don't think he would join us. He's just as hard as _____.

　　(A) walls　　　　　(B) nails　　　　(C) nuts

正確解答：(B) 我覺得他不會參加，他是個鐵石心腸的傢伙。

 原來應該這樣說！

as hard as nails 鐵石心腸

　　這個由來已久的慣用語起初是用flint stone（打火石），後來因為打火石愈來愈少見，而且有很多東西都比它硬，所以就逐漸被改成as hard as nails。hard有時指難以改變的，有時指困難的，有時指冷酷的，使用時要特別注意。

 **對話練習 Let's Talk!**

Wendy: Tony, come and help me move the wardrobe.

Tony: I can't. I have to study now.

Wendy: Come on, just five minutes. I can't move it myself.

Tony: Yes, you can. Just try harder.

Wendy: You're really **as hard as nails**. I could hurt my back!

Tony: All right. I'm coming now.

溫蒂：東尼，來幫我搬衣櫃。

東尼：不行，我要唸書。

溫蒂：來啦，五分鐘就好，我自己搬不動。

東尼：你可以的，用力一點就行了。

溫蒂：你很無情耶，我可能會傷到背部的！

東尼：好啦，我現在就過去。

字彙／片語充電區 Words and Phrases

hard-boiled 形 強硬的 / indifferent 形 漠不關心的 / compassionate 動 同情
a cold fish 冷漠無情的人 / couldn't care less 毫不關心 / be all heart 仁慈慷慨的

UNIT
180

「貪多嚼不爛」，與digest有關？

🎧 180

暖身猜猜看 Warming Up

情境：朋友兼職過多，把自己累壞了，你想勸他，這時應該怎麼說？

(　　) You shouldn't bite off more than you can _____.

　　(A) chew　　　　(B) choose　　　　(C) eat

正確解答：(A) 你不應該忙這麼多事。

原來應該這樣說！

bite off more than sb. can chew 貪多嚼不爛

　　吃東西的時候如果咬得太大口，嘴巴滿到嚼不動，最後也是得吐出來一些，所以這個慣用語用來形容「接太多工作或做太多事，多到自己無法承受」；要注意bite off才有咬掉、咬下來的意思，bite只是咬。

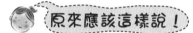

Allen: Have you seen Grace this morning?

Amy: Actually, she called in sick today.

Allen: It's not because of her part-time jobs, is it?

Amy: I'm afraid so. She **bites off more than she can chew**.

Allen: I can't blame her. She's in financial difficulty now.

亞倫：你今天早上看到葛瑞絲了嗎？

艾咪：其實呢，她今天請病假。

亞倫：該不會是因為她的兼差吧？

艾咪：恐怕是，她工作過度，貪多嚼不爛囉。

亞倫：這也不能怪她，她有經濟困難。

字彙／片語充電區 Words and Phrases

overdo 動 使過勞 / wade 動 費力做完 / extreme 名 極限 / capable 形 有能力的
keep one's nose to the grindstone 埋頭苦幹 / be engaged in 努力從事於⋯

UNIT 181 覺得某人「本性難移」，說won't change就足夠？

🎧 181

 暖身猜猜看 Warming Up

情境：你的個性急躁，但你自覺改不了，這時應該怎麼說？

(   ) I know I should slow down, but a leopard can't change its _____.

　　(A) steps 　　　　　 (B) spots 　　　　 (C) shape

正確解答：(B) 我知道我應該放慢速度，可是江山易改，本性難移。

 原來應該這樣說！

a leopard can't change its spots 本性難移

　　美洲豹一身的斑紋是牠最顯眼也無法改變的特徵，所以這個慣用語是用來表示一個人固有的特色、個性或習慣無法輕易改變，特別是指不好的事物。如果要用簡單一點的說法，可以說"This is who I am."

 對話練習 Let's Talk!

Helen: You look tired. Did you stay up late again?

Dylan: Uh...the book I've been reading is so exciting.

Helen: I guess **a leopard can't change its spots**.

Dylan: Come on. I am going to change.

Helen: Well, it's your life. Just don't indulge yourself too much.

海倫：你看起來很累，又熬夜了嗎？

狄倫：呃…我在讀的那本書實在太吸引人了。

海倫：我看你實在是本性難移。

狄倫：別這樣嘛，我一定會改的。

海倫：那是你的生活，總之不要太放縱自己。

字彙/片語充電區 Words and Phrases

stubborn 形 頑固的；倔強的 / entrenched 形 根深蒂固的 / pliable 形 能變通的
set in one's ways 積習難改 / turn over a new leaf 改頭換面 / turn into 使變成

UNIT 182　某人過於「自大無禮」，只想得到rude？

🎧 182

暖身猜猜看 *Warming Up*

情境：某同事太自以為是，惹人厭，這時應該怎麼說？

(　　) We all think Mark is too big for his ＿＿＿＿.

　　(A) feet　　　　　(B) boots　　　(C) head

正確解答：(B) 我們都認為馬克太自大了。

原來應該這樣說！

too big for one's boots 自大

　　這個慣用語當中的boots也可以用britches（馬褲）替換，都是用來比喻一個人過度自我膨脹，最後連靴子或馬褲都塞不下。要注意big用來表示抽象的意思時，除了可以當「浮誇」解釋，還有「心胸寬大」的意思。

對話練習 *Let's Talk!*

Roy: I think the new girl has a crush on me.

Tina: No, she doesn't. You're **too big for your boots**.

Roy: She told me I'm the most dependable guy she knows.

Tina: I think she just wants people to like her.

Roy: I don't believe you. I'm going to ask her out.

羅伊：我覺得那個新來的女生對我有意思。

蒂娜：才沒有哩，你太自大了。

羅伊：她跟我說，我是她見過最可靠的人。

蒂娜：我覺得她只是想要讓大家喜歡她而已。

羅伊：我才不信，我去約她。

字彙／片語充電區 *Words and Phrases*

arrogant 形 傲慢的 / cocky 形 太過自信的；驕傲的 / self-abased 形 自卑的
be puffed up 自負的 / on an ego trip 自吹自擂 / have a big heart 寬宏大量

UNIT 183 講人只會「虛張聲勢」，和boast的用法差不多？

🎧 183

 暖身猜猜看 *Warming Up*

情境：朋友自信滿滿地掛保證，卻是空頭支票，這時應該怎麼說？

(　　) It turned out that he is all _____ and no steak.

　　(A) sizzle　　　　　(B) smell　　　　　(C) spice

正確解答：(A) 結果他只是虛張聲勢而已。

 原來應該這樣說！

all sizzle and no steak 虛張聲勢

　　當你聽到鐵板嘶嘶作響，自然會期待吃到一客美味多汁的牛排，但如果牛排到頭來都沒出現，那可就令人失望了，這個慣用語就是在「形容人虛張聲勢，只會誇誇而談」；牛肉常用來比喻好處或利益，此處也有類似的意味。

 對話練習 *Let's Talk!*

Greg: Did you hear anything about the raise our boss promised us?

Ivy: Well, he made the same promise last year, too.

Greg: So he is **all sizzle and no steak**?

Ivy: For now, asking for a raise is pie in the sky.

Greg: That's a bummer. I was thinking about getting a new car.

葛瑞格：你有聽到任何有關老闆答應加薪的後續消息嗎？

艾　薇：其實，他去年也答應給我們加薪。

葛瑞格：所以他只是開空頭支票，說說而已？

艾　薇：就現在的情況來說，要求加薪不太可能。

葛瑞格：真沒意思，我原本還準備買輛新車呢。

字彙／片語充電區 *Words and Phrases*

bluff 動 虛張聲勢／boaster 名 自誇的人／grandiose 形 浮誇的／pledge 名 保證

all mouth and no trousers 光說不練／a man of his word 說到做到的人

UNIT 184

「廢話連篇」的人，
說的話太useless了？

🎧 184

暖身猜猜看 *Warming Up*

情境：某位友人對性別平等的言論簡直都在鬼扯，這時應該怎麼說？

(　　) Tom's thoughts about gender equality are so full of _____.

(A) hot trash　　　(B) hot words　　　(C) hot air

正確解答：(C) 湯姆對於性別平等的想法簡直是廢話連篇。

原來應該這樣說！

full of hot air 廢話連篇；空口說白話

　　這個源自美國的慣用語，最早開始使用的時候只有hot air，用來形容冗長的說話，有如一陣熱空氣，令人不悅又空泛不實際；演變到今天，可以將hot air用it代替，簡化成我們在電視中常聽到的full of it。

Vicky: Didn't Bill help you with the paper? I saw you two talking.	維琪：比爾沒有要幫你準備報告嗎？我看到你們在談話。
Adam: Don't mention it. He is so **full of hot air**.	亞當：別提了，他都在鬼扯。
Vicky: True. I can't help rolling my eyes whenever I talk to him.	維琪：這倒是，每次和他說話，我都忍不住翻白眼。
Adam: I wonder where he got his confidence from.	亞當：不知道他哪來的自信。
Vicky: It could be the Mustang he's driving.	維琪：可能是來自他開的那輛野馬跑車吧。

字彙／片語充電區 *Words and Phrases*

nonsense 名 胡言亂語 / absurd 形 荒謬的 / brag 動 吹噓 / blowhard 名 吹牛大王
a know-it-all 自以為什麼都知道的人 / be all hat and no cattle 浮誇而不實際

UNIT 185 叫人「有話直說」，就是straight一點？

🎧185

 暖身猜猜看 Warming Up

情境：你想和生氣的朋友解釋某人只是有話直說，這時應該怎麼說？

(　　) He didn't mean to offend. He's just a guy who calls a _____ a
_____.

  (A) grape   (B) square   (C) spade

正確解答：(C) 他不是故意要惹你不高興的，他只是有話直說。

 原來應該這樣說！

call a spade a spade 有話直說

  這個慣用語源自於古老的希臘，起初是用來形容一個人不懂得說話，演變到今天，意指有話直說。至於為什麼要用spade（鏟子）這個字呢？據說原始的用法不是這個字，但因為後來翻譯上的謬誤，才這麼延用下來。

 **對話練習** *Let's Talk!*

Kevin: What do you think about my article? Do you like it?

Irene: I think that's...not bad.

Kevin: It's OK. Just be honest with me.

Irene: OK. I think your message is too obscure for most readers.

Kevin: Hmm...Maybe I should just **call a spade a spade**.

凱文：你覺得我的文章寫得如何？你喜歡嗎？

艾琳：我覺得…還不錯。

凱文：沒關係，你就老實說吧

艾琳：好，我覺得你所傳達的訊息對大部分的讀者來說很模糊。

凱文：嗯…也許我應該有話直說才對。

字彙／片語充電區 *Words and Phrases*

candid 形 直言不諱的 / **guileless** 形 誠實的 / **embellish** 動 修飾 / **portray** 動 描繪
nail it down 講明白 / **be up-front** 直截了當的 / **beat about the bush** 拐彎抹角

UNIT 186 某人「舌燦蓮花」，就用lotus形容？

🎧 186

 暖身猜猜看 Warming Up

情境：你和朋友提起你遇到一個口才很好的推銷員，這時應該怎麼說？

( ) That salesman was so silver-_____ that I almost took out my wallet.

(A) tongued　　　(B) mouth　　　(C) teeth

正確解答：(A)那名銷售員的口才很好，我差點就要掏出錢包了。

 原來應該這樣說！

silver-tongued 口才很好；舌燦蓮花

　　silver在英文當中隱含「精煉出來的物質」，而silver-tongued就是藉此印象來形容一個人舌燦蓮花的特質，擅長表達和説服他人。類似此處「形容詞+名詞+-ed」的英文變化很常見，ex. broken-hearted（傷心的）。

 *Let's Talk!*

Nina: Did your dad agree to loan you money for a car?

Larry: No. I guess I'm not as **silver-tongued** as my sister.

Nina: So your sister got money from your dad?

Larry: He said she needs a car where she studies.

Nina: That makes sense. We can get around by subway.

妮娜：你爸爸答應借錢給你買車了嗎？

賴瑞：沒有，可能我的口才沒有我妹妹那麼好吧。

妮娜：所以你妹妹成功跟你爸爸拿到錢了？

賴瑞：他說我妹妹唸書的地方須要開車。

妮娜：有道理，我們可以搭地鐵趴趴走。

字彙/片語充電區 *Words and Phrases*

eloquent 形 有說服力的 / glib 形 善辯的 / slick 形 油嘴滑舌的 / convince 動 説服
bring around 使信服 / twist one's arm 強迫某人 / flowery language 花言巧語

UNIT 187 「告密者」與「抓耙子」，與tell或say有關係嗎？

🎧 187

暖身猜猜看 Warming Up

情境：有抓耙子向主管透漏事情，這時應該怎麼說？

( ) Some _____-blower told our manager about the problem.

　　(A) wind　　　　　(B) bubble　　　　(C) whistle

正確解答：(C) 有告密者向我們經理透漏這個問題。

原來應該這樣說！

whistle-blower 告密者；舉發人

　　whistle-blower指的是揭露不當或不法行為的人，這個字的使用範圍很廣，無論是在組織內部舉發，或是向警察檢舉、向新聞媒體揭發都可以適用，因此可以視情況翻譯成「抓耙子」或「爆料者」。

對話練習 Let's Talk!

Renee: You look so upset. What happened?

Mike: I believe Steve stole my idea.

Renee: Did you two talk about the idea before?

Mike: No. But I suspect that he peeped at my proposal.

Renee: If you want to be a **whistle-blower**, you need solid proof.

芮妮：你看起來情緒很差，怎麼了？

麥克：我覺得史提夫偷了我的點子。

芮妮：你們之前討論過你的點子嗎？

麥克：沒有，但我懷疑他偷看了我的企劃書。

芮妮：如果你想告發他，那就得有確切的證據。

字彙／片語充電區 Words and Phrases

canary 名 告密者 / disclose 動 揭發 / prosecute 動 檢舉 / accomplice 名 共犯
stool pigeon 線民 / break the news 爆料 / let the cat out of the bag 洩露秘密

UNIT 188 「面面俱到」的人，用nice足夠嗎？

🎧 188

暖身猜猜看 Warming Up

情境：你想提醒朋友，人無法面面俱到，這時應該怎麼說？

(　　) Your problem is that you're trying to be all things to all ＿＿＿.

    (A) parts　　　　　(B) people　　　(C) groups

正確解答：(B) 你的問題在於你想要面面俱到。

原來應該這樣說！

all things to all people 面面俱到

　　這個慣用語出自《新約聖經》的〈哥林多前書〉，用來表示滿足所有人的一切，即面面俱到之意，常用於否定句，因為在現實生活中，要面面俱到的確很難；people可以視情況換成其他複數名詞（ex. members）。

對話練習 Let's Talk!

Nick: You've been helping others the whole morning.

Maggie: And I forgot Mr. Lee's document! I wish I had a double.

Nick: You can't be **all things to all people**.

Maggie: Right. I'm afraid I have to cancel the lunch date with you.

Nick: That's not what I mean!

尼克：你整個早上都在幫忙其他人耶。

瑪姬：我忘了李經理的文件！真希望有個分身。

尼克：你沒辦法面面俱到的。

瑪姬：說的對，我看我得取消跟你的午餐約會了。

尼克：我不是那個意思！

字彙／片語充電區 Words and Phrases

ingratiate 動 迎合 / soft-hearted 形 心腸軟的 / fawn 動 巴結 / offend 動 得罪
smooth and slick 八面玲瓏 / Catch-22 (俚)兩難的局面 / fall foul of 冒犯；衝突

UNIT 189
說到「狀態良好」，就會提到condition？

🎧 189

暖身猜猜看 *Warming Up*

情境：你今天的狀態良好，這時可以怎麼說？

(　　) I had a good sleep last night and I'm totally on the ＿＿＿ now.

(A) call　　　　　(B) roll　　　　　(C) ball

正確解答：(C) 我昨晚睡得很好，現在狀態絕佳。

原來應該這樣說！

on the ball 機靈；狀態良好

這個慣用語的起源來自於運動用語，為keep your eyes on the ball的簡略說法。在球類比賽中，要時時留意球的位置和去向，才能反應；在日常生活中，這個說法可用來表示反應靈敏、很靈光的意思。

Let's Talk!

Fanny: Are you ready for the game?	芬妮：你準備好要比賽了嗎？
Eddy: Can I rest today? I'm not feeling **on the ball**.	艾迪：我今天可以休息嗎？我狀況不太好。
Fanny: Absolutely. Are you all right?	芬妮：當然可以，你還好吧？
Eddy: I don't think so. I've been under great stress lately.	艾迪：不太好，我最近壓力很大。
Fanny: You really need something to relax.	芬妮：你實在必須找個方法放鬆才行。
Eddy: Yeah. That's why I'm going home now.	艾迪：是啊，所以我現在要回家了。

字彙/片語充電區 *Words and Phrases*

vigorous 形 精力充沛的 / **reaction** 名 反應 / **blunt** 形 遲鈍的 / **beware** 動 留心
up to speed 表現佳 / **as sharp as a tack** 聰明敏捷的 / **know one's stuff** 有能力

UNIT 190

「某人非常珍愛的人」，
一定會與love有關？

🎧 190

 暖身猜猜看 *Warming Up*

情境：你的表弟是祖母最疼愛的孫子，這時應該怎麼說？

(　　) Victor is indeed the _____ of my grandmother's eye.

(A) pearl　　　　(B) peach　　　(C) apple

正確解答：(C) 維克多真是祖母最疼愛的人。

 原來應該這樣說！

apple of one's eye 某人非常珍愛的人

　　apple of one's eye是個相當古老的慣用語，在莎士比亞的作品和《聖經》都出現過，用來指某人相當珍視的人或物，但以指人的情況較多，而且這個慣用語通常帶有比較的意味，也就是「在某一群人當中最受喜愛的」。

 *Let's Talk!*

Roger: Boy, that girl sure is the **apple of your eye**.

Peter: Look at her smile. I think I'm totally captivated.

Roger: I've never seen you like this. Maybe she's the one.

Peter: What about you?

Roger: All I know is my apple is waiting for me at home, and I've got to go.

羅傑：哇，看來你真的特別喜歡那個女孩。

彼德：看看她的笑容，我覺得我被她征服了。

羅傑：我從來沒看你這樣過，搞不好她就是你的真命天女喔。

彼德：那你怎麼樣？

羅傑：我只知道我的寶貝現在在家等我，我得走了。

字彙/片語充電區 *Words and Phrases*

preference 名 偏好 / **partial** 形 偏愛的 / **favoritism** 名 偏袒 / **value** 動 重視
dote on 溺愛 / **Beauty is in the eye of the beholder.** 情人眼裡出西施。

UNIT 191 稱讚人有「吸引人的特質」，只懂personality？

🎧 191

 暖身猜猜看 Warming Up

情境：班上的新同學很有魅力，這時應該怎麼說？

（　　）Jessica has such ＿＿＿ ways that even I adore her.

　　(A) catching　　　　(B) winning　　　　(C) loving

正確解答：(B) 潔西卡真的很有魅力，連我都喜歡她。

 原來應該這樣說！

winning ways 吸引人的特質；魅力

　　如果你有魅力、能言善道，而且可以不費吹灰之力就讓大家喜歡你，那基本上你就算得上是人生勝利組，而這些為人所喜愛的特質，就可以用winning ways來表示，指吸引人的魅力所在。

 **對話練習 Let's Talk!**

Esther: How long have you been working for your company?

Teresa: Let me see. I'm in my 4th year.

Esther: Will you get a promotion in the near future?

Teresa: I'm not sure. Maybe I'm not that experienced.

Esther: I think what you need is to develop your **winning ways**.

艾絲特：你在你的公司工作多久了？

泰瑞莎：我想想看，今年是我在公司的第四年了。

艾絲特：你在不久的未來會升職嗎？

泰瑞莎：我不確定，也許我的經驗還不足夠。

艾絲特：我覺得你需要的是培養你的吸引力。

字彙／片語充電區 Words and Phrases

charisma 名 領袖氣質；魅力 / magnetize 動 吸引 / idolize 動 把…當偶像崇拜
drawing power 吸引力 / have a fascination for 使著迷 / hard to resist 難拒絕

UNIT 192

講人個性「正直」，就說a straight man？

🎧 192

暖身猜猜看 *Warming Up*

情境：某人很正直，不會對女朋友不忠，這時應該怎麼說？

( ) Carl is a straight _____. He would never cheat on you.

    (A) arrow   (B) road   (C) string

正確解答：(A) 卡爾是個正直的人，他不會背著你亂來。

原來應該這樣說！

straight arrow 正直的人

    一支箭要做得直，射出去的箭也得直直地飛，才能射中目標，所以straight arrow用來比喻一個人的個性正直，行事作風直來直往，也可以用來形容一個人生活嚴謹，無不良嗜好（菸酒不沾、不縱情聲色等）。

對話練習 *Let's Talk!*

Tracy: Should I ask Josh to my party?

Steven: Are you serving beer and liquor at your party?

Tracy: Are you kidding? What kind of party doesn't serve those?

Steven: If so, I don't think a **straight arrow** like him would go.

Tracy: Okay. Maybe I can brew some tea for him.

崔　西：我該不該邀請賈許來我的派對啊？

史蒂芬：你的派對裡會提供啤酒和烈酒嗎？

崔　西：開什麼玩笑？沒有酒還能叫派對嗎？

史蒂芬：那他那種正派的人應該就不會去。

崔　西：好吧，也許我可以為他泡點茶。

字彙／片語充電區 *Words and Phrases*

upright 形 正直的 / moral 名 道德 / crooked 形 不正派的 / decadent 形 頹廢的
a square shooter 老實人 / flat out 坦率地 / by hook or by crook 不擇手段地

UNIT 193 想叫人「別掃興」，真與掃把broom有關？

🎧 193

 暖身猜猜看 Warming Up

情境：在KTV唱得正高興，朋友卻談起公事，這時可以怎麼說？

(　　) Come on! We're here to have fun. Don't be a _____ kill.

(A) fizz　　　　　(B) buzz　　　　　(C) sizzle

正確解答：(B) 拜託！我們是來玩的，別掃興。

 原來應該這樣說！

buzz kill 掃興的人

　　buzz是指談話的嘈雜聲，也可以指愉悅、興奮感，而扼殺這種感覺的人就是掃興的人。動詞kill因為本身也可以當名詞，所以後面加不加-er的說法都有。buzz kill也可以寫成buzzkill/buzz killer/buzzkiller。

 **對話練習** Let's Talk!

Brian: Have you finished your report?

Carol: I stayed up and got it done. I can finally go on my trip.

Brian: Good for you. I'm going to have some fun tonight.

Carol: But I heard that your team has to work overtime today.

Brian: No! I forgot! Thanks for being a **buzz kill**!

布萊恩：你的報告完成了嗎？

卡　蘿：我熬夜做完了，終於可以去度假了。

布萊恩：有你的，我今晚要去好好放鬆一下。

卡　蘿：可是我聽說你的團隊今天要加班。

布萊恩：糟糕！我忘了！謝謝喔，你這個掃興鬼！

字彙/片語充電區 *Words and Phrases*

dampener 名 掃興的人或事物 / **bummer** 名 令人不愉快的事物 / **spoil** 動 搞糟

throw a wet blanket 潑冷水 / **put a damper on** 掃興 / **liven up** 助興；活躍

UNIT 194 「為人順從」的羔羊，用lamb形容最精確？

🎧 194

暖身猜猜看 Warming Up

情境：想勸人別老順從、被佔便宜，這時應該怎麼說？

(　　) Don't be a ＿＿＿＿. You're not their servant.

    (A) pullover　　　　(B) pushover　　　(C) pushup

正確解答：(B) 別當濫好人，你不是他們的僕人。

原來應該這樣說！

pushover 順從的人；容易打敗的人

　　pushover是指很好說話，很容易放棄立場，也因此容易被佔便宜的人。要注意這是一個字，不可分開來寫成push over（推倒），意思不同。這個慣用語也可以用來比喻很容易完成或獲得的事物。

對話練習 *Let's Talk!*

Anna: Bill said that I should wear more yellow.

Chad: Did you know that he said you're a **pushover**?

Anna: That's not true. I say no to him sometimes.

Chad: Yeah? When was the last time you did that?

Anna: When he asked me if he needed to give back the five dollars I lent him.

安娜：比爾說我應該多穿黃色的衣服。

查德：你知道他說你很好欺負嗎？

安娜：我才沒有，我有時候也會對他說不。

查德：是嗎？你上次拒絕他是什麼時候？

安娜：是他問我需不需要把借給他的五元還我的時候。

字彙/片語充電區 *Words and Phrases*

submissive 形 順從的 / **breeze** 名 輕而易舉的事 / **headstrong** 形 固執的；任性的
duck soup 小事一樁 / **easy pickings** 易說服的人 / **an opinion-maker** 有主見的人

UNIT
195

「無視常規的人」，
會和rule有關嗎？

🎧 195

暖身猜猜看 *Warming Up*

情境：同事這陣子行為老是脫序，這時可以怎麼提醒他？

( ) You are a loose _____. You're going to get into trouble!

    (A) boat   (B) cannon   (C) knot

正確解答：(B) 你的行為老是脫軌，會惹上麻煩的！

原來應該這樣說！

a loose cannon 無視常規、無責任感的人

　　這個慣用語從字面來看是「鬆掉的大砲」，古代的戰船上都會裝載大砲做為武器，而且要牢牢地綁在船身上，如果大砲鬆掉，在船上亂滑動的話，就會是件很危險的事；藉此來形容一個不可信賴、無責任感，且會帶來麻煩的人。

對話練習 *Let's Talk!*

Leon: This paper is good work. Sean really put his mind to it.

Peggy: Can you believe he was **a loose cannon** a year ago?

Leon: Really? I wonder what changed him.

Peggy: I think the credit goes to his girlfriend.

Leon: Ah, the power of love. Isn't that lovely?

里昂：這份報告寫得真好，西恩真的很用心。

佩姬：你能相信一年前他還像個不定時炸彈嗎？

里昂：真的嗎？不知道是什麼改變了他。

佩姬：我想這是他女朋友的功勞。

里昂：啊，愛情的力量，真好。

字彙/片語充電區 *Words and Phrases*

inattentive 形 漫不經心的 / **sensible** 形 明智的 / **troublemaker** 名 惹麻煩的人
be absent-minded 恍神 / **put oneself together** 振作 / **sharp as a needle** 敏銳的

UNIT 196 形容一個人像「拼命三郎」，是什麼樣的person？

🎧 196

暖身猜猜看 *Warming Up*

情境：為了存錢，朋友像個拼命三郎般工作，這時應該怎麼說？

(　　) You work really hard. You are such an eager _____.

　　(A) boar　　　　　(B) bear　　　　　(C) beaver

正確解答：(C) 你真的很認真工作，真是個拼命三郎。

原來應該這樣說！

an eager beaver 勤於工作的人；拼命三郎

　　beaver是河狸，牠們會花很多時間用牙齒啃斷樹枝，蒐集材料，並在水上築巢，給人忙碌的感覺，所以人們就用牠來比喻很忙碌的人，再加上押韻的形容詞eager，就形成了這個慣用語，用來形容對工作很認真的人。

Oliver: Hi, how are you feeling now?

Peggy: I feel a lot better. I was just too tired.

Oliver: Being too much of **an eager beaver** is not so good.

Peggy: I know. I'll come up with something to balance my life.

Oliver: That would be better for you.

奧利佛：嗨，你現在覺得如何？

佩　姬：我覺得好多了，我只是太累了。

奧利佛：對工作過度投入可不太好。

佩　姬：我知道，我會想辦法找些能調劑生活的事情做。

奧利佛：那對你來說會比較好。

字彙／片語充電區 *Words and Phrases*

workaholic 名 工作狂 / go-getter 名 幹勁十足的人 / lethargic 形 懶洋洋的
ball of fire 企圖心旺盛的人 / a live wire 生龍活虎的人 / bent on 有…的決心

UNIT 197 「入不敷出」的生活，就用without money？

🎧 197

暖身猜猜看 Warming Up

情境：室友常常入不敷出，你想勸他，這時應該怎麼說？

(　　) You have to try to spend less and stop living _____ your means.

(A) on　　　　　　(B) beyond　　　　　　(C) over

正確解答：(B) 你要試著少花一點，別再入不敷出了。

原來應該這樣說！

live beyond one's means 入不敷出

　　這個慣用語的重點是要用beyond來表示「超出」，用means表示「收入或財產」，注意means不是複數形，前面可以加所有格表示某人的收入或財產；生活方式超過擁有的財產，表示一個人花的比賺的多，即入不敷出。

Let's Talk!

Kate: Is that a new laptop? I thought your budget is pretty tight.

Jack: My old one was stolen. I had no choice but to buy a new one.

Kate: Where did you get the money?

Jack: I emptied my savings account.

Kate: I guess you don't mind **living beyond your means**.

凱特：那是新筆電嗎？我以為你手頭很緊。

傑克：我的舊筆電被偷了，只好買台新的。

凱特：你哪來的錢？

傑克：我用光了戶頭裡的積蓄。

凱特：我想你並不介意過入不敷出的日子吧。

字彙/片語充電區 Words and Phrases

overdraw 動 透支 / deplete 動 用盡 / lavish 動 揮霍；浪費 / well-off 形 富裕的
be in debt 欠債 / make ends meet 收支平衡 / tighten one's belt 縮衣節食

UNIT 198 某人「大禍臨頭」, 會提到trouble？

🎧 198

 暖身猜猜看 Warming Up

情境：對於大禍臨頭、肯定要下台的政府官員，可以怎麼說？

(　　) I think now that politician is a dead man _____. We'll see.

    (A) dying   (B) rising   (C) walking

正確解答：(C) 我覺得那名政客大禍臨頭了，等著看吧。

 原來應該這樣說！

dead man walking 大禍臨頭的人

    這個慣用語表面上好像在說殭屍，其實此處的dead man是指遭逢災難的人，walking則用來形容dead man，表示雖然這個人還能走路，但實際上已經形同死人，所以是「大禍臨頭」的意思。

 *Let's Talk!*

Harry: Do you know that Mr. Lee is going to fire Jack?

Sara: Are you sure about that?

Harry: Definitely. He is a **dead man walking** now.

Sara: But he's been doing pretty well at work.

Harry: Until yesterday. We lost an important client because of him.

哈利：你知道李經理要辭掉傑克嗎？

莎拉：你確定嗎？

哈利：百分之百確定，他要大禍臨頭了。

莎拉：但是，他的工作表現一直都相當不錯。

哈利：昨天之前是都不錯，但他昨天讓我們損失了一名重要的客戶。

字彙／片語充電區 *Words and Phrases*

catastrophe 名 災難；不幸 / doomed 形 注定失敗的 / control 動 支配；管理
as dead as a dodo 沒救 / make amends for 贖罪 / walk on eggshells 戰戰兢兢

UNIT 199 說人「走下坡」，會用walk down？

🎧 199

暖身猜猜看 Warming Up

情境：某位選手的表現每況愈下，這時應該怎麼說？

(　　) I think that player is _____ the hill now.

    (A) over　　　　　(B) past　　　　(C) down

正確解答：(A) 我覺得那名選手開始走下坡了。

原來應該這樣說！

over the hill 走下坡

    over the hill是指人到了一個年紀，體力各方面都不如以往，就像爬到了山頂之後，剩下的都是下坡路，也可以用來指過時的東西；要注意hill不能改用mountain，go over the mountain為克服困難和挑戰的意思。

Let's Talk!

Anna: Why do you want to borrow my laptop?

Todd: I guess mine is just old. It's **over the hill** now.

Anna: Or you saw something newer and faster.

Todd: Ha, you read my mind! I'm saving up for it.

Anna: You're such a technomaniac.

安娜：你怎麼會想要和我借筆記型電腦？

陶德：我覺得我的那台已經太老舊，它已經開始走下坡了。

安娜：我看是你發現更新更快的玩意兒了吧。

陶德：哈，你真了解我！我正在存錢準備買下它。

安娜：你真是個科技狂。

字彙／片語充電區 Words and Phrases

decline 動 衰退 / senescent 形 衰老的 / summit 名 顛峰 / surpass 動 超過
past one's prime 過了顛峰期 / stage a comeback 東山再起 / make a mess 出錯

UNIT 200 踩到他人的「痛腳」，會是什麼樣的feet？

🎧 200

 暖身猜猜看 *Warming Up*

情境：你的缺點是生氣時會失控，這時可以怎麼說？

(　　) I lose control when I get angry. That's my feet of _____.

　　(A) cement　　　　　(B) clay　　　　(C) wood

正確解答：(B) 我生氣的時候會失控，這是我的弱點。

 原來應該這樣說！

feet of clay 痛腳

　　feet of clay是指不為人知的弱點或缺點，典故出自《聖經》。當一座雕像的全身都由金、銀和鐵鑄成，但腳卻是黏土，這裡當然就是全身最脆弱的地方；可以寫成clay feet，但還是以此處的feet of clay較為常見。

 *Let's Talk!*

Sara: Hey, are you listening to me? I'm talking to you!

Robert: I'm so sorry. I think I was distracted.

Sara: What distracted you? There's no one else here.

Robert: That's my **feet of clay**. I can't focus for too long.

Sara: You can train yourself. If possible, do one thing at a time.

莎　拉：嘿，你有在聽嗎？我在跟你說話！

羅伯特：抱歉，我剛剛分心了。

莎　拉：有什麼好分心的？這裡又沒有別人。

羅伯特：這是我的缺點，我無法專心太久。

莎　拉：你可以訓練自己，可以的話，一次只做一件事情。

字彙／片語充電區 *Words and Phrases*

vulnerable 形 有弱點的 / flaw 名 缺點 / spotless 形 無瑕疵的 / conceal 動 隱瞞
Achilles' heel 致命傷 / dig the dirt 揭人瘡疤 / have one's number 握有某人把柄

UNIT 201 常見的「笑柄」，和handle有關嗎？

🎧 201

暖身猜猜看 Warming Up

情境：朋友戴了一頂奇怪的帽子，你怕他被人取笑，這時應該怎麼說？

( ) You're going to become the laughing _____ of your class.
   (A) stock　　　　(B) thing　　　　(C) story

正確解答：(A) 你會成為班上的笑柄。

原來應該這樣說！

laughing stock 笑柄

　　stock在中世紀是用於刑罰的刑具（架住受刑人的頭與雙手），但這裡是指工具用來握持的那一端；一個成為笑柄的人，就是因為有他，事情才好笑，就像一個工具，要先握住把手，才能讓它起作用。

Let's Talk!

Chris: You look so upset. What in the world is going on?	克里斯：你看起來很心煩，到底怎麼了？
Amber: That phony girl in my class and I wore the same shirt today!	安　珀：班上那個很假的女生今天和我穿一樣的襯衫！
Chris: So what? Maybe it's a popular shirt.	克里斯：那又怎樣？也許那件襯衫很流行。
Amber: It means my taste is as bad as hers. I'm going to be a **laughing stock**.	安　珀：這表示我的品味跟她一樣差，我會成為大家的笑柄。
Chris: Relax. Maybe she's crying for the same reason now.	克里斯：放輕鬆，她或許也正為了同一件事在哭訴呢。

字彙／片語充電區 Words and Phrases

dupe 名 容易被愚弄的人 / tease 動 戲弄 / gullible 形 易受騙的 / humiliate 動 羞辱
a fall guy 容易受騙的人 / die laughing 笑死了 / make fun of 取笑；嘲弄

「毅然決定」的態度，用decide強度不足怎麼辦？

UNIT 202

🎧 202

暖身猜猜看 Warming Up

情境：一直拿不定主意的你，終於下定決心買車，這時應該怎麼說？

( ) I finally took the _____ and bought a car yesterday.

(A) plunge   (B) drop   (C) plan

正確解答：(A) 我昨天終於下定決心，買了一台車。

原來應該這樣說！

take the plunge 毅然決定做某事

    take the plunge指的是決定做某件很重要或很困難的事（特別是在經過一段長時間的思考之後），plunge（跳入）在此處為名詞；plunge當動詞的慣用語plunge in的意思則不同，通常指未經仔細思考而一時衝動去做某事。

Let's Talk!

Rachel: I have something big to share with you. I mean really big.

Henry: I was going to ask you. I saw the ring. So you...

Rachel: Yes! I **took the plunge** and decided to marry Terry.

Henry: Congratulations! I'm happy for you.

Rachel: Thank you. Finally, I'm going to start a family.

瑞秋：我有件大事要跟你分享，真的很重大的大事。

亨利：我正想問你，我看到戒指了，所以你…

瑞秋：沒錯！我下定決心要嫁給泰瑞了。

亨利：恭喜你！我真為你高興。

瑞秋：謝謝，我終於要建立自己的家庭了。

字彙/片語充電區 Words and Phrases

commence 動 著手 / undertake 動 進行 / resolute 形 毅然的 / decisive 形 果斷的
take upon oneself 開始 / set about 著手進行 / make a run at 試著達成某個目標

UNIT 203 「破釜沉舟」的決心， 是要break the boat嗎？

🎧 203

 暖身猜猜看 Warming Up

情境：鮑伯下了破釜沉舟的決心向安告白，這時應該怎麼說？

( ) Bob burned his _____ by telling Ann how he really feels about her.

    (A) cars   (B) roads   (C) bridges

正確解答：(C) 鮑伯下了破釜沉舟的決心，對安告白了。

 原來應該這樣說！

burn one's bridges 破釜沉舟；斷絕退路

    burn one's bridges的意思近似中文的破釜沉舟，但破釜沉舟有表示「決心」的意味，而burn one's bridges可單純表示「做了某件無法回頭或斷絕後路的事」；這個慣用語中的bridges若換成boats，則為英式用法。

 **對話練習** Let's Talk!

Allen: I quit my job. Now I can devote myself to my own business.

Donna: Wow, you officially **burned your bridges**.

Allen: If you don't give it your best shot, you don't deserve to succeed.

Donna: But I still think you need something to fall back on.

Allen: I'm sure I can come up with something when I need it.

亞倫：我辭職了，現在可以專心投入自己的事業了。

唐娜：哇，你還真是正式斷絕後路了。

亞倫：如果不盡全力，就沒資格成功。

唐娜：不過我還覺得你需要留個後路。

亞倫：我相信當我需要的時候，就能找到的。

字彙／片語充電區 Words and Phrases

resolution 名 決心／**boldness** 名 勇敢／**elastic** 形 有彈性的／**undo** 動 取消
kick down the ladder 斷絕後路／**go for broke** 孤注一擲／**iron will** 堅定的意志

UNIT 204 中文的「浴火重生」，就說reborn from the fire ?

🎧 204

 暖身猜猜看 *Warming Up*

情境：希望球隊今年能有「浴火重生」的表現，這時應該怎麼說？

( ) I hope we will rise from the _____ this year.

　　(A) flames　　　　　(B) fire　　　　(C) ashes

正確解答：(C) 希望我們今年能浴火重生。

 原來應該這樣說！

rise from the ashes 浴火重生

　　西方傳說中的鳳凰，在五百歲後會引火自焚，再從灰燼中重生。rise from the ashes就來自於這個傳說，用來比喻人或事物受到重創之後再度復出或重建，展現新的面貌；注意物體燃燒後的殘留物通常要用複數形的ashes。

 *Let's Talk!*

Lara: Your new bicycle looks awesome. I like the color.

Kenny: Actually, it's not brand-new. I had my old bicycle remodeled.

Lara: What? You turned that piece of junk into this?

Kenny: Yeah. I just don't have the heart to recycle it.

Lara: It indeed has **risen from the ashes**.

拉拉：你的新腳踏車看起來真棒，我喜歡它的顏色。

肯尼：其實它不是新的，我改裝了我的老腳踏車。

拉拉：什麼？你把那堆廢鐵變成這個？

肯尼：對啊，我實在不忍心把它拿去資源回收。

拉拉：它可真的是浴火重生了。

字彙 / 片語充電區 *Words and Phrases*

regenerate 動 重建 / comeback 名 重整旗鼓 / perish 動 消滅 / stumble 動 失足
raise from the dead 重生 / wipe out 摧毀 / screw up 一團糟 / tear down 拆除

UNIT 205 說到「冒險一試」，會提到risk這個字？

🎧 205

暖身猜猜看 Warming Up

情境：看著烏雲密佈的天氣，不帶雨傘實在很冒險，這時應該怎麼說？

( ) Don't _____ it. Take an umbrella with you.

    (A) cheat   (B) bet   (C) chance

正確解答：(C) 別冒險，帶把雨傘吧。

原來應該這樣說！

chance it 冒險一試

    chance當名詞的用法大家都很熟悉（意指機會），它當動詞時，意思則為冒險，後面接冒險的事，常見的用法是用代名詞it代替前面所提到的事，以避免語句冗長的情況，這個慣用語能夠加強說話者的語氣。

Dale: Are you still thinking about entering the singing contest?

Eve: I am. But I'm scared that I might make a fool of myself.

Dale: I say you should **chance it**. It could be a great experience.

Eve: Maybe you are right. I would hate myself if I held back.

Dale: Yeah. Practice as much as you can and give it your best shot.

戴爾：你還在考慮參加歌唱比賽的事嗎？

伊芙：是有在考慮，但我好怕出醜。

戴爾：我覺得你應該去試試，這會是個很棒的經驗。

伊芙：也許你說得對，如果我退縮了，我會恨我自己。

戴爾：沒錯，盡可能地多練習，拿出你最好的表現。

字彙／片語充電區 Words and Phrases

hazard 名 危險 / **daring** 形 敢於冒險的 / **boldness** 名 大膽 / **discreet** 形 謹慎的
tempt fate 冒險；涉險 / **at the risk of** 冒著危險 / **a sure bet** 肯定會發生的事

UNIT 206 「一頭栽進某事」，是因為focus得太專心？

🎧 206

暖身猜猜看 Warming Up

情境：你每天回家都迫不及待地翻閱一本書，這時應該怎麼說？

( ) The book is such a page-turner. I can't wait to ＿＿＿＿ into it every day.

(A) dive　　　　　　(B) see　　　　　　(C) plunge

正確解答：(A) 這本書真是引人入勝，我每天都等不及要讀它。

原來應該這樣說！

dive into 一頭栽進去

　　dive常見的意思是跳水或潛水，也有飛機向下俯衝的意思，兩者都有一股腦兒往一個方向前進的意象在，所以dive into在日常生活中可以用來表示很熱心地投入某事物或潛心鑽研某事物，也可以用dive in替換。

對話練習 Let's Talk!

Flora: I've been **diving into** cooking. I spend lots of time in my kitchen.

Glenn: That's wonderful. I used to cook a lot, too.

Flora: Why don't you come over this weekend? I'll make lunch for us.

Glenn: Sounds good. I can bring some nice wine.

Flora: Be prepared to be amazed by my specialty fried rice.

芙蘿拉：我最近在鑽研廚藝，在廚房花了不少時間。

葛　倫：那很好啊，我以前也經常下廚。

芙蘿拉：你這個週末到我家如何？我來準備午餐。

葛　倫：聽起來很棒，我可以帶瓶不錯的紅酒。

芙蘿拉：準備被我的特製炒飯嚇一跳吧。

字彙／片語充電區 Words and Phrases

avidly 副 熱心地 / **obsess** 動 著迷 / **fling** 動 熱心投入 / **listless** 形 無精打采的

buckle down 認真地埋首於 / **tear into** 充滿幹勁地投入 / **in low spirits** 沒精神

UNIT 207 「竭盡全力」的說法，和work hard差不多？

🎧 207

暖身猜猜看 Warming Up

情境：在朋友有困難的時候，你想盡全力幫他，這時應該怎麼說？

( ) I would bend over _____ to help you if you need me. Don't worry.

(A) leftwards (B) forwards (C) backwards

正確解答：(C) 如果你需要我，我會盡全力幫你，別擔心。

原來應該這樣說！

bend over backwards 竭盡全力

　　這個慣用語原本是指身體往後彎的動作，也就是下腰。因為下腰對許多人來說都是需要花很多力氣的事，所以便用這個慣用語表示「非常努力或竭盡心力」，特別是用在幫助、滿足或取悅他人的時候。

對話練習 Let's Talk!

Julia: I heard that your brother got the scholarship. Congratulations!

Kent: Thanks. My mom has been **bending over backwards** to support him.

Julia: He has been working very hard at school. He deserves it.

Kent: Well, he always tries his best not to let my mom down.

Julia: I wish my brother could be as thoughtful as yours.

茱莉亞：聽說你弟弟拿到獎學金了，恭喜！

肯　特：謝謝你，我媽一直都竭盡全力地在支持他。

茱莉亞：他在學業上一直都很認真，這是他應得的。

肯　特：嗯，他總是盡力不讓我媽失望。

茱莉亞：真希望我弟弟也可以像他一樣善解人意。

字彙／片語充電區 Words and Phrases

attempt 動 努力；嘗試 / endeavor 動 盡力 / hassle 名 困難 / hesitate 動 猶豫
go out of the way 煞費苦心 / break one's back 拼命工作 / lie down on 偷懶

UNIT 208　叫人「提起幹勁」，當然就是cheer up？

🎧 208

 暖身猜猜看 Warming Up

情境：你想督促朋友提起幹勁把報告完成，這時應該怎麼說？

(　　) If you want to meet the deadline, you'd better get _____.

　　(A) breaking　　　(B) cracking　　　(C) tracking

正確解答：(B) 如果你想趕上截止時間，最好提起幹勁完成。

 原來應該這樣說！

get cracking 提起幹勁開始做某事

　　get後面加動名詞有開始做某事的意思，而crack在此處是指發出霹啪的聲響，像鞭炮一樣，所以get cracking的意思就是「很有幹勁地開始做某事」；使用時也可以在get和cracking之間加一個名詞表示要做的事。

 *Let's Talk!*

Martin: Now I know the importance of a good sleep.

Laura: See? Staying up for days just affects your efficiency.

Martin: Yeah. My head hasn't been this clear for a long time.

Laura: Great. Now let me get you some nice breakfast.

Martin: Thanks. I think I'm totally ready to **get cracking**.

馬丁：我現在知道好好睡一覺的重要性了。

蘿拉：看吧，熬夜只會影響你的效率而已。

馬丁：是啊，我的頭腦好久沒這麼清楚了。

蘿拉：太好了，那我現在來幫你準備一頓豐盛的早餐。

馬丁：謝謝，我想我完全準備好要好好幹活了。

字彙/片語充電區 Words and Phrases

embark 動 從事 / vigor 名 活力 / willpower 名 意志力 / passive 形 消極的
kick off 開始 / get one's feet wet 動手做 / get steam up 振作 / cut it out 停止

UNIT 209 「休兵和解」的說法，只懂得勸人要peace？

🎧 209

 暖身猜猜看 Warming Up

情境：跟朋友吵完架後又冷戰，你希望能和好，這時應該怎麼說？

( ) I shouldn't have said that. Let's bury the _____, shall we?

  (A) hammer   (B) fight   (C) hatchet

正確解答：(C) 我不應該說那些話，我們休兵和解，好嗎？

 原來應該這樣說！

bury the hatchet 休兵和解

  根據北美原住民的傳統，當部落之間達成和平協議時，要將作戰用的短斧埋起來，作為停止戰爭的象徵，這就是bury the hatchet這個慣用語的起源，用來表示「和解」或「言歸於好」的意思。

 **對話練習** *Let's Talk!*

Ned: Peter sent me a nice message after our argument.

Mindy: How sweet! So you two **buried the hatchet**?

Ned: Yeah. Actually, there's so much we can talk about.

Mindy: Well, good for you. You saved yourself a friend.

Ned: No, he's the one with a big heart.

奈德：在爭吵過後，彼德傳了一封友善的簡訊給我。

明蒂：真貼心！所以你們和好了？

奈德：對啊，而且我發現，我們可以聊的東西很多。

明蒂：太好了，你替自己留住了一個朋友。

奈德：不，他才是那個比較寬宏大量的人。

字彙／片語充電區 Words and Phrases

apologize 動 道歉 / compromise 名 妥協 / appease 動 姑息 / instigate 動 慫恿
make peace 講和 / hold out the olive branch 釋出善意 / bear no malice 無惡意

UNIT 210　與人「合作」，最簡單生動的說法是？

🎧 210

暖身猜猜看 Warming Up

情境：你在電視上看到某部長拒絕合作，這個情境應該怎麼說？

(　　) It's surprising that the minister refused to play ＿＿＿＿.

　　(A) ball　　　　(B) together　　　　(C) the case

正確解答：(A) 那個部長竟然拒絕合作，真令人驚訝。

原來應該這樣說！

play ball 合作

　　play ball很明顯是來自運動用語。一場球賽需要多人合作才玩得起來，所以這個慣用語帶有「合作」的意思，也可表示「答應照他人的要求做某事」；另外，在棒球賽開始時，裁判會大喊"Play ball!"，用來表示「球賽開始」。

對話練習 Let's Talk!

Penny: God! Steve doesn't want to work on this project anymore.

Owen: I'm not surprised. He's not a guy you should **play ball** with.

Penny: I've learnt my lesson. But where can I find a new partner?

Owen: You can join my team if you want.

Penny: Thank you. You're a lifesaver!

潘妮：天啊！史提夫不想再做這個案子了。

歐文：不意外，你不應該跟他合作。

潘妮：我學到教訓了，可是我上哪兒去找新的夥伴啊？

歐文：如果你願意的話，可以加入我的小組。

潘妮：謝謝，你真是個救星！

字彙/片語充電區 Words and Phrases

collaborate 動 合作 / conspire 動 協力 / comply 動 遵從 / disregard 動 不理會
pull together 同心協力 / throw in with 入夥 / hook up with 與某組織或單位合作

UNIT 211 「密切合作」的關係，當然會提到close？

🎧 211

暖身猜猜看 *Warming Up*

情境：你和同事密切合作，談成了案子，這時應該怎麼說？

(　　) Peter and I worked hand in ＿＿＿＿ and we got the case.

(A) hand　　　　(B) pocket　　　　(C) glove

正確解答：(C) 彼德和我通力合作，談成了這個案子。

原來應該這樣說！

hand in glove 關係緊密；密切合作

　　就像手套戴在手上那麼密合，hand in glove若用來比喻人際關係，意指關係非常緊密；若用來比喻合作關係，則指相當密切的合作；要注意此慣用語中的手和手套都是單數型，也可以用hand and glove取代。

Let's Talk!

Vera: Your parents really have a good relationship.

Tim: Yeah. After forty years of marriage, they're still **hand in glove**.

Vera: That's amazing. What's the secret?

Tim: Well, they've always been best friends with each other.

Vera: I think they are what they call lifetime partners.

薇拉：你父母的關係真的很好。

提姆：是啊，他們都結婚四十年了，關係還是很親密。

薇拉：真令人驚奇，他們的祕訣是什麼？

提姆：他們一直以來都是彼此最好的朋友。

薇拉：我想這就是所謂的終身伴侶吧。

字彙／片語充電區 *Words and Phrases*

intimate 形 親密的 / jointly 副 共同地 / synergy 名 合力 / aloof 形 遠離的；冷漠的
on good terms with 與…關係良好 / side by side 相互支持 / on the beat 合拍

UNIT 212 「白忙一場」的辛勞，是gain nothing？

🎧 212

 暖身猜猜看 *Warming Up*

情境：朋友想說服父母買車給他，你認為不可能，這時可以怎麼說？

( ) Forget it. It's going to be a wild _____ chase.

    (A) horse   (B) goose   (C) dog

正確解答：(B) 算了吧，說了也是白說。

 原來應該這樣說！

wild goose chase 徒勞；無意義的追求

    這個慣用語最早出自莎翁名著《羅密歐與茱麗葉》，直到十九世紀才演變成「徒勞」之意。由於野雁很容易受到驚嚇，想要追逐的話，到頭來可能只能眼睜睜看著牠們飛走，所以wild goose chase就被用來形容「白忙一場」。

 *Let's Talk!*

Lynn: Here's my proposal for selling our new product to teenagers.

Ben: But it's designed for adults. I'm afraid you've been on a **wild goose chase**.

Lynn: Not necessarily. Over 10 percent of our buyers are under 18.

Ben: Why would they want to use it?

Lynn: It's probably because a lot of them can't wait to grow up.

琳：這是我的企劃，內容包含如何把新產品賣給青少年。

班：但那個產品是針對成年人設計的，可能會白忙一場。

琳：不見得，我們的購買者當中，有百分之十未滿十八歲。

班：他們怎麼會想要用這個產品呢？

琳：可能是因為他們等不及想長大吧。

字彙／片語充電區 *Words and Phrases*

vain 形 徒然的 / **pursue** 動 追求 / **outcome** 名 結果；結局 / **fruitful** 形 收穫豐富的
fool's errand 白費力氣的奔波 / **doom and gloom** 沒有希望 / **false trail** 錯誤方向

UNIT 213 「贏面最大的選擇」，是某種choice？

🎧 213

暖身猜猜看 Warming Up

情境：約會快遲到，搭計程車似乎是最好的選擇，這時應該怎麼說？

( ) We only have twenty minutes. I think taking a cab is our best

_____.

(A) chance　　　　(B) set　　　　(C) bet

正確解答：(C) 我們只有二十分鐘，我覺得搭計程車是最好的選擇。

原來應該這樣說！

best bet 贏面最大的選擇

　　bet源自賭博用語，指下注的對象，best bet從字面上來看是「最有可能贏的選擇」，引申為「最有可能達成目標的選擇」；best choice也有相同的意思，但用bet更能表現出做選擇時的不確定感。

Walter: We need one more member for our research team.	華特：我們的研究小組還得再找一個成員。
Dana: How about Alison? She has some connections.	黛娜：找艾莉森如何？她有一些人脈。
Walter: I just called her. She's on Frank's team now.	華特：我剛才打給她，她加入了法蘭克那一組。
Dana: We can try Bert. He's knowledgeable about the field.	黛娜：我們可以試試伯特，他很了解這個領域。
Walter: Yeah, I think he is our **best bet**. I don't know him well, though.	華特：對，我想他是我們最好的選擇了，但我和他不熟。

字彙／片語充電區 Words and Phrases

odds 名 機會 / **vantage** 名 優勢 / **contender** 名 角逐者 / **weigh** 動 權衡
the top horse 最好的選擇 / **an odds-on favorite** 勝算很大的人或事物

UNIT 214 看到某人「極力殺價」，可以說bargain a lot？

🎧 214

暖身猜猜看 *Warming Up*

情境：想稱讚某位客人真會殺價，這時應該怎麼說？

( ) One of your customers really _____ a hard bargain.

(A) drove (B) took (C) carried

正確解答：(A) 你其中一名顧客砍價砍得真兇。

原來應該這樣說！

drive a hard bargain 極力殺價

　　bargain當動詞指討價還價；名詞則有交易或買賣的意思；drive a hard bargain意指「買方盡力壓低價格，而賣方在仍有獲利的情況下同意成交」；如果只是一般的買賣，可用make a bargain描述。

對話練習 *Let's Talk!*

Chloe: Come take a look at my new car. What do you think?

Bobby: Wow! It must have cost you a fortune.

Chloe: I **drove a hard bargain** and saved myself 1,500 dollars.

Bobby: That's awesome! Maybe you can help me get a good price, too.

Chloe: Sure. Now hop in and let's go for a ride.

克蘿伊：來看看我的新車，你覺得如何？

鮑　比：哇！一定花了你不少錢。

克蘿伊：我殺價殺得可兇了，最後省了一千五百元。

鮑　比：太棒了！搞不好你也可以幫我要到好價錢。

克蘿伊：沒問題，上車吧！我們去兜風。

字彙/片語充電區 *Words and Phrases*

haggle 動 討價還價 / slash 動 削減 / closeout 名 清倉大拍賣 / profit 名 利潤
knock off 減價 / mark down 降價 / a good buy 划算交易 / invoice price 進貨價

UNIT 215 「欺騙」某人，與lie大同小異？

🎧 215

暖身猜猜看 Warming Up

情境：一位你很信任的朋友竟然欺騙了你，這時應該怎麼說？

( ) I trusted him with my heart, but he took me for a _____.

(A) treat　　　　(B) ride　　　　(C) trip

正確解答：(B) 我全心地信任他，但他卻騙了我。

原來應該這樣說！

take sb. for a ride 欺騙

　　試想，當你信任一個人，照著他的話去做，到頭來卻發現是他騙了你，感覺就好像他載著你兜了一圈，結果到了一個錯的地方，這就是take sb. for a ride的意思，這個慣用語其實也有殺人之意，但生活中還是較常用來表示欺騙。

對話練習 Let's Talk!

Fred: Harry said he can help me get a new laptop at a very low price.

Grace: Take my advice. Stay away from him.

Fred: Why? He showed me the picture. It's a pretty good laptop.

Grace: He once said the same thing to me, but he **took me for a ride**.

Fred: Thank God I haven't given him my money!

弗瑞德：哈利說他可以幫我用超低價買到新筆電。

葛瑞絲：聽我的，離他遠一點。

弗瑞德：為什麼？他給我看過照片，是一台很棒的筆電。

葛瑞絲：他曾經跟我說過同樣的事，結果他騙了我。

弗瑞德：幸好我還沒給他錢！

字彙／片語充電區 Words and Phrases

betray 動 背叛 / ungrateful 形 不領情的 / hoax 名 騙局 / trustworthy 形 能信賴的
double-cross 詐欺 / take to cleaners 騙光錢財 / lead on 慫恿 / reckon on 指望

UNIT 216

愛「刁難、找碴」的人，就是有很多problem？

🎧 216

暖身猜猜看 *Warming Up*

情境：你和朋友抱怨另一個同事老是刁難你，這時應該怎麼說？

(　　) James can always find something to give me a _____ time with.
　　(A) hard 　　　　　(B) bad 　　　　　(C) sad

正確解答：(A) 詹姆士永遠可以找事情刁難我。

原來應該這樣說！

give sb. a hard time 為難；責備

　　give sb. a hard time主要有兩個意思，第一個是為難、刁難；第二個是責備、嘲笑或開玩笑；當第二個意思使用時，後面可用about加上原因。注意time在這裡指的是一段時間，所以可數，記得要加上冠詞a。

對話練習 *Let's Talk!*

Gordon: I just can't stand the guy who was reassigned to my team!

Heather: You mean Joseph? What don't you like about him?

Gordon: It seems like he loves to **give me a hard time**.

Heather: Maybe it's not what you think. He's strict with himself, too.

Gordon: Alright. Maybe I'll give him a second chance.

戈登：我真受不了那個被重新分配到我小組的傢伙！

海瑟：你是說喬瑟夫嗎？他哪裡惹你不高興了？

戈登：他似乎喜歡刁難我。

海瑟：事情也許不是你想的那樣，他對自己也很嚴格。

戈登：好吧，也許我會再給他一次機會。

字彙／片語充電區 *Words and Phrases*

irritate 動 使難受；使煩躁 / **nag** 動 糾纏不休 / **heckle** 動 刁難 / **spite** 動 惡意對待
pick on 找碴 / **get on one's nerves** 使心煩 / **drive sb. up the wall** 使某人大怒

UNIT 217　提到「推卸責任」，肯定與responsibility有關？

🎧 217

暖身猜猜看 *Warming Up*

情境：看到一則市政府推卸責任的新聞，這時應該怎麼說？

(　　) It's obvious that the city government is trying to pass the _____.

(A) card　　　　　(B) pot　　　　　(C) buck

正確解答：(C) 市政府很明顯想推卸責任。

原來應該這樣說！

pass the buck 推卸責任

　　這個慣用語源自於撲克牌遊戲。為了防止作弊，遊戲的每一輪都要換人發牌，輪到發牌的人，會拿到一個識別物（稱為buck），所以pass the buck在牌桌上是指不擔任發牌的工作，引申為推卸責任。

對話練習 *Let's Talk!*

Karen: God! When is the last time you cleaned up the living room?

Jimmy: Don't look at me. I hardly use the living room.

Karen: So it's your roommate? He should clean up the mess.

Jimmy: I've told him that. But he always **passes the buck**.

Karen: If I were you, I would move out as soon as possible.

凱倫：天哪！你上次打掃客廳是什麼時候？

吉米：別看我，我幾乎沒在用客廳。

凱倫：所以是你室友弄的？他真該清理這些髒亂。

吉米：我和他說過了，但他總是推卸責任。

凱倫：如果我是你，我肯定會盡早搬走。

字彙／片語充電區 *Words and Phrases*

dodge 動 躲避；閃避／**shirk** 動 逃避義務或責任／**inequitable** 形 不公平的
cop out 放棄；逃避／**duck out of** 避免做某事／**take upon oneself** 承擔責任

UNIT 218 某人「不告而別」，leave接下來該說什麼？

🎧 218

暖身猜猜看 *Warming Up*

情境：參加舞會時，朋友沒跟任何人說就離開，這時應該怎麼說？

(　　) I saw John a few minutes ago. I think he took a _____ leave.

　　(A) French　　　　(B) British　　　　(C) Chinese

正確解答：(A) 我幾分鐘前看到約翰，我想他不告而別了。

原來應該這樣說！

take a French leave 不告而別

　　據說在十八世紀的法國，要從一個宴會或正式場合離開時，習慣上不用向邀請你來的人打招呼，所以take a French leave就被用來表示不告而別；這個慣用語也可以用來形容未經請假或通知就擅離職位的情況。

對話練習 *Let's Talk!*

Toby: Sam's briefcase is missing. I think he **took a French leave**.

Sharon: What? He said he would go to the party with us.

Toby: Maybe he has something more important to do.

Sharon: Or maybe he is just shy. I'm going to call him now.

Toby: Give him a break. Parties are not for everyone.

陶比：山姆的公事包不在，我猜他先走了。

莎朗：什麼？他說他會跟我們去參加派對的。

陶比：也許他有更重要的事要處理。

莎朗：也可能是他太害羞，我來打電話給他。

陶比：你放他一馬吧，不是每個人都愛參加派對。

字彙／片語充電區 *Words and Phrases*

sneak 動 偷偷地走 / truancy 名 曠課；逃學 / absence 名 缺席 / notify 動 告知
skip school 翹課 / out on duty 出勤；執行任務 / take a leave of absence 請假

UNIT 219 「慫恿」他人的說法，比想像中更簡單？

🎧 219

暖身猜猜看 *Warming Up*

情境：店員一直慫恿朋友買衣服，你想提醒他，這時應該怎麼說？

(　　) The clerk is just _____ you on. Don't fall for that.

　　(A) egging　　　　(B) cheesing　　　　(C) buttering

正確解答：(A) 那個店員只是在慫恿你，不要上當。

原來應該這樣說！

egg on 慫恿

　　蛋和慫恿有什麼關係？其實，egg在這裡不是指蛋，而是另一個字edge的變體。edge當動詞有將物體慢慢往某方向移動的意思，在此引申為引導或慫恿某人去做某事，特別是不當的事或壞事。

Ruby: Why did you lie to me and say you had to work last weekend?

Scott: Oh, God. I didn't want to, but Terry kept **egging** me **on**.

Ruby: So you'd rather lie than have dinner with my family.

Scott: I'm so sorry. I had a rough week. I really needed to relax.

Ruby: I would have understood if you had told me the truth.

露　比：你為什麼騙我說你上個週末要工作？

史考特：天啊，我也不想騙你，可是泰瑞一直慫恿我。

露　比：所以你寧願騙我，也不願意跟我的家人吃飯。

史考特：真的很抱歉，可是我上週很辛苦，我需要好好放鬆一下。

露　比：如果你跟我實話實說，我就會體諒的。

字彙／片語充電區 *Words and Phrases*

pander 動 慫恿 / abet 動 煽動；教唆 / dissuade 動 勸阻 / wrongdoing 名 做壞事
stir up 鼓動 / prevail upon 勸說 / whip up 激發；激勵 / talk out of 勸人勿做某事

UNIT 220 看到「起哄」的眾人，能說noisy嗎？

🎧 220

 暖身猜猜看 Warming Up

情境：想描述某位客人在店內大吵大鬧，這時應該怎麼說？

(　　) A man was kicking up a ＿＿＿＿ and yelling at the clerk.

　　(A) chaos　　　　(B) noise　　　　(C) fuss

正確解答：(C) 有一個人在製造騷亂，對店員大吼大叫。

 原來應該這樣說！

kick up a fuss 起哄；製造騷亂

　　kick up的意象相當生動，想像你往地面一踢，揚起一陣沙塵；fuss則表示驚慌或不安，所以kick up a fuss有「製造騷亂」或「吵吵嚷嚷」的意思。這個慣用語當中的fuss可用row（吵嚷）或storm（激動）替換，意思相同。

 Let's Talk!

Teresa: How's your steak? I don't really enjoy mine.

Frank: It's kind of overcooked. Thank God I have sharp teeth.

Teresa: This is not right. I'm going to call for the manager.

Frank: Okay. But just take it easy and try not to **kick up a fuss**.

Teresa: Don't worry. It's your birthday. I'm not going to ruin it.

泰瑞莎：你的牛排好吃嗎？我不太喜歡我的。

法蘭克：煮得有點太老了，還好我牙齒夠利。

泰瑞莎：這樣不對，我要請他們的經理過來。

法蘭克：好吧，不過你要心平氣和一點，別引起騷動。

泰瑞莎：別擔心，今天是你的生日，我不會搞砸。

字彙／片語充電區 Words and Phrases

nuisance 名 麻煩事 / gripe 動 抱怨；惹惱 / protest 動 抗議 / yield 動 屈服；投降
sound off 大發牢騷 / take exception to 表示不滿 / pat on the back 鼓勵；讚揚

UNIT 221　某人表現「失常」，會和unusual有關嗎？

🎧 221

 暖身猜猜看 *Warming Up*

情境：同事在會議上的發言與平常個性不符，這時可以怎麼說？

(　　) What Larry said at the meeting is quite out of ＿＿＿＿.

　　(A) soul　　　　(B) character　　　　(C) head

正確解答：(B) 賴瑞今天在會議上的發言跟他平常很不一樣。

 原來應該這樣說！

out of character 失常；言行與平日的個性不同

　　想把中文的失常翻成英文，很可能會因為把焦點放在「常」這個字，而使用normal和common等字；其實，所謂失常，就是「言行和某人的個性不符」，所以適合用out of character，out of在此可解釋成悖離。

 **對話練習** *Let's Talk!*

Will: Mr. Lee did a hilarious talk show. That was totally **out of character**.

Erin: Your manager? I thought he was a serious man.

Will: That's what I thought, too. I guess I didn't know him very well after all.

Erin: Well, it usually takes time to know what a person is really like.

Will: True. My co-workers sometimes surprise me by what they do.

威爾：李經理講了一段好好笑的脫口秀，一點都不像他。

艾琳：你的經理？我以為他的個性很嚴肅。

威爾：我也這麼以為，我想我對他的了解太少了。

艾琳：真正要了解一個人通常需要一段時間。

威爾：這倒是，我同事有時做的事會讓我嚇一大跳呢。

字彙/片語充電區 *Words and Phrases*

unseemly 形 不宜的 / clash 動 抵觸 / deviate 動 脫離常規 / accordant 形 一致的
jar with 與…不一致 / tally with 吻合；符合 / bargain on 意料(常與否定句連用)

UNIT 222

「失去理智」的情緒化，
會用到rational這個字？

🎧 222

暖身猜猜看 *Warming Up*

情境：馬文因為車被偷而非常難過，這時應該怎麼說？

(　　) Marvin might lose his ＿＿＿＿ if you mention his lost car.

　　(A) marbles 　　　　(B) jewel 　　　　(C) gold

正確解答：(A) 如果你跟馬文提到他車子被偷，他可能會抓狂。

原來應該這樣說！

lose one's marbles 失去理智；抓狂

　　在早期，彈珠（marble）是孩童的主要玩具之一，很多小朋友是靠著遊戲來贏得彈珠，所以這些小玻璃球對他們來說很重要，而marble就被借用來比喻人身上很重要的東西，也就是理智，可別以為是在講丟失的彈珠。

對話練習 *Let's Talk!*

Emma: Hello? Mr. Simpson? This is your tenant, Emma.

Alfred: Hello, Emma. What can I do for you?

Emma: Mr. Lin's dog likes to bark at night. I'm going to **lose my marbles**.

Alfred: Okay. I'll ask him to do something about it.

Emma: Thank you, Mr. Simpson. I really need a good night's sleep.

艾　瑪：喂？辛普森先生嗎？我是你的房客艾瑪。

艾佛瑞：你好，艾瑪，有什麼事情嗎？

艾　瑪：林先生的狗喜歡在晚上叫，再這樣下去，我會發瘋的。

艾佛瑞：好，我會請他改善。

艾　瑪：謝謝你，辛普森先生，我真的需要好好睡個覺。

字彙／片語充電區 *Words and Phrases*

flip 動 因激動而失去控制 / **wit** 名 理智 / **devastate** 動 崩潰 / **regain** 動 恢復
crack up 精神崩潰 / **freak out** 發瘋 / **hit the roof** 勃然大怒 / **let it out** 宣洩

UNIT 223 在「太歲頭上動土」，真與head有關？

🎧 223

 暖身猜猜看 *Warming Up*

情境：想勸人不要因一時的氣憤得罪上位者，這時應該怎麼說？

(　　) Calm down. It's just like bearding the lion in his ＿＿＿＿.

(A) cave　　　　(B) den　　　　(C) place

正確解答：(B) 冷靜一點，這簡直就是在太歲頭上動土。

 原來應該這樣說！

beard the lion in his den 太歲頭上動土

　　這個慣用語的來源可能綜合了兩個故事，都和聖經有關。跟獅子待在同一個籠子裡，還要去拔牠的鬍鬚，可以想見這有多危險；beard the lion in his den就是在某人的地盤上面對他或衝突，也可以單用beard the lion。

 對話練習 *Let's Talk!*

Glenn: Hey, where are you going? The TV show is about to start.

Judy: Didn't you hear the barking? I've got to talk to Mr. Banks.

Glenn: He's a grumpy man. You're **bearding the lion in his den**.

Judy: Maybe I am. But we just can't always put up with him and his animal.

Glenn: If you must go, I'll go with you.

葛蘭：嘿，你要去哪裡？電視節目快開始了。

茱蒂：你沒聽到狗叫聲嗎？我要去跟班克斯先生談談。

葛蘭：他的脾氣很差，你這是在太歲頭上動土。

茱蒂：也許吧，但我們不能總是縱容他和他的寵物。

葛蘭：如果你一定要去的話，那我陪你去。

字彙/片語充電區 *Words and Phrases*

jeopardy 名 險境 / bold 形 大膽的；無畏的 / reckless 形 魯莽的 / peril 名 危險
face down 面對 / stick up for 捍衛 / stand up to 敢於面對 / submit to 屈服

UNIT 224 說到「有樣學樣」，
可能和imitate差不多？

🎧 224

 暖身猜猜看 *Warming Up*

情境：你勸朋友戒菸，以免小孩有樣學樣，這時應該怎麼說？

( ) Remember the saying "_____ see, _____ do"?

　　(A) puppy　　　　　(B) people　　　(C) monkey

正確解答：(C) 還記得「有樣學樣」這個諺語嗎？

 原來應該這樣說！

Monkey see, monkey do. 有樣學樣。

　　Monkey see, monkey do.是一個近代才出現的用法，主要的意思有兩種：第一種是指學習一樣東西時只學表面，不知道其原理；第二種是指模仿，特別是在技術和知識不如被模仿者的情況下。

 *Let's Talk!*

Hannah: This new phone looks so much like the one I have!	漢　娜：這支新手機看起來跟我的好像！
Oscar: It just looks like yours, but it's not the same one.	奧斯卡：它只是看起來像，和你的並非同一支。
Hannah: Thank goodness. Because it's much cheaper than mine.	漢　娜：太好了，因為這支比我的便宜多了。
Oscar: **Monkey see, monkey do.** They copied the look.	奧斯卡：他們只是有樣學樣，抄襲外觀而已。
Hannah: It could have fooled me.	漢　娜：差點就被騙了。

字彙/片語充電區 *Words and Phrases*

mimic 動 模仿；學樣子 / **forgery** 名 偽造 / **duplicate** 動 複製 / **contrast** 名 差異
do likewise 照著做 / **rip off** 剽竊；偷竊 / **a carbon copy** 非常相像的人或物

UNIT 225 將危機「化險為夷」，會是become safe？

🎧 225

暖身猜猜看 Warming Up

情境：送進加護病房的病人終於化險為夷，這時應該怎麼說？

(　　) He has turned the ＿＿＿＿ and will be discharged next week.

(A) corner　　　　(B) head　　　　(C) situation

正確解答：(A) 他現在已經好轉，下星期就可以出院。

原來應該這樣說！

turn the corner 化險為夷

在賽跑、賽馬或賽車等場合，最後一個彎道往往是關鍵，很多反敗為勝的情況都在此發生，所以turn the corner就被用來形容「某人或某件事經過了一個困難的時刻之後，情況開始好轉」的情況。

對話練習 Let's Talk!

Calvin: My restaurant has finally **turned the corner**.

Doris: Congratulations. I heard the past few months weren't easy.

Calvin: Yeah. We never had over fifty customers per day.

Doris: That was bad indeed. What happened then?

Calvin: Well, some bloggers' articles just changed everything.

卡　文：我餐廳的生意終於好轉了。

桃莉絲：恭喜你，我聽說過去幾個月很不容易。

卡　文：對啊，每天的客人不超過五十個。

桃莉絲：真的很慘，那後來發生了什麼事？

卡　文：這個嘛…部落客的推薦讓一切都不同了。

字彙／片語充電區 Words and Phrases

upturn 名 好轉 / **crisis** 名 危機；緊急關頭 / **plight** 動 承諾 / **deteriorate** 動 使惡化

straighten out 解決 / **pull through** 度過難關 / **go downhill** 走下坡；形勢愈來愈糟

UNIT 226 「忍氣吞聲」的模樣，就用endure形容？

🎧 226

 暖身猜猜看 *Warming Up*

情境：面對壞脾氣的老闆，你決定忍氣吞聲，這時可以怎麼說？

(　　) I decide to eat ＿＿＿＿＿ whenever my boss gets mad at me.

　　(A) sand　　　　　(B) dirt　　　　　(C) anger

正確解答：(B) 我決定在上司發飆的時候忍氣吞聲。

 原來應該這樣說！

eat dirt 忍氣吞聲

　　eat dirt直接翻成中文是吃土，不過它當然和台灣人說的吃土不一樣。dirt原指灰塵或泥巴，這裡的dirt則指「屈辱」或「不友善的對待」，eat dirt則用來形容「擺出低聲下氣的姿態」，即「忍氣吞聲」之意。

 對話練習 *Let's Talk!*

Bella: Your sister is really upset. What did you do?

Henry: I promised to send a package for her, but it totally slipped my mind.

Bella: Did you apologize?

Henry: Yes, I did. But she was still mad. So I just **ate dirt**.

Bella: I see. Let me buy you some ice cream.

貝拉：你姊姊很不悅，你做了什麼？

亨利：我答應要幫她寄包裹，但我完全忘記了。

貝拉：你跟她道歉了嗎？

亨利：道歉了，可是她還是很生氣，所以我只能低聲下氣囉。

貝拉：原來如此，來吧，我請你吃冰淇淋。

字彙/片語充電區 *Words and Phrases*

cringe 動 卑躬屈膝 / coward 形 膽怯的 / abide 動 忍受；容忍 / confront 動 對抗
tuck one's tail 忍受 / put up with 容忍 / knuckle under 屈服 / find fault 挑剔

UNIT 227 「摸摸鼻子接受」，會提到某人的nose？

🎧 227

暖身猜猜看 *Warming Up*

情境：想換貨時發現店倒了，只好自認倒楣，這時應該怎麼說？

( ) I guess I have to _____ it up and sew up the hole myself.

(A) eat　　　　　　(B) take　　　　　(C) suck

正確解答：(C) 我想我得自認倒楣，自己把洞縫起來。

原來應該這樣說！

suck it up 摸摸鼻子接受；面對現實

　　suck一般的意思是吸入，它有一個常見的俚語用法，表示「很爛」或「令人討厭」，ex. This place sucks.（這個地方真爛。）；依照這個意思，suck it up所指的是「無奈地接受或面對不怎麼令人滿意的現實」。

對話練習 *Let's Talk!*

Lenny: Man! I have rebooted my laptop three times this morning.

Marian: You can try to reformat your hard drive.

Lenny: I did it a few months ago. Maybe it's time to do it again.

Marian: Or maybe it's time to shop for a new one.

Lenny: Nah. I'll just **suck it up** and stick to my old pal for now.

藍　尼：天哪！我今天早上已經重開機三次了。

瑪莉安：你可以試著重灌硬碟。

藍　尼：我幾個月前重灌過，也許該再次重灌。

瑪莉安：或許你根本就該買台新電腦了。

藍　尼：不了，我會先忍一忍，繼續使用我的老伙伴。

字彙／片語充電區 *Words and Phrases*

endure 動 容忍 / loath 形 勉強的 / discontent 形 不滿的 / acceptable 形 能接受的
bow to fate 向命運低頭 / **hit a bad patch** 倒楣；不好過 / **strive against** 反抗

UNIT 228 「深受情緒所苦」，是某一種suffering？

🎧 228

 暖身猜猜看 Warming Up

情境：朋友的小狗過世之後，就一直非常傷心，這時應該怎麼說？

(　　) Mark has been _____ his heart out since his dog died.

　　(A) crying　　　　(B) beating　　　　(C) eating

正確解答：(C) 自從馬克的狗過世之後，他就一直沉浸在悲傷中。

 原來應該這樣說！

eat one's heart out 因悲傷、嫉妒等情緒而受苦

　　此慣用語是指內心被悲傷、憂慮、嫉妒等強烈的情緒佔據而感到痛苦，有如這些情緒在啃咬自己的內心；另外在炫耀時，若想讓對方嫉妒，就會用命令句表現，ex. Eat your heart out! I won the prize.（嫉妒吧？我中獎了。）

 **對話練習** *Let's Talk!*

Vince: What happened to George? He looks unhappy.

Zoe: The girl he likes is dating Bill. Now he is **eating his heart out**.

Vince: What's with that girl? She's got so many guys crazy about her.

Zoe: You're not? She knows how to make guys feel they're special.

Vince: I guess I don't need anybody to prove myself.

文斯：喬治怎麼了？他看起來很不開心。

柔伊：他喜歡的那個女生和比爾在一起，他正為愛所苦。

文斯：那個女生有什麼好？她讓很多男生為她著迷。

柔伊：你不會嗎？她知道如何讓男性覺得他們很特別。

文斯：我想我不需要任何人來證明我自己。

字彙／片語充電區 *Words and Phrases*

vexation 名 苦惱 / **anguish** 名 極度的痛苦 / **corrode** 動 侵蝕 / **gnaw** 動 啃咬
in a stew over 為…焦急或憂慮 / **hang crepe** 悲傷；苦惱 / **dwell upon** 放不下

UNIT 229
「故意冷落」他人的態度，就是冷冰冰的coldly？

🎧 229

暖身猜猜看 *Warming Up*

情境：朋友整天冷落你，你想問他原因，這時應該怎麼說？

(　　) Why did you give me the cold ＿＿＿＿ for the whole day?

(A) eyes　　　　(B) shoulder　　　　(C) back

正確解答：(B) 為什麼你整天都故意忽視我？

原來應該這樣說！

give the cold shoulder 故意忽視；冷落

　　這個源自十九世紀初期的慣用語其實很容易望文生義，它從一開始就是指在故意忽視某人的時候，用背對著他，只讓他看肩膀，藉以表示冷漠。要注意的是，雖然所有人都有兩個肩膀，但在這裡要用單數。

對話練習 *Let's Talk!*

Paula: Simon **gave** me **the cold shoulder** for the whole week.

Nelson: Did you try to figure out why?

Paula: I texted him, but he hasn't texted me back yet.

Nelson: Maybe you can ask him in person tomorrow in class.

Paula: I sure will. It's been bugging me the whole week.

寶　拉：賽門整個禮拜都故意冷落我。

尼爾森：你有試著找出原因嗎？

寶　拉：我傳了簡訊，但他還沒回覆我。

尼爾森：也許明天上課的時候，你可以當面問他。

寶　拉：我一定會問，這件事已經困擾我整個星期了。

字彙／片語充電區 *Words and Phrases*

snub 動 冷落；怠慢／**disregard** 動 漠視／**distantly** 副 冷淡地／**disdain** 名 輕蔑 **keep aloof from** 不友善／**put the chill on** 忽視／**turn up one's nose** 嗤之以鼻

UNIT 230

「笑得合不攏嘴」，會用到laugh嗎？

🎧 230

暖身猜猜看 Warming Up

情境：聽到年終獎金，都笑得合不攏嘴了，這時應該怎麼說？

( ) I grinned from _____ to _____ when I heard about the annual bonus.

(A) cheek   (B) ear   (C) eye

正確解答：(B) 聽到年終獎金，我都笑得合不攏嘴了。

原來應該這樣說！

grin from ear to ear 笑得合不攏嘴

　　英文當中用來表示笑容的字有很多，grin就是其中一個，指露出牙齒的笑容。這個慣用語是以誇張的說法「笑得嘴角都跑到耳邊了」來形容一個人「笑得很開的模樣」，即笑得合不攏嘴。

對話練習 Let's Talk!

Carl: You're **grinning from ear to ear**. Did you win a big prize?

Della: How did you know? I won an iPad in a contest.

Carl: No way! I'm so jealous. I've always wanted an iPad.

Della: I have one more raffle ticket if you want it.

Carl: Ha. Thanks, but I don't think I am as lucky as you are.

卡爾：你笑得合不攏嘴，是中了什麼大獎嗎？

黛拉：你怎麼知道？我參加比賽，贏了一台iPad。

卡爾：不會吧？真令人忌妒，我一直都很想要一台iPad。

黛拉：我還有一張抽獎券，你想要的話可以給你。

卡爾：哈，謝了，但我覺得我不會有你那麼幸運。

字彙／片語充電區 Words and Phrases

beam 動 眉開眼笑 / **titter** 名 竊笑 / **radiate** 動 流露出 / **giggle** 動 咯咯地笑
split one's sides 捧腹大笑 / **roll in the aisles** 樂不可支 / **light up** 面露喜色

UNIT 231　開心得「手舞足蹈」，會提到dance嗎？

🎧 231

 暖身猜猜看 Warming Up

情境：某樂團要開演唱會，你高興得不得了，這時應該怎麼說？

(　　) I _____ for joy when I heard that the band is having a concert.

(A) drove　　　　(B) ran　　　　(C) jumped

正確解答：(C) 聽到那個樂團要開演唱會，我樂得手舞足蹈。

 原來應該這樣說！

jump for joy 手舞足蹈

　　這個慣用語是從人樂得手舞足蹈的姿態而來，藉以表達快樂與喜悅；名詞 **joy**可以解釋為快樂的感覺，也可以指讓人快樂的人或事物。另外補充**jump the gun**，同樣從**jump**衍生，但所表達的是操之過急之意。

 **對話練習 Let's Talk!**

Emma: What's the noise about? Are we having a party?

Gavin: Sort of. Mary is now **jumping for joy**.

Emma: I heard that she got into the school she had dreamed about.

Gavin: Yeah. We plan to celebrate tonight. Are you coming?

Emma: Sure. I wouldn't miss it.

艾瑪：在吵什麼？開派對嗎？

蓋文：差不多，瑪莉正高興地手舞足蹈。

艾瑪：我聽說她考上了她一直想讀的學校。

蓋文：是啊，我們計劃今晚出去慶祝，你要來嗎？

艾瑪：當然，我一定到。

字彙／片語充電區 Words and Phrases

ecstasy 名 欣喜若狂 / **jubilate** 動 歡呼 / **elated** 形 興高采烈的 / **exult** 動 歡欣鼓舞
in seventh heaven 極高興 / **be on fire** 在興頭上 / **stars in one's eyes** 充滿期待

246

UNIT 232
快要「笑破肚皮」，會提到belly這個字嗎？

🎧 232

暖身猜猜看 *Warming Up*

情境：你想推薦一部令人大笑不止的喜劇片，這時應該怎麼說？

(　　) You've got to see this movie. It's going to have you in _____.

    (A) stitches   (B) surgery   (C) hospital

正確解答：(A) 你一定要看這部電影，它會讓你笑破肚皮。

原來應該這樣說！

in stitches 笑破肚皮

    stitch一般指縫衣服的針數，也就是每縫一針後，產生在布面上的一小段線，它還有一個特別的意思，就是因跑步或大笑所導致的身體疼痛，因為笑得太大力，導致像被針刺般，感到疼痛，比喻「大笑而無法控制的狀態」。

對話練習 *Let's Talk!*

Flora: Your brother is such a funny guy.

Hal: That's his specialty. He is good at making people laugh.

Flora: We were not only laughing. He had us **in stitches**.

Hal: Ha. I'm glad you guys like him.

Flora: We've got to have dinner again. I could really use some more laughs.

芙蘿拉：你弟弟真是一個很風趣的人。

哈　爾：那是他的專長，他很會逗別人笑。

芙蘿拉：不只是笑而已，我們都快笑破肚皮了。

哈　爾：哈，很高興你們喜歡他。

芙蘿拉：我們一定要再一起吃晚餐，我真的很需要多笑一笑。

字彙／片語充電區 *Words and Phrases*

side-splitting 形 滑稽的 / **hysterical** 形 歇斯底里的 / **thigh-slapper** 名 爆笑笑話
burst into laughter 爆笑 / **bust a gut** 大笑不止 / **a rib tickler** 很好笑的笑話或故事

UNIT 233 常聽到的「欣喜若狂」，與joyful差不多吧？

🎧 233

 暖身猜猜看 Warming Up

情境：期待的日本之旅讓你欣喜若狂，這時應該怎麼說？

( ) I've finally saved enough to go to Japan. That put me over the

_____.

    (A) moon   (B) cloud   (C) wind

正確解答：(A) 我終於存夠錢去日本，那讓我高興得不得了。

 原來應該這樣說！

over the moon 樂翻了；欣喜若狂

    這個慣用語據說來自一首童謠裡的歌詞："...the cow jumped over the moon..."，如果一個人欣喜至極，甚至都可以飛到月球上去，那真是無法形容的快樂吧！注意這個慣用語的欣喜程度比delighted要高，小心別言過其實。

對話練習 Let's Talk!

David: You'll never guess what just happened to me!

Sandy: What is it?

David: Well, I was checking the lottery results, and guess what?

Sandy: Don't tell me you won! Really?

David: Yes, I did! It really put me **over the moon**!

大衛：你絕對猜不到我發生了什麼事！

仙蒂：發生什麼事了？

大衛：嗯，我剛剛在查看樂透開獎的結果，你猜怎麼著？

仙蒂：別告訴我你中獎了！真的嗎？

大衛：沒錯！真讓我樂翻了！

字彙 / 片語充電區 *Words and Phrases*

thrilled 形 興奮的 / **exultation** 名 得意洋洋 / **marvel** 動 使驚奇 / **pitifully** 副 悲戚地
be on cloud nine 欣喜若狂 / **a blessed event** 喜事 / **to borrow trouble** 自尋煩惱

UNIT 234 某人「氣得跳腳」，就說be mad to jump？

🎧 234

暖身猜猜看 Warming Up

情境：你因為會議上的事情而氣得跳腳，這時應該怎麼說？

( ) I was _____ out of shape because Jack didn't back me up.

(A) bent　　　(B) snapped　　　(C) twisted

正確解答：(A) 因為傑克沒有支持我，所以我氣得要死。

原來應該這樣說！

be/get bent out of shape 氣得不得了；氣得跳腳

　　人在生氣到無法控制時，是沒有辦法好好思考或做事的，就像釘子彎掉，就無法發揮作用一樣。bent是bend（彎曲）的過去分詞，out of shape的意思是變形或走樣，兩者合起來意指「氣得不得了」，通常與get或be動詞連用。

對話練習 Let's Talk!

Iris: My brother lied to me again. I was so angry!

Glenn: You don't need to **get bent out of shape** over this.

Iris: But I've told him many times not to lie.

Glenn: Maybe you've made it too difficult for him to tell the truth.

Iris: God! It's so hard to be a good sister.

艾芮絲：我弟弟又騙我了，我超生氣的！

葛　蘭：你不需要為了這個而氣得跳腳。

艾芮絲：可是我跟他說過很多次，叫他不要說謊。

葛　蘭：也許你讓他覺得說實話很困難。

艾芮絲：天哪！當個好姊姊真難。

字彙/片語充電區 Words and Phrases

enrage 動 激怒 / incensed 形 極為憤怒的 / uncontrollable 形 控制不住的
have a cow 氣炸了 / blow one's top 勃然大怒 / be hopping mad 暴跳如雷的

UNIT 235 「大受打擊」的情緒，想必令人shocking吧？

🎧 235

暖身猜猜看 Warming Up

情境：好友因為親戚過世，而大受打擊，這時應該怎麼說？

( ) Janet took it really _____ when her beloved uncle passed away.

　　(A) strong　　　　　(B) tough　　　(C) hard

正確解答：(C) 自己親愛的叔叔過世了，珍妮特非常傷心。

原來應該這樣說！

take it hard 受打擊；傷心

很多人都知道take it easy是放輕鬆，那如果用easy的相反詞hard替換呢？hard這個單字的意思很多，加一加超過十五個字義；take it hard當中的hard則是指「難受的」，整個慣用語表示「受到打擊而傷心或難受」。

對話練習 Let's Talk!

Jack: Congratulations on the exhibit. It's really impressive.

Carol: Thank you. But I was kind of depressed this afternoon.

Jack: It's not because of those critiques, is it?

Carol: Yes. I really hoped that people would like my paintings.

Jack: Don't **take it** too **hard**. I don't think those critics ever like anything.

傑克：恭喜你辦了畫展，我真的很佩服你。

卡蘿：謝謝，可是我今天下午滿沮喪的。

傑克：該不會是因為那些評論吧？

卡蘿：是啊，我真的很希望大家都會喜歡我的畫。

傑克：別太難過，我覺得那些評論家看什麼都不順眼。

字彙／片語充電區 Words and Phrases

lament 動 哀悼；悲嘆 / sorrow 名 傷心事 / wail 動 嚎啕大哭 / gloat 動 幸災樂禍
cast down 沮喪 / a bolt from the blue 突如其來的打擊 / on a downer 感到沮喪

UNIT 236 「觸及他人的痛處」，只能用hurt嗎？

🎧 236

暖身猜猜看 Warming Up

情境：你因為他人不友善的言語而感到受傷，這時應該怎麼說？

(　　) Your harsh words have cut me to the _____.

　　(A) skin　　　　　(B) quick　　　　　(C) heart

正確解答：(B) 你這些惡劣的話語傷到我了。

原來應該這樣說！

cut to the quick 觸及痛處

　　cut to the...意指「切到某個地方」，但quick不是用來描述「很快」的形容詞嗎？其實它可以當名詞，指的是指甲下面那塊特別柔軟脆弱的肉，當你在剪指甲時，如果不小心剪太深，會感覺很痛，衍生出的意思即為「觸及痛處」。

對話練習 Let's Talk!

Paul: I need someone for my team, but I can't find anyone I trust.

Maggie: You just **cut** me **to the quick**. I thought you trusted me.

Paul: I do, but I'm looking for a man. That's why I never asked you.

Maggie: Oh, I see. Did you ask Allen?

Paul: Allen! How did I miss him? I'm going to call him now.

保羅：我需要一位組員，可是我找不到可以信任的人。

瑪姬：你傷到我了，我以為你信任我。

保羅：我是信任你啊，不過我要找的是男生，所以才沒問你。

瑪姬：哦，原來如此，你問過亞倫了嗎？

保羅：亞倫！我怎麼會漏掉他？我現在就打給他。

字彙／片語充電區 Words and Phrases

sting 動 傷害 / **afflict** 動 使痛苦 / **trauma** 名 創傷 / **alleviate** 動 減輕；緩和
step on one's toe 得罪某人 / **cast a slur on** 中傷 / **be sick at heart** 傷心

UNIT 237 情緒「崩潰」的說法，應該與break有關？

🎧 237

 暖身猜猜看 *Warming Up*

情境：主管嚴厲的批評讓你崩潰大哭，這時應該怎麼說？

(　　) I came apart at the ＿＿＿＿ and cried after work.

　　(A) cracks　　　　　(B) gaps　　　　　(C) seams

正確解答：(C) 下班後，我崩潰大哭。

 原來應該這樣說！

come apart at the seams 崩潰；失控

　　come apart是破裂，seam是接縫或縫合處，當人承受很大的壓力或心情非常不好的時候，就像一件衣物被用力地拉扯，當承受不住的時候，針線的縫合處就會撕裂破碎，用來比喻「情緒上的崩潰和失控」。

 *Let's Talk!*

Cathy: I haven't seen Peter for a while.

Nathan: That accident really made him **come apart at the seams**.

Cathy: I would have felt the same if I had lost my brother.

Nathan: I have written him some emails, and he finally wrote me back.

Cathy: That's very sweet of you to be there for him.

凱西：我已經好一陣子沒見到彼德了。

納森：當時那場意外真的讓他崩潰了。

凱西：我如果失去了兄弟，也會和他一樣的。

納森：我寫了幾封電子郵件給他，他終於回信了。

凱西：你人真好，一直陪著他。

字彙/片語充電區 *Words and Phrases*

disintegrate 動 崩潰 / undertake 動 承受 / shatter 動 打擊 / sustain 動 禁得起
break down 崩潰 / lose one's cool 沈不住氣 / tear sth. to pieces 嚴厲批評某物

UNIT 238 「因情緒激動而哽咽」，能用哽住的choke嗎？

🎧 238

暖身猜猜看 Warming Up

情境：某部電影的其中一幕每次都讓你哽咽，這時應該怎麼說？

(　) I have a ＿＿＿＿＿ in my throat every time I watch this scene.

　　(A) lump　　　　　(B) swelling　　　　(C) bump

正確解答：(A) 每次我看到這一幕都會哽咽。

原來應該這樣說！

have a lump in one's throat 因情緒激動而哽咽

　　lump的意思是隆起或腫塊，當情緒激動時，會感覺喉嚨彷彿被一塊東西塞住，這就是哽咽，英文以have a lump in one's throat表示；如果主詞是讓人哽咽的事物，可說這個東西bring a lump to one's throat。

Let's Talk!

Wayne: Thanks for the birthday party. Is this my gift?

Victor: Yes. Open it up. I'm sure you'll like it.

Wayne: God! I've been thinking about getting this watch for a while.

Victor: I know. Enjoy it. You're not crying, are you?

Wayne: I **have a lump in my throat**. This is such a great gift.

韋　恩：謝謝你幫我慶生，這是給我的禮物嗎？

維克多：沒錯，打開吧，你一定會喜歡。

韋　恩：天哪！我想買這隻錶想了好一陣子。

維克多：我知道，好好享用吧，你該不會是在哭吧？

韋　恩：我哽咽了，這真是一份很棒的禮物。

字彙/片語充電區 Words and Phrases

choke 動 哽住 / emotional 形 感情的 / affecting 形 令人感動的 / tear 名 眼淚
choke with sobs 哽咽 / burst out 突然激動起來 / lost for words 說不出話來

UNIT 239 「哪壺不開提哪壺」，只知道壺叫 kettle？

🎧 239

 暖身猜猜看 Warming Up

情境：你想制止同事討論某人的過失，這時應該怎麼說？

(   ) It's none of our business. Don't air her dirty _____ in public.

    (A) stove   (B) closet   (C) laundry

正確解答：(C) 這跟我們沒有關係，別哪壺不開提哪壺。

 原來應該這樣說！

air one's dirty laundry 哪壺不開提哪壺

    如果有人把你的 dirty laundry（骯髒待洗的衣物）晾（air）出來給大家看，那應該挺尷尬的吧？這個慣用語就是從此義引申出「不該提的事卻提出來」的意思；慣用語中的 air 可以用 wash 取代。

 **對話練習** Let's Talk!

Bill: Let's go see a movie tonight. I've booked the tickets.

Jenny: Ah...You know what they said about our office romance?

Bill: Well, what did they say?

Jenny: They said people shouldn't mix love and work.

Bill: Why do some people just love to **air others' dirty laundry**?

比爾：今天晚上一起去看電影吧，我訂好票了。

珍妮：呃⋯你知道大家怎麼說我們的辦公室戀情嗎？

比爾：他們怎麼說？

珍妮：說人不應該把愛情與工作混為一談。

比爾：為何有些人就是喜歡哪壺不開提哪壺？

字彙／片語充電區 *Words and Phrases*

privacy 名 隱私 / scandal 名 醜聞 / gossip 名 閒話 / tight-lipped 形 守口如瓶的
take it personally 感情用事 / zip one's lip 保守秘密 / not in the zone 在狀況外

UNIT 240
「玩火自焚」的說法，用burn oneself適當嗎？

🎧 240

暖身猜猜看 *Warming Up*

情境：想勸朋友別惹禍上身，這時應該怎麼說？

(　　) You'll probably get your ＿＿＿＿＿ burnt and be sorry forever.

(A) toes　　　　(B) fingers　　　　(C) legs

正確解答：(B) 你可能會惹禍上身，後悔一輩子。

原來應該這樣說！

get one's fingers burnt 惹禍上身；玩火自焚

　　「get/have + N + P.P.」是一種使役動詞句型的運用，表示「使/讓…被…」，所以get fingers burnt也可以説成burn fingers，字面上的意思是「燒傷手指」，引申為「玩火自焚」，通常指愚蠢或不當的行為導致不利的後果。

Diane: Look at you! So how long will you be on crutches?

　　Bill: The doctor figures that it'll be many months.

Diane: So what happened? Did you hit a tree or something?

　　Bill: I sped a bit too fast on the freeway and hit the barrier.

Diane: You must abide by the law, or you'll **get your fingers burnt**.

黛安：看看你！你要撐拐杖撐到什麼時候啊？

比爾：醫生估計要好幾個月的時間。

黛安：所以是發生什麼事？你撞到一棵樹還是怎樣？

比爾：我在高速公路上飆得有點太快，撞到護欄。

黛安：你得遵守交通規則，否則就會自食惡果啊。

字彙／片語充電區 *Words and Phrases*

rash 形 魯莽的 / **consequence** 名 後果 / **repent** 動 後悔 / **caution** 名 小心謹慎
ask for trouble 自食惡果 / **learn a lesson** 學到教訓 / **tread on thin ice** 如履薄冰

UNIT 241 「死路一條」，是can't cross的路嗎？

🎧 241

暖身猜猜看 Warming Up

情境：朋友頑固的作法可能會走進死胡同，這時應該怎麼說？

(　　) Back out from the _____ street and try my suggestion.

　　(A) two-way　　　　(B) narrow-minded　　　　(C) dead-end

正確解答：(C) 退出死胡同，試試我的建議。

原來應該這樣說！

a dead-end street 死路一條

　　dead（死亡）的衍生義最早出現於十九世紀，用來指稱關閉著的水管，由此引申出「不用的」之意；dead-end則結合dead（死的）與end（盡頭），當名詞可表示「死巷」（具體），也可指「不可能成功的計畫」（抽象）。

對話練習 Let's Talk!

Rick: My boss is on my back every day.

Judy: Really? Why is that?

Rick: He wants me to cut costs because we are over budget.

Judy: Well, the prices of raw materials have skyrocketed recently.

Rick: Yeah. So I have to avoid running on **a dead-end street**.

瑞克：我老闆每天都盯著我。

茱蒂：真的嗎？為什麼？

瑞克：因為公司的花費超過預算，他要我減少成本。

茱蒂：嗯，原物料的價格最近都在飆漲。

瑞克：是啊，所以我必須避免走進死胡同。

字彙 / 片語充電區 Words and Phrases

hair-splitting 形 鑽牛角尖的 / flexible 形 彈性的 / alternative 名 替代方案
a blind alley 絕路 / split hairs 鑽牛角尖 / light the way to 指引…的明路

UNIT 242 「焦慮不安」的心情，有比anxious更簡單的描述？

🎧 242

 暖身猜猜看 *Warming Up*

情境：聊到畢業即失業的恐慌與擔心，這時應該怎麼說？

(   ) I've been all in a _____ over my career recently.

    (A) protest   (B) stew   (C) moment

正確解答：(B) 我最近一直為了工作的事情焦慮不安。

 原來應該這樣說！

in a stew 焦躁；焦慮不安

    stew當名詞表示正處於「悶、燉、煮」的狀態。想像一個人待在大悶鍋裡，或一直處於煩悶的狀態或環境中，肯定坐立難安。這個慣用語也常見於put sb. in a stew（使某人焦慮不安）、get into a stew（顯得不安）。

對話練習 *Let's Talk!*

Kelly: Bob! I'm running into trouble. You must help me this time!

Bob: Aren't I always trying to help you? First, you have to chill out.

Kelly: Ok. I'm a little bit calmer now.

Bob: Good. Now tell me what you are again **in a stew** about?

Kelly: I'm getting old, Bob. I found more lines around my eyes!

凱莉：鮑伯！我慘了，這次你一定要幫我！

鮑伯：我哪一次沒有幫你？你得先冷靜一點。

凱莉：好，我現在比較冷靜了。

鮑伯：很好，那麼告訴我，你又在焦慮個什麼勁？

凱莉：鮑伯，我變老了，我發現我眼睛周圍的魚尾紋變多了！

字彙 / 片語充電區 *Words and Phrases*

irritable 形 煩躁的 / anxiety 名 焦慮 / dread 動 懼怕 / collected 形 鎮定的
sit on thorns 如坐針氈 / be worried sick 擔心死了 / feel at ease 一派輕鬆

UNIT 243 「嚇得心臟快跳出來了」，heart到底在哪裡？

🎧 243

 暖身猜猜看 Warming Up

情境：坐雲霄飛車真是讓你的驚嚇指數破表，這時應該怎麼說？

(　　) I almost felt my heart in my ＿＿＿＿＿＿ when I rode the roller coaster.

(A) liver　　　　(B) blood　　　　(C) mouth

正確解答：(C) 當我玩雲霄飛車時，我嚇得心臟都快跳出來了。

 原來應該這樣說！

heart in one's mouth 嚇得心臟快跳出來了

　　這個起源於十六世紀中期的慣用語，字面上的意思是「心臟跑到嘴巴裡」，即俗話說「心都要跳出來了」的意思，在修辭學上，類似的用法稱為「誇飾法」，也可以用heart in one's throat表示相同的意思。

 對話練習 Let's Talk!

Dave: My stocks got whacked last week!

Tara: I'm in the same boat as you. I got hit pretty hard, too.

Dave: Big money was sometimes made in waiting.

Tara: But my **heart** was **in my mouth**, so I sold out all my stocks.

Dave: I know. The financial crisis has really shaken the markets.

戴夫：上週我的股票大跌！
塔拉：我可以感同身受，我也賠得很慘。
戴夫：賺大錢有時候需要等待。
塔拉：但我真的嚇死了，把我的股票全數脫手。
戴夫：我能理解，金融危機撼動了全球股市。

字彙／片語充電區 *Words and Phrases*

petrified 形 嚇得目瞪口呆的 / sedate 形 沉著的；平靜的 / unaffected 形 不受影響的
be in a panic 陷入恐慌 / be scared out of one's wits 嚇破膽 / freak sb. out 嚇死

UNIT 244

一個人「坐立難安」，要描述sit的狀態嗎？

🎧 244

暖身猜猜看 *Warming Up*

情境：想勸人沉著些，別老是坐立難安，這時應該怎麼說？

(　　) Would you calm down? You're on the ＿＿＿＿ of your seat.

　　(A) side　　　　　(B) brink　　　　(C) edge

正確解答：(C) 你可以冷靜一點嗎？你一直坐立不安耶。

原來應該這樣說！

on the edge of one's seat 坐立難安

　　字面意義是「在某人座位的邊緣」，用來描述一個人坐立難安；當你在看緊張刺激的電影，被片中的情節吸引時，也可以這個慣用語表示，ex. The movie had me on the edge of my seat.（這部電影真是引人入勝。）

對話練習 *Let's Talk!*

John: The seats in the theater were crowded! My legs kept cramping up.

Mary: It sounds like you were **on the edge of your seat**.

John: I guess that I shouldn't complain so much.

Mary: Why? It's okay to me.

John: Because I sat next to the most beautiful girl in the whole theater.

約翰：那間戲院的座位好擠，我的腳一直抽筋。

瑪莉：聽起來你剛剛似乎一直坐立難安。

約翰：我想我不應該抱怨這些。

瑪莉：為什麼？我不介意啊。

約翰：因為坐在我旁邊的，是全戲院最漂亮的女孩。

字彙／片語充電區 *Words and Phrases*

fidget 動 坐立不安 / **edgy** 形 煩躁不安的 / **fret** 動 使煩躁 / **restless** 形 心神不寧的
be on tenterhooks 憂慮不安 / **be keyed up** 緊張的 / **keep one's head** 保持鎮定

UNIT 245 急得像「熱鍋上的螞蟻」，是ant on the hot pot？

🎧 245

 暖身猜猜看 Warming Up

情境：要結帳時找不到錢包，真是心急如焚，這時應該怎麼說？

( ) I was like a cat on hot ＿＿＿＿ after I found my wallet had been stolen.

    (A) bricks   (B) stoves   (C) pots

正確解答：(A) 在我發現我的皮夾被偷了之後，我心急如焚。

 原來應該這樣說！

a cat on hot bricks 熱鍋上的螞蟻；心急如焚

    這個慣用語源自十七世紀的一本諺語集，原來的説法是a cat on a hot bake-stone（烘爐上的貓）。中文所謂「急得像熱鍋上的螞蟻」就如同英文的「貓在火燙的磚頭上」，另外也可以説have/get ants in one's pants。

 Let's Talk!

Linda: My base salary cannot cover my monthly bills.	琳達：我的底薪無法支付我每個月的開銷。
Mark: Maybe you should consider finding a more stable job.	馬克：你也許應該考慮找另一份更穩定的工作。
Linda: I'm going to seriously think it over.	琳達：我會認真考慮這件事情的。
Mark: Keep your chin up! Let's go for a cup of coffee.	馬克：振作點！我們去喝杯咖啡吧。
Linda: Good idea. This conversation has made me feel like **a cat on hot bricks**.	琳達：好主意，談起這件事就讓我感到心急如焚。

字彙／片語充電區 Words and Phrases

stammer 動 結巴 / **frantic** 形 發狂似的 / **patience** 名 耐性 / **carefree** 形 無憂慮的 **lose one's presence of mind** 亂了方寸 / **keep straight in the head** 思緒有條理

UNIT 246
緊張到「心跳加速」，會用speed up嗎？

🎧 246

 暖身猜猜看 *Warming Up*

情境：被老闆叫去問話，你緊張得心跳加速，這時應該怎麼說？

( ) When I was summoned by the boss, my heart missed a _____.

　　(A) jump　　　　　(B) beat　　　　(C) breath

正確解答：(B) 當老闆找我去問話的時候，我的心跳得好快。

原來應該這樣說！

one's heart misses/skips a beat 心跳加速；心跳漏了一拍

　　正常人的心跳（heart beat）都有一定的規律，如果「漏跳一拍」的話，肯定是因為太緊張、害怕或興奮。這裡的動詞misses也可以用skips來取代；另外，one's heart stands still也有類似的意思。

 **對話練習** *Let's Talk!*

Jill: You'll never guess who just called me. My ex-boyfriend Luke!

Jack: **Your heart** must have **missed a beat** at that moment.

Jill: Yeah. I was taken by surprise.

Jack: Is he seeing anybody now? I think you two made a good couple.

Jill: Actually, I don't expect to rekindle any old sparks between us.

吉兒：你絕對猜不到剛才誰打電話給我，我的前男友路克！

傑克：你當時一定心跳加速了吧。

吉兒：嗯，我是滿吃驚的。

傑克：他現在有和其他人交往嗎？我覺得你們很配。

吉兒：老實說，我不想再和他有什麼火花了。

字彙/片語充電區 *Words and Phrases*

accelerate 動 使加速 / tense 形 緊繃的 / startled 形 受驚嚇的 / calm 形 鎮定的
drive sb. crazy 令某人為之瘋狂 / take a firm hold on oneself 使自己鎮定下來

UNIT 247 已經「無計可施」，是can do nothing？

🎧 247

 暖身猜猜看 Warming Up

情境：能做的都做了，問題還是無法解決，這時應該怎麼說？

( ) I'm at my ＿＿＿＿＿ in trying to increase the sales volume.

(A) wits' end　　　(B) last straw　　　(C) bee's knees

正確解答：(A) 對於增加銷售量，我已經無計可施了。

原來應該這樣說！

at one's wits' end 無計可施；黔驢技窮

　　這個說法源自聖經，wit表示一個人的「智能」，也就是處理或解決事情的智慧，那麼「在某人智能的尾端」就是指一個人已經想不出解決的辦法了；注意wit常以複數形出現，所有格會在s後加上一撇（wits'）。

 **對話練習** Let's Talk!

Jeff: The boss definitely got on my nerves after only one day!

Cindy: Come on! She's not that bad.

Jeff: To be honest, I'm **at my wits' end** in trying to get along with her.

Cindy: Well, break is over. She said that she needs to talk to me.

Jeff: Maybe you're going to get canned!

傑夫：那個老闆只須一天就可以把我惹毛！

辛蒂：幹嘛這樣！她沒有那麼壞。

傑夫：老實說，我實在不知道該如何與她相處。

辛蒂：嗯，休息時間結束了，她說要跟我談談。

傑夫：搞不好你會被炒魷魚！

字彙／片語充電區 Words and Phrases

intelligence 名 智慧 / solve 動 解決 / strategy 名 策略 / aggressive 形 積極的
leave sth. to chance 聽天由命 / In the end, things will mend. 船到橋頭自然直。

UNIT 248
「瞠目結舌」的表情，會用上eye與tongue？

🎧 248

暖身猜猜看 *Warming Up*

情境：友人穿上婚紗的模樣令你瞠目結舌，這時應該怎麼說？

(　　) My ＿＿＿＿ dropped at the sight of you in this wedding dress.

　　(A) jaw　　　　　　(B) teeth　　　　　　(C) eyes

正確解答：(A) 看到你穿上這套婚紗的樣子，我簡直目瞪口呆。

原來應該這樣說！

one's jaw drops 目瞪口呆；瞠目結舌

　　jaw是「下巴」，大部分人感到驚訝的時候，嘴巴會張開，如果非常驚訝，就可以用這個說法強調驚訝的程度。主詞如果是人，要改成drop one's jaw；另外，要形容令人驚訝的人事物時，可以用jaw-dropping。

對話練習 *Let's Talk!*

Monica: It was a perfect candle-lit dinner. What a great birthday present!

Bruce: Hold on! I got you something else for a gift.

Monica: What? Are you trying to spoil me?

Bruce: Here. I had to pull a few strings to get my hands on this.

Monica: The new fall LV bag! You are always able to make **my jaw drop**.

莫妮卡：真是完美的燭光晚餐，好棒的生日禮物喔！

布魯斯：等一下！我還有其他的禮物給你。

莫妮卡：什麼？你是打算要寵壞我嗎？

布魯斯：拿去吧，我動用了一些私人關係才拿到的。

莫妮卡：LV的新秋季包！你總是能讓我大為驚喜。

字彙／片語充電區 *Words and Phrases*

unexpected 形 意外的 / abnormal 形 不尋常的 / commonplace 形 司空見慣的
out of this world 出類拔萃；精彩極了 / take one's breath away 令人屏息、感動

UNIT 249 「心情跌到谷底」，會down到什麼地方？

🎧 249

暖身猜猜看 *Warming Up*

情境：朋友一副悶悶不樂的樣子，這時應該怎麼說？

( ) You look down in the _____. What happened?

　　(A) slumps 　　　　(B) dumps 　　　　(C) dumplings

正確解答：(B) 你看起來心情跌到谷底了，發生了什麼事？

原來應該這樣說！

down in the dumps 心情跌到谷底

　　dump當名詞可表示垃圾堆或髒亂的地方，但它的原意並非如此。這個慣用語起源於十八世紀，在當時，dumps指的是depression，也就是沮喪，而in the dumps再加上down（心情不佳），就能表示「跌到谷底的心情」。

對話練習 *Let's Talk!*

Kevin: Why do you look so **down in the dumps**?

　Tina: Things haven't been going smoothly for me at the car dealership.

Kevin: Are you still not getting along well with your boss?

　Tina: It's not that. Well, I haven't sold a single car in over six weeks!

Kevin: Wow! That is terrible. What about the other sales people?

凱文：為什麼你看起來這麼沮喪呢？

蒂娜：我在汽車代理商做得不是很好。

凱文：你跟老闆還是處得不好嗎？

蒂娜：不是那樣的，我這六週多來沒賣出一輛車！

凱文：哇！還真糟，那其他銷售員怎麼樣？

字彙/片語充電區 *Words and Phrases*

moody 形 鬱鬱寡歡的 / downcast 形 心情低落的 / light-hearted 形 心情愉快的
down in the mouth 心情低落 / with a sense of melancholy 帶著一點憂鬱氣息

UNIT 250
「心情七上八下」，就是不斷up and down？

🎧 250

暖身猜猜看 Warming Up

情境：參加面試的你，緊張得忐忑不安，這時應該怎麼說？

(　　) I had ＿＿＿＿ in my stomach as my turn was soon coming.

　(A) butterflies　　　(B) ants　　　(C) cockroaches

正確解答：(A) 當快輪到我的時候，我心情七上八下的。

原來應該這樣說！

butterflies in one's stomach 心情七上八下

　　這個慣用語最早起源於二十世紀初的文學作品。字面上的意思是「胃裡有許多蝴蝶在飛舞」，用以形容人內心感到驚慌或焦慮；如果要表示「讓某人心情七上八下」，則可用give sb. butterflies in one's stomach。

對話練習 Let's Talk!

Frank: Hi. I'm new here. My name's Frank.

Patty: Nice to meet you. So what are you going to do today?

Frank: Well, I have some kind of training later.

Patty: Relax. They won't be too hard on you on your first day.

Frank: Fortunately, the **butterflies in my stomach** seem to be gone now.

法蘭克：嗨，我是新來的，我叫法蘭克。

佩　蒂：很高興認識你，那你今天要做什麼呢？

法蘭克：我等一下會有個職訓課程。

佩　蒂：放輕鬆，才第一天，他們不會對你太嚴苛。

法蘭克：幸運的是，我現在似乎不再那麼坐立不安了。

字彙／片語充電區 Words and Phrases

jumpy 形 提心吊膽的；神經質的 / flutter 動 使不安 / uneasiness 名 侷促不安
air of tension 緊張 / with an easy grace 神情自若 / take a deep breath 深呼吸

UNIT 251 「令人極度恐懼」，只能用very強調程度？

🎧 251

 暖身猜猜看 Warming Up

情境：某部恐怖片挑起你極大的恐懼，這時應該怎麼說？

(　　) I won't see this movie again. It made my _____ run cold.

　　(A) finger 　　　　(B) blood 　　　　(C) heart

正確解答：(B) 我不想再看一次這部電影，它把我嚇得半死。

原來應該這樣說！

make one's blood run cold 令人極度恐懼

　　就醫學的角度而言，當一個人恐懼到極點時，體溫將急速下降，降至30°C以下時，即瀕臨死亡的狀態，所以blood run cold被引申為「被嚇死」或「嚇破膽」之意，類似的說法還有make one's blood freeze。

 **對話練習 Let's Talk!**

May: What do you think about the Grand Canyon?

Joe: It's pretty neat. People can stand on its platform and view the great scenery.

May: So...let's go there for our next trip!

Joe: No way! That view will surely **make my blood run cold**.

May: Right. You've suffered from acrophobia. What a shame!

梅：你覺得大峽谷怎麼樣？

喬：不錯啊，你可以站在那裡的平台觀賞美景。

梅：那…我們下次旅遊就去那裡吧！

喬：不行！那會讓我嚇破膽的。

梅：對喔，你有懼高症，真可惜！

字彙／片語充電區 Words and Phrases

horrify 動 使恐懼；使驚恐 / frightened 形 受驚嚇的 / detached 形 無動於衷的
be scared out of one's wits 被嚇破膽 / be daredevil on sth. 在…(方面)膽大妄為

UNIT 252 向人「傾訴心事」，用tell就好？

🎧 252

 暖身猜猜看 Warming Up

情境：某位朋友是你最能傾訴心事的對象，這時應該怎麼說？

( )　You are the one that I can _____ my heart out to.

　　(A) pour　　　　　(B) pick　　　　(C) place

正確解答：(A) 你是我可以傾訴心事的好朋友。

 原來應該這樣說！

pour one's heart out 傾訴心事

　　pour是用來描述將液體倒入某處的動作，如果將心事比擬成液體，pour one's heart out就是將內心深處的想法說出來；也可以把out往前移，變成pour out one's heart，如果要說明傾訴的對象，可在後面加上to sb.。

 對話練習 *Let's Talk!*

Brenda: Barbara is someone you can **pour your heart out** to.

Arnold: That's how I feel about her, too. I'm going to ask her out.

Brenda: But I think she is like the sunshine.

Arnold: What do you mean by that?

Brenda: You can enjoy it, but you can't take it home.

布蘭達：芭芭拉是個可以傾訴心事的對象。

阿　諾：我也這麼覺得，我準備約她出去。

布蘭達：可是我覺得她就像陽光一樣。

阿　諾：什麼意思？

布蘭達：你可以享受陽光的溫暖，但卻無法擁有它。

字彙/片語充電區 *Words and Phrases*

vent 動 吐露 / unleash 動 宣洩 / confide 動 吐露秘密 / innermost 形 內心深處的
a load off one's mind 如釋重負 / give away 洩露；露出馬腳 / hush up 秘而不宣

UNIT 253 一時「語塞」而支支吾吾，用stammer準沒錯？

🎧 253

暖身猜猜看 Warming Up

情境：暗戀對象讓你緊張得支支吾吾，這時應該怎麼說？

(　　) I was so excited that I got ＿＿＿＿＿ at first.

(A) tongue-caught　　　(B) mouth-tied　　　(C) tongue-tied

正確解答：(C) 起初我因為太興奮而說不出話來。

原來應該這樣說！

tongue-tied　語塞；舌頭打結

　　tongue-tie原本是一個醫學名詞，指的是舌繫帶過短，導致說話不清楚。將tie改成過去分詞tied，tongue-tied引申出「舌頭打結」或「結巴」的意思，通常是由緊張、興奮、害羞或尷尬的情緒所造成的現象。

對話練習 Let's Talk!

Bruce: You seemed **tongue-tied** about something.

Monica: There's something that I think it's time I told you about.

Bruce: OK. Get it off your chest, Sweetie.

Monica: Before we get more serious, I must tell you that I'm infertile.

Bruce: Oh! ......You are? That's not the end of the world!

布魯斯：你似乎支支吾吾的？

莫妮卡：有件事我覺得是時候告訴你了。

布魯斯：好，說吧，親愛的。

莫妮卡：在我們的關係變得更深入以前，我得告訴你，我有不孕症。

布魯斯：噢！……是嗎？那又不是世界末日！

字彙/片語充電區 Words and Phrases

speechless 形 無言的 / **awkward** 形 尷尬的 / **stutter** 名 口吃 / **eloquent** 形 流利的
a twist in one's tongue 口齒不清 / **argue sb. down** 把某人駁倒 / **think over** 三思

UNIT 254 「面不改色」，當然與face有關？

🎧 254

 暖身猜猜看 *Warming Up*

情境：聽到裁員的消息，有人面不改色，這時應該怎麼說？

(　　) John kept doing his work, not turning a ＿＿＿＿.

　　(A) finger　　　　　(B) hair　　　　(C) head

正確解答：(B) 約翰面不改色地繼續做他的工作。

 原來應該這樣說！

not turn a hair 面不改色

　　這個慣用語來自賽馬用語，通常馬在跑完一場比賽後，身上的毛會蓬亂外翻，如果一根毛都沒亂，看起來就好像什麼事都沒發生；引申為「在應該表現出生氣或難過等情緒時卻面不改色」；注意一定要用否定形。

 *Let's Talk!*

Charles: I love this movie. Great story and totally spine-chilling.

Yvonne: Yeah? I think it's just OK.

Charles: How could you be so calm? You **didn't turn a hair**.

Yvonne: I am immune to horror movies. I mean, they're just movies.

Charles: But this one is a piece of art that arouses your deepest fear.

查爾斯：我愛這部片，故事讚，恐怖到骨子裡。

伊　芳：是嗎？我覺得還好。

查爾斯：你怎麼這麼冷靜？完全面不改色。

伊　芳：我對恐怖片免疫，我是說，它們就只是電影而已嘛。

查爾斯：但這是一部能激起你最深層恐懼的藝術之作耶。

字彙/片語充電區 *Words and Phrases*

level-headed 形 冷靜的 / **poise** 名 鎮定 / **suppress** 動 忍住 / **tranquil** 形 安詳的
keep one's shirt on 冷靜 / **keep a stiff upper lip** 不動聲色 / **at a loss** 不知所措

269

UNIT 255 請某人「鎮定下來」，有比calm down更生動的說法？

🎧 255

暖身猜猜看 Warming Up

情境：你想讓車輛發生擦撞的朋友鎮定下來，這時應該怎麼說？

(　　) Get a _____ on yourself. Call the police and take some pictures.

(A) grip　　　　(B) handle　　　　(C) grab

正確解答：(A) 鎮定一點，打電話報警，並且拍幾張照片。

原來應該這樣說！

get a grip on oneself 鎮定下來

　　如果只看get a grip on，它的意思為掌握或瞭解某事物，而如果on的後面加上反身代名詞，意思就變成控制自己的行為和情緒，也就是鎮定；這個慣用語可以用get a hold of oneself替換，意思不變。

對話練習 Let's Talk!

Anna: Bert, you've got to help me. The hospital called me and...

Bert: Hey! **Get a grip on yourself**. Tell me what's going on.

Anna: The hospital told me that my brother had a car accident.

Bert: Let me drive you to the hospital. We'll figure out what to do then.

Anna: Thank you. I'm totally lost now.

安娜：伯特，你一定要幫我，醫院剛剛打給我說…

伯特：嘿！鎮定一點，告訴我怎麼回事。

安娜：醫院的人跟我說，我弟弟出車禍了。

伯特：我載你去醫院，到了那裡，我們就會知道該怎麼做。

安娜：謝謝你，我現在完全六神無主。

字彙 / 片語充電區 Words and Phrases

composure 名 鎮靜 / assuage 動 使安靜 / reassure 動 安撫 / rational 形 理性的
chill out 冷靜下來 / cool off 鎮靜 / simmer down 息怒 / sort out 解決問題

UNIT 256 「擺脫某種情緒或念頭」，與get rid of相同？

🎧 256

暖身猜猜看 *Warming Up*

情境：想勸朋友買下筆電，免得想個不停，這時應該怎麼說？

( ) You should just buy the laptop and get it out of your _____.

    (A) heart   (B) system   (C) chest

正確解答：(B) 你應該把那台筆電買下來，別再牽腸掛肚了。

原來應該這樣說！

get sth. out of one's system 擺脫某種情緒或念頭

　　這裡的system是指身體或整個人，get sth. out of one's system字面上有「從身體出來」的意思，藉以表示「擺脫某種情緒或念頭」（特別是藉著表達念頭或實際做出來）；get後面的名詞常用it表示，以避免冗長的句子。

對話練習 *Let's Talk!*

Vicky: Hi, Tracy. Do you have a minute? I need to talk to you.	薇琪：嗨，崔西，你有空嗎？我得和你談談。
Tracy: Hi, roomy. Sure. What is it?	崔西：嗨，親愛的室友，當然有空，有什麼事嗎？
Vicky: Uh...Can you keep your dog out of the living room?	薇琪：呃…你可以不要讓你的狗跑到客廳嗎？
Tracy: Oh! I forgot that you are not a dog person. I'm sorry.	崔西：喔！我忘了你不喜歡狗，真不好意思。
Vicky: Thank you so much. I'm glad I **got that out of my system**.	薇琪：太謝謝你了，真高興我有說出來，現在可以放下心中的大石了。

字彙/片語充電區 *Words and Phrases*

confess 動 坦白；承認 / **candid** 形 坦言的；直率的 / **relieved** 形 不再憂慮的
carry out 實行；進行 / **spit out** 坦率地說出來 / **put sth. behind** 將…拋在腦後

UNIT 257 「對⋯產生好感」，會用feeling形容？

🎧 257

 暖身猜猜看 Warming Up

情境：你想大膽對某人表示好感，這時應該怎麼說？

(　　) I think I have really taken a ＿＿＿＿ to you.

(A) fancy　　　　　(B) chance　　　　　(C) risk

正確解答：(A) 我對你真的很有好感。

 原來應該這樣說！

take a fancy to 對⋯產生好感

　　fancy是一種「渴望」或「愛戀」的心情，但它特別指「剛萌芽的感覺」，所以它與desire或yearn所表達的渴望不同，程度並非相當強烈；此處的to為介系詞，其後須接名詞或動名詞。

 Let's Talk!

Mandy: All right. What did your girlfriend say?

Jack: She said she **took a fancy to** another guy.

Mandy: I'm sorry to hear that. But there are plenty of fish in the sea.

Jack: It's just hard for me to get her out of my mind.

Mandy: I don't know why. You're such a sincere guy with a cute haircut...

曼蒂：好吧，你女朋友說了什麼？

傑克：她說她喜歡上別人了。

曼蒂：真令人遺憾，不過，天涯何處無芳草。

傑克：但是我很難忘記她。

曼蒂：我真不明白，你個性老實，頭髮又剪得這麼可愛⋯

字彙/片語充電區 Words and Phrases

charm 名 魅力 / attractive 形 迷人的 / yearn 動 渴望 / gruesome 形 令人厭惡的
be deeply trapped in 無法自拔於⋯ / be sold on 看中 / be grossed out on 討厭

UNIT 258

「白紙黑字」的承諾，
是handwriting on paper？

🎧 258

暖身猜猜看 *Warming Up*

情境：想說明規定都白紙黑字印在合約裡，這時應該怎麼說？

( ) The details are all in ＿＿＿＿ and white in the contract.

(A) red　　　　　(B) blue　　　　　(C) black

正確解答：(C) 所有的細節都清清楚楚地寫在合約上。

原來應該這樣說！

in black and white 白紙黑字；清清楚楚

　　這個慣用語當中的black指的是墨水，white則是紙，in black and white 就是將事情以書寫或印刷的方式呈現；black and white有另一個意思，就是形容事情簡單明瞭，ex. a black and white issue（簡單明瞭的議題）。

對話練習 *Let's Talk!*

Earl: Hello, Mrs. Thompson. Can I hang a painting on the wall?

Jill: Sorry, Earl. You can't hammer nails on the wall.

Earl: Why not? It's just a small nail. Nobody would notice it.

Jill: No, Earl. It's all **in black and white** in the lease.

Earl: All right. I won't do it.

厄爾：哈囉，湯普森太太，我可以在牆上掛一幅畫嗎？

吉兒：抱歉，厄爾，你不能在牆上釘釘子。

厄爾：為什麼不行？只是一根小小的釘子，不會有人注意到的。

吉兒：不行，厄爾，這條規定清清楚楚地印在合約上。

厄爾：好吧，我不釘就是了。

字彙／片語充電區 *Words and Phrases*

certification 名 證明 / visible 形 可看見的；明白的 / straightforward 形 明確的
printed matter 印刷品 / solid gold 確定無疑的 / without dispute 沒有爭議的

UNIT 259 描述得「一清二楚」，該如何強調clear的程度？

🎧 259

暖身猜猜看 *Warming Up*

情境：想解釋自己在溝通時已經講得很清楚，這時應該怎麼說？

(　　) I believe I've made my request _____ clear.

(A) cloudy　　　　(B) crazy　　　　(C) crystal

正確解答：(C) 我相信我已經把我的要求說得一清二楚了。

原來應該這樣說！

crystal clear 晶瑩剔透；一清二楚

　　從十五世紀開始，crystal（水晶）就被用來比喻透明度非常高的事物，crystal clear這個慣用語中的crystal則為形容詞，即「水晶般的」，這個慣用語將兩個形容詞擺在一起，以強調「清晰」與「清澈」的語意。

對話練習 *Let's Talk!*

Cindy: Did you check out the want ads I told you about yesterday?

Taylor: Yeah, there were so many sales positions posted there.

Cindy: I'm sure that you can find a better job.

Taylor: I really need something that is more challenging.

Cindy: I guess your motive is **crystal clear**; you want a way out!

辛蒂：你看過我昨天告訴你的求職廣告了嗎？

泰勒：有，上面刊登了好多銷售人員的職缺。

辛蒂：我相信你一定可以找到更好的工作。

泰勒：我真的需要一些比較有挑戰性的工作。

辛蒂：我想你的動機已經很明顯了；你要另尋出路！

字彙／片語充電區 *Words and Phrases*

clear-cut 形 輪廓清晰的 / ambiguous 形 含糊不清的 / complicated 形 複雜的
open and above board 光明正大的 / for sure 確切地 / out of focus 模糊焦點

UNIT 260　和人說「大致了解」了，只有understand可用？

🎧 260

暖身猜猜看 Warming Up

情境：在經由解說後，你大致了解了情況，這時應該怎麼說？

(　　) I appreciate your explanation, and I can get the _____ of it.

(A) drift　　　　(B) draft　　　　(C) dread

正確解答：(A) 謝謝你的解釋，我大致可以了解。

原來應該這樣說！

get the drift 大致了解

　　drift當名詞指「漂流物」，引申為「要旨」之意，因此get the drift (of)能用以表示「了解某件事的概要」，動詞get可用catch取代；另外，這個慣用語中的the也可以用所有格呈現，ex. I get your drift.（我懂你的意思。）

對話練習 Let's Talk!

Kevin: When is Mr. Jackson's second interview?

Laura: Well...he said that he wasn't interested when I called him.

Kevin: I'm really surprised. I thought he wanted this job badly.

Laura: Maybe the salary and benefits are his first priority.

Kevin: Okay. I **get the drift**.

凱文：傑克森先生的第二次面試是什麼時候？

蘿拉：嗯…我打電話給他的時候，他說他沒有興趣了。

凱文：真令我訝異，我以為他很想要這份工作。

蘿拉：或許薪水和福利才是他的首要考量。

凱文：好吧，這樣我大概了解情況了。

字彙／片語充電區 Words and Phrases

apprehend 動 理解；領會 / preliminary 形 初步的；預備的 / outline 名 概要

make a summary of 對…概要說明 / tell sb. every last word 一五一十說明清楚

UNIT 261 大家「各說各話」，會與different扯上關係？

🎧 261

暖身猜猜看 Warming Up

情境：你想提醒部屬不要爭功諉過，這時應該怎麼說？

(　　) Hold on! Let's stop talking at ＿＿＿＿-purposes.

(A) crash　　　　(B) cream　　　　(C) cross

正確解答：(C) 等一下！我們不要再各說各話了。

原來應該這樣說！

at cross-purposes 各說各話；別有用心

　　cross當形容詞時有「交叉的、橫貫的」之意，更貼切的說法是「相反的」（opposed）。這個慣用語有兩種解釋：第一種是雙方認為說的或做的是同一件事，但實則不然；另一種是雙方分別做不同的事，且彼此互不認同。

對話練習 Let's Talk!

Helen: What a chaotic meeting!	海倫：真是亂七八糟的會議！
Tommy: True! Everyone seemed to speak **at cross-purposes**.	湯米：真的！每個人似乎都有不同的意見。
Helen: Yeah. Nobody was willing to give an inch.	海倫：是啊，沒有人願意讓步。
Tommy: Did you see Jane's face when David told her off?	湯米：大衛臭罵珍的時候，你看到她的表情了嗎？
Helen: I sure did! I think she was utterly stunned!	海倫：當然了！我想她完全嚇傻了！

字彙／片語充電區 Words and Phrases

opposed 形 反對的 / opinionated 形 堅持己見的 / coordinate 動 協調一致
get one's wires crossed 誤解他人的話 / be firm in one's opinion 堅持己見

UNIT 262 「對某人所說的話予以保留」，與untrustworthy差不多？

🎧 262

暖身猜猜看 *Warming Up*

情境：擔心朋友被人欺騙，想要提醒他，這時應該怎麼說？

(　　) We really don't know anything about him. You have to _____ his words.

    (A) reduce   (B) weigh   (C) lighten

正確解答：(B) 我們並不認識他，不要輕易相信他的話。

原來應該這樣說！

weigh one's words 對某人所說的話予以保留

    weigh one's words的字面意思為「秤秤某人言語的重量」，也就是「謹慎衡量、不輕易相信」的意思。weigh經常與介系詞against合用，ex. weigh the benefits against the risks，意思是「權衡利益與風險」。

對話練習 *Let's Talk!*

Mike: So, did you get any suitable applicants?

Jenny: I did interview an eloquent lady, but I don't think she's serious.

Mike: So actually, you **weighed her words**, didn't you?

Jenny: You got it. I'll make a decision after a few more interviews.

Mike: Yeah. We have to be more cautious.

麥克：你有面試到合適的應徵者嗎？

珍妮：有一位口才很好的女士，不過我不認為她是認真的。

麥克：所以你對她的話有所保留，是嗎？

珍妮：是啊，我想再多面試幾位再做決定。

麥克：也對，我們都得更謹慎一點。

字彙／片語充電區 *Words and Phrases*

deliberate ⑱ 謹慎的 / deceptive ⑱ 騙人的；虛偽的 / scrutiny ⑬ 仔細觀察
follow up with 持續觀察 / be fair and square 公正的 / put one's faith in 有信心

UNIT 263　想要「鄭重發誓」，十之八九會用到swear？

🎧 263

 暖身猜猜看 *Warming Up*

情境：你對朋友發誓你說的話句句屬實，這時應該怎麼說？

(　　) I _____ my heart and swear that every word I just said is true.

　　(A) press　　　　　(B) cross　　　　　(C) beat

正確解答：(B) 我發誓我說的每一句話都是真的。

 原來應該這樣說！

cross one's heart 鄭重發誓

　　cross在這裡是動詞，意思是「在某處畫十字」。這個慣用語的用法與西方的宗教信仰有關，用於發誓的情境中；如果想發重誓，可以說cross my heart and hope to die，意思類似「如果違背誓言就不得好死」。

 對話練習 *Let's Talk!*

Paula: Weren't you supposed to be in the office last night? I saw you in a restaurant.

　Ned: That's impossible.

Paula: But the guy I saw wore the green coat I bought for you.

　Ned: **Cross my heart**, that was Bill. I lent him my coat.

Paula: I see. He looked just like you from the back.

寶拉：你昨晚不是應該在辦公室嗎？我在餐廳看到你。

奈德：那不可能。

寶拉：但是我看到的那個人穿著我送你的綠色外套。

奈德：我發誓，那是比爾，我把外套借給他了。

寶拉：原來如此，他的背影看起來跟你好像。

字彙／片語充電區 *Words and Phrases*

vow 動 發誓 / warrant 動 保證 / vouch 動 確定 / sincerity 名 真心誠意
take an oath 發誓 / give one's word 保證 / pledge oneself 發誓；保證

UNIT 264 表達「同意參與」，要agree、也要attend？

🎧 264

暖身猜猜看 *Warming Up*

情境：你不同意參與一項不合法的聯署活動，這時應該怎麼說？

( ) I'm sorry, but I won't _____ myself to an unjust petition.

    (A) lend   (B) borrow   (C) let

正確解答：(A) 抱歉，但我不會同意參與不正當的連署。

原來應該這樣說！

lend oneself to 同意參與；贊同

    lend oneself to後面接事件或活動時，表示「某人同意參與它」；但若主詞為物品，寫成lend itself to時，則必須解釋為「適合」，ex. The car doesn't lend itself to bright colors.（這輛車不適合明亮的顏色。）

Let's Talk!

Harry: Our boss is holding a contest for ideas related to the annual banquet.

Irene: Yeah? I'm not **lending myself to** the contest.

Harry: Why not? The winner can win ten thousand dollars.

Irene: I don't enjoy going to banquets that the boss attends.

哈利：我們老闆要舉行一項關於尾牙點子的競賽。

艾琳：是嗎？我可不參加。

哈利：為什麼？冠軍可以得到一萬元耶。

艾琳：我不喜歡參加有老闆在場的宴會。

字彙/片語充電區 *Words and Phrases*

consent 動 贊成 / endorse 動 背書 / alliance 名 結盟 / dissuade 動 勸阻
count sb. in 算某人一份 / take part in 參加；參與 / talk sb. out of sth. 勸退

UNIT 265　彼此「口徑一致」，就用same表達一致性？

🎧 265

 暖身猜猜看 Warming Up

情境：想讓老闆了解加薪是大家共同的想法，這時應該怎麼說？

(　　) All divisions spoke with one _____, asking for a pay raise.
　　(A) voice　　　　　(B) sound　　　(C) tone

正確解答：(A) 所有的部門都口徑一致，要求加薪。

 原來應該這樣說！

with one voice 口徑一致

　　voice表示一個人說話的「聲音」，與物品碰撞而發出的sound不同；所以能用one voice來表示大家「意見一致」；voice還有一個常見的意思是「發言的權利」，ex. have a voice in the group是指在團體中有發言權。

 **對話練習** Let's Talk!

Brian: They are lying through their teeth!

Tracy: I've seen the financials. The company made a lot of profit!

Brian: I think those big wigs just want to line their own pockets.

Tracy: Yeah. We must protest **with one voice** and go on a strike.

Brian: Well, we can't take this lying down.

布萊恩：他們根本就是睜眼說瞎話！

崔　西：我看過財務報表，公司的獲利其實很高！

布萊恩：我看那些大人物根本想要中飽私囊吧。

崔　西：是啊，我們必須口徑一致地表示抗議，並罷工。

布萊恩：嗯，我們絕不罷休。

字彙／片語充電區 Words and Phrases

unity 名 一致性 / mutual 形 相互間的 / approval 名 贊同 / unilateral 形 單方的
pull together 團結起來 / comply with 與…一致 / split on an opinion 意見分歧

UNIT 266
想替別人「加油打氣」，怎麼想都只有cheer？

🎧 266

 暖身猜猜看 *Warming Up*

情境：你想請人去替朋友打氣，這時應該怎麼說？

( ) Bill looks down in the dumps. Can you help get him _____ up?

    (A) puffed   (B) rounded   (C) pumped

正確解答：(C) 比爾的情緒非常低落，你可以去給他打打氣嗎？

 原來應該這樣說！

pump up 加油打氣

    pump意指「用幫浦打氣」，充氣之後的輪胎或氣球是不是會越來越大、越來越高（up）呢？因此pump up引申有「鼓勵」之意；另外，pump也可指「將物體快速地上下移動」，所以口語中的pump iron是指舉重。

 **對話練習** *Let's Talk!*

Gina: I've got some bad news. We are going to get laid off.

Eric: I know. I feel really depressed.

Gina: How did you know about that before I told you?

Eric: Bad news travels fast.

Gina: I'll collect pogey for a few months and then try to find another job.

Eric: Me, too. Let's get **pumped up** together!

吉 娜：我有一個壞消息，我們要被裁員了。
艾瑞克：我知道，我很沮喪。
吉 娜：我還沒告訴你，你怎麼知道？
艾瑞克：壞事傳千里。
吉 娜：我會先領幾個月的失業救濟金，再找工作。
艾瑞克：我也是，我們一起加油吧！

字彙 / 片語充電區 *Words and Phrases*

morale 名 士氣 / **inflatable** 形 膨脹的 / **frustrate** 動 挫敗 / **discourage** 動 使洩氣
a shot in the arm 強心針；為之振奮 / **spray salts into one's wound** 落井下石

UNIT 267 能「接受不同的意見」，就說這個人很open-minded？

🎧 267

 暖身猜猜看 Warming Up

情境：想勸大家接受彼此不同的意見，這時應該怎麼說？

(　　) There's no point discussing this. Let's agree to _____.

(A) dislike　　　(B) disagree　　　(C) accept

正確解答：(B) 繼續討論沒有意義，讓我們尊重彼此的意見吧。

 原來應該這樣說！

agree to disagree 接受彼此的意見不同

　　這個慣用語普遍被認為源自於美國的文學作品（1785年），當時出現的詞彙為agree to differ，直到後來才衍生出agree to disagree的用法；意思是「雖然彼此不同意對方的意見，但同意接受這個狀況，不再強要說服對方」。

 **對話練習 Let's Talk!**

Bella: That movie is one of the greatest in the genre!

Duke: I can't say I agree with you. The actors were terrible.

Bella: No, they're not. They are all very good actors.

Duke: They are teenage idols. All they need to do is look good.

Bella: All right. Let's just **agree to disagree**.

貝拉：那部電影是同類型當中拍得最好的其中一部！

杜克：這我可不同意，演員的表現很糟糕。

貝拉：才不會，他們都是很棒的演員。

杜克：他們是青少年偶像，只需要看起來又帥又美的就好。

貝拉：好啦，就讓我們求同存異吧。

字彙/片語充電區 Words and Phrases

conflict 名 分歧 / tolerate 動 容忍 / amicable 形 友好的 / concede 動 承認；容許
make peace with 講和 / live with 接受 / stand for 支持 / break with 與…決裂

UNIT 268 常講的「實話實說」，用honest就能表達？

🎧 268

暖身猜猜看 *Warming Up*

情境：你要隱瞞事實的朋友從實招來，這時應該怎麼說？

( ) I want you to come _____ with me about the case.

　　(A) clean 　　　　(B) empty 　　　　(C) clear

正確解答：(A) 我要你老實說。

原來應該這樣說！

come clean 實話實說；全盤托出

　　come在這個慣用語中有「達到某種狀態」的意思，clean則指「心理上的乾淨」，也就是無所隱瞞或欺騙，慣用語come clean就是將藏在心裡的話全部說出來，後面可用with接說話的對象，用about接內容。

Mike: Do you know who took my piece of chocolate cake?	麥克：你知道誰拿走了我的巧克力蛋糕嗎？
Nora: I...don't know.	諾拉：我⋯不知道。
Mike: Now **come clean** with me, or you can forget about the concert.	麥克：快老實說，不然就不帶你去演唱會。
Nora: All right. Peter ate it. But he said he would bring you another piece today.	諾拉：好啦，彼德吃掉了，但他說今天會帶一塊新的來給你。
Mike: You'd better call him. I want the cake now.	麥克：你最好打電話給他，我現在就要那塊蛋糕。

字彙／片語充電區 *Words and Phrases*

disclose 動 透露 ／ acknowledge 動 承認 ／ transparent 形 透明的 ／ cloak 動 掩飾
own up 坦承(小錯) ／ keep back 隱瞞 ／ keep one's hands clean 避免招惹麻煩

UNIT 269　提到「直言不諱」，就用speak開頭？

🎧 269

 暖身猜猜看 Warming Up

情境：你想直接說出你對某藝術品的看法，這時應該怎麼說？

(　　) I'm going to pull no _____ here. I think it needs a lot of work.

　　(A) beats　　　　　(B) hits　　　　　(C) punches

正確解答：(C) 我就直說了，我覺得它很多地方要改進。

 原來應該這樣說！

pull no punches 直言不諱；毫不保留

　　這個慣用語源自於拳擊用語，pull在這裡形容收的動作，當你pull your punches，表示你收斂了力道，沒有用全力出拳；pull no punches用在生活中的引申義是「直接說出心裡話，沒有保留」。

 Let's Talk!

Penny: I saw your article in the school paper. Congratulations!

Oscar: Thanks. What do you think?

Penny: It's great. You **pulled no punches** on the issue of high tuition.

Oscar: I just hope that I won't be in trouble because of it.

Penny: I don't think you will. You didn't defame anyone.

佩　妮：我看到你的文章被刊在校刊上了，恭喜！

奧斯卡：謝謝，你覺得如何？

佩　妮：很棒啊，你對高學費的問題直言不諱。

奧斯卡：希望我不會因為這篇文章而惹上麻煩。

佩　妮：應該不會吧，你並沒有抹黑任何人。

字彙/片語充電區 Words and Phrases

blast 動 嚴厲批評 / unrestrained 形 沒有限制的；無拘束的 / euphemistic 形 委婉的 talk cold turkey 直言不諱 / lay it on the line 老實說 / incriminate oneself 認罪

UNIT 270 問人「你在想什麼？」最簡單的說法是什麼？

🎧 270

暖身猜猜看 Warming Up

情境：你想問沉思的朋友在想什麼，這時應該怎麼說？

( ) A _____ for your thoughts. Is there something bothering you?

    (A) quarter   (B) dollar   (C) penny

正確解答：(C) 你在想什麼？有什麼煩心的事嗎？

原來應該這樣說！

A penny for your thoughts. 你在想什麼？

　　這個慣用語基本上是一種請求，可視為委婉的說法，當你看到某人陷入沉思或似乎很煩惱時，就可以用這個慣用語詢問對方在想什麼，是有別於What are you thinking about?的另一種說法。

Sam: Rose? Rose? **A penny for your thoughts.**

Rose: What? Oh, hi, Sam. I'm sorry. I was thinking about the test.

Sam: You're really a hard-working student, aren't you?

Rose: This is my favorite subject, so I try to do the best I can in it.

Sam: You know what? A fresh cup of coffee might help you think.

山姆：蘿絲？蘿絲？你在想什麼？

蘿絲：什麼？喔嗨，山姆，不好意思，我在想剛才的小考。

山姆：你真是個很認真的學生耶。

蘿絲：這是我最喜愛的科目，所以我特別下了功夫。

山姆：你知道嗎？一杯現泡的咖啡或許可以幫助你思考。

字彙／片語充電區 Words and Phrases

contemplate 動 沉思 / ponder 動 默想 / concern 動 擔心 / inquisitive 形 好奇的
chew the cud 深思 / in a daze 發呆 / lost in abstraction 出神 / hold back 保留

UNIT 271 「直截了當」而傷人，會用direct形容嗎？

🎧 271

 暖身猜猜看 *Warming Up*

情境：朋友欲言又止，你想請他直接說出心裡話，這時應該怎麼說？

(　　) Just tell me straight from the ＿＿＿＿＿ about everything, OK?

    (A) neck   (B) shoulder   (C) bottom

正確解答：(B) 直截了當地跟我說，好嗎？

 原來應該這樣說！

straight from the shoulder 直截了當；一針見血

    shoulder是「肩膀」，straight from the shoulder本來是指直接從肩膀處瞄準對方，揮拳打過去，這樣出拳可使出全身力氣，所以又狠又重；而後被引申為說話直截了當，甚至有些傷人喔！

 對話練習 *Let's Talk!*

Jennifer: Have you heard about...oh, it's no good to gossip.

Brian: Come on! Just tell me **straight from the shoulder**.

Jennifer: Oh, it's about Sam and Joyce. They are seeing each other.

Brian: Well, I don't think it's a big deal.

Jennifer: It is! Sam dated three girls at the same time before.

珍妮佛：你聽說…喔，說閒話不是很好。

布萊恩：什麼啊？直截了當地告訴我吧。

珍妮佛：就是山姆和喬伊絲的事，他們兩個在交往。

布萊恩：那沒什麼大不了的吧。

珍妮佛：這事才大條！山姆以前曾經同時和三個女孩子交往。

字彙/片語充電區 *Words and Phrases*

explicit 形 直截了當的 / **artless** 形 無虛飾的；自然的 / **frankness** 名 坦白；率直
let it all hang out 坦承 / **double talk** 顧左右而言他 / **be hem and haw** 吞吞吐吐的

UNIT 272 「用膝蓋想也知道的事情」，用easy開頭就差不多了？

🎧 272

暖身猜猜看 Warming Up

情境：針對朋友的問題，你覺得答案顯而易見，這時可以怎麼說？

(　) Of course you can't give in. It's a _____.

    (A) dog-walker　　(B) left-hander　　(C) no-brainer

正確解答：(C) 你當然不能讓步，這用膝蓋想都知道。

原來應該這樣說！

no-brainer 用膝蓋想也知道的事情

　　no-brainer的字面意思指「不必花費大腦的事」，引申為「用膝蓋想也知道」的簡單事情。這個慣用語從1950年代開始出現，一開始只是用來形容不花腦力的事，之後才被用來解釋為理所當然的答案。

Jennifer: I think a suitable dress is needed for an interview.

  Frank: That's a **no-brainer**. What happened?

Jennifer: The interviewee wore a backless top and a mini-skirt.

  Frank: Wow. That's not appropriate for sure.

Jennifer: Yeah. I wonder how she could be so inappropriate!

珍妮佛：我認為面試的服裝還是必須得體才對。

法蘭克：這是無庸置疑的，怎麼了嗎？

珍妮佛：剛剛那名應徵者穿了一件露背裝和迷你裙。

法蘭克：哇，那確實不適當。

珍妮佛：是啊，真不知道她怎麼會穿得怎麼不恰當！

字彙/片語充電區 Words and Phrases

pushover 名 輕而易舉的事 / simplicity 名 單純 / sophisticated 形 複雜的
like a duck to water 如同鴨子划水般容易 / low-hanging fruit 簡單可以做到的事

UNIT 273 「從小道消息得知」，小道真的用alley嗎？

🎧 273

暖身猜猜看 *Warming Up*

情境：分享八卦時說的「這可是小道消息」，應該怎麼說？

( ) I heard it from the _____ that Mr. Wang has divorced recently.

　　(A) bananas　　　　(B) grapevine　　　　(C) lemonade

正確解答：(B) 我聽到小道消息說，王先生最近離婚了。

原來應該這樣說！

hear from the grapevine 從小道消息得知

　　這個慣用語起源於沒有電話的古代，當時多用電報來傳遞通訊，卻有人誤把交錯纏結的電報線路比喻為葡萄藤（grapevine），後來hear from/through the grapevine就被引申指「聽到小道消息」，通常為親朋好友間的私房話。

對話練習 *Let's Talk!*

Jack: What did you want to talk to me about?

Lulu: I think it's time for us to call it quits.

Jack: What? Is there some kind of problem you want to talk about?

Lulu: I **heard** it **from the grapevine** that you went to a movie with a lady.

Jack: God! Who said that? I really hate gossipers.

傑克：妳想和我談什麼呢？

露露：我想我們該分手了。

傑克：什麼？你願意和我說是哪裡出了問題嗎？

露露：我聽說你和一個女生去看電影。

傑克：天啊！是誰說的？我真討厭那些亂傳流言的人。

字彙／片語充電區 *Words and Phrases*

rumor 名 謠言／**whisper** 動 竊竊私語／**tabloid** 名 八卦雜誌／**reality** 名 真實性
back-fence talk 閒言閒語／**play safe** 謹言慎行；不冒險／**brass tacks** 事實真相

UNIT 274 「口碑」很好或很差，可以說people say？

🎧 274

暖身猜猜看 *Warming Up*

情境：有一家店靠著客人之間的好口碑而出名，這時應該怎麼說？

(　　) This shop has become very popular, largely by word of _____.

　　(A) mouth 　　　　(B) talk 　　　　(C) speech

正確解答：(A) 這家店主要是靠口碑建立起知名度。

原來應該這樣說！

word of mouth 口碑；口耳相傳

　　這個慣用語字面上的意思為「嘴巴說出來的話」，引申為「口碑」；word of mouth經常與介系詞by搭配，by word of mouth就是通過口頭來傳播；要注意的是，雖然我們通常用複數words表示話語，但在這裡要用單數。

Let's Talk!

Waiter: May I take your order now?

Jocelyn: Do you recommend anything special? I'm new here.

Waiter: Sure, you could try the Norwegian smoked salmon.

Jocelyn: Okay. I'll order that. How's the prawn cocktail?

Waiter: It's also very popular. Most of our customers have heard of it through **word of mouth**.

侍　者：我可以幫您點餐了嗎？

約瑟琳：你有什麼特別推薦的嗎？我第一次來。

侍　者：有的，您可以試試挪威煙燻鮭魚。

約瑟琳：好，我要來一份，那明蝦冷盤沙拉怎麼樣？

侍　者：它也很受歡迎，大部分的客人都聽聞過這道菜的好口碑。

字彙／片語充電區 *Words and Phrases*

recommendation 名 推薦 / **promotion** 名 促銷；晉升 / **orally** 副 口頭地；口述地
spread from mouth to mouth 一傳十，十傳百 / **few and far between** 門可羅雀

UNIT 275 「重要的人」或「最棒的東西」，用important或good形容？

🎧 275

暖身猜猜看 Warming Up

情境：你提到某個總認為自己最棒的人，這時應該怎麼說？

(　　) Larry always thinks he's the bee's _____.

　　(A) arms　　　　　(B) fingers　　　　(C) knees

正確解答：(C) 賴瑞總是認為自己最重要、最了不起。

原來應該這樣說！

bee's knees 重要的人物；最棒的東西

　　蜜蜂的膝蓋怎麼會與best扯上關係呢？有兩種說法：一是因為諧韻，念起來順口；二是因為蜜蜂在採蜜時，膝部常沾滿了大量蜜粉，所以引申為「最精華的部分」；注意這個慣用語現今較不常見。

對話練習 Let's Talk!

Lena: You look in high spirits. Why's that?

Jim: There's a new girl in our division. I think she's the **bee's knees**.

Lena: That tall and thin girl? She seems all right, I guess.

Jim: She has a unique appeal to me. I can't stop thinking about her.

Lena: If you like her so much, you should try asking her out.

莉娜：你看起來神采飛揚的樣子，怎麼啦？

吉姆：我們部門來了個新女生，我覺得她棒透了。

莉娜：那個身材高挑的女生？我覺得她還好啦。

吉姆：她對我有一股特別的吸引力，我沒辦法不去想她。

莉娜：如果你真的那麼喜歡她，就該試著約她出去。

字彙/片語充電區 Words and Phrases

paramount 形 最重要的；主要的 / **self-esteem** 名 自尊 / **weighty** 形 重量級的
be second to none 當仁不讓；第一名 / **drop sth. like a hot potato** 避之唯恐不及

「說話不得體」，就用否定型not？

UNIT 276

🎧 276

 暖身猜猜看 Warming Up

情境：你想禮貌地提出反對意見，這時應該怎麼說？

( ) Excuse me if I speak out of _____, but I don't agree with you.

　　(A) shape 　　　　　(B) turn 　　　　　(C) tune

正確解答：(B) 原諒我說話不得體，但我不同意你的話。

原來應該這樣說！

speak out of turn 說話不得體

　　turn在此為名詞，意思是「行為舉止」；out of有「偏離」的意思，所以 speak out of turn可以解釋為「說話不得體」，通常是指說話的時機、身分不適當；如果將speak改成behave，behave out of turn則指「行為不得體」。

 **對話練習 Let's Talk!**

Lance: I heard that Uncle Willie was here. Is everything okay?

Martha: He's been a little short of money lately, so I gave him some.

Lance: Again? He should go get a real job. What a loser!

Martha: Watch your language, Lance. You're **speaking out of turn**.

Lance: I'm sorry, Mom. I just hate to see you becoming his ATM.

藍斯：我聽說威利叔叔來過了，一切都還好嗎？

瑪莎：他最近手頭有點緊，所以我給了他一些錢。

藍斯：又給？他應該去找份實在的工作，真是個遜咖！

瑪莎：說話小心點，藍斯，你說得太過分了。

藍斯：對不起，媽，我只是不想看到你變成他的提款機。

字彙／片語充電區 Words and Phrases

amiss 副 不得體地 / imprudently 副 輕率地 / unfavorably 副 令人不快地
befit the occasion 得體 / on the nose 恰到好處 / draw one's horns in 謹慎

UNIT 277　說某事「無趣又沒用」，只能用and連接兩個詞？

🎧 277

 暖身猜猜看 *Warming Up*

情境：你想叫朋友別看沒營養的電視節目，這時應該怎麼說？

(　) This TV show is for the _____. You should stop watching it.

　　(A) pigs　　　　(B) monkeys　　　　(C) birds

正確解答：(C) 這個電視節目真無聊，你不應該再看了。

 原來應該這樣說！

for the birds 無趣又沒用

　　這個慣用語源自於二次大戰末期的美軍陣營，它原來的說法是shit for the birds，因為有些鳥類為了找尋種子，會去啄馬的糞便，所以有此說法；This is for the birds.就是This is shit.的另一種說法，藉此避開不文雅的用字。

 對話練習 *Let's Talk!*

Sally: Hello, Ralph. What are you reading?

Ralph: My roommate highly recommended this novel.

Sally: Judging from your face, it's not exactly your kind of book.

Ralph: Actually, I think it's strictly **for the birds**.

Sally: So are you going to tell your roommate you don't like it?

莎莉：哈囉，拉夫，你在看什麼？

拉夫：我室友大力推薦這本小說。

莎莉：從你的表情看來，你不怎麼喜歡這本書吧。

拉夫：事實上，我覺得這本書沒什麼可讀的價值。

莎莉：所以你打算跟你室友說你不喜歡嗎？

字彙/片語充電區 *Words and Phrases*

valueless 形 無價值的 / ludicrous 形 滑稽的 / absurd 形 愚蠢的；可笑的
be good for nothing 一無是處 / of no account 沒用的 / kid stuff 簡單的事

UNIT 278 「插嘴應和」，馬上就想到cut in？

🎧 278

暖身猜猜看 Warming Up

情境：別人在討論時，你想插話表達想法，這時可以怎麼說？

(　　) Pardon me for ＿＿＿＿ in, but there's something I have to say.

  (A) chiming   (B) cutting   (C) jingling

正確解答：(A) 抱歉，我插個話，有件事我必須說一下。

原來應該這樣說！

chime in 插嘴應和

  chime是指門鈴或是有報時裝置的時鐘發出聲響，教堂響起鐘聲也可以叫chime。這個慣用語指「在談話當中加入自己的意見」，也就是「插嘴」；但若加上介系詞with，chime in with則有「同意」或「與…一致」之意。

對話練習 Let's Talk!

Wendy: What are you watching? A talk show? Who's that speaking?

Vincent: Some critic who always **chimes in** while others are talking.

Wendy: That's kind of annoying. But it's quite common.

Vincent: This is bad. Listening is just as important as speaking.

Wendy: Maybe the show is just too short for him to listen quietly.

溫蒂：你在看什麼？談話節目嗎？在說話的那個人是誰？

文森：某個總會在別人講話時插嘴的評論家。

溫蒂：是挺煩人，但這很常見。

文森：這樣很不好，傾聽和說話同樣重要。

溫蒂：也許是因為節目的播放時間太短，所以他沒時間靜靜地聽吧。

字彙/片語充電區 Words and Phrases

interrupt 動 打斷他人說話 / echo 動 附和 / heckle 動 激烈質問 / abrupt 形 唐突的
cut short 打斷談話 / intrude oneself into 硬插入談話 / apply one's ears to 傾聽

UNIT 279 「責罵不休」的模樣，用yell at就足夠？

🎧 279

暖身猜猜看 *Warming Up*

情境：想制止朋友的責罵不休，這時應該怎麼說？

(　　) Can you stop busting my ＿＿＿＿＿ and give me a break?

    (A) clips   (B) chops   (C) claps

正確解答：(B) 你就不能別再罵個沒完，讓我休息一下嗎？

原來應該這樣說！

bust one's chops 責罵不休

    chop在舊時代的英語中表示「嘴邊的鬢角」，bust是「猛擊」之意，所以這個慣用語的意思就是「猛擊某人的鬢角」，意思與slap in one's face（打巴掌）雷同，引申為「不斷地責罵」，並帶有「侮辱」的意味在內。

Wayne: I see that you went out shopping again!

Wendy: Don't worry. It's not like it came out of your pocket.

Wayne: Wow! That was not fair. I'm not a tightwad.

Wendy: Listen. Stop **busting my chops**.

Wayne: I am not. I just believe being frugal is better for us.

韋恩：我看到你又出去購物了！

溫蒂：別擔心，錢又不是從你的口袋掏的。

韋恩：哇！那樣說真不公平，我不是小器鬼。

溫蒂：聽著，別再罵個沒完了。

韋恩：我沒有要罵個沒完，我只是覺得節儉一點會比較好。

字彙 / 片語充電區 *Words and Phrases*

nag 動 不斷嘮叨 / incessant 形 不停的 / continual 形 連續的 / forgive 動 寬恕
call one's names 責罵 / be fed up with 受夠… / forgive and forget 既往不究

UNIT 280 講人行為「太過分」，難道也說too much？

🎧 280

暖身猜猜看 *Warming Up*

情境：你認為弟弟說話太過分，這時應該怎麼說？

(　　) You overstepped the ＿＿＿＿ by teasing your friend's family.

(A) side　　　　　(B) land　　　　　(C) mark

正確解答：(C) 取笑你朋友的家人實在太過分了。

原來應該這樣說！

overstep the mark 太過分

　　overstep有超出某個限度的意思，而mark是標記，在這裡指可容許範圍的標記，所以overstep the mark就是指「超過可容許的範圍」，也就是「太過分」之意；overstep the line也有相同的意思。

對話練習 *Let's Talk!*

Emma: What are you doing? Writing a letter?

Bart: Sort of. It's a sorry note to Linda.

Emma: What did you do to her?

Bart: We had a fight yesterday, and what I said **overstepped the mark**.

Emma: Maybe you can buy her a gift and give it to her with that sorry note.

艾瑪：你在幹嘛？寫信嗎？

巴特：差不多，這是給琳達的道歉信。

艾瑪：你對她做了什麼？

巴特：我們昨天吵了一架，當時我說的話太過分了。

艾瑪：也許你可以買份禮物，和道歉信一起送給她。

字彙／片語充電區 *Words and Phrases*

outrageous 形 令人難以接受的 / detestable 形 可惡的 / moderate 形 不過分的
go too far 太過分 / the last straw 忍耐的極限 / be off-limits 不可逾越；禁止入內

UNIT 281 「大肆吹捧」近似炫耀，所以可以用show off？

🎧 281

 暖身猜猜看 Warming Up

情境：鄰居又在炫耀她新買的包包了，這時應該怎麼說？

(　　) She's _____ her designer handbag again, but I know it's a fake.

(A) pumping up　　(B) burning out　　(C) puffing up

正確解答：(C) 她又在吹噓自己的名牌包了，但我知道那是仿冒品。

 原來應該這樣說！

puff up 大肆吹捧

puff意指「吹」或「噴」，puff up字面上的意思為「向上吹」，故引申出「吹噓」、「（使）驕傲自滿」或「（使）趾高氣昂」的意思；如果用來表示身體狀況，puff up則指因受傷或受感染而「腫起來」。

 Let's Talk!

Jason: So it's said some ghosts haunt the place?

Diane: David said there are a lot of poltergeist-like activities going on there!

Jason: I think he just wanted to reduce the price of the house.

Diane: Is that so?

Jason: He tends to **puff up** everything for certain purposes.

傑森：所以據說那棟房子裡有鬼魂出沒？

黛安：大衛說那裡有很多靈異現象！

傑森：我想他只是想壓低房子的價錢吧。

黛安：是這樣嗎？

傑森：他喜歡為了某些目的而吹噓一些事情。

字彙／片語充電區 *Words and Phrases*

brag 動 吹噓 / boastful 形 自誇的 / humble 形 謙虛的 / practical 形 實在的
oversell oneself 自我吹噓 / lay one's feet on the ground 腳踏實地；實實在在

UNIT 282

「假意的恭維」，
會用fox這個字嗎？

🎧 282

 暖身猜猜看 *Warming Up*

情境：你想提醒朋友某人的讚美並非出於真心，這時應該怎麼說？

( ) When he said that your hair is "truly different", that's a _____ compliment.

(A) left-handed   (B) blonde-haired   (C) short-armed

正確解答：(A) 他說你的髮型「很特別」，那是假意的恭維。

 原來應該這樣說！

left-handed compliment 假意的恭維

我們總喜歡以數目的多寡，來決定什麼是主流。慣用左手的人數比慣用右手的人數少，因而在許多文化裡，左撇子（left-hander）會受到歧視，因此產生這個慣用語，表示「似褒實貶的恭維」，與back-handed compliment同義。

 對話練習 *Let's Talk!*

Jodie: My mother-in law just complains too much!

Paul: If you learn to speak honeyed words, things might be better.

Jodie: What can I say? She's far too shrewd.

Paul: Well, listening is the highest form of **left-handed compliment**.

Jodie: Sounds reasonable. I could try that first.

喬蒂：我婆婆太愛抱怨了！

保羅：如果你學著說些好話，情況可能會好轉。

喬蒂：我能說什麼？她很精明的。

保羅：這個嘛，聆聽是阿諛奉承的最高境界。

喬蒂：聽起來有點道理，我可以先試著那樣做。

字彙/片語充電區 *Words and Phrases*

sarcasm 名 挖苦 / pretend 動 假裝 / praise 動 稱讚 / plain-spoken 形 有話直說的
cater to 迎合 / speak honeyed words 甜言蜜語 / cut no ice with 對⋯起不了作用

297

UNIT 283 視野如「井蛙之見」般狹隘，用frog比喻準沒錯？

🎧 283

暖身猜猜看 *Warming Up*

情境：想鼓勵朋友把視野放開一點，這時應該怎麼說？

( ) People with _____ vision often make mistakes.

(A) tunnel　　　(B) one-sided　　　(C) funnel

正確解答：(A) 目光短淺的人經常會犯錯。。

原來應該這樣說！

tunnel vision 視野狹隘；井蛙之見

　　tunnel是「隧道」，想像自己站在隧道的一端，往另一端出口看過去，是不是只看到一個很小的視野呢？tunnel vision這個慣用語即用來形容一個人「只看到事情的一面，無法全方位看待整件事情」。

對話練習 *Let's Talk!*

Carl: I think Lisa is too pessimistic and has **tunnel vision** about everything.

Fanny: I feel the same way. Jack told me that she has some mental problems.

Carl: I hope that she can get some help.

Fanny: Actually, Jack has suggested to her that she see a shrink.

Carl: Good. I hope she follows his advice.

卡爾：我覺得麗莎太悲觀，視野太狹隘。

芬妮：我也這麼覺得，傑克覺得她的心理有問題。

卡爾：我希望她能夠尋求一些幫助。

芬妮：事實上，傑克已經建議她去看心理醫生了。

卡爾：太好了，我希望她能接納他的建議去看醫生。

字彙／片語充電區 *Words and Phrases*

outlook 名 視野 / comprehensive 形 全面性的 / extensive 形 廣大的；廣闊的
a frog in the well 井底之蛙 / open the doors wide on every side 全方位看待

UNIT 284 「偷偷在一旁觀察的人」，會用什麼來形容person？

🎧 284

暖身猜猜看 *Warming Up*

情境：你希望能聽到同事們的悄悄話，這時應該怎麼說？

(　　) I'd love to be ＿＿＿＿ on the wall and hear what they're talking about.

　　(A) an ant　　　　　(B) a fly　　　　　(C) a bug

正確解答：(B) 我真想變成牆上的蒼蠅，聽他們在說什麼。

原來應該這樣說！

a fly on the wall 偷偷在一旁觀察的人

　　這個慣用語指一個人「可以觀察到他人的言行，同時又不被注意到」，用法起源於1920年代的美國，到了1960年代，這個詞開始用來指一種紀錄片的類型，拍攝者將攝影機放在不容易被發現的地方，以最自然的方式拍攝。

對話練習 *Let's Talk!*

Kent: Why are you leaning your ear against the door?

Laura: Quiet. I'm trying to find out what Mom and Dad are talking about.

Kent: What do you think they're talking about?

Laura: I guess it's Bill. God! I wish I could be **a fly on the wall**.

Kent: Your boyfriend? Don't bother. They don't like him at all.

肯特：你幹嘛把耳朵貼在門上？

蘿拉：安靜點，我想知道媽和爸在房間裡說什麼。

肯特：你覺得他們在談什麼？

蘿拉：我猜他們在談比爾，天哪！真希望能在旁邊偷聽。

肯特：你男朋友？別忙了，他們一點都不喜歡他。

字彙／片語充電區 *Words and Phrases*

snoop 動 窺探 / pry 動 刺探 / overhear 動 無意間聽到 / bystander 名 旁觀者
poke one's nose into 管閒事 / peep at 偷看 / hole up 藏匿 / enquire into 調查

UNIT 285 「中看不中用的東西」，只有useless可形容？

🎧 285

 暖身猜猜看 Warming Up

情境：你認為某支股票不怎麼樣，沒有投資價值，這時應該怎麼說？

( ) Don't invest in unnecessary bells and _____.

(A) watches (B) rings (C) whistles

正確解答：(C) 不要把錢投資在中看不中用的東西上。

 原來應該這樣說！

bells and whistles 中看不中用的東西

　　bells and whistles（鈴與汽笛）這個慣用語據說與古代的交通工具有關。汽車與火車的汽笛聲有叫人留心的作用，而鈴可以作裝飾；在現代美語中，其褒貶意思都有，可引申為吸引使用者的附加設施，或無聊沒價值的東西。

 **對話練習** *Let's Talk!*

Henry: This new sports car looks so flashy, doesn't it?

Bonnie: Why do you care? We don't even have a garage.

Henry: But take a look at all its cool features!

Bonnie: You are too easily impressed by **bells and whistles**.

Henry: Come on! You know how much I've longed for a car like this.

亨利：這款新跑車看起來真炫，是不是？

邦妮：你看這個做什麼？我們連車庫都沒有。

亨利：但它看上去超酷的！

邦妮：你太容易被中看不中用的東西吸引了。

亨利：別這樣！你知道我有多想擁有一台類似的車的。

字彙/片語充電區 *Words and Phrases*

superficial 形 膚淺的 / showy 形 浮華的；華麗的 / spectacle 名 令人羨慕的人事物
pleasant to the eye 中看的 / to no avail 無益 / live up to one's name 名符其實

UNIT 286　所謂的「瑕疵品」，用一個單字就能表達？

🎧 286

 暖身猜猜看 Warming Up

情境：你買了部二手車，卻發現是部瑕疵品，這時應該怎麼說？

(　　) This car is a real _____. I have spent more time fixing it than driving it.

(A) apple　　　　(B) lemon　　　　(C) grape

正確解答：(B) 這車有夠破，我花在修理它的時間比開的時間還多。

 原來應該這樣說！

a lemon 瑕疵品；無價值的東西

　　lemon（檸檬）是一種酸酸的水果，過去人們常以lemon形容尖酸刻薄的人，後來被引申為有缺陷或損壞的事物；另外，lemon在現代美語裡常被用來指「泡水車」；經濟學有lemon market，表示市場上充斥品質低劣的商品。

 *Let's Talk!*

Cathy: Is there something wrong with your car? I just smelled a strange odor.

Frank: I think it came from outside. I drove near a refuse burner.

Cathy: Wait, do you see that smoke in front of us?

Frank: Oh no! Let's get out of the car!

Cathy: What a close call! And what **a lemon** you have!

凱　西：你的車還好嗎？我剛剛聞到一股怪味。

法蘭克：我想是外面的味道，剛才經過一個焚化爐。

凱　西：等等，你看見前面冒煙了嗎？

法蘭克：喔不！我們快下車！

凱　西：真是驚險！你這是什麼大爛車啊！

字彙／片語充電區 *Words and Phrases*

sour 形 酸味的 / defect 名 瑕疵 / shortcoming 名 缺點 / functional 名 實用的
a piece of junk 爛貨 / knock it off 扔掉；丟棄 / cooked data 動過手腳的數據

UNIT 287 「物超所值的商品」，就是value很高？

🎧 287

 暖身猜猜看 *Warming Up*

情境：買了個「俗又大碗」的好東西，這時應該怎麼說？

(　　) It only costs one hundred dollars! It's almost a ＿＿＿＿ at this price.

(A) steal (B) penny (C) gift

正確解答：(A) 這東西才一百元！價格實在太便宜了。

 原來應該這樣說！

a steal 物超所值的商品

　　steal當動詞是「偷」，在棒球比賽中則有「盜壘」之意，如果盜壘成功，就有「賺到」的意味，藉以形容「商品便宜到讓人感覺賺到」的意思，下次聽到有人說It's a steal!，可別以為它是「偷來的」喔！

 *Let's Talk!*

William: My wife and I went to Crete, and I highly recommend it!

Joyce: I've always wanted to visit the Mediterranean.

William: Crete is very romantic, and it is full of history.

Joyce: But I think it's very expensive to travel there, right?

William: Maybe you can get **a steal** at this travel fair.

威　廉：我太太跟我去了趟克里特島，我強烈推薦這個地方！

喬伊絲：我一直都很想去地中海。

威　廉：克里特島非常浪漫，而且擁有悠久的歷史。

喬伊絲：但到那裡旅遊應該很貴吧？

威　廉：也許你能在這個旅遊展中撈到個好價錢。

字彙 / 片語充電區 *Words and Phrases*

sell-off 名 被以廉價出售的東西 / **auction** 名 拍賣 / **steep** 形 價格過高或不合理的
a real buy 物超所值的商品 / **buy...for a song** 以低價購得 / **at a premium** 以高價

UNIT 288
熱銷一空的「搶手貨」，只知道best-seller？

🎧 288

暖身猜猜看 Warming Up

情境：你想請朋友幫忙買熱門比賽的門票，這時應該怎麼說？

( ) Go get the tickets right now! The match is a _____.

    (A) rip-off   (B) time-killer   (C) hot ticket

正確解答：(C) 現在就去買票！這場比賽很搶手。

原來應該這樣說！

a hot ticket 搶手貨

    hot除了有「熱」的意思之外，還有「熱門的、搶手的」之意。hot ticket 大約從1950年代才開始出現，來自運動賽事的用語，指很熱門的比賽，其門票熱銷的情況，後來廣泛指任何受歡迎的事物，也就是「搶手貨」。

Let's Talk!

Laura: Hi, I'd like to see a good movie. Any suggestions?	蘿 拉：嗨，我想看一部好電影，有什麼建議嗎？
Clerk: If you're a fan of action films, "Hero" is very popular.	售票員：如果您喜歡動作片，《英雄》最近很流行。
Laura: Sounds good. Give me two tickets, please.	蘿 拉：聽起來不錯，請給我兩張票。
Clerk: Okay...I'm sorry, but there are no tickets left for today.	售票員：好的…我很抱歉，今天的票已經售完了。
Laura: Wow, looks like it's **a hot ticket**. Now I'm really interested.	蘿 拉：哇，看起來這部片子很熱門，我開始感興趣了。

字彙／片語充電區 Words and Phrases

sought-after 形 受歡迎的 / vogue 名 風行 / inconspicuous 形 不引人注目的
a hot shot 大紅人 / **sell like hot cakes** 熱銷 / **lash out one's fortune** 花大錢

UNIT 289 「賣太貴」的負面意涵，用expensive就能表達？

🎧 289

 暖身猜猜看 *Warming Up*

情境：貴得嚇人的商品，簡直與搶錢無異，這時可以怎麼說？

( ) That shirt is indeed a _____. I'm not going to buy it.

    (A) rip-off   (B) robbery   (C) ripper

正確解答：(A) 那件襯衫貴得嚇人，我不會買。

 原來應該這樣說！

a rip-off 賣太貴的東西

　　rip這個動詞本來是「撕」或「剝」的意思，rip off就是「扯下」或「剝掉」，所以當你說I got ripped off!就是「我被坑了」（如同被剝了一層的感覺）；若以名詞的rip-off呈現，則表示「買的物品不值它的價格」。

 *Let's Talk!*

Kevin: Hey, Sara! Mr. Wang has given me a quote for the materials.

Sara: That's great! How much?

Kevin: $2,500 in total. Twenty percent off, according to him.

Sara: That's **a rip-off**! The quote from Mr. Lin is $1,000.

Kevin: What?! How could Wang charge us so much then?

凱文：嘿，莎拉！王先生已給我材料的報價了。

莎拉：太好了！那是多少錢？

凱文：總共2,500元，他說給我們打八折了。

莎拉：敲竹槓啊！林先生說可以算我們1,000元。

凱文：什麼？！王先生怎麼能賣我們這麼貴呢？

字彙／片語充電區 *Words and Phrases*

bogus 形 假冒的；偽造的 / **quality** 名 品質 / **deserve** 動 值得；該得 / **grift** 名 詐騙 **squeeze sth. out of sb.** 敲詐 / **a sugar daddy** 凱子 / **a good deal** 物超所值之物

UNIT 290 媲美印鈔機的「金雞母」，真的是golden hen？

🎧 290

暖身猜猜看 *Warming Up*

情境：老闆想要讚賞公司的忠實客戶，這時可能怎麼說？

( ) Let's pay respect to our ＿＿＿＿－ those loyal clients.

  (A) top tickets   (B) smoking guns   (C) cash cows

正確解答：(C) 讓我們對本公司的金雞母 — 忠實客戶們表達敬意。

原來應該這樣說！

a cash cow 金雞母；搖錢樹

  這個慣用語的來源來自於印度傳統對牛的尊敬，會將錢奉獻給牛隻。演變到後來，「現金牛」衍生出「搖錢樹」之意；請注意這裡使用「母牛（cow）」，而非公牛（bull），這是因為母牛才能擠牛奶（有生產力）。

對話練習 *Let's Talk!*

Emily: This beverage shop is **a cash cow**.	艾蜜莉：這家飲料店真是一棵搖錢樹。
Jeffrey: I agree. Look how crowded it is.	傑佛瑞：我同意，店裡人潮洶湧啊。
Emily: That must be very profitable! I wish I owned a business like this.	艾蜜莉：一定很好賺！真希望我也能擁有這樣的生意。
Jeffrey: You know what? They even opened a fried chicken stand near our campus.	傑佛瑞：你知道嗎？他們甚至在我們學校附近開了一家炸雞排攤位。
Emily: No wonder I often see customers standing in long lines there.	艾蜜莉：難怪我常常看到顧客在大排長龍。

字彙/片語充電區 *Words and Phrases*

profit 名 利潤；盈利 / **lucrative** 名 有利可圖的；盈利的 / **worthless** 形 無價值的
make a fortune 大賺一筆 / **beat the drum for** 推銷 / **take pains to** 慘淡經營

UNIT 291 努力存起來的「老本」，是什麼money？

🎧 291

 暖身猜猜看 Warming Up

情境：勸人別把存款全數投入股市中，這時應該怎麼說？

(　　) Don't invest all of your ＿＿＿＿ in the stock market.

　　(A) brain-turner　　　(B) nest egg　　　(C) hot penny

正確解答：(B) 別把你所有的老本都投入股市。

 原來應該這樣說！

nest egg 退休金；老本

　　nest egg（窩裡的蛋）原本指的是假蛋，放著騙家禽多生蛋的，從這個意思引申，用來指錢，就好像是中文裡說的「錢滾錢」，更進一步說，nest egg 常用來指「退休金、老本」，隱含「為特定目的而存的錢」。

 **對話練習** *Let's Talk!*

Jason: I think that we should start planning for our retirement.

Julie: You mean like starting a **nest egg** or something?

Jason: That's exactly what I'm talking about.

Julie: OK. Tell me what you have in mind. I'm all ears.

Jason: Well, I think we can make some investments from now on.

傑森：我想我們應該開始規劃退休生活了。

茱莉：你是指開始存錢之類的嗎？

傑森：是啊，就是這個意思。

茱莉：好吧，你有什麼想法嗎？我洗耳恭聽。

傑森：嗯，我覺得從現在開始，我們可以做點投資。

字彙／片語充電區 *Words and Phrases*

pension ❷ 養老金 / bankroll ❷ 資金；鈔票 / manage ❶ 管理 / inventory ❷ 庫存
save for a rainy day 未雨綢繆 / put away in reserve 另存 / easy money 好賺

UNIT 292 要描述「一大筆錢」，一定會用a great amount？

🎧 292

暖身猜猜看 *Warming Up*

情境：死薪水族的你，負擔不起現今的房價，這時應該怎麼說？

（　　）I'd really love to buy an apartment, but it costs a _____.

(A) pretty penny　　　(B) big cash　　　(C) great money

正確解答：(A) 我很想買棟公寓，但那要花一大筆錢。

原來應該這樣說！

a pretty penny 一大筆錢

除了我們熟知的cost a lot of money（花很多錢）以外，這個慣用語也能強調「錢的量」。penny是英國最小的貨幣單位，pretty在此則表達「大量」，大量的一分錢，就是「一大筆錢」。

對話練習 *Let's Talk!*

Phil: So do you feel like going to the new vegetarian restaurant?	菲爾：有一間新開幕的素食餐廳，要去嗎？
Lucy: Is it the one close by? I heard each dish costs **a pretty penny**.	露西：在附近那間嗎？聽說它每一道菜都非常貴耶。
Phil: I think it's no big deal spending some of your fortune occasionally.	菲爾：我覺得偶爾花錢享受一下也無妨。
Lucy: Well, I'm trying to cut back on expenses.	露西：嗯，我想試著減少開銷。
Phil: No wonder you brown-bag it every day to work now.	菲爾：難怪你現在每天上班都自己帶午餐。

字彙／片語充電區 *Words and Phrases*

cost 名 費用 / extravagant 形 奢侈的 / invaluable 形 無價的 / frugal 形 簡樸的
live in luxury 奢侈 / dig into one's pocket 花錢不手軟 / a penny pincher 鐵公雞

UNIT
293

「一本引人入勝的書」，用attractive行嗎？

🎧 293

暖身猜猜看 Warming Up

情境：精彩的小說讓你很想一口氣把它看完，這時應該怎麼說？

(　　) This book's such a ＿＿＿＿＿ that I can't put it aside for a while.

　　(A) page-brainer　　(B) page-ruler　　(C) page-turner

正確解答：(C) 這本書真是好看，讓我愛不釋手。

原來應該這樣說！

a page-turner 一本引人入勝的書

　　本來turn a page叫作「翻一頁」，而「翻到第幾頁」可以說turn to page No...。所以，我們可以想見a page-turner就是讓你在看一本書時看到忘我，這本書彷彿可以自動翻頁，引申為一本「好看得不得了的書」。

對話練習 Let's Talk!

Linda: This novel is **a real page-turner**.

Gordon: Oh really? Is it sort of like a Sherlock Holmes novel or something?

Linda: Not exactly. It's a suspense novel.

Gordon: If it's so interesting, then I'll get a copy.

Linda: Don't bother. They just made a movie out of it. Want to go and see it?

琳達：這本小說相當引人入勝。

戈登：真的嗎？是像福爾摩斯那一類的嗎？

琳達：不完全相同，它是本懸疑小說。

戈登：如果這麼有趣，那我也去買一本來看。

琳達：別麻煩了，他們剛把小說翻拍成電影呢，要去看嗎？

字彙／片語充電區 Words and Phrases

must-read 形 必讀的 / **tribute** 名 稱頌；貢獻 / **neglected** 形 被忽略的；冷門的
make a movie out of 改編成電影 / **make a stir** 引起騷動 / **thumb through** 隨便翻

UNIT 294 「老掉牙的故事」，用boring形容到位嗎？

294

暖身猜猜看 Warming Up

情境：朋友說了一個你已經聽過好幾次的笑話，這時可以怎麼說？

(　　) That joke is an old _____ that I've heard at least a dozen times.

(A) fame　　(B) chestnut　　(C) glory

正確解答：(B) 這是個老掉牙的笑話，我已經聽過十幾次了。

原來應該這樣說！

an old chestnut 老掉牙的故事

nut是果仁，chestnut就是讓你口水直流的栗子，那如果是放了很久的栗子，肯定不會有人想吃吧？因此，an old chestnut（放了很久的栗子）就被引申為一個笑話或故事被說過太多次，變得沒有意思或不吸引人。

對話練習 Let's Talk!

Monica: Bruce is dull and talks about the same things every day.

Derek: There you go again! Those stories are **old chestnuts** to me.

Monica: But I would much rather hear something new.

Derek: Something new? Like what?

Monica: To be frank, I'd like to hear that you want to take me out on a date.

莫妮卡：布魯斯真的很無趣，每天都在說相同的事情。

德瑞克：你又來了！這些抱怨對我來說都是老掉牙了。

莫妮卡：但我期望你有些新的回應。

德瑞克：新的回應？例如？

莫妮卡：坦白說，我比較希望你來邀我去約會呢。

字彙/片語充電區 Words and Phrases

cliche 名 陳腔濫調 / **repetitive** 形 重複的 / **stale** 形 無新意的 / **novelty** 名 創新
fall into a pattern 一成不變 / **out of date** 落伍的 / **be weary of** 對…感到厭倦

UNIT 295 我們常喝的「水」，除了water以外的說法是？

🎧 295

暖身猜猜看 Warming Up

情境：想勸開車的朋友別喝酒，喝水就好，這時可以怎麼說？

(　　) Don't drink and drive. Adam's _____ is the best beverage.

(A) rib　　　　　　(B) ale　　　　　　(C) apple

正確解答：(B) 開車不喝酒，水是最好的飲料。

原來應該這樣說！

Adam's ale 水

這個慣用語來自聖經的典故。ale本來是一種麥芽酒，但在伊甸園裡的亞當（Adam）只能喝水，所以Adam's ale就是指「水」，不過它背後的意義是「苦水」，有「禁慾」與「節制」的涵義；注意這個慣用語現在較少用。

Molly: You have high blood pressure. Beer isn't good for you!

Kent: I know, but I just cannot refrain from drinking it.

Molly: Having more **Adam's ale** will do good to you.

Kent: I guess you're right. It's time to make a change.

Molly: I can help you prepare some healthy meals if you want, too.

莫莉：你有高血壓，喝啤酒對你不好！

肯特：我知道，但我就是無法克制自己。

莫莉：多喝水對你才有幫助。

肯特：我想你是對的，是該做點改變了。

莫莉：如果你想要的話，我可以幫你準備一些健康的餐點。

字彙／片語充電區 Words and Phrases

beverage 名 飲料 / refrain 動 克制；節制 / liquid 名 液體 / alcohol 名 酒精
hold back from 克制住不去做(某事) / in poor shape 身體不舒服；狀況不佳

UNIT 296 讓人視線不清的「濃霧」，會用fog還是mist？

🎧 296

 暖身猜猜看 *Warming Up*

情境：開車遇到濃霧，一定要特別注意，這時應該怎麼說？

(　　) Watch out! The fog was as thick as _____.

　　(A) fruit jam　　　(B) herbal tea　　　(C) pea soup

正確解答：(C) 小心點！這霧很濃。

 原來應該這樣說！

pea soup 濃霧

　　這個慣用語起源於十九世紀的英國，工業革命的發展除了帶來便利之外，也帶來工廠廢氣的汙染，這些廢氣與霧（fog）結合，帶有混濁不清的黃色，所以用pea soup（豆羹，呈黃色）形容，以便與自然的白色霧氣區隔。

 對話練習 *Let's Talk!*

Mike: Did you hear what that couple were talking about?

Kelly: No. What were they talking about?

Mike: They said the flight was delayed because of the **pea soup** conditions.

Kelly: Are you sure they're taking the same flight that we are going to take?

Mike: Yeah. I heard them mention the flight number.

麥克：你有聽到那對夫妻說的話嗎？

凱莉：沒有，他們說了什麼？

麥克：他們說班機因為遭遇濃霧而延誤了。

凱莉：你確定他們搭的和我們搭的是同一班飛機嗎？

麥克：確定，我聽到他們提到班機號碼。

字彙/片語充電區 *Words and Phrases*

dense 形 濃厚的 / mist 名 霧 / blurred 形 難以辨識的 / searchlight 名 探照燈
be pitch-dark 黑漆漆 / a toss-up 難預料的事 / see...through a mist 霧裡看花

UNIT 297 影集中常出現的「鐵證」，用evidence可以嗎？

🎧 297

 暖身猜猜看 *Warming Up*

情境：男友偷吃，恰巧被你抓到把柄，這時應該怎麼說？

( ) Don't try to explain it. The _____ was the lipstick on your collar.

　　(A) smoking gun 　　(B) firing gun 　　(C) loaded gun

正確解答：(A) 別想解釋，你領子上的口紅就是鐵證。

 原來應該這樣說！

smoking gun 鐵證

　　smoking不是「抽菸」，而是「正在冒煙」的意思。這個慣用語使用了某種意象，剛射擊過的手槍會冒煙，所以，當你手上握住一支正在冒煙的槍，前面又躺著一名死者，而警察又正好出現，這真是賴都賴不掉的鐵證囉！

 *Let's Talk!*

Lily: I found out that my husband has been cheating on me.

Jeff: How do you know that? How can you be so sure?

Lily: Well, I found a lipstick stain on his collar while I was doing the laundry.

Jeff: So...did you ask him about it?

Lily: Isn't a lipstick stain considered a **smoking gun**?

莉莉：我發現我丈夫對我不忠。

傑夫：你怎麼知道是這樣？怎麼能這麼確定？

莉莉：我洗衣服的時候，發現他的襯衫領子有口紅印。

傑夫：所以，你有問他這件事嗎？

莉莉：口紅印不就是鐵證嗎？

字彙／片語充電區 *Words and Phrases*

evident 形 明顯的 ／ **undisputable** 形 無庸置疑的 ／ **suspected** 形 有嫌疑的
leave sb. speechless 令某人啞口無言 ／ **talk one's way out of sth.** 狡辯擺脫

UNIT 298　提到「男生廁所」，想委婉一點可以嗎？

🎧 298

暖身猜猜看 *Warming Up*

情境：想委婉表達自己在找男廁所，這時可以怎麼說？

(　　) Excuse me. May I use the little boy's _____?

(A) room 　　　　(B) house 　　　　(C) door

正確解答：(A) 不好意思，請問我可以用男生廁所嗎？

原來應該這樣說！

little boy's room 男生廁所

　　英文裡的「廁所」有很多種説法，**little boy's room**字面上的意思為「男孩的房間」，藉此表示「男廁」，為委婉的説法，等同於**gentleman's room**；如果是女廁，可以説**little girl's room**或**lady's room**。

對話練習　*Let's Talk!*

Kent: God! I've run to the **little boy's room** several times this morning.

Tina: That's terrible! Are you all right?

Kent: Not really. I've been having abdominal cramps all morning.

Tina: What did you have for dinner last night?

Kent: I ate a lot of shellfish. That probably wasn't a smart move.

肯特：天啊！我今天早上已經跑了好幾趟廁所了。

蒂娜：真慘！你還好嗎？

肯特：不怎麼好，我腹部絞痛了整個早上。

蒂娜：你昨天晚餐吃了什麼啊？

肯特：我吃了很多帶殼海鮮，這大概不是什麼明智之舉。

字彙／片語充電區 *Words and Phrases*

washroom 名 洗手間 / **flush** 動 沖水；使臉紅 / **lavatory** 名 (飛機、火車上的)廁所
wash one's hands 上廁所 / **hold one's water** 某人憋尿 / **take a dump** 上大號

UNIT 299 「精神奕奕」的樣子，與spirit有關嗎？

🎧 299

 暖身猜猜看 Warming Up

情境：看到一位八十歲的老先生精神奕奕，這時可以怎麼說？

(   ) I'm so amazed that the old guy is so alive and _____.

    (A) beating   (B) running   (C) kicking

正確解答：(C) 那名老先生如此精神奕奕，真令人吃驚。

 原來應該這樣說！

alive and kicking 活得好好的；精神奕奕

    alive常用於表示「劫後餘生」的「活著」，那如果不只是活著，還能踢人（kick）的話，就真是可喜可賀了！alive and kicking通常用來表示「令人驚訝」的活力或生命力，kicking也可用well取代，但用kicking較生動。

 *Let's Talk!*

Winnie: What's with that bandage on your forehead?

Robert: I got in a car wreck last week and I bumped my head.

Winnie: That's terrible! Was it a minor accident or...?

Robert: It was a head-on collision. My car was totaled.

Winnie: At least you're still **alive and kicking**.

維　妮：	你額頭上的繃帶是怎麼回事？
羅伯特：	我上禮拜出車禍，撞到頭。
維　妮：	真糟啊！是小車禍還是…？
羅伯特：	迎面對撞，我的車全毀了。
維　妮：	至少你還活得好好的。

字彙／片語充電區 *Words and Phrases*

lively 形 活潑的 / **animated** 形 活躍的 / **conscious** 形 清醒的 / **lifeless** 形 死的 / **in the pink** 健康的 / **as fresh as daisy** 精神飽滿的 / **at one's last gasp** 奄奄一息

UNIT 300

「（身體、運作）狀況良好」，只想得出用well形容？

🎧 300

暖身猜猜看 *Warming Up*

情境：想告訴朋友押注一匹神采奕奕的馬，這時應該怎麼說？

(　　) The No. 2 horse looks in fine _____ and should win the race.
　　(A) fettle　　　　(B) saddle　　　　(C) rattle

正確解答：(A) 二號馬看起來狀況很好，應該會贏。

原來應該這樣說！

in fine fettle 神采奕奕；（身體、運作）狀況良好

　　fettle這個字有「修補」的意思，in fine fettle就是從一個較不好的狀態，經過調整、修繕之後，轉為良好狀態；可以用來形容人或事物；其中形容詞fine可以用good或excellent等形容詞取代。

David: Where are you headed? Do you need a lift somewhere?

Irene: No thanks. I'm going to the gym, and it's out of your way.

David: Good for you to regularly do workouts.

Irene: And that's why I'm always **in fine fettle**.

David: I guess I should do exercise with you sometimes.

大衛：你要去哪裡？要我載你一程嗎？

艾琳：不，謝了，我正要去健身房，那裡對你來說不順路。

大衛：你有運動的習慣真棒。

艾琳：所以我總是精神奕奕啊。

大衛：我想我有時候應該要跟你一起去運動。

字彙／片語充電區 *Words and Phrases*

energetic 形 精力旺盛的 / stout 形 粗壯的 / sluggish 形 懶散的 / collapse 動 累倒
a red glow on one's face 容光煥發 / keel sb. over 使暈倒 / (be) run down 累壞

UNIT 301　上了年紀的人「身體硬朗」，和strong有差嗎？

🎧 301

暖身猜猜看 Warming Up

情境：朋友的爺爺年近八十，身體仍非常硬朗，這時應該怎麼說？

（　　）Your grandfather looked _____ and hearty.

　　(A) hale　　　　　(B) male　　　　　(C) pale

正確解答：(A) 你爺爺看起來非常健壯。

原來應該這樣說！

hale and hearty 非常健壯

　　這個說法源自古英語，hale源自hal，原意是安全的、無病痛的，現在通常用來形容一個上了年紀的人身體還相當硬朗，再加上hearty有精力充沛的意思，因此，這個慣用語就表示「一個人看起來不但健康，且過得很開心」。

Joseph: Mrs. Lee had plastic surgery to make herself look young.	約瑟夫：李太太做了整形手術，想藉此讓自己恢復年輕的容貌。
Nancy: She spent so much money on this. That's insane!	南　西：她花了很多錢在這上面，真是瘋狂啊！
Joseph: Her family almost ended up in the poorhouse because of her.	約瑟夫：就因為她，她的家人差點窮到走投無路。
Nancy: We'll all be old one day. I don't think it's a big deal.	南　西：我們都會變老，那根本沒什麼大不了。
Joseph: Take my grandma for instance. She looks so **hale and hearty**.	約瑟夫：像我奶奶，身體很硬朗，也過得很開心呢。

字彙/片語充電區 Words and Phrases

peppy 形 精神充沛的 / **physique** 名 體格 / **feeble** 形 虛弱的 / **fragile** 形 虛弱的 / **be wrapped tight** 身體狀況良好；頭腦健全的 / **strong as an ox** 壯得跟牛一樣

UNIT 302 什麼都能吃的「鐵胃」，用healthy stomach？

🎧 302

暖身猜猜看 *Warming Up*

情境：朋友的鐵胃總讓你感到羨慕不已，這時應該怎麼說？

(　) You can eat everything, and you really have an _____ stomach!

　　(A) sugar coated　　　(B) solid gold　　　(C) cast iron

正確解答：(C) 你什麼都能吃，真是個鐵胃！

原來應該這樣說！

a cast iron stomach 鐵胃；健康的胃

　　cast當名詞指「模子」，cast iron就是「鐵打的」，所以cast iron stomach意思就是很強的胃（鐵胃）；有時會在食譜或菜單上看到餐點旁邊註明cast iron stomach required，表示這道菜口味很重，胃弱的人不宜。

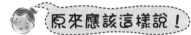  *Let's Talk!*

Ann: I have loose bowels! It must be the hot pot last night.

Ken: Your stomach is so weak! I made a pig of myself, too.

Ann: Then you have **a cast iron stomach**. You can eat everything.

Ken: I think my physique is the key.

Ann: Cut it out! You have high blood pressure and high cholesterol.

安：我拉肚子了！一定是昨晚的火鍋害的。

肯：你的胃太虛了！我不也大吃大喝了一番？

安：那你的胃是「鐵胃」，什麼都能吃。

肯：我想個人體質是關鍵吧。

安：得了吧！你有高血壓和高膽固醇耶。

字彙/片語充電區 *Words and Phrases*

devour 動 吃光 / gulp 動 大吃大喝 / digestion 名 消化；吸收 / diarrhea 名 腹瀉
make a pig of oneself 大快朵頤 / go stale (食物)過期 / have loose bowels 腹瀉

317

UNIT 303 瘦到不成人樣的「皮包骨」，還是用too thin描述？

🎧 303

 暖身猜猜看 *Warming Up*

情境：你看到一位瘦得不像話的明星，這時應該怎麼說？

(　　) She is simply a _____ of bones. That's not beautiful at all.

　　(A) set　　　　　　(B) bag　　　　　　(C) pack

正確解答：(B) 她簡直是皮包骨，那樣一點都不美。

原來應該這樣說！

a bag of bones 皮包骨

　　這個慣用語是用來比喻人的身材，當一個人瘦到幾乎可以透過皮膚看見骨頭的形狀，就可以這樣描述；另外，用實際物品來形容瘦子的説法還有skinny as a rail，意思是「瘦得跟欄杆一樣」。

 *Let's Talk!*

Colin: Tara! It's so good to see you. You've lost so much weight.

Tara: Yeah, but not in a healthy way. I had a serious disease.

Colin: I'm sorry. How are you now?

Tara: I'm all better now, but I was like **a bag of bones** before.

Colin: Let's have a big meal and celebrate your recovery.

科林：塔拉！真高興見到你，你瘦了好多。

塔拉：是啊，不過並非健康瘦下來的，我生了一場重病。

科林：真令人遺憾，那你現在的身體狀況如何？

塔拉：我現在已經全好了，可是之前瘦得像皮包骨。

科林：我們去吃一頓大餐，慶祝你的康復吧。

字彙/片語充電區 *Words and Phrases*

skeletal 形 骨瘦如柴的 / sallow 形 氣色不好的 / malnourished 形 營養不良的
be peak and pine 消瘦 / be skin and bones 瘦巴巴 / waste away 消瘦下去

UNIT 304 「腰間的脂肪游泳圈」，真的用a swim ring嗎？

🎧 304

暖身猜猜看 *Warming Up*

情境：腰間的「游泳圈」實在太難消除，這時應該怎麼說？

( ) I tried to lose weight, but it is hard to get rid of my _____ tire.

（A) rest （B) spare （C) other

正確解答：(B) 我試著減肥，但腰間這圈肥肉很難消。

原來應該這樣說！

spare tire 腰間贅肉；備胎

　　spare tire（多餘的輪胎）有兩個意思：一是車子爆胎時可以使用的「備胎」，另一個則是常常拿來開胖子玩笑的「游泳圈」，它還有一個有趣的說法 love handle，源自於情侶擁抱時，會玩笑性地捏腰間的肥肉。

Lucy: I'm going on a diet, and I think you should go on one, too.

Bob: What? Are you kidding? I'm in great shape.

Lucy: Very funny. I can see your **spare tire** so clearly.

Bob: Oh yeah? I'll think about it.

Lucy: From now on, I'm going to monitor what you eat.

露西：我在實行減重計畫，我覺得你也需要。

鮑伯：什麼？你在開玩笑嗎？我身材很棒的。

露西：真好笑，我都可以清楚看見你腰間的游泳圈了。

鮑伯：是這樣嗎？那我考慮一下。

露西：從現在起，我會監督你吃的東西。

字彙／片語充電區 *Words and Phrases*

beer belly 名 啤酒肚 / potbelly 名 肥胖的大肚皮 / waistline 名 腰圍 / slim 形 纖細的
bay window 胖肚子 / middle-aged spread 中年發福 / abdominal muscles 腹肌

UNIT 305　滿布的「瘀青」，會用bruise形容？

🎧 305

暖身猜猜看 Warming Up

情境：看到人因為被痛扁，身上瘀青，這時應該怎麼說？

(　) Poor boy! He was beaten black-and-_____.

　　(A) blue　　　　　　(B) red　　　　　　(C) green

正確解答：(A) 真可憐！他被打得遍體鱗傷。

原來應該這樣說！

black-and-blue 瘀青；遍體鱗傷

　　black-and-blue顧名思義就是「黑與青」，也就是青一塊紫一塊（台語「黑青」）的意思；另外，可別把blue in the face誤以為是被打得「黑青」喔，它是指因氣急敗壞或精疲力竭而「臉色發青」。

對話練習 Let's Talk!

Paul: Are the arguments between you and Mike getting better now?

Jenny: No. Actually, he gets really angry and starts throwing things.

Paul: Are you serious? That's terrible!

Jenny: I'm afraid I'll be beaten **black-and-blue** one day.

Paul: You should seek counseling before things get really out of hand!

保羅：你跟麥克爭執的情況有改善了嗎？

珍妮：沒有，事實上，他真的動怒，還開始摔東西。

保羅：你是說真的嗎？那太糟糕了！

珍妮：我怕有一天會被打得青一塊紫一塊。

保羅：在情況失控之前，你應該去尋求諮商。

字彙 / 片語充電區 Words and Phrases

bruise 名 青腫 / blemish 名 (身上的)瘀點 / abrasion 名 擦傷 / swelling 名 腫大

cuts and bruises all over 遍體鱗傷 / chip on one's shoulder 向某人挑釁

UNIT 306 身體不適而「臉色發青」，會說turn blue嗎？

🎧 306

暖身猜猜看 *Warming Up*

情境：看到因暈船而臉色發青的乘客，這時應該怎麼說？

(　　) Many passengers on the boat looked blue around the _____.

    (A) beards　　　　(B) gills　　　　(C) jaws

正確解答：(B) 船上的許多乘客都看起來一臉病懨懨的樣子。

原來應該這樣說！

blue around the gills 臉色發青；一臉病容

    gill指「腮」，想像人的這個部位四周爆青筋的樣子，肯定極不舒服，也就是「臉色發青」之意，慣用語中的blue可以用green替換；反義詞為rosy around the gills（氣色紅潤的）。

對話練習 *Let's Talk!*

Marcy: Are you okay? You look **blue around the gills**.

Bruce: My dad had a heart attack last night.

Marcy: That's terrible. How is he doing now?

Bruce: He's feeling a lot better and he'll be home tomorrow.

Marcy: I guess you didn't sleep a wink all night.

瑪　西：你還好嗎？看起來一臉病容。
布魯斯：我爸爸昨晚心臟病發。
瑪　西：真是糟糕，那他現在怎麼樣了？
布魯斯：他好多了，明天就會回家。
瑪　西：我猜你整個晚上都沒闔眼吧。

字彙／片語充電區 *Words and Phrases*

ailing 形 身體不舒服的 / lackadaisical 形 懶散的；無精打采的 / hardy 形 強壯的
sick to one's stomach 反胃 / spit up 嘔吐；吐出來 / up to snuff 身體狀況良好

UNIT 307　身體某處「發麻」，用什麼來形容最道地？

🎧 307

 暖身猜猜看 Warming Up

情境：天氣冷颼颼，手都凍得發麻，這時應該怎麼說？

(　　) It's so cold that I had pins and ＿＿＿＿ in my fingers.

　　(A) nails　　　　(B) needles　　　　(C) spikes

正確解答：(B) 天氣好冷，我的手指都發麻了。

 原來應該這樣說！

have pins and needles 發麻

　　pin是「大頭釘」，而needle是縫衣用的「針」，身體的某一部位長久保持某一姿勢之後，產生大小針刺的感覺，不就是所謂的「發麻」嗎？另外，on pins and needles指心情焦慮或七上八下，通常搭配be動詞使用。

 _Let's Talk!_

Jeff: It's freezing cold! I **had pins and needles** in my fingers!

Ivy: I told you to wear gloves and bundle up.

Jeff: I guess I should have taken your advice this time.

Ivy: It looks like you have frostbite on your nose and cheeks!

Jeff: That's highly possible. My cheeks were numb.

傑夫：外面冷到凍僵！我騎車時手都麻痺了！

艾薇：我就叫你戴手套、多穿點的啊。

傑夫：我想這次我應該聽你的建議才對。

艾薇：你的鼻子和臉頰看起來都凍傷了！

傑夫：很有可能，我的臉頰都麻痺了。

字彙/片語充電區 _Words and Phrases_

numb 形 麻痺的 / paralyze 動 使麻痺 / stiff 形 僵硬的 / senseless 形 失去知覺的
have a dull pain 隱隱作痛 / be stock still 無法動彈 / be chilled to the bone 凍僵

UNIT 308 睡覺睡到「落枕」，會用到pillow這個字嗎？

🎧 308

暖身猜猜看 Warming Up

情境：一早醒來發現自己落枕，脖子僵硬，這時應該怎麼說？

(　　) This morning, I woke up with a ＿＿＿＿ in my neck.

　　(A) kink　　　　　　(B) knit　　　　　　(C) knock

正確解答：(A) 今天早上起床時，發現自己落枕了。

原來應該這樣說！

a kink in one's neck 落枕；頸部痠痛

　　kink指「抽筋」，所以a kink in one's neck就是「脖子抽筋」，通常是指睡覺姿勢不正確，早上一醒來所感到的脖子痠痛現象（我們常說的「落枕」）；現代美語裡也常見a crick in the neck，crick指「（頸或背的）痛性痙攣」。

Let's Talk!

Sherry: I think that I've aggravated an old injury.

　Allen: What do you mean by an old injury?

Sherry: I had a car accident before and received a direct blow to my neck.

　Allen: That sounds really terrible!

Sherry: That's why I often wake up with **a kink in my neck**.

雪莉：我覺得我的舊傷似乎又更嚴重了。

亞倫：你說的舊傷是什麼意思？

雪莉：我以前出過車禍，那時候我的頸部直接受到撞擊。

亞倫：聽起來真恐怖！

雪莉：這也是為什麼我起床時，頸部常會感到痠痛的原因。

字彙／片語充電區 Words and Phrases

stiffness 名 僵硬 / sore 形 痛的 / ointment 名 藥膏 / soothe 動 緩和；撫慰
get a stiff neck 脖子僵硬 / be off color 氣色差 / a fit of dizziness 一陣暈眩

UNIT 309 「走累而造成的腳痛」，當然與feet有關？

🎧 309

 暖身猜猜看 *Warming Up*

情境：登山走到腳起水泡，實在走不動了，這時應該怎麼說？

(　　) Hey! Can we sit back here? My dogs are _____.

　　(A) barking　　　　(B) running　　　　(C) jumping

正確解答：(A) 嘿！我們可以在這裡坐下嗎？我的腳好痛。

 原來應該這樣說！

one's dogs are barking 腳痛；腳走累了

　　dogs are barking（狗在吠）與腳痛扯得上關係嗎？想像你出去遛狗（walk a dog）卻不知道要休息，搞得狗都累到走不下去而喊叫，這才發現自己的腳真的累了；難怪英文裡有dog-tired（累翻了）這個形容詞。

 *Let's Talk!*

Jessie: You really danced gracefully today.

Greg: Stop flattering me! I wish that I were half as good as you.

Jessie: I sprained my ankle yesterday so **my dogs are barking** today.

Greg: Oh really? You hid it very well.

Jessie: I could have canceled class today, but I decided to grin and bear it.

潔　西：你今天的舞步看起來很優雅。

葛瑞格：別恭維我了！真希望我跳的有你一半好。

潔　西：我昨天扭到腳踝，所以今天腳很痛。

葛瑞格：真的嗎？那你隱藏得真好。

潔　西：我可以取消今天的課程，但我還是決定咬緊牙關忍耐。

字彙／片語充電區 *Words and Phrases*

footsore 形 (因走路過多而)腳酸的 / twinge 名 抽痛；劇痛 / drained 形 精疲力盡的
walk a thousand miles 千里迢迢；風塵僕僕 / **a long day's walk** 走了一整天的路

UNIT 310 想明確講出「得…病」，catch a cold顯得不足？

🎧 310

 暖身猜猜看 *Warming Up*

情境：因為染上流感，所以想跟公司請病假，這時應該怎麼說？

( ) I'd like to take a day off because I _____ with the flu.

    (A) walked out   (B) made up   (C) came down

正確解答：(C) 我得了流行性感冒，想請一天假。

 原來應該這樣說！

come down with 得…病

    come down的字面意思是「下來」，其後接不同的介系詞時，會帶出不同的意思；而介系詞with可表示「原因」，所以come down with等同於contract（罹患），意指「因為某個原因而感到不適」。

 對話練習 *Let's Talk!*

Frank: Good morning. Is this Jenny speaking? This is Frank.

Jenny: Frank? You don't sound well.

Frank: Yeah. I think I have **come down with** the flu.

Jenny: I see. I didn't even recognize your voice on the phone.

Frank: I just wanted to let you know that I won't be in today.

法蘭克：早安，請問是珍妮嗎？我是法蘭克。

珍　妮：法蘭克？你聽起來不太好。

法蘭克：是啊，我想我感冒了。

珍　妮：原來如此，在電話裡幾乎認不出你的聲音。

法蘭克：只是要告訴你，我今天不會進辦公室。

字彙／片語充電區 *Words and Phrases*

infect 動 感染 / undergo 動 接受(治療) / antibody 名 抗體 / mending 形 康復中
catch a cold 感冒 / be immune to 對…免疫 / in fine feather 健康狀況良好

UNIT 311 某人「狀態不佳」，就用bad或not good？

🎧 311

 暖身猜猜看 *Warming Up*

情境：明明做好萬全準備，卻臨場表現不佳，這時可以怎麼說？

( ) I don't know why, but I just felt out of _____ from the start.

(A) kinds　　　　(B) types　　　　(C) sorts

正確解答：(C) 不知道為什麼，我從一開始就覺得不對勁。

 原來應該這樣說！

out of sorts 心情不佳；身體不適

　　這個說法的起源，其中一個和古時候的活字印刷術有關，當時印刷機中的活字稱為sorts，如果印刷人員找不到要用的字，感覺肯定很不好，所以out of sorts有「不對勁」之意，用來形容心情不好、身體不適，或狀態不佳。

 對話練習 *Let's Talk!*

Kyle: I feel a bit **out of sorts**. It must be the lunch.

Joyce: My goodness. What did you have?

Kyle: A lot. I was so hungry. I think I ate too much.

Joyce: Poor thing. Looks like you can't go to the party with me tonight.

Kyle: Don't worry about me. You go ahead and have fun.

凱　爾：我有點不舒服，一定是因為午餐的關係。

喬伊絲：天哪，你吃了什麼？

凱　爾：很多，我當時很餓，我想我是吃太多了。

喬伊絲：好可憐，看來今晚你是無法和我一起參加派對了。

凱　爾：別擔心我，好好去玩吧。

字彙／片語充電區 *Words and Phrases*

downcast 形 低落的 / prostrate 形 疲憊的 / languid 形 倦怠的 / husky 形 健壯的
below par 狀況不及一般水準 / get the bug 得病 / full of pep 心情愉快；精神佳

UNIT 312 所謂的「冒冷汗」，究竟cold在哪裡？

🎧 312

暖身猜猜看 Warming Up

情境：卡費繳不停，想到這個就冒冷汗，這時應該怎麼說？

(　　) Thinking about money makes me break out in a cold _____!

(A) shoulder　　　(B) sweat　　　(C) feet

正確解答：(B) 想到錢就讓我直冒冷汗。

原來應該這樣說！

break out in a cold sweat 冒冷汗

　　cold sweat表示「冷汗」，通常是在我們感到非常緊張或驚慌時，會有的生理現象；另外，break out是指事件或災難突然發生，這個慣用語用在身體方面，則是指疹子或汗突然佈滿全身。

Amy: Where have you been? I've been worried sick about you!	艾咪：你去哪了？我擔心死了！
Will: I had a little accident and was rushed to the hospital.	威爾：我出了一點小意外，被緊急送往醫院。
Amy: Are you OK? You don't look very well.	艾咪：你還好嗎？你看起來不是很好。
Will: I **broke out in a cold sweat** before passing out.	威爾：我狂冒冷汗，後來就昏倒了。
Amy: Here. Take your coat off and grab a seat.	艾咪：來吧，把外套脫下來，拿張椅子坐。

字彙／片語充電區 Words and Phrases

agitated 形 慌張的 / panic 名 慌張 / aghast 形 驚駭的 / petrified 形 目瞪口呆的
in a blue funk 在惶恐中 / in a dither 慌亂 / no sweat 輕而易舉 / step on it 趕快

UNIT
313

突然「失去知覺」，只知道faint這個字？

🎧 313

暖身猜猜看 *Warming Up*

情境：你突然不舒服，感覺快昏過去了，這時應該怎麼說？

(　　) I think I'm going to _____ out. Please help me sit down.

　　(A) white　　　　　　(B) black　　　　　(C) light

正確解答：(B) 我覺得我快昏倒了，請扶我坐下。

原來應該這樣說！

black out 失去知覺

　　black在這裡是動詞，有「變黑」的意思；black out用於描述身體狀況時，意思是「昏倒或失去知覺」，就好像房間的燈突然熄掉一樣，中文有「眼前一黑」的說法，意思與這個慣用語相近。

Vince: Wendy? Are you all right? Thank God you're back!

Wendy: What's going on? Oh, my head. It hurts.

Vince: You suddenly passed out when we were walking.

Wendy: I remember I felt a headache, and then I **blacked out**.

Vince: You should go get a thorough physical exam.

文斯：溫蒂？你還好嗎？謝天謝地，你醒了！

溫蒂：發生什麼事了？噢，我的頭好痛。

文斯：我們剛才在走路的時候，你突然昏倒。

溫蒂：我記得我感到一陣頭痛，然後就暈倒了。

文斯：你應該去做個徹底的健康檢查。

字彙／片語充電區 *Words and Phrases*

unconscious 形 失去知覺的 / swoon 動 昏厥 / whirl 動 頭暈 / smother 動 窒息
in a dead faint 不省人事 / slip into coma 陷入昏迷 / on the rocks 岌岌可危

UNIT 314 「痛得快死了」，真是hurt too much？

🎧 314

暖身猜猜看 *Warming Up*

情境：你牙齒突然痛起來，快痛死人了，這時應該怎麼說？

( ) I'm _____ with pain because of the decayed tooth.

　　(A) racked 　　　　(B) tracked 　　　(C) hacked

正確解答：(A) 我因為蛀牙而痛得要死。

原來應該這樣說！

be racked with pain 痛得快死了

　　rack本來是指「架子」，當動詞時表示「把…釘在架子上」，想像如果人被釘在架子上，懸在那兒，自然是苦不堪言吧！和單純的feel pain或painful相比，be/feel racked with pain可以更明顯地將「痛」的感覺發揮至極致。

Joyce: What's the matter? Did you get brain freeze?

John: No. It's my tooth.

Joyce: Are your teeth sensitive to cold things?

John: No. I think I've got a cavity. Oh! I'm **being racked with pain**.

Joyce: Well, you should go to the dentist and get a check-up.

喬伊絲：怎麼了？你吃太快頭痛了嗎？

約　翰：不是，是我的牙齒。

喬伊絲：你的牙齒會對冰冷的東西敏感喔？

約　翰：不會，我想我應該是蛀牙了。噢！我快痛死了。

喬伊絲：嗯，你應該要去看牙醫，做個檢查。

字彙／片語充電區 *Words and Phrases*

agony 名 痛苦 / torture 動 使折磨；使苦惱 / afflict 動 使承受痛苦 / soothe 動 緩和
beyond description 難以言喻 / pain reliever 止痛藥 / take the edge off 使緩和

UNIT 315 「聲音沙啞說不出話」，說了can't talk，那沙啞呢？

🎧 315

 暖身猜猜看 Warming Up

情境：準備演講的你，聲音卻沙啞得不得了，這時應該怎麼說？

(   ) Sorry, but I just have a ＿＿＿＿ in my throat now.

(A) frog   (B) fish   (C) shrimp

正確解答：(A) 不好意思，現在我的聲音沙啞，說不出話來。

 原來應該這樣說！

a frog in one's throat 聲音沙啞說不出話

　　「喉嚨裡的青蛙」（a frog in one's throat）怎麼會與「喉嚨沙啞」有關呢？據說以前人們常從小溪直接取水飲用，可能無意中將青蛙的卵吞下肚，當時的人會相信，卵會在人的喉嚨裡面孵化成青蛙，哽住你的喉嚨，使你說不出話。

 對話練習 Let's Talk!

Jerry: Ladies and gentlemen, thank you...uh...umm...I...

Vicky: What's wrong with you? Why are you stuttering?

Jerry: I just wanted to say — I mean, to...

Vicky: Take it easy. Everybody, let's give him some time.

Jerry: Thanks. I think I definitely have **a frog in my throat**.

傑瑞：各位先生女士，感謝您…呃…嗯…我…

薇琪：你怎麼了？怎麼結結巴巴的？

傑瑞：我想要說—我的意思是，我要說…呃…

薇琪：放輕鬆，各位，我們再給他一點時間吧。

傑瑞：謝謝，我想我一定是嗓子啞了說不出話。

字彙/片語充電區 Words and Phrases

rustiness 名 沙啞 / raucous 形 聲音沙啞的 / fluent 形 流利的 / talkative 形 健談的 throat drop(s) 喉糖 / sore throat 喉嚨痛 / loud and clear voice 爽朗的聲音

UNIT 316 感到「疲憊不堪、累壞了」，又是用very形容tired？

🎧 316

暖身猜猜看 *Warming Up*

情境：連續工作的你真的快累壞了，這時應該怎麼說？

(　　) Now I'm completely ＿＿＿＿＿ and need a thorough rest.

　　(A) fed up　　　　(B) run down　　　　(C) taken aback

正確解答：(B) 現在我疲憊不堪，需要充分的休息。

原來應該這樣說！

run down 累壞了；疲憊不堪

　　run down本來是指機器或時鐘等因故障或老舊，而逐漸停下來不動，用在「人」身上則引申為因身體的疲憊而導致不舒服；這個慣用語還有「撞倒」的意思，ex. I ran down the mailbox.（我把信箱撞倒了。）

對話練習 *Let's Talk!*

Karen: God! It's so busy back in the kitchen.

Danny: I bet. A lot of customers have been coming in with those 2-for-1 coupons.

Karen: I know. I can't wait for that promotion to be over with!

Danny: It's been so hectic. Sometimes, I feel **run down** by this job!

Karen: It sounds like you're fed up, too.

凱倫：天啊！廚房都要忙翻了。

丹尼：我同意，一直有很多客人拿買二送一的優惠券來消費。

凱倫：我明白，真恨不得促銷活動趕快結束！

丹尼：最近實在超忙碌，有時候，我快被這工作搞死了！

凱倫：聽起來你也受不了囉。

字彙／片語充電區 *Words and Phrases*

exhausted 形 筋疲力盡的 / worn-out 形 疲倦的 / depleted 形 耗盡的；用盡的
wan and sallow 憔悴的 / suffer from 患(病) / feel up to par 覺得狀況良好

UNIT 317 快被「累垮」，就是超過limit？

🎧 317

暖身猜猜看 Warming Up

情境：工時長壓力又大，都快被累垮了，這時應該怎麼說？

( ) I will ＿＿＿＿＿ if I don't drop out.

　　(A) lay down　　　　(B) burn out　　　　(C) flow away

正確解答：(B) 如果我不離開，我會累垮的。

原來應該這樣說！

burn out 累垮

　　簡單的說，burn out就是「燃燒殆盡」，它可以用來形容人的體力、精神耗盡，也可以形容一部機器因老舊而失去作用；如果要強調的是「累垮自己」，可用主動的burn oneself out，也可以用wear out表達相同的意思。

Luke: Jane has become really possessive lately. We argue a lot.	路克：珍最近佔有慾很強，我們吵得很兇。
Fanny: It sounds like your relationship is on the rocks.	芬妮：看來你們的關係岌岌可危。
Luke: It's almost impossible to communicate with her.	路克：要和她溝通幾乎是不可能的事。
Fanny: Are you sick and tired of feeling this way?	芬妮：你已經厭倦這樣的感覺了嗎？
Luke: Honestly, I'm almost **burning** myself **out** in this relationship.	路克：老實說，我在這段關係中快累垮了。

字彙／片語充電區 Words and Phrases

fatigue 名 疲勞；疲乏 / **drooping** 形 萎靡不振的 / **bleary-eyed** 形 睡眼惺忪的
burn the midnight oil 熬夜 / **be run off one's leg** 累垮 / **a ball of fire** 有精神者

UNIT 318　喝酒隔天的「宿醉」，用drunk形容？

🎧 318

暖身猜猜看 *Warming Up*

情境：你想勸朋友別猛灌酒，免得宿醉，這時應該怎麼說？

(　　) Don't drink too much, or you'll definitely have a bad ＿＿＿＿.

　　　(A) turnaround　　　(B) makeup　　　(C) hangover

正確解答：(C) 別喝太多，不然你一定會宿醉得很嚴重。

原來應該這樣說！

have a hangover 宿醉

　　hang over字面上的意思是「掛在那裡」，指一件不好的事情產生持續性的影響；名詞hangover就是從此義引申而來，表示「宿醉」，且帶有身體不舒服之意；須注意別與drunk（喝醉的）的意思搞混了。

對話練習 *Let's Talk!*

Lucy: So, what brings you here tonight?

Danny: It's not my day today. Please make mine a double.

Lucy: Here's your drink. Hey! You should slow down a bit.

Danny: Cheers, and don't nag. I took a taxi here anyway.

Lucy: You have to work tomorrow, right? I'm afraid you'll **have a hangover**.

露西：你今晚怎麼會來呢？

丹尼：我今天過得很不順，請給我兩倍的量。

露西：這是你的酒，嘿！你應該喝慢一點。

丹尼：乾啦，別囉嗦，反正我搭計程車來的。

露西：你明天還要上班吧？我擔心你會宿醉。

字彙／片語充電區 *Words and Phrases*

alcoholic 名 酒鬼 / dizzy 形 頭暈的 / falter 動 (走路)搖搖晃晃 / recover 動 復原
under the influence 喝醉酒 / be seeing double (因酒醉而)眼花 / throw up 嘔吐

UNIT 319 「暈船」的說法，一定會提到boat？

🎧 319

暖身猜猜看 Warming Up

情境：搭乘渡輪時，暈船的你感到頭暈想吐，這時應該怎麼說？

( ) I'm feeling like _____ the fishes.

　　(A) kicking　　　　(B) dropping　　　　(C) feeding

正確解答：(C) 我想我暈船了。

原來應該這樣說！

feed the fishes 暈船

　　feed the fishes照字面翻譯，意思是「餵魚」，但如果暈船得很嚴重，因而掉入水，那也是「餵魚」囉！所以這個慣用語就被用來指稱「暈船」的狀態，也可以說seasick，但這個慣用語不能用於搭車或搭飛機喔！

對話練習 Let's Talk!

Matt: Excuse me. Do you have anything for seasickness?

Emma: Yes, I have some in my bag. Please wait a bit.

Matt: Thank you. My brother felt faint. I think he has **fed the fishes**.

Emma: Poor boy! Don't worry. This pill is really effective.

Matt: I should take some with me next time, just in case.

麥特：不好意思，請問你有暈船藥嗎？

艾瑪：有的，在我包包裡，你等我一下。

麥特：謝謝你，我弟弟感到暈眩不適，我想他暈船了。

艾瑪：可憐的男孩！別擔心，這個藥片很有效。

麥特：我下次應該帶一點在身上，以防萬一。

字彙/片語充電區 Words and Phrases

faint 動 暈厥；暈倒 / carsick 形 暈車的 / nausea 名 作嘔；暈船 / rocky 形 晃動的
not firm on one's feet 站不穩 / take a pill 服用一顆藥丸 / knock out 敲昏

UNIT 320
「讓某人清醒過來」，和叫醒的wake up不同？

🎧 320

暖身猜猜看 *Warming Up*

情境：你想潑點冷水讓酒醉的人清醒過來，這時可以怎麼說？

(　) Splash some cold water in his face to ＿＿＿＿ him around.

　　(A) make　　　　　(B) take　　　　　(C) bring

正確解答：(C) 潑點冷水在他臉上，讓他清醒過來。

原來應該這樣說！

bring sb. around 把某人救醒；讓某人清醒過來

　　bring around有幾個常見的意思：第一個是「把…帶過來」，第二個是「說服」，這裡介紹的則是「讓某人清醒過來」；因為「清醒」是consciousness，所以也可以改成bring sb. to consciousness。

對話練習 *Let's Talk!*

Diane: Thank God that Dad was **brought around** by Ben.

　Hank: Yeah. Dad can count himself lucky that he's still alive.

Diane: We owe Ben. We should express our gratitude to him.

　Hank: Dad said that Ben pulled him out of the frigid water by himself.

Diane: He's old, but he's still as strong as a horse.

黛安：謝天謝地，爸被班救了回來。

漢克：是啊，爸這條命算是撿回來的。

黛安：我們欠班一份人情，我們應該表達對他的感謝。

漢克：爸說班一個人就將他從冰冷的湖水中拉出來。

黛安：他算是老當益壯了。

字彙/片語充電區 *Words and Phrases*

awaken 動 喚醒；覺醒 / sober 形 清醒的；沒喝醉的 / level-headed 形 清醒的
in right mind (人)清醒 / fall unconscious 不醒人事 / to no avail 回天乏術

UNIT 321 健康情況「康復中」，只知道與health有關？

🎧 321

 暖身猜猜看 Warming Up

情境：你為好友的康復情況感到高興，這時應該怎麼說？

(　　) I'm happy to see that your health is on the _____.

  (A) mess   (B) mend   (C) matter

正確解答：(B) 看到你的病情好轉，我很高興。

 原來應該這樣說！

on the mend 康復中；好轉

 mend是名詞，表示「修繕」、「變好」，這個字也可以當動詞，on the mend不但可以指身體狀況的好轉，也可用在其他方面，ex. The economy is on the mend gradually.（經濟正在好轉。）

 **對話練習** *Let's Talk!*

Gavin: Ann has been constantly nagging me to get married.

 Lisa: Don't you want to get married?

Gavin: Well, I'm not ready to tie the knot yet. So we had a fight.

 Lisa: I believe your relationship will be **on the mend** soon.

Gavin: Thanks. I guess I'll try communicating with her again.

蓋文：安一直吵著要結婚。

麗莎：你不想結婚嗎？

蓋文：我還沒準備好要結婚，所以我們大吵了一架。

麗莎：我相信你們的關係很快就會好轉的。

蓋文：謝謝你，我想我會再找她溝通吧。

字彙／片語充電區 *Words and Phrases*

improving 形 改善中的 / convalesce 動 病後療養 / deteriorate 動 惡化；退化
over the hump 否極泰來 / operating room 手術室 / safe and sound 安然無恙

UNIT 322 「動手術」的動作，用surgery表現得出來嗎？

🎧 322

暖身猜猜看 *Warming Up*

情境：醫生想告訴病人只要動點小手術就會痊癒，這時應該怎麼說？

( ) You only have to go under the _____ to have it removed. It's very fast.

(A) knife　　　　(B) scalpel　　　　(C) table

正確解答：(A) 你只需要動個手術把它切除，很快就好。

原來應該這樣說！

go under the knife 動手術

　　knife是「刀子」，但go under the knife可不是「要被砍」，而是「動手術」的意思，通常用於口語中；至於正式用法，可以說undergo a surgery或undergo an operation（補充：手術刀為scalpel）。

Let's Talk!

Doctor: That little ball you feel in your hand is a tumor.

Kevin: God! I thought that's what it might be.

Doctor: Take it easy. Most of these growths are benign tumors.

Kevin: So...do I still need to **go under the knife**?

Doctor: Yes. We'll remove it just to be on the safe side.

醫師：你手上的小腫塊是腫瘤。

凱文：天啊！我之前就感覺它是個腫瘤。

醫師：不用緊張，大部分的腫瘤都是良性的。

凱文：所以…我還需要開刀嗎？

醫師：是的，安全起見，我們還是建議割除它。

字彙/片語充電區 *Words and Phrases*

operation 名 手術 / surgery 名 外科手術 / remove 動 切除 / failure 名 (手術)失敗
operate on 對…動手術 / plastic surgery 整形手術 / local anesthetic 局部麻醉

UNIT 323 有人「受重傷」，
injury的程度要如何表現？

🎧 323

暖身猜猜看 *Warming Up*

情境：發生車禍，你發現有人受重傷，這時應該怎麼描述？

(　　) He'd copped a ＿＿＿＿＿ in the car accident.

    (A) pocket   (B) packet   (C) poker

正確解答：(B) 他因為車禍受了重傷。

原來應該這樣說！

cop a packet 受重傷；遭逢不幸

    cop表「抓住」，packet是「包裹」（美式英文用package）。那麼，「抓住包裹」與「受重傷」有何關係？這個慣用語源自過去的軍中術語，當受了傷的士兵必須拿著包袱到醫院去時，想必很嚴重；也可以形容人突遭變故。

對話練習 *Let's Talk!*

Gina: I think that I'm going to find a place on a lower floor.

Albert: Why? You're scared of earthquakes?

Gina: Don't you know about the terrible earthquake in Taiwan in 1999?

Albert: I know about that one. I think it measured 7.6 on the Richter scale.

Gina: Yeah. Around 1,800 people died and many **copped a packet**.

吉　娜：我想要找個樓層低一點的住家。

艾伯特：為什麼？你很怕地震嗎？

吉　娜：你不知道台灣1999年發生的大地震嗎？

艾伯特：我知道，好像是芮氏規模 7.6 級的大地震。

吉　娜：是啊，大約有一千八百人死亡，還有許多人受重傷。

字彙／片語充電區 *Words and Phrases*

injured 形 受傷的 / **wound** 名 傷口 / **impaired** 形 受損的 / **adverse** 形 逆境的
beyond cure 回天乏術 / **on the brink of** 瀕臨…的邊緣 / **invalid first-aid** 急救無效

UNIT 324

「幾乎崩潰」的情緒，
是瀕臨理智的edge嗎？

🎧 324

 暖身猜猜看 *Warming Up*

情境：想安慰朋友他無須崩潰，只需要冷靜一點，這時可以怎麼說？

( ) I don't think you're on your _____. Just calm down.

　　(A) last straw　　　(B) last legs　　　(C) second hand

正確解答：(B) 我不覺得你快崩潰了，冷靜一點。

 原來應該這樣說！

on one's last legs 快掛了；幾乎崩潰

　　on one's last legs是指一個人的腿抽筋，或者腿的機能已達極限，無法再動；引申為「幾乎崩潰」的意思（無法再冷靜處事），也可以用來形容車子或機器設備等，ex. My old car is on its last legs.（我的老爺車快掛了。）

 **對話練習** *Let's Talk!*

Jenny: What's going on? You look terrible.

Bill: I'm not sure. Maybe my sales pitch wasn't convincing enough.

Jenny: Maybe you scare people off because you're too aggressive.

Bill: Or maybe I'm the worst car salesman on the planet!

Jenny: You'll be **on your last legs** if you keep worrying this way.

珍妮：怎麼了？你臉色好差。

比爾：我不知道，也許我的銷售手法不夠有說服力。

珍妮：或許是你太積極，把客人都嚇跑了。

比爾：也或者我根本就是這世界上最糟的售車員！

珍妮：你再這樣擔心下去，會發瘋的。

字彙/片語充電區 *Words and Phrases*

dog-tired 形 筋疲力盡的；累垮的 / strained 形 緊張的 / insistence 名 堅持
at death's door 死到臨頭 / at the end of rope 走投無路 / in extremis 絕境

UNIT 325 說人「一命嗚呼」，想避開die要怎麼說？

🎧 325

暖身猜猜看 Warming Up

情境：某個罪犯的死刑判決終於履行了，這時應該怎麼說？

( ) That scum of the earth finally kicked the _____.

(A) bucket　　　　(B) baggage　　　(C) blogger

正確解答：(A) 那個敗類終於一命嗚呼了。

原來應該這樣說！

kick the bucket 一命嗚呼；死翹翹

　　bucket指「桶子」，但kick the bucket可不是「踢桶子」喔！這個典故來自古代，處犯人絞刑時，腳下都會先墊個桶子，當你把桶子踢開時，罪犯就完蛋了。不過，這個用法並不正式，一般是對死者較為不尊重，或是委婉的講法。

Let's Talk!

Carter: Are you OK? You look as pale as a ghost.

Karen: My uncle **kicked the bucket** because of oral cancer.

Carter: Oral cancer? I wonder what caused it.

Karen: Betel nuts, most likely. He chewed betel nuts all day long.

Carter: I'm sorry to hear that.

卡特：妳還好嗎？妳的臉色看起來像鬼一樣蒼白。

凱倫：我的叔叔過世了，口腔癌惹的禍。

卡特：口腔癌？他怎麼會得口腔癌呢？

凱倫：檳榔的可能性最大，他整天都在嚼檳榔。

卡特：聽到這消息真令人難過。

字彙/片語充電區 Words and Phrases

demise 名 死亡 / repose 動 安息；長眠 / perish 動 毀滅 / survival 名 倖存(者)
pass away 過世 / give up the ghost 死亡 / tough it out 撐過去 / pass out 昏倒

UNIT 326

「剎那間」與「一瞬間」，用quick強調就可以了？

🎧 326

暖身猜猜看 *Warming Up*

情境：你想告訴朋友，你的頭痛一下就會好，這時可以怎麼說？

(　　) My headache is not serious, and I'm sure it will be gone in ＿＿＿＿.

(A) an instant　　　(B) a distance　　　(C) an insistence

正確解答：(A) 我的頭痛不很嚴重，應該一下子就會好。

原來應該這樣說！

in an instant 剎那間；一瞬間

　　instant當形容詞時，意思是「立即的」，例如大家熟知的泡麵，英文是 instant noodles；另外，有個常見的說法是take an instant dislike，意思是「第一眼就不喜歡」；此慣用語中的instant則為名詞，意思是「頃刻間」。

對話練習 *Let's Talk!*

Hal: I've read the draft of your new book. I'm truly touched.

Lucy: Thank you, I'm glad you like it.

Hal: I believe the first edition will be sold out **in an instant**.

Lucy: Wow. You sure have faith in me. I'll send you a copy when it's published.

Hal: Thanks. I'll recommend it to all my friends.

哈爾：我讀了你新書的稿子，看完真的很感動。

露西：謝謝你，很高興你喜歡。

哈爾：我相信初版肯定馬上就會銷售一空。

露西：哇。你對我真有信心，出版之後我會送一本給你。

哈爾：謝謝，我會把它推薦給我所有的朋友。

字彙／片語充電區 *Words and Phrases*

jiffy 名 瞬間 / forthwith 副 立即 / prompt 形 迅速的 / gradually 副 漸漸地
in the blink of an eye 一眨眼的時間 / at a blow 立刻 / bit by bit 一點一點地

UNIT 327 「趕在最後一刻」，用last minute就行？

🎧 327

暖身猜猜看 Warming Up

情境：你與朋友在最後一刻趕到機場，這時應該怎麼說？

(　　) We got to the airport in the ＿＿＿＿ of time.

    (A) crack   (B) last   (C) nick

正確解答：(C) 我們趕在最後一刻抵達機場。

原來應該這樣說！

nick of time 趕在最後一刻；及時

　　nick原本指的是刻痕，和notch的意思相同，有精準和確切的意涵在，其實nick本身就可以解釋為「關鍵時刻」或是「最後一刻」，後面加上time只是為了強調這個慣用語的時間概念。

對話練習 Let's Talk!

Karen: I turned in my paper in the **nick of time**.

Leon: That's great! But what made you turn in your paper so late?

Karen: Well, my computer was infected with a virus.

Leon: You must have been depressed.

Karen: Yes, but luckily, I kept my draft. That's why I could finish it on time.

凱倫：我在最後一刻交了報告。

里昂：太棒了！可是你怎麼會這麼晚才交報告？

凱倫：因為我的電腦中毒了。

里昂：你一定很沮喪。

凱倫：是啊，但幸好我保留了草稿，所以才能及時完成。

字彙/片語充電區 Words and Phrases

duly 副 準時地 / vital 形 極為重要的 / precise 形 準確的 / propitious 形 順利的 / in a split second 剎那間 / under the wire 及時 / by happy chance 幸運地

UNIT 328 講「時間緊迫」時，用得著emergent嗎？

🎧 328

 暖身猜猜看 Warming Up

情境：你手邊正有份緊急的工作要完成，這時應該怎麼說？

( ) I am now working _____ the clock to meet the deadline.

    (A) across   (B) against   (C) on

正確解答：(B) 我現在正為了趕上截止日期而加緊工作。

 原來應該這樣說！

against the clock 時間緊迫

    介系詞against含有與某人或事物對立或對抗的意思，而clock在這裡代表時間（相當於time），所以against the clock就用來表示「非常緊急、盡可能地快」，猶如與時間對抗，看誰比較快。

 **對話練習 Let's Talk!**

Adam: Hi, Becky. How's your writing project going?

Becky: There are only three weeks left. I have to work **against the clock**.

Adam: Is there anything I can do to help?

Becky: I guess you can do the proofreading for me.

Adam: Okay. Just send me the files, and I'll make time for it.

亞當：嗨，貝琪，你的寫作計畫進行得如何？

貝琪：只剩三個禮拜，我得加緊趕工了。

亞當：我可以幫什麼忙嗎？

貝琪：我想你可以幫我校對。

亞當：沒問題，把檔案寄給我，我會抽空校對。

字彙／片語充電區 Words and Phrases

hustle 動 趕緊 / **briskly** 副 迅速地 / **urgency** 名 緊急；迫切 / **linger** 動 拖延；磨蹭 / **be pressed for time** 時間緊迫 / **make haste** 趕緊 / **top priority** 第一優先的事情

UNIT 329 「和時間賽跑」，真用run來比喻嗎？

🎧 329

暖身猜猜看 Warming Up

情境：經驗告訴你，考試要分秒必爭，這時應該怎麼說？

(　　) Taking an exam is a ＿＿＿＿ against time.

(A) fight 　　　　 (B) race 　　　　 (C) test

正確解答：(B) 考試是件要和時間賽跑的事。

原來應該這樣說！

race against time 分秒必爭；和時間賽跑

　　這個慣用語與前一個單元的意思相似，使用動詞race後，就是「和時間競賽」，也就是非常緊急、分秒必爭的意思。這個慣用語特別的地方在於它可以當名詞，也可以當動詞，當名詞時記得前面要加上不定冠詞a。

Let's Talk!

Penny: Hey, Oliver. Slow down. Where are you running to?

Oliver: Sorry, I can't stop now. I'm **racing against time** to get to the post office.

Penny: Are you sending a package or something?

Oliver: Yeah. I've got to send this gift today.

Penny: Well, I can give you a ride. My car is over there.

佩　妮：嘿，奧利佛，慢一點，你趕著去哪裡？

奧利佛：抱歉，我現在不能停下來，我正趕著去郵局。

佩　妮：你要寄包裹之類的東西嗎？

奧利佛：對啊，我今天必須把這個禮物寄出去。

佩　妮：我可以載你一程，我的車就停在那裡。

字彙 / 片語充電區 Words and Phrases

rush 動 急速行動 / bustle 動 奔忙 / tension 名 緊張的狀況 / exigent 形 緊急的
lose no time 分秒必爭 / mile a minute 非常快速 / beat a deadline 在時限內趕上

UNIT 330 「爭取時間」做事，就是fight for time？

🎧 330

 暖身猜猜看 *Warming Up*

情境：想辦驚喜派對，你得爭取時間準備，這時應該怎麼說？

(　　) I'll _____ for time while you get everything ready.

(A) fool　　　　　　(B) play　　　　　(C) drag

正確解答：(B) 我會爭取時間，你們就趁機準備。

 原來應該這樣說！

play for time 爭取時間

　　play for time特別指「以拖延的手段爭取時間」；play在這裡有「處理」或「應付」的意思，ex. I played the situation carefully.（我小心地處理這個狀況。）由於這個慣用語有拖延之意，所以也可以用stall for time取代。

 對話練習 *Let's Talk!*

Rita: The assignment is due next week. Can you meet the deadline?

Sean: Hardly. I'm afraid I'll have to **play for time**.

Rita: What's your plan? It's not easy to fool our supervisor.

Sean: I won't fool anyone. I'm thinking about getting some help.

Rita: You can ask Tim. He's pretty good at statistics.

芮塔：這項任務下週就得完成，你趕得上截止日嗎？

西恩：不太可能，我想我必須爭取時間。

芮塔：你有什麼計畫？要騙我們的主管可沒那麼容易。

西恩：我才沒有要騙人，我是想找幫手。

芮塔：你可以問提姆，他很擅長統計。

字彙／片語充電區 *Words and Phrases*

temporize 動 拖延以爭取時間；迎合潮流 / **withhold** 動 阻擋；抑制 / **balk** 動 妨礙
buy time 以拖延的方式爭取時間 / **hold over** 留住 / **put off** 拖延 / **rein in** 使放慢

UNIT 331 「時間抓得太緊」，可以用tight形容？

🎧 331

 暖身猜猜看 *Warming Up*

情境：你想勸朋友不要把時間抓得剛剛好，這時可以怎麼說？

(　　) Don't cut things too ＿＿＿＿. You'd better leave some extra time.

　　(A) sharp　　　　　(B) fine　　　　　(C) thin

正確解答：(B) 不要把時間抓得太剛好，你最好多留點時間。

原來應該這樣說！

cut things fine 時間抓得太緊

　　fine在這裡指的是細的、薄的。切東西的時候，如果切得很細很薄，就很容易切壞，由此引申出的cut things fine就用來表示「時間抓得剛好，一不小心就可能會不夠」；其中things可以用it代替，說成cut it fine。

 *Let's Talk!*

Danny: I don't want to rush you, but we're about to run out of time.

Carol: Trust me. We'll get there on time.

Danny: As far as I know, you're not always on time.

Carol: I **cut things fine** just because I don't want to waste time.

Danny: This type of thinking could ruin you. Accidents happen, you know.

丹尼：我不想催你，但我們快沒時間了。

卡蘿：相信我，我們會準時抵達的。

丹尼：就我所知，你不是每次都準時。

卡蘿：我把時間抓得剛好，因為我不想浪費時間。

丹尼：這個想法可能會害了你，意外總是會發生。

字彙／片語充電區 *Words and Phrases*

hairbreadth 形 間不容髮的 / imminent 形 迫在眉睫的 / manage 動 勉強達成
just get by 剛好過關 / by the skin of one's teeth 勉強 / more than enough 充足

UNIT 332

要說「等待機會」，用wait for chance？

🎧 332

暖身猜猜看 *Warming Up*

情境：這次沒升遷的你打算繼續等待機會，這時應該怎麼說？

(　　) I will keep doing my best and _____ my time.

　　(A) hold　　　　　(B) keep　　　　　(C) bide

正確解答：(C) 我會繼續拿出最好的表現，等待機會。

原來應該這樣說！

bide one's time 等待機會

　　bide在此為「等待」之意，time指時機，所以bide one's time如同字面上的意思，就是等待時機和機會；bide另外可解釋為禁得起，ex. The house can bide the typhoon.（這房子禁得起颱風。）

對話練習 *Let's Talk!*

Terry: My girlfriend and I had a quarrel about living together.

Emma: I'm sorry to hear that. Did you try to text her?

Terry: Yeah. I've tried everything, but she doesn't respond at all.

Emma: So what are you going to do?

Terry: I think I'll just **bide my time** until she is willing to talk.

泰瑞：我女友和我為了同居的事吵了一架。

艾瑪：我很遺憾，你試過傳訊息給她嗎？

泰瑞：傳了，我什麼都試過，但她完全不回應。

艾瑪：那你打算怎麼辦？

泰瑞：我看我就等待機會，直到她願意談為止。

字彙／片語充電區 *Words and Phrases*

anticipate 動 期望；預料 / **patiently** 副 耐心地 / **abide** 動 等候 / **await** 動 期待 **stick around** 在某處等待 / **lie low** 潛伏 / **be up for grabs** 大家都有機會爭取的

UNIT 333 「時機成熟」的時刻，應該與ripe有關？

🎧 333

暖身猜猜看 Warming Up

情境：「對的人會在時機成熟的時候出現」，這句話應該怎麼說？

( ) Your Mr. Right will show up in the _____ of time.

(A) goodness　　　(B) fatness　　　(C) fullness

正確解答：(C) 你的真命天子會在對的時間出現。

原來應該這樣說！

fullness of time 對的時間；時機成熟

　　這個慣用語在基督教世界很常見，fullness有充分的意思，也可以解釋為成熟，所以fullness of time意思就是時機成熟，或是等到足夠的時間過去之後，通常會在前面加上in the，in在此指「過了某段時間」。

對話練習 Let's Talk!

Betty: I think I should quit this job as soon as possible.

Eric: If I were you, I would keep doing my best in this position.

Betty: But this is not the company I want to stay at forever!

Eric: Trust me. A good opportunity will come in the **fullness of time**.

Betty: I sure hope so. I don't have too much time to waste.

貝　蒂：我覺得我應該盡早辭職。

艾瑞克：如果我是你，我會繼續在崗位上努力。

貝　蒂：可是我不想永遠待在這家公司啊！

艾瑞克：相信我，等到時機成熟，機會就會來了。

貝　蒂：希望如此，我沒有太多時間可以浪費。

字彙/片語充電區 Words and Phrases

destined 形 注定的 / eventually 副 終於 / opportune 形 恰好的 / timely 形 適時的
Time is ripe. 時機成熟。/ in the long run 終究 / when all is said and done 畢竟

UNIT 334 重要的「關鍵時刻」，是什麼moment嗎？

🎧 334

暖身猜猜看 *Warming Up*

情境：有個球員在比賽的關鍵時刻得了分，這時可以怎麼說？

(　) Johnson made two 3-point shots at ＿＿＿＿ time.

(A) crispy　　　　(B) crunch　　　　(C) clash

正確解答：(B) 強森在關鍵時刻投進兩顆三分球。

原來應該這樣說！

crunch time 關鍵時刻

　　crunch time主要有兩個意思：第一個是在某個截止日期之前需要全力衝刺的時間；第二個是在某個重大事件發生之前的一段時間；此外，crunch當名詞使用時，本身就有緊要關頭或危機的意思。

Let's Talk!

Allen: We're having a party this weekend. Are you coming?

Emily: I wish I could, but this week is **crunch time** for my proposal.

Allen: I see. How is it going now?

Emily: Quite well. Now I'm making some amendments.

Allen: Well, good luck with your work.

亞　倫：我們這個週末要辦派對，你要來嗎？

愛蜜莉：我很希望我能去，可是這週是我企劃案的關鍵時刻。

亞　倫：原來如此，那你的企劃案目前進行得如何？

愛蜜莉：滿順利的，現在我要再修改一些內容。

亞　倫：那就祝你好運了。

字彙／片語充電區 *Words and Phrases*

crucial 形 重要的 / decisive 形 關鍵的 / strait 名 困境 / sprint 名 衝刺；全速疾跑
a defining moment 決定性時刻 / a turning point 轉捩點 / all of a sudden 突然間

UNIT 335 「非常規律」的狀態，一定會用到routine？

🎧 335

暖身猜猜看 Warming Up

情境：你每天準時上下班，非常規律，這時可以怎麼說？

( ) I clock in at nine and clock out at six every day, just like _____.

(A) artwork　　(B) clockwork　　(C) brickwork

正確解答：(B) 我每天很規律地九點打卡上班，六點打卡下班。

原來應該這樣說！

like clockwork 非常規律；很順利

　　clockwork原本的意思是發條，早期的時鐘都是用發條驅動的，所以clockwork給人一種規律、準確與平穩的感覺；因此，like clockwork就被用來形容很有規律性的人或事物，常與動詞go或run一起使用。

對話練習 Let's Talk!

Nina: Hi, Matt. How's the restaurant business?

Matt: It was hard at first, but now it's running **like clockwork**.

Nina: I've been there several times. The sandwiches are delicious.

Matt: I can give you the recipe if you like. Just don't tell anyone else.

Nina: Wow. That's very generous of you. Thanks.

妮娜：嗨，麥特，餐廳的生意如何？

麥特：一開始很辛苦，但現在很順利。

妮娜：我去過幾次，你們的三明治真是美味。

麥特：你要的話，我可以把食譜給你，但別跟其他人說。

妮娜：哇，你真大方，謝謝。

字彙／片語充電區 Words and Phrases

regularity 名 規律性 / consistency 名 一致 / smoothness 名 平穩；順利
in apple-pie order 井然有序 / with accuracy 準確地 / in a mess 一團亂

UNIT 336　「依某人的步調和時間」，就用pace來形容？

🎧 336

暖身猜猜看 Warming Up

情境：想提醒朋友，做事不能只按自己的步調，這時應該怎麼說？

(　　) You can't do everything in your own _____ time.

(A) sweet　　　　　(B) hot　　　　(C) cool

正確解答：(A) 你不能什麼事都只照自己的步調去做。

原來應該這樣說！

in one's own sweet time 依某人的步調和時間

　　sweet常見的意思是「甜的」，在口語英文中，則可以解釋為「愉快的、愜意的」，所以in one's own sweet time就是「依某人覺得合適的時間」（令他感到最愜意的時間或步調），也可以改成in one's own good time。

Mandy: Relax. The tour bus will wait. We're their responsibility.

Willie: We're in a group! You can't just do things **in your own sweet time**.

Mandy: All right. Just give me two more minutes. I'm going to the bathroom.

Willie: You have one minute and a half.

Mandy: Yes, sir. Be right back.

曼蒂：放輕鬆，遊覽車會等我們的，我們是他們的責任。

威利：我們是在一個團體裡！你不能只按照自己的時間做事。

曼蒂：好啦，再給我兩分鐘，我跑個廁所。

威利：給你一分半鐘。

曼蒂：是的，長官，馬上回來。

字彙/片語充電區 Words and Phrases

pleased 形 高興的 / agreeably 副 愜意地 / casual 形 隨便的 / willful 形 任性的
pace oneself 調整做事的步調 / fritter away time 浪費時間 / goof off 混日子

UNIT 337 「有的是時間」，用 have a lot of time？

🎧 337

 暖身猜猜看 Warming Up

情境：想鼓勵比賽落選的朋友，告訴他來日方長，這時應該怎麼說？

(   ) You have time on your ＿＿＿＿. You can always start over.

    (A) side   (B) end   (C) part

正確解答：(A) 你有的是時間，隨時都可以重頭來過。

原來應該這樣說！

time on one's side 不趕時間；有的是時間

    on one's side 是跟某人站在同一邊，也就是「對某人有利」，所以，time on one's side 是在表達「某人有充分的時間」（時間對他有利），通常與動詞 have 連用；這個慣用語也可以用句子表示，說成 Time is on one's side.。

 *Let's Talk!*

Gary: Why are you still here? You should be working on your paper.

Holly: Prof. Lin gave us an extra week, so I have **time on my side**.

Gary: So are you planning to finish it in the nick of time?

Holly: No. It's half written already. I'll finish it in no time.

Gary: Anyway, you'd better do it early.

蓋瑞：你怎麼還在這裡？你應該在寫報告才對吧。

荷莉：林教授多給我們一個星期，所以我有的是時間。

蓋瑞：所以你打算在最後一刻才完成嗎？

荷莉：不是啦，我已經寫一半了，很快就能寫完。

蓋瑞：無論如何，你最好早點完成。

字彙／片語充電區 *Words and Phrases*

unhurried 形 不慌不忙的 / amble 動 從容地漫步 / stressed 形 感到有壓力的
in favor of 有利於 / in no lack of 不缺乏 / go easy on 寬容 / be hard on 嚴苛

UNIT 338 「比指定時間早」，只會講early這個單字？

🎧 338

暖身猜猜看 *Warming Up*

情境：你想提醒弟弟盡早完成暑假作業，這時應該怎麼說？

(　　) You'd better finish your summer homework in _____ time.

　　(A) fine　　　　　　(B) nice　　　　　(C) good

正確解答：(C) 你最好提早完成你的暑假作業。

原來應該這樣說！

in good time 比指定時間早；提早

　　in good time指的是「比預期或指定的時間還早」，也就是在時間還很充裕的時候。如果在這個慣用語前面加上all，all in good time是用來安撫人的說法，告訴對方「馬上」或者「就快好了」，和soon的意思相近。

對話練習 Let's Talk!

Henry: A quarter to twelve! We arrived **in good time**.

Jenny: That taxi driver is really good. He saved us twenty minutes.

Henry: Yeah. Now we even have time for a quick lunch.

Jenny: We should check in and get to the boarding gate first.

Henry: But I'm really hungry after all the tension.

亨利：十一點四十五分！我們提早抵達了。

珍妮：那個計程車司機真厲害，幫我們省了二十分鐘。

亨利：對啊，我們現在甚至還有時間吃個簡單的午餐。

珍妮：我們應該先去報到，然後去登機門。

亨利：但經過剛才的一陣緊張之後，我真的餓了。

字彙/片語充電區 *Words and Phrases*

beforehand 副 提前地 / anticipative 形 先發制人的 / untimely 形 過早的
in advance 預先 / in due course 在適當的時候 / in the offing 即將來臨的

UNIT 339 「很久之後」的時間，誇張的比喻怎麼說？

🎧 339

 暖身猜猜看 Warming Up

情境：你不想做無效率的冗長討論，這時應該怎麼說？

(　　) I don't want to discuss this till the ＿＿＿＿ come home.

　　(A) birds 　　　　　(B) cows 　　　　　(C) sheep

正確解答：(B) 我不想針對這件事一直討論下去。

 原來應該這樣說！

till the cows come home 很久

　　這個可能起源於十九世紀蘇格蘭的說法，意思很容易理解。牛是步調緩慢的動物，可以想像牠們回家要花很長的時間，所以till the cows come home的意思就是指「一段很久且不確定的時間」，其中till可以換成until。

 **對話練習** Let's Talk!

Andy: Are you still looking for your pink sweater?

Tess: Yes. I just can't find it anywhere.

Andy: You can look for it **till the cows come home**, but you won't find it.

Tess: Why are you so sure?

Andy: Because I saw your sister wearing it this morning.

安迪：你還在找你的粉紅色毛衣啊？

泰絲：對啊，我怎麼樣都找不到。

安迪：你可以繼續這樣找下去，但你找不到的。

泰絲：為什麼你能這麼確定？

安迪：因為我今天早上看到你姊穿著那件毛衣。

字彙／片語充電區 Words and Phrases

abiding 形 持續的 / **persisting** 形 持續的；堅持的 / **endlessly** 副 無止盡地
on and on 繼續不停地 / **over the long haul** 長時間以來 / **by and by** 不久之後

UNIT 340 「很長的一段時間」，只想得出long time？

🎧 340

暖身猜猜看 *Warming Up*

情境：舊地重遊，你看著許久不見的景色，這時可以說什麼？

(   ) I haven't been here in _____ years.

　　(A) horse's　　　(B) donkey's　　　(C) goat's

正確解答：(B) 我已經好長一段時間沒來了。

原來應該這樣說！

donkey's years 很長一段時間

　　這個慣用語最早的說法是donkey's ears，為同韻俚語（rhyming slang），以與years押同韻的donkey's ears來比喻時間，後來才改為donkey's years；這是因為驢子很長壽，且用years更能點出「時間」的概念。

對話練習 *Let's Talk!*

Molly: Blake? My God! It really is you. Remember me? I'm Molly.

Blake: Molly! I don't believe it! I'm so happy!

Molly: I was pretty sure it was you when I saw you from the back.

Blake: How are you? I haven't seen you in **donkey's years**.

Molly: I'm doing fine. How about having dinner together?

莫　莉：是布萊克嗎？天哪！真的是你，記得我嗎？我是莫莉。

布萊克：莫莉！太不可思議了，我真高興！

莫　莉：光看到背影，我就相當確定是你了。

布萊克：你過得好嗎？我好久沒看到你了。

莫　莉：我很好，一起吃頓晚餐如何？

字彙／片語充電區 *Words and Phrases*

long-winded 形 冗長的 / **extended** 形 長期的；延伸的 / **eon** 名 極長的時間
coon's age 很長一段時間 / **a month of Sundays** 很長的時間 / **in a snap** 頃刻之間

UNIT 341　時間上的「漸漸」，如何強調一點一點推進的過程？

🎧 341

暖身猜猜看 Warming Up

情境：看到大廈漸漸愈蓋愈多的城市，可以怎麼說？

(　　) I think we'll see some more buildings by _____.

　　(A) scales　　　　(B) grades　　　　(C) degrees

正確解答：(C) 我相信公寓大廈漸漸地會愈來愈多。

原來應該這樣說！

by degrees 漸漸

　　degree除了「等級」之外，還可以當單位詞，意思是「度」（例如攝氏零度是zero degree Centigrade），從此義衍生，by degrees就解釋為「一點一點地」；此外，degree還有「程度」之意（ex. to a degree 非常）。

Cindy: There's a hole in my bag! All my change in it is gone.	辛蒂：我的包包破了個洞！裡面的零錢都掉光了。
Teddy: Let me see. I think it has worn out **by degrees**.	泰迪：我看看，我覺得它是漸漸被磨破的。
Cindy: I thought it could last longer.	辛蒂：我以為它可以撐得更久。
Teddy: Looks like its bottom touched the ground very often.	泰迪：看起來它的底部常常磨到地板。
Cindy: Yeah. The strap is kind of long. I should have adjusted it.	辛蒂：對啊，帶子太長了，我應該把它調短一點的。

字彙／片語充電區 Words and Phrases

successive 形 依次的 / **piecemeal** 副 逐個地；逐漸地 / **unhurried** 形 悠閒的
in stages 漸次地 / **in small doses** 短暫地 / **by fits and starts** 間歇性地

UNIT 342 頻率上的「每一次」，除了 every time以外的說法是？

🎧 342

暖身猜猜看 Warming Up

情境：你有個同學每次都忘了你的名字，這時可以怎麼說？

(　　) I have to remind Jack of my name at every _____.

(A) chance 　　　 (B) run 　　　 (C) turn

正確解答：(C) 我每次都要提醒傑克我叫什麼名字。

原來應該這樣說！

at every turn 每一次

　　at every turn除了可以解釋為「每一次」之外，也有「處處」的意思；turn當名詞有許多解釋，可以是「一次機會」，ex. It's my turn.（輪到我了。）也可以是「轉角」，ex. a sharp turn（急轉彎）。

對話練習 Let's Talk!

Owen: I heard that you passed the exam. Congratulations!

Peggy: Thank you for helping me with my studying.

Owen: No problem. I just answered a few questions for you.

Peggy: That helped a lot! Thanks for being there for me **at every turn**.

Owen: That's what friends are for.

歐文：我聽說你通過考試了，恭喜你！

佩姬：謝謝你幫我準備考試。

歐文：不用客氣，我只是回答了你幾個問題而已。

佩姬：你的幫助很大！謝謝你每次都幫我。

歐文：朋友就是要互相幫忙嘛。

字彙/片語充電區 Words and Phrases

unexceptionally 副 沒有例外地 / periodical 形 間歇的 / frequency 名 頻率
at any moment 隨時 / on any occasion 在任何情況下 / all over the place 到處

UNIT
343

「一見到就…」的說法，還只知道as soon as嗎？

🎧 343

暖身猜猜看 Warming Up

情境：你一眼就認出許多年不見的朋友，這時可以怎麼說？

(　　) Although you look a bit different now, I can recognize you on

_____.

(A) sight　　　　(B) spot　　　(C) sense

正確解答：(A) 即使你變得不太一樣了，我還是能一眼認出你。

原來應該這樣說！

on sight 一見到就…

　　sight在這裡解釋為看見；on則有「在…的同時」之意，因此，on sight 就表示看到的同時，可以用at sight替換；sight也有「視覺、視力」之意，ex. have good sight（視力很好）、lose one's sight（失明）。

對話練習 Let's Talk!

George: How was your blind date? Did you recognize him **on sight**?

Stella: Yes. He wore a red sweater as he mentioned in the email.

George: So would you go out with him again?

Stella: I think so. He is sweet and funny. That's always a plus.

George: It sounds like you two might be good together.

喬　治：你的盲目約會如何？你第一眼就認出他了嗎？

史黛拉：是啊，他穿紅色毛衣，就像他在信裡說的。

喬　治：那你還會跟他出去嗎？

史黛拉：應該會，他很貼心，也滿幽默的，這些都是加分點啊。

喬　治：聽起來你們應該很適合交往。

字彙／片語充電區 Words and Phrases

thereupon 副 隨即 / simultaneously 副 同時地 / concurrently 副 同時發生
upon seeing 一見到就… / in a flash 立即；瞬間 / straight away 馬上；即刻

UNIT 344 「久久才發生一次」，只能用頻率副詞表示？

🎧 344

暖身猜猜看 *Warming Up*

情境：遇到難得一見的好老師，這時可以怎麼說？

(　　) Mr. Johnson is a professor you meet once in a blue _____.

(A) sun (B) moon (C) star

正確解答：(B) 強森老師是個很難得遇到的好教授。

原來應該這樣說！

once in a blue moon 久久一次；很少發生

　　這個看似浪漫的慣用語，其中一個起源來自美國的農民曆。一年四季當中，一季通常只有三個滿月，當某一季出現四個滿月時，當季的第三個滿月就稱為 blue moon，這種情況通常幾年才有一次，所以用來比喻很少發生的事。

對話練習 *Let's Talk!*

Anna: Guess what my sister did yesterday. She bought me lunch!

Kevin: No kidding? Again? I thought she only did that **once in a blue moon**.

Anna: She did it because she wanted to borrow my red high heels.

Kevin: But those are your lucky high heels.

Anna: So I told her I'll let her wear them when pigs fly.

安娜：你猜我姊昨天做了什麼？她請我吃午餐！

凱文：有沒有搞錯？又請你？她很少請吃飯的。

安娜：她請客是因為想借我的紅色高跟鞋。

凱文：那是妳的幸運高跟鞋耶。

安娜：所以我跟她說，除非豬會飛，不然不可能。

字彙／片語充電區 *Words and Phrases*

infrequently 副 稀少地 / scarcely 副 幾乎不 / long-awaited 形 盼望已久的
fat chance 不太可能發生 / out of the blue 出人意料地 / when pigs fly 絕不可能

UNIT 345 午夜剛過的「凌晨」，只能用1:00 A.M.表示嗎？

🎧 345

 暖身猜猜看 *Warming Up*

情境：朋友的生日派對持續到凌晨，這時應該怎麼說？

(　　) Ann's birthday party went on into the _____ hours.

(A) new　　　　(B) dark　　　　(C) small

正確解答：(C) 安的生日派對持續到凌晨。

 原來應該這樣說！

the small hours 午夜剛過的一段時間；凌晨

　　the small hours這個說法直至十九世紀才出現，它指的是午夜之後到黎明之前的幾個小時，大約在凌晨一點到四點左右；因為這幾個小時在時鐘刻度的最前面，數字最小，所以用small這個字形容。

 對話練習 *Let's Talk!*

Judy: Did you stay up late last night?

Zack: Yeah. I was watching a movie on TV and went to bed in **the small hours**.

Judy: That must have been a good movie. You don't usually go to sleep that late.

Zack: The movie totally sucked me in right until the end.

Judy: Will there be a rerun of it today?

茱蒂：你昨晚熬夜了嗎？

柴克：對啊，我在看一部電視上播的電影，到凌晨才睡。

茱蒂：那部電影一定很精彩，你不常那麼晚睡。

柴克：我完全被那部片吸引住了。

茱蒂：那今天會有重播嗎？

字彙／片語充電區 *Words and Phrases*

daybreak 名 破曉 / sunup 名 日出 / soundless 形 無聲的 / gloom 名 陰暗
before dawn 黎明之前 / the witching hour 子夜 / deep in the night 深夜

UNIT 346 「一大清早」的黎明時刻，就是sunrise之前？

🎧 346

暖身猜猜看 Warming Up

情境：參加旅遊的你們，一大清早就要起床，這時應該怎麼說？

(　　) I'm afraid we have to get up at the ＿＿＿＿ of dawn.

　　(A) crack　　　　　(B) open　　　　(C) crash

正確解答：(A) 我們恐怕一大早就要起床了。

原來應該這樣說！

crack of dawn 一大清早

　　crack of dawn精確地說，指的是早晨出現第一道曙光的瞬間，在這之後，就是早晨時光，所以可以用來泛指「一大清早」；crack在此處為名詞，意思是裂縫（用來指稱破曉的狀態），可以用break取代，即break of dawn。

Doris: You look tired. Did you sleep well last night?	桃莉絲：你看起來好累，昨晚有睡好嗎？
Craig: Actually, no. Some noise woke me up at the **crack of dawn**.	克雷格：其實沒有，我一大早就被某個聲音吵醒
Doris: Have you figured out what the noise was?	桃莉絲：你有找出那是什麼聲音嗎？
Craig: No. And I couldn't get back to sleep after that.	克雷格：沒有，而且我被吵醒之後，就再也睡不著了。
Doris: Maybe you can take a nap for a few minutes.	桃莉絲：或許你可以小睡幾分鐘。

字彙／片語充電區 Words and Phrases

aurora 名 曙光 / daylight 名 日光 / sunshine 名 陽光；晴天 / twilight 名 黃昏的天色
peep of day 破曉 / the wee hours 凌晨 / break of day 破曉 / at daybreak 黎明時

UNIT 347 「開始著手進行某事」，用start準沒錯？

🎧 347

暖身猜猜看 Warming Up

情境：你想鼓勵無精打采的同事動起來，這時應該怎麼說？

(　　) Let's get _____ to work. We don't have much time to lose.

(A) in　　　　　　(B) down　　　　　(C) over

正確解答：(B) 開始幹活吧，我們沒剩多少時間了。

原來應該這樣說！

get down to 開始

　　get down to後面加名詞，表示「開始認真做某件事」，常見的用法是在後面加上business/work/it，表示「開始辦正事」；但如果只是get down，意思則是「記下、寫下」。

對話練習　Let's Talk!

Colin: I have a deadline to meet, but I can't seem to **get down to** it.

Cathy: Are you alright? Do you want to take some aspirin?

Colin: I took some already. I think I need to take a nap.

Cathy: Yeah. Sleep is always the best medicine.

Colin: And a good meal, too.

科林：我要趕一個快截稿的稿件，可是我卻不想動。

凱西：你還好嗎？要不要吃點阿斯匹靈？

科林：我已經吃了，我想我需要去睡一下。

凱西：嗯，睡眠是最好的藥。

科林：還有好好地吃一頓飯也是。

字彙/片語充電區 Words and Phrases

embark 動 使從事 / immerse 動 埋首於 / implement 動 實施 / earnest 形 認真的
give oneself to 專心致力於 / enter into 開始；著手 / go all out for 盡全力爭取

UNIT 348　連續好幾個小時的「老半天」，要怎麼形容hours呢？

🎧 348

 暖身猜猜看 *Warming Up*

情境：你必須開好幾個小時的車才能抵達某景點，這時可以怎麼說？

(　) We need to drive for hours on ＿＿＿ to get there.

(A) top　　　　(B) end　　　　(C) bottom

正確解答：(B) 我們得要連續開好幾個小時的車才能抵達。

 原來應該這樣說！

for hours on end 連續好幾個小時；老半天

　　on end接在一段時間之後，可用來表示「一段連續而不中斷的時間」，ex. three days on end（一連三天）；on end單獨使用時，則有「豎立」的意思，ex. Can you place the stand on end?（你可以把架子立起來嗎？）

 *Let's Talk!*

Bert: My God! We've been walking **for hours on end**.

Abby: Come on. We are so close to the tourist center.

Bert: I'm not going one more step until I feel better.

Abby: We should do this more often. It will be easier for you next time.

Bert: Oh, spare me. You said that we wouldn't have to walk very long!

伯特：天哪！我們已經連續走了好幾個小時了。

艾比：拜託，我們已經很接近遊客中心了。

伯特：在我覺得好一點之前，我連一步都不想走了。

艾比：我們應該多出來健行，下次你就會覺得輕鬆多了。

伯特：饒了我吧，你說我們不用走很久的！

字彙／片語充電區 *Words and Phrases*

successively 副 連續地 / lengthy 形 冗長的 / interruption 名 中斷 / awhile 副 片刻 / in a row 連續 / forever and a day 似無止盡的時間 / on and off 斷斷續續地

UNIT 349　每天「打卡上班」，card與動詞搭配就行了？

🎧 349

 暖身猜猜看 Warming Up

情境：你想說明公司規定早上九點前要打卡，這時應該怎麼說？

(　　) We clock _____ by nine every morning during the weekdays.
　　　(A) into　　　　　　(B) to　　　　　　(C) in

正確解答：(C) 我們每週一到週五，每天早上九點前要打卡上班。

 原來應該這樣說！

clock in 打卡上班

　　紀錄上下班時間的打卡鐘，英文有兩種說法，time recorder或time clock。而打卡上班的動作（將卡放進打卡鐘）就是clock in，也可以用clock on表示；至於下班，就說clock out或clock off。

 **對話練習** *Let's Talk!*

Emma: Do you have a minute, Frank?

Frank: Sure, Mrs. Porter. What can I do for you?

Emma: The record says you didn't **clock in** last Monday.

Frank: I must have forgotten to **clock in**. But I did clock out.

Emma: So when did you come to work on that day? I'll fill in the time for you.

艾　瑪：你有空嗎，法蘭克？

法蘭克：有的，波特太太，有什麼事嗎？

艾　瑪：這份紀錄說你上週一沒有打卡上班。

法蘭克：我上班時肯定忘了打卡，但我下班有打卡。

艾　瑪：你那一天是幾點來上班的？我幫你填上時間。

字彙/片語充電區 *Words and Phrases*

attendance 名 出席；參加 / **punctual** 形 準時的 / **binding** 形 必須遵守的
punch in 打卡上班 / **turn up** 出現 / **on the dot** 準時 / **ahead of time** 提前

UNIT 350 食品的「保存期限」，可以用due date表示？

🎧 350

暖身猜猜看 *Warming Up*

情境：朋友請你吃東西，但你發現它過期了，這時應該怎麼說？

(　　) The snack is past its ＿＿＿＿＿ life. We'd better not eat it.

(A) store (B) shelf (C) purchase

正確解答：(B) 這零食已經過了保存期限，我們最好不要吃。

原來應該這樣說！

shelf life 保存期限

　　shelf life從字面上很像是「架子的使用期」，很讓人困惑，其實，它指的是食品等商品的使用期限（注意對象必須為會壞的食品類）；在商品包裝上，通常會在日期前面加上use by/best by/best if used by表示保存期限。

Let's Talk!

Josh: How about we get some of these crackers? They look good.

Ivy: Yeah, they do. Let me see...But their **shelf lives** are about to expire.

Josh: I think the best before date is only for reference.

Ivy: You go ahead and buy them if you want, but I won't eat them.

Josh: Forget it. I'll just get a soda.

喬許：我們買點這種餅乾好不好？看起來滿好吃的。

艾薇：是不錯，我看看…可是保存期限快到了。

喬許：我覺得保存期限只是參考用的。

艾薇：你要買的話，隨你便，但我可不吃。

喬許：算了，我買罐汽水就好。

字彙/片語充電區 *Words and Phrases*

guarantee 動 保證 / **stale** 形 不新鮮的 / **preservative** 名 防腐劑 / **expire** 動 到期 / **the best before date** 最佳期限 / **prior to** 在…之前 / **food poisoning** 食物中毒

UNIT 351 「兩件事之間的空檔」，會用到between嗎？

🎧 351

暖身猜猜看 Warming Up

情境：你提議在新工作開始之前的空檔去旅行，這時應該怎麼說？

(　　) How about we take a short trip in the _____?

 (A) interim   (B) intersection   (C) interline

正確解答：(A) 我們在這期間來一趟短期的旅程如何？

原來應該這樣說！

in the interim 兩件事之間的空檔

  interim當名詞時，指的是「兩個事件之間的空檔或過渡期」，加上介系詞與定冠詞的in the interim，就表示在空檔時間內；interim也可以當形容詞，表示某事物是「臨時的」，ex. an interim government（臨時政府）。

對話練習 Let's Talk!

Maggie: My team just closed a deal. Do you want to have dinner with us?	瑪姬：我的小組剛結束一個案子，要不要和我們共進晚餐啊？
Larry: Congratulations! Sure. If it's okay with you guys.	賴瑞：恭喜！好啊，如果你們覺得可以的話。
Maggie: Of course it's okay. They will be happy to have you.	瑪姬：當然可以啊，他們會很高興有你加入的。
Larry: So is your next case coming soon?	賴瑞：那你們馬上就會進行下一個案子嗎？
Maggie: No. I'm thinking about taking a vacation **in the interim**.	瑪姬：不會，我想趁這個空檔放個假。

字彙／片語充電區 Words and Phrases

amid 介 在…之間 / **pending** 介 到…為止 / **interval** 名 間隔 / **recess** 名 學校的假期
in the meanwhile 其間 / **for the time being** 現在 / **in the course of** 在…期間

UNIT 352 期限之外的「寬限期」，只想到more time？

🎧 352

暖身猜猜看 *Warming Up*

情境：你向新房客解釋房租有一週的寬限期，這時應該怎麼說？

(　　) You have a one week ＿＿＿＿＿ period after the due date for your rent.

    (A) mercy   (B) kind   (C) grace

正確解答：(C) 房租在繳納期限過後，有一個禮拜的寬限期。

原來應該這樣說！

grace period 寬限期

    grace本身有慈悲或恩惠的意思，grace period從字面上來看，是法外開恩的期間，也就是「寬限期」；這個詞可以用在許多地方，例如繳納帳單、還債、執行命令或履行義務等。

Greg:	Uh, Ellie. I'm kind of short. Can I give you the money next month?	葛瑞格：	呃，艾莉，我手頭有點緊，我可以下個月再給你錢嗎？
Ellie:	No problem. Take your time.	艾　莉：	沒問題，慢慢來。
Greg:	Thanks for the **grace period**!	葛瑞格：	謝謝你願意讓我晚點還錢！
Ellie:	It's not like you owe me a million or anything. Is everything okay?	艾　莉：	你又不是欠我一百萬還是什麼的，一切都還好嗎？
Greg:	My car broke down last week, and it cost me a lot.	葛瑞格：	我的車上週拋錨，花了我好多錢。

字彙／片語充電區 *Words and Phrases*

suspension 名 暫緩執行 / **deferment** 名 延期 / **due** 形 到期的 / **penalty** 名 罰款
behind schedule 延遲 / **in arrears** 拖欠 / **to be paid** 待繳的 / **time out** 暫停

國家圖書館出版品預行編目資料

超強關鍵慣用語口說提升術 / 張翔 著. -- 初版. -- 新
北市：知識工場出版 采舍國際有限公司發行，
2021.03面； 公分. -- (Excellent；90)
ISBN 978-986-271-898-8 (平裝)

1.英語　2.慣用語　3.會話

805.123　　　　　　　　　　　110000242

 知識工場 · Excellent 90

超強關鍵慣用語口說提升術

出 版 者／全球華文聯合出版平台 · 知識工場
作　　者／張翔　　　　　　　　　印 行 者／知識工場
出版總監／王寶玲　　　　　　　　英文編輯／何牧蓉
總 編 輯／歐綾纖　　　　　　　　美術設計／蔡億盈

· ·

台灣出版中心／新北市中和區中山路2段366巷10號10樓
電話／（02）2248-7896　　　　　　傳真／（02）2248-7758
ISBN-13／978-986-271-898-8
出版日期／2021年3月初版

· ·

全球華文市場總代理／采舍國際
地址／新北市中和區中山路2段366巷10號3樓
電話／（02）8245-8786　　　　　　傳真／（02）8245-8718

· ·

港澳地區總經銷／和平圖書
地址／香港柴灣嘉業街12號百樂門大廈17樓
電話／（852）2804-6687　　　　　　傳真／（852）2804-6409

· ·

全系列書系特約展示
新絲路網路書店
地址／新北市中和區中山路2段366巷10號10樓
電話／（02）8245-9896　　　　　　傳真／（02）8245-8819
網址／www.silkbook.com

素人崛起，
從出書開始！

全國最強 4 天培訓班，
見證人人出書的奇蹟。

讓您借書揚名，建立個人品牌，
晉升專業人士，帶來源源不絕的財富。

**擠身暢銷作者四部曲，
我們教你：**

**企劃怎麼寫／ 撰稿速成法／
出版眉角／ 暢銷書行銷術／**

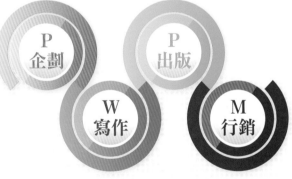

P 企劃

P 出版

W 寫作

M 行銷

保證出書

Publish for You,
king Your Dreams
Come True.

★ 如何讓別人在最短時間內對你另眼相看？
★ 要如何迅速晉升 A 咖、專家之列？
★ 我的產品與服務要去哪裡置入性行銷？
★ 快速成功的捷徑到底是什麼？
★ 生命的意義與價值要留存在哪裡？

答案就是出一本書！

當名片式微，出書取代名片才是王道！

人人適用的成名之路：出書

當大部分的人都不認識你，不知道你是誰，他們要如何快速找到你、了解你、與你產生連結呢？試想以下的兩種情況：

➲ **不用汲汲營營登門拜訪，就有客戶來敲門，你覺得如何？**

➲ **有兩個業務員拜訪你，一個有出書，另一個沒有，請問你更相信誰？**

無論行銷任何產品或服務，當你被人們視為「專家」，就不再是「你找他人」，而是「他人主動找你」，想達成這個目標，關鍵就在「出一本書」。

透過「出書」，能迅速提升影響力，建立「專家形象」。在競爭激烈的現代，「出書」是建立「專家形象」的最快捷徑。

想成為某領域的權威或名人？出書就是正解！

體驗「名利雙收」的12大好處

　　暢銷書的魔法，絕不僅止於銷售量。當名字成為品牌，你就成為自己的最佳代言人；而書就是聚集粉絲的媒介，進而達成更多目標。當你出了一本書，隨之而來的，將是 12 個令人驚奇的轉變：

01 增強自信心

　　對每個人來說，看著自己的想法逐步變成一本書，能帶來莫大的成就感，進而變得更自信。

02 提高知名度

　　雖然你不一定能上電視、錄廣播、被雜誌採訪，但卻絕對能出一本書。出書，是提升知名度最有效的方式，出書＋好行銷＝知名度飆漲。

03 擴大企業影響力

　　一本宣傳企業理念、記述企業如何成長的書，是一種長期廣告，讀者能藉由內文，更了解企業，同時產生更高的共鳴感，有時比花錢打一個整版報紙或雜誌廣告的效果要好得多，同時也更能讓公司形象深入人心。

04 滿足內心的榮譽感

　　書，向來被視為特別的存在。一個人出了書，便會覺得自己完成了一項成就，有了尊嚴、光榮和地位。擁有一本屬於自己的書，是一種特別的享受。

05 讓事業直線上衝

　　出一本書，等於讓自己的專業得到認證，因此能讓求職更容易、升遷更快捷、加薪有籌碼。很多人在出書後，彷彿打開了人生勝利組的開關，人生和事業的發展立即達到新階段。出書所帶來的光環和輻射效應，不可小覷。

06 結識更多新朋友

在人際交往愈顯重要的今天，單薄的名片並不能保證對方會對你有印象；贈送一本自己的書，才能讓人眼前一亮，比任何東西要能讓別人記住自己。

07 讓他人刮目相看

把自己的書，送給朋友，能讓朋友感受到你對他們的重視；送給客戶，能贏得客戶的信賴，增加成交率；送給主管，能讓對方看見你的上進心；送給部屬，能讓他們更尊敬你；送給情人，能讓情人對你的專業感到驚艷。這就是書的魅力，能讓所有人眼睛為之一亮，如同一顆糖，送到哪裡就甜到哪裡。

08 塑造個人形象

出書，是自我包裝效率最高的方式，若想成為社會的精英、眾人眼中的專家，就讓書替你鍍上一層名為「作家」的黃金，它將持久又有效替你做宣傳。

09 啟發他人，廣為流傳

把你的人生感悟寫出來，不但能夠啟發當代人們，還可以流傳給後世。不分地位、成就，只要你的觀點很獨到，思想有價值，就能被後人永遠記得。

10 闢謠並訴說心聲

是否曾經對陌生人的中傷、身邊人的誤解，感到百口莫辯呢？又或者，你身處於小眾文化圈，而始終不被理解，並對這一切束手無策？這些其實都可以透過出版一本書糾正與解釋，你可以在書中盡情袒露心聲，彰顯個性。

11 倍增業績的祕訣

談生意，尤其是陌生開發時，遞上個人著作＆名片，能讓客戶立刻對你刮目相看，在第一時間取得客戶的信任，成交率遠高於其他競爭者。

12 給人生的美好禮物

歲月如河，當你的形貌漸趨衰老、權力讓位、甚至連名氣都漸趨平淡時，你的書卻能為你留住人生最美好的的黃金年代，讓你時時回味。

書的面子與裡子，全部教給你！

★出版社不說的暢銷作家方程式★

P 說服出版社的神企劃

W 加速寫作的方程式

P 增加優勢的出版眉角

M 衝上排行榜的行銷術

暢銷書都是這麼煉成的！

P PLANNING 企劃 好企劃是快速出書的捷徑！

投稿次數＝被退稿次數？對企劃毫無概念？別擔心，我們將在課堂上公開出版社的審稿重點。從零開始，教你神企劃的 NO.1 方程式，就算無腦套用，也能讓出版社眼睛為之一亮。

W WRITING 寫作 卡住只是因為還不知道怎麼寫！

動筆是完成一本書的必要條件，但寫作路上，總會遇到各種障礙，靈感失蹤、沒有時間、寫不出那麼多內容……在課堂上，我們教你主動創造靈感，幫助你把一個好主意寫成暢銷書。

P PUBLICATION 出版　　懂出版，溝通不再心好累！

為什麼某張照片不能用？為什麼這邊必須加字？我們教你出版眉角，讓你掌握出版社的想法，研擬最佳話術，讓出書一路無礙；還會介紹各種出版模式，剖析優缺點，選出最適合你的出版方式。

M MARKETING 行銷　　100% 暢銷保證，從行銷下手！

書的出版並非結束，而是打造個人品牌的開始！資源不足？知名度不夠？別擔心，我們教你素人行銷招式，搭配魔法講盟的行銷活動與資源，讓你從第一本書開始，創造素人崛起的暢銷書傳奇故事。

魔法講盟出版班：優勢不怕比

		魔法講盟 出書出版班	普通寫作出書班
①	課程完整度	完整囊括 PWPM 勝	只談一小部分
②	講師專業度	各大出版社社長 勝	不一定是業界人士
③	課堂互動	理論教學＋分組實作 勝	只講完理論就結束
④	課後成果	有實際的 SOP 與材料 勝	聽完之後還是無從下手
⑤	學員指導程度	多位社長分別輔導 勝	一位講師難以照顧學生
⑥	上完課是否能 直接出書	● 是出版社，直接談出書 ● 出版模式最多元，保證出書 勝	上課歸上課，要出書還是必須自己找出版社

Planning 一鼓作氣寫企劃

　　大多數人都以為投稿是寄稿件給出版社的代名詞，NO！所謂投稿，是要投一份吸睛的「出書企劃」。只要這一點做對了，就能避開80% 的冤枉路，超越其他人，成功簽下書籍作品的出版合約。

　　企劃，就像是出版的火車頭，必須由火車頭帶領，整輛火車才會行駛。那麼，什麼樣的火車頭，是最受青睞的呢？要提案給出版社，最重要的就是讓出版社看出你這本書的「市場價值」。除了書的主題 & 大綱目錄之外，也千萬別忘了作者的自我推銷，比如現在很多網紅出書，憑藉的就是作者本身的號召力。

　　光憑一份神企劃，有時就能說服出版社與你簽約。先用企劃確定簽約關係後，接下來只需要將你的所知所學訴諸文字，並與編輯合作，就能輕鬆出版你的書，取得夢想中的斜槓身分 — 作家。

　　企劃這一步成功後，接下來就順水推舟，直到書出版的那一天。

關於 Planning，我們教你：

- 提案的方法，讓出版社樂意與你簽約。
- 具賣相的出書企劃包含哪些元素 & 如何寫出來。
- 如何建構作者履歷，讓菜鳥寫手變身超新星作家。
- 如何鎖定最夯議題 or 具市場性的寫作題材。
- 吸睛、有爆點的文案，到底是如何寫出來的。
- 如何設計一本書的架構，並擬出目錄。
- 投稿時，如何選擇適合自己的出版社。
- 被退稿或石沉大海的企劃，要如何修改。

寫作沒有絕對的公式，平凡、踏實的口吻容易理解，進而達到「廣而佈之」的效果；匠氣的文筆則能讓讀者耳目一新，所以，寫書不需要資格，所有的名作家，都是從素人寫作起家的。

雖然寫作是大家最容易想像的環節，但很多人在創作時還是感到負擔，不管是心態上的過不去（自我懷疑、完美主義等），還是技術面的難以克服（文筆、靈感消失等），我們都將在課堂上一一破解，教你加速寫作的方程式，輕鬆達標出書門檻的八萬字或十萬字。

課堂上，我們將邀請專業講師 & 暢銷書作家，分享他們從無到有的寫書方式。本著「絕對有結果」的精神，我們只教真正可行的寫作方法，如果你對動輒幾萬字的內文感到茫然，或者想要獲得出版社的專業建議，都強烈推薦大家來課堂上與我們討論。

學會寫作方式，就能無限複製，創造一本接著一本的暢銷書。

關於 Writing，我們教你：

- 了解自己是什麼類型的作家 & 找出寫作優勢。
- 巧妙運用蒐集力或 ghost writer，借他人之力完成內文。
- 運用現代科技，讓寫作過程更輕鬆無礙。
- 經驗值為零的素人作家如何寫出第一本書。
- 有經驗的寫作者如何省時又省力地持續創作。
- 如何刺激靈感，文思泉湧地寫下去。
- 完成初稿之後，如何有效率地改稿，充實內文。

找靈感
產出內文
借助寫手
IDEA

Publication 懂出版的作家更有利

完成書的稿件，還只是開端，要將電腦或紙本的稿件變成書，需要同時藉助作者與編輯的力量，才有可看的內涵與吸睛的外貌，不管是封面設計、內文排版、用色學問，種種的一切都能影響暢銷與否；掌握這些眉角，就能斬除因不懂而產生的誤解，提升與出版社的溝通效率。

另一方面，現在的多元出版模式，更是作家們不可不知的內容。大多數人一談到出書，就只想到最傳統的紙本出版，如果被退稿，就沒有其他辦法可想；但隨著日新月異的科技，我們其實有更多出版模式可選。你可以選擇自資直達出書目標，也可以轉向電子書，提升作品傳播的速度。

條條道路皆可圓夢，想認識各個方案的優缺點嗎？歡迎大家來課堂上深入了解。你會發現，自資出版與電子書沒有想像中複雜，有時候，你與夢想的距離，只差在「懂不懂」而已。

出版模式沒有絕對的好壞，跟著我們一起學習，找出最適解。

關於 Publication，我們教你：

- 依據市場品味，找到兼具時尚與賣相的設計。
- 基礎編務概念，與編輯不再雞同鴨講。
- 身為作者必須了解的著作權注意事項。

- 電子書的出版型態、製作方式、上架方法。
- 自資出版的真實樣貌 & 各種優惠方案的諮詢。
- 取得出版補助的方法 & 眾籌出書，大幅減低負擔。

Marketing 行銷布局，打造暢銷書

一路堅持，終於出版了你自己的書，接下來，就到了讓它大放異彩的時刻了！如果你還以為所謂的書籍行銷，只是配合新書發表會露個臉，或舉辦簽書會、搭配書店促銷活動，就太跟不上二十一世紀的暢銷公式了。

要讓一本書有效曝光，讓它在發行後維持市場熱度、甚至加溫，刷新你的銷售紀錄，靠的其實是行銷布局。這分成「出書前的布局」與「出書後的行銷」。大眾對於銷售的印象，90% 都落在「出書後的行銷」（新書發表會、簽書會等），但許多暢銷書作家，往往都在「布局」這塊下足了功夫。

事前做好規劃，取得優勢，再加上出版社的推廣，就算是素人，也能秒殺各大排行榜，現在，你可不只是一本書的作者，而是人氣暢銷作家了！

好書不保證大賣，但有行銷布局的書一定會好賣！

關於 Marketing，我們教你：

- 新書衝上排行榜的原因分析 & 實務操作的祕訣。
- 善用自媒體 & 其他資源，建立有效的曝光策略。
- 素人與有經驗的作家皆可行的出書布局。
- 成為自己的最佳業務員，延續書籍的熱賣度。
- 如何善用書腰、贈品等周邊，行銷自己的書。
- 網路 & 實體行銷的互相搭配，創造不敗攻略。
- 推廣品牌 & 服務，讓書成為陌生開發的利器。

布局

周邊

網路

活動

掌握出版新趨勢，保證有結果！

　　在現今愈來愈多元的出版模式下，你只知道一種出書方式嗎？魔法講盟的出版班除了傳授傳統投稿的撇步，還會介紹出版新趨勢——自資出版與電子書。更重要的是，我們不僅上課，還提供最完整的出版服務 & 行銷資源，成果看得見！

一、傳統投稿出版： 理論 & 實作的 NO.1 選擇

　　魔法講盟出版班的講師，包括各大出版社的社長，因此，我們將以業界的專業角度 & 經驗，100% 解密被退稿或石沉大海的理由，教你真正能打動出版社的策略。

　　除了 PWPM 的理論之外，我們還會以小組方式，針對每個人的選題 & 內容，悉心個別指導，手把手教學，親自帶你將出書夢化為暢銷書的現實。

二、自資出版： 最完整的自資一條龍服務

　　不管你對自資出版有何疑惑，在課堂上都能得到解答！不僅如此，我們擁有全國最完整的自費出版服務，不僅能為您量身打造自助出版方案、替您執行編務流程，還能在書發行後，搭配行銷活動，將您的書廣發通路、累積知名度。

　　別讓你的創作熱情，被退稿澆熄，我們教你用自資管道，讓出版社後悔打槍你，創造一人獨享的暢銷方程式。

三、電子書： 從製作到上架的完整教學

　　隨著科技發展，每個世代的閱讀習慣也不斷更新。不要讓知識停留在紙本出版，但也別以為電子書是萬靈丹。在課堂上，我們會告訴你電子書的真正樣貌，什麼樣的人適合出電子書？電子書能解決 & 不能解決的面向為何？深度剖析，創造最大的出版效益。

　　此外，電子書的實際操作也是課程重點，我們會講解電子書的製作方式與上架流程，只要跟著步驟，就能輕鬆出版電子書，讓你的想法能與全世界溝通。

紙電皆備的出版選擇，圓夢最佳捷徑！

ESBIH課程

真健康＋大財富＝真正的成功

你還在汲汲營營於累積財富嗎？
「空有財富，健康堪虞」的人生，
絕不能算是真正的成功！
如今，有一種新商機現世了！
它能助你在調節自身亞健康狀態的同時，
也替你創造被動收入，賺進大把鈔票。

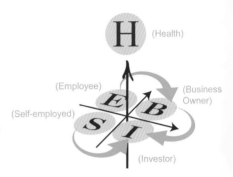

現在，給自己一個機會，積極了解這個「賺錢、自用兩相宜」的新商機，如何為你創造ESBIH三維「成功」卦限！

歡迎在每月的 ｛第一個週五下午2：30～8：30 第二個週五晚上5：30～8：30｝前來中和魔法教室！

魔法講盟特聘台大醫學院級別醫師會同Jacky Wang博士與David Chin醫師共同合作開始一連串免費授課講座。

課中除了教授您神秘的回春大法，

還為您打造一台專屬的自動賺錢機器！

讓您在逆齡的同時也賺進大筆財富，

完美人生的成功之巔就等你來爬！

詳情開課日期及授課資訊，請掃描QR Code或撥打真人客服專線

02-8245-8318，亦可上新絲路官網 silkbook com www.silkbook.com

14

原來逆齡可以這麼簡單！

利人利己，共好雙贏

眾所周知，現今的「抗衰老」方法，只有「幹細胞」與「生長激素」兩大方向。

但，無論從事哪一種療法，都所費不貲，甚至還可能造成人體額外的負擔！

那麼，有沒有一種既省錢，又能免去副作用的回春大法？

有！風靡全歐洲的「順勢療法」讓您在後疫情時代活得**更年輕、更健康**！

現在，　**魔法講盟**　特別開設一系列**免費**課程，為您解析抗衰老奧秘！

☆ 參加這門課程，可以學到什麼？

- ☑ 剖析逆齡回春的奧秘
- ☑ 掌握改善亞健康的方式
- ☑ 窺得延年益壽的天機
- ☑ 跟上富人的投資思維
- ☑ 打造自動賺錢金流
- ☑ 獲得真正的成功

時間	**2020**	9/4(五)14:30	9/11(五)17:30	11/6(五)14:30
		11/13(五)17:30	12/4(五)14:30	12/11(五)17:30
	2021	1/8(五)17:30	2/5(五)14:30	3/5(五)14:30
		3/12(五)17:30	4/9(五)17:30	5/7(五)14:30
		5/14(五)17:30	6/4(五)14:30	6/11(五)17:30
		7/2(五)14:30	7/9(五)17:30	……
地點	**中和魔法教室** 新北市中和區中山路二段366巷10號3樓 （位於捷運環狀線中和站與橋和站間， **COSTCO** 對面郵局與 Ⓥ 福斯汽車間巷內）			

課中除了教你如何轉換平面的ESBI象限，

更為你打造完美的H（Health）卦限！

ESBIH構成的三維空間，才是真正的成功！

真永是真

本世紀全球華人圈最偉大的高端演講

Knowledge Feast Lecture

真理指引の知識服務

～王晴天與您講道理的人生大夢

讀萬卷書，
不如行萬里路，
行萬里路，不如閱人無數，
閱人無數，不如名師指路，
名師指路，不如跟隨成功者的腳步，
跟隨成功者腳步，不如高人點悟！
經過歷史實踐和理論驗證的真知，
蘊藏著深奧的道理與大智慧。
晴天大師用三十年的體驗與感悟，
為你講道理、助你明智開悟！
為你的工作、生活、人生「導航」，
從而改變命運、實現夢想，
成就最好的自己！

台灣版《時間的朋友》
「真永是真」知識饗宴
邀您一同追求真理 ‧
分享智慧 ‧ 慧聚財富！

時間 ▶ 2020場次 11/7（六）13:30～
　　 ▶ 2021場次 11/6（六）13:30～
地點 ▶ 新店台北矽谷國際會議中心

（新北市新店區北新路三段223號 🚇 捷運大坪...

報名或了解更多、2022年日程請掃碼查詢
或撥打真人客服專線 (02) 8245-8318

台灣最大培訓機構&學習型組織　魔法講...